THE SPELLMAN FILES

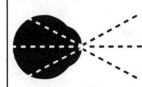

This Large Print Book carries the
Seal of Approval of N.A.V.H.

THE SPELLMAN FILES

LISA LUTZ

THORNDIKE PRESS

An imprint of Thomson Gale, a part of The Thomson Corporation

Detroit • New York • San Francisco • New Haven, Conn. • Waterville, Maine • London

LIBRARY OF CONGRESS CATALOGING-IN-PUBLICATION DATA

Lutz, Lisa.
  The Spellman files / by Lisa Lutz.
    p. cm. — (Thorndike Press large print core)
  ISBN-13: 978-0-7862-9406-0 (alk. paper)
  ISBN-10: 0-7862-9406-X (alk. paper)
    1. Private investigators — Fiction. 2. Large type books. 3. Domestic
  fiction. I. Title.
  PS3612.U897S67 2007b
  813'.6—dc22   2007005785

Published in 2007 by arrangement with Simon & Schuster, Inc.

Printed in the United States of America on permanent paper
10 9 8 7 6 5 4 3 2 1

For David Klane

PROLOGUE

San Francisco, Night

I duck into the parking garage, hoping to escape. But my boots echo on the slick cement, broadcasting my location to anyone listening. And I know they are listening. I make a mental note to myself not to wear these shoes again if there is a chance I'll get involved in a pursuit.

I start to run up the spiral driveway of the garage, knowing they'll never match my pace. The sound of my strained breath now masks the echo of my footsteps. Behind me, I hear nothing.

I stop in my tracks to listen more closely. One car door, then another, shuts and an engine turns over. I try to predict their next move as I scan the lot for Daniel's car.

Then I spot it — a midnight blue BMW — eclipsed on either side by two enormous SUVs. I rush to the newly waxed four-door sedan and put the key in the lock.

The scream of the car alarm hits me like a punch in the stomach. I'm breathless for a moment as I recover. I had forgotten about the security system. I drive a twelve-year-old Buick that unlocks with a *freakin' key!* the way it's supposed to.

My thumb fumbles with the remote device until the siren stops. I can hear the other car inching up the driveway, moving slowly just to torture me. I finally press the button that unlocks the door.

Car Chase #3

The nondescript Ford sedan cuts past my vehicle, giving me enough time to screech out of the parking space before it blocks my path down the driveway. As I zoom out of the garage, I check my rearview mirror and see the Ford right on my tail.

I shoot across the street, making a sharp left. My foot hits the floor. I am surprised by the smooth, rapid acceleration of the luxury vehicle. I realize there are reasons people buy these cars beyond concerns of vanity. I remind myself not to get used to it.

The speedometer reads 50 mph in no time flat. The Ford is about a hundred meters back, but closing in. I slow down to get them close on my tail and then overshoot the right turn onto Sacramento Street, but they know all my tricks and stay right behind me.

Speeding over two hills, the BMW, followed by the Ford, reaches downtown in record time. I check the fuel gauge. Maybe an hour of high-speed driving left. I turn right into an alley and sweep through to the other side, making a left turn onto a one-way street, going the wrong way. Two cars sound their horns and career out of my trajectory. I check my mirror, expecting to have made some headway, but I can't shake them.

Driving south of Market Street, I accelerate one last time, more as an act of showmanship than an attempt to escape. I follow it up by slamming on my brakes. I do it just to rattle them, just to remind them that I am still in control.

The Ford screeches to a halt about ten feet behind the BMW. I turn off the ignition and take a few deep breaths. I casually get out of the car and walk over to the sedan.

I knock on the driver's-side window. A moment passes and the window rolls down. I put my hand on the hood of the car and lean in just a bit.

"Mom. Dad. This has to stop."

The Interview:
Chapter 1

Seventy-two Hours Later

A single lightbulb hangs from the ceiling, its dull glow illuminating the spare decor of this windowless room. I could itemize its contents with my eyes closed: one wooden table, splintered and paint-chipped, surrounded by four rickety chairs; a rotary phone; an old television; and a VCR. I know this room well. Hours of my childhood I lost in here, answering for crimes I probably did commit. But I sit here now answering to a man I have never seen before, for a crime that is still unknown, a crime that I am too afraid to even consider.

Inspector Henry Stone sits across from me. He places a tape recorder in the center of the table and switches it on. I can't get a good read on him: early forties, short-cropped salt-and-pepper hair, crisp white shirt, and a perfectly tasteful tie. He might be handsome, but his cold professionalism feels like a mask. His suit seems too pricey for a civil servant and makes me suspicious. But everyone makes me suspicious.

"Please state your name and address for the record," says the inspector.

"Isabel Spellman. Seventeen ninety-nine Clay Street, San Francisco, California."

"Please state your age and date of birth."

"I'm twenty-eight. Born April 1, 1978."

"Your parents are Albert and Olivia Spellman, is that correct?"

"Yes."

"You have two siblings: David Spellman, thirty, and Rae Spellman, fourteen. Is that correct?"

"Yes."

"Please state your occupation and current employer for the record."

"I am a licensed private investigator with Spellman Investigations, my parents' PI firm."

"When did you first begin working for Spellman Investigations?" Stone asks.

"About sixteen years ago."

Stone consults his notes and looks up at the ceiling, perplexed. "You would have been twelve?"

"That is correct," I respond.

"Ms. Spellman," Stone says, "let's start at the beginning."

I cannot pinpoint the precise moment when

it all began, but I can say for sure that the beginning didn't happen three days ago, one week, one month, or even one year ago. To truly understand what happened to my family, I have to start at the very beginning, and that happened a long time ago.

■ ■ ■ ■

PART ONE:
ANTEBELLUM

■ ■ ■ ■

A Long Time Ago

My father, Albert Spellman, joined the San Francisco Police Department when he was twenty and one-half years old, just as his father, grandfather, and brother had done before him. Five years later he made inspector and was transferred to vice. Two years after that, while telling his informant a joke, Albert tripped and fell down two flights of stairs. The fall left him with an unreliable back that would cause him to collapse in pain without warning.

Forced into early retirement, Albert immediately went to work for Jimmy O'Malley, a one time robbery inspector turned private investigator. The year was 1970. Although Jimmy was nearing eighty, O'Malley Investigations was still pulling in a respectable caseload. With my father on board, the business took off. Albert has an unusual gift with people, a goofy, affable charm that elicits immediate trust. His sense of humor is purely cheap vaudeville, yet everyone falls for it. Some of his routines — like sneezing Eastern European names — he never grows tired of. Only his children have suggested he work up some new material.

At six foot three and two hundred twenty pounds, you might imagine his physique would intimidate, but his easy gait always masked the strength beneath. His face seemed to defy description with features so mismatched, they looked like a collage of other faces. My mother used to say, *If you stared at him long enough, he was handsome.* And my father would continue, *But your mother was the only one who had the patience.*

In 1974, during a routine insurance-company surveillance that concluded in Dolores Park, Albert spotted a petite brunette lurking behind a set of bushes flanking the Muni tracks. Intrigued by her unusual behavior, he dropped his paid surveillance detail to follow this mysterious woman. Within a short time, Albert determined that the suspiciously behaving brunette was doing some surveillance of her own. He came to this conclusion when she pulled a camera and an enormous telephoto lens out of her purse and began taking snapshots of a young couple embroiled on a park bench.

Her camerawork was unsteady and amateurish and Albert decided to offer some professional assistance. He approached, either too quickly or too closely (the details are now a blur to both parties), and got kneed in the groin. My father would later say he fell in love as the pain subsided.

Before the brunette could plant another debilitating blow, Albert rattled off his credentials to subdue the surprisingly strong woman. The brunette, in turn, apologized, introduced herself as Olivia Montgomery, and reminded my father that sneaking up on women is both impolite and potentially dangerous. Then she offered an explanation for her amateurish spying and solicited some advice. It was revealed that the man still entangled on the park bench was Ms. Montgomery's future brother-in-law. The woman, however, was not her sister.

Albert played hooky the rest of the afternoon to aid and instruct Ms. Montgomery in her surveillance of one Donald Finker. Their efforts began at Dolores Park and ended at an Irish pub in the Tenderloin. Finker was none the wiser. Olivia would later call the day a great success, although her sister Martie would not. Several bus tokens, cab fares, and two rolls of film later, Olivia and Albert managed to catch Donald in the arms of three separate women (some he'd paid) and slipping money in the pockets of two separate bookies. Albert was impressed with Olivia's acumen and discovered that having a petite, quick-on-her-feet, twenty-one-year-old brunette working a surveillance job was an invaluable asset. He didn't know whether to ask her out or offer her a job. Too torn to make that decision, Albert did both.

Three months later, Olivia Montgomery became Olivia Spellman in a small Las Vegas ceremony. Martie caught the bouquet, to her great astonishment, but thirty-three years later would still be unmarried. A year after that, Albert bought the business from Jimmy and changed its name to Spellman Investigations.

THE FIRSTBORN

David Spellman was born perfect. Eight pounds even, with a full head of hair and unblemished skin, he cried for a brief moment right after his birth (to let the doctor know he was breathing), then stopped abruptly, probably out of politeness. Within two months, he was sleeping seven hours straight and occasionally eight or nine.

While Albert and Olivia automatically considered their first child the picture of perfection, it wasn't until two years later, when I came along to provide a point of comparison, that they realized how flawless David really was.

David grew more attractive the older he got. While he bore no real resemblance to anyone in my family, his features were a collection of my mother's and father's best attributes, with a few of Gregory Peck's thrown in. He never suffered through an awkward stage, just an occasional black eye brought on by a jealous classmate (which somehow looked fetching on him). David excelled in school with little or no effort, possessing a brain for academics that has not been duplicated anywhere in our entire family tree. A natural athlete, he declined being captain of just about every sports team in high school to avoid the covetous backlashes that would often ensue. There was nothing sinister in his ungodly perfection. In fact, he possessed modesty beyond his years. But I was determined to kick out the legs of every chair he ever sat on.

The crimes I committed against my brother were manifold. Most went unpunished, as David was never a snitch, but there were others that could not escape the careful scrutiny of my ever-vigilant parents. As soon as I developed language skills, I began to document my crimes, not unlike a shop clerk logs inventory. The record of my crimes took the form of lists, followed by relevant details. Sometimes there were thumbnail sketches of a misdeed, like, "12-8-92. Erased hard drive on David's computer." Other times the lists were followed by a detailed rendering of the event, usually in the case of crimes for which I was caught. The details were necessary so that I could learn from my mistakes.

THE INTERROGATION ROOM

That is what we came to call it, but it was, in fact, our unfinished basement. Contents: one lightbulb, one table, four chairs, a rotary phone, and an old TV. Since it had the lighting and spare furnishings of a noir film, my parents could not resist staging all of our sentencing hearings in this primitive space.

I held a long-term reservation on the room, being my family's primary agitator. Below is a sampling of my basement interrogations. The list is by no means exhaustive:

Isabel, Age 8

I sit in one of the unbalanced chairs, leaning to one side. Albert paces back and forth. Once he is certain that I am beginning to squirm, he speaks.

"Isabel, did you sneak into your brother's room last night and cut his hair?"

"No," I say.

Long pause.

"Are you sure? Maybe you need some time to refresh your memory."

Albert takes a seat across the table and looks me straight in the eye. I quickly look down but try to maintain my ground.

"I don't know anything about a haircut," I say.

Albert places a pair of safety scissors on the table.

"Do these look familiar?"

"Those could be anyone's."

"But we found them in your bedroom."

"I was framed."

In fact, I was grounded for one week.

Isabel, Age 12

This time my mother does the pacing, carrying a laundry basket under her left arm. She puts the basket on the table and pulls out a wrinkled oxford shirt in a shade of pink so pale it is clearly not its intended color.

"Tell me, Isabel. What color is this shirt?"

"It's hard to say in this light."

"Hazard a guess."

"Off-white."

"I think it's pink. Are you willing to give me that?"

"Sure. It's pink."

"Your brother now has five pink shirts and not one white shirt to wear to school." (The school uniform code strictly says *white shirts only.*)

"That's unfortunate."

"I think you had a hand in this, Isabel."

"It was an accident."

"Is that so?"

"A red sock. I don't know how I missed it."

"Produce the sock in ten minutes. Otherwise, you're paying for five new shirts."

I couldn't produce the sock, because it didn't exist. However, I did manage to get the red food coloring out of my bedroom and into the neighbor's trash can without detection in that time frame.

I paid for those shirts.

Isabel, Age 14

By now my father has been permanently elected interrogator. Frankly, I think he was just missing his cop days; sparring with me kept him fresh.

Fifteen minutes pass in silence as he tries to make me sweat. But I'm getting better at this game and manage to look up and hold his gaze.

"Isabel, did you doctor the grades on your

brother's report card?"

"No. Why would I do that?"

"I don't know. But I know you did it."

He places the report card on the table and slides it in front of me. (These were the old handwritten cards. All you had to do was pinch a blank one and solicit the services of a decent forger.)

"It's got your fingerprints all over it."

"You're bluffing." (I wore gloves.)

"And we had the handwriting analyzed."

"What do you take me for?"

Albert sighs deeply and sits down across from me. "Look, Izzy, we all know you did it. If you tell me why, we won't punish you."

A plea bargain. This is new. I decide to go for it, since I don't want to be trapped at home all week. I take a moment to respond, just so the confession doesn't come too easily.

"Everyone should know what it's like to get a C."

It took some time, but eventually I grew tired of trying to dethrone King David. There had to be a better way to pave my own path. No one could deny that I was a difficult child, but my true life of crime did not begin until I met Petra Clark in the eighth grade. We met in detention and bonded over our mutual (and fanatical) love for the 1960s sitcom *Get Smart.* I couldn't begin to estimate the number of hours we spent, stoned, watching repeats on cable, laughing so hard it hurt. It was only natural that we would soon become inseparable. It was a friendship based on common interests — Don Adams, beer, marijuana, and spray paint.

In the summer of 1993, when we were both fifteen, Petra and I were suspected of committing a string of unsolved vandalisms in the Nob Hill district of San Francisco. Despite the numerous Neighborhood Watch meetings in our honor, none of the cases could be proven. At the time we would reflect upon our transgressions the way an artist might admire his own paintings. Petra and I challenged each other to push the boundaries of our misdemeanors. Our crimes were childish, yes, but they possessed a kind of creative energy that was absent from your everyday vandalism. The following is the first co-list Petra and I created; however, many more would follow.

1. 6-25-93   Relandscaped Mr. Gregory's backyard.[1]
2. 7-07-93   Drive-by.
3. 7-13-93   Stole 5 basketballs, 3 field hockey sticks, 4 baseballs, and 2 baseball gloves from phys ed storage closet at Mission High School.
4. 7-16-93   Dyed Mrs. Chandler's toy poodle cobalt blue.
5. 7-24-93   Drive-by.
6. 7-21-93   Deposited a case of beer outside an AA meeting on Dolores Street.[2]
7. 7-30-93   Drive-by.
8. 8-10-93   Filled out subscription cards for *Hustler* magazine on behalf of an assortment of married men in the neighborhood.

[1] Petra, having a way with scissors — even the garden-variety kind — created a topiary that resembled a hand with an extended middle finger.
[2] Paid homeless man to buy beer.

Our staple activity was what we called the "drive-by." When lack of inspiration limited our nightly activities, garbage night provided a backup plan. It was simple, really: We'd sneak out of our homes after midnight. Petra would pick me up in her mom's 1978 Dodge Dart (which Petra had stolen), and we'd sideswipe trash cans left out for the garbage truck. It wasn't so much the rush of destruction that appealed to me and Petra, but more the narrow escapes. By the end of summer, however, my luck had run out.

I found myself in the interrogation room once again. This time it was different, since it was a real interrogation room in a real police department. My father wanted me to give up my source and I refused.

8-16-93

The crime: Six hours earlier, I had snuck out of the house past midnight, hitched a ride to a party in the Mission, and picked up a guy who wanted to score some blow. Although cocaine wasn't my thing, the guy was sporting a leather jacket and a Kerouac novel and I have a weakness for tough guys who read. So I told him I knew a dealer — for reasons I'll get to later — and I made a call, asking if I could "cash in on that favor." Driving to my source's house, I made the leather jacket guy from the party as an undercover cop and demanded he drive me home. Instead, he drove me to the police station. When it was established that I was the daughter of Albert Spellman, a deco-rated ex-cop, Dad was called in.

Albert entered the Box still groggy with sleep.

"Give me a name, Izzy," he said, "and then we can go home and punish you for real."

"Any name?" I asked coyly.

"Isabel, you told an undercover police officer that you could score him some blow. You then made a phone call to a man you claimed was a dealer and asked if you could cash in on a favor. That doesn't look good."

"No, it doesn't. But the only real crime you've got me on is breaking curfew."

Dad offered up his most threatening gaze and said one last time, "Give me his name."

The name the cops wanted was Leonard Williams, Len to his friends, high school senior. The truth was, I barely knew the guy and had never bought drugs from him. What I did know I pieced together through years of eavesdropping, which is how I learn most things. I knew Len's mother was on disability and addicted to painkillers. I knew his father had been killed in a liquor store shooting when Len was six years old. I knew that he had two younger brothers and the welfare checks did not feed them all. I knew Len dealt drugs like some kids get after-school jobs — to put food on the table. I knew Len was gay, and I never told anyone about it.

It was the night of Unpunished Crime #3. Petra and I broke onto school property to steal from the phys ed storage closet (I was convinced that a secondhand sporting-goods business would solve our cash-flow problem). I picked the lock to the storage closet and Petra and I moved the inventory into her car. But then I got greedy and remembered that Coach Walters usually kept a bottle of Wild Turkey in his desk drawer. While Petra waited in the car, I returned to the school grounds and caught Len and a football player making out in Coach Walters's office. Because I never said anything, Len thought he owed me. What he didn't know was that I was good at keeping secrets, having so many of my own. One more made no difference to me.

"I am not a snitch" was all I ever said.

My father took me home that night without uttering a single word. Nothing happened to Len. They had only a nickname to go on. As for me, I got off easy, at least compared to my father, who endured endless jeering from his former colleagues; they found it infinitely amusing that Al couldn't crack his own daughter as an informant. Yet I know that for a man who spent years working the streets, he understood the codes that criminals live by and to a certain extent respected my silence.

If you can imagine me without my litany of crimes or my brother as a point of comparison, you might be surprised to find that I stand up all right on my own. I can enter a room and have its contents memorized within a few minutes; I can spot a pickpocket with the accuracy of a sharpshooter; I can bluff my way past any currently employed night watchman. When inspired, I have a doggedness you've never seen. And while I'm no great beauty, I get asked out plenty by men who don't know any better.

But for many years, my attributes (for what they're worth) were obscured by my defiant ways. Since David had cornered the market on perfection, I had to settle for mining the depths of my own imperfection. At times it seemed the only two sentences spoken in our household were *Well done, David* and *What were you thinking, Isabel?* My teenage years were defined by meetings at the principal's office, rides in squad cars, ditching, vandalism, smoking in the bathroom, drinking at the beach, breaking and entering, academic probation, groundings, lectures, broken curfews, hangovers, blackouts, illegal drugs, combat boots, and unwashed hair.

Yet I could never do as much damage as I intended, because David was always undoing it. If I missed a curfew, he covered for me. If I lied, he corroborated. If I stole, he returned. If I smoked, he hid the butts. If I passed out on the front lawn, he moved my lifeless body into my bedroom. If I refused to write a paper, he wrote it for me, even dumbing down the language to make it believable. When he discovered that I wasn't turning in his work on my behalf, he took to delivering the papers directly to the teachers' mailboxes.

What was so infuriating about David was that he *knew.* He knew that — to a certain extent — my failure was a reaction to his perfection. He understood that I was his fault and he genuinely felt contrite. My parents would occasionally ask me why I was the way I was. And I told them: They needed balance. Added together and divided evenly, David and I would be two exceedingly normal children. Rae would eventually throw everything off balance, but I'll get to that later.

1799 Clay Street

The Spellman residence is located at 1799 Clay Street on the outskirts of the Nob Hill district of San Francisco. If you walk half a mile to the south, you'll reach the Tenderloin — San Francisco's heterosexual redlight district. If you head too far north, you'll land in some variety of tourist trap, whether it's Lombard Street or Fisherman's Wharf or, if you're really unfortunate, the Marina.

Spellman Investigations is conveniently located at the same address. (My father loves to joke about his commute down the stairs.) The building itself is an impressive four-level Victorian, painted blue with white trim, that my parents could never have afforded had it not been passed down from three generations of Spellmans. The property itself is valued at close to two million, which means my parents threaten to sell at least four times a year. But those are empty threats. My parents would rather have old furniture, chipped paint, and economic uncertainty than European vacations, retirement funds, and a home in the suburbs.

At the entrance to my family's home/business, you will find four mailboxes that read, from left to right: Spellman, Spellman Investigations (we've only had one mail carrier who routinely differentiated between the two), Marcus Godfrey (my father's long-lived undercover name), and Grayson Enterprises (a dummy business name that our firm uses for lighter cases). There are also two or three PO boxes around the Bay Area that the business sustains when more camouflage is necessary.

Once inside the Spellman home, you come upon a staircase that winds up to the second level, where all three bedrooms are located. To the right of the staircase is a door with a hanging sign that says SPELLMAN INVESTIGATIONS. The door is locked during all nonbusiness hours. Left of the staircase is the entrance to the living room. A threadbare couch with a worn zebra-skin pattern once provided the centerpiece to the room. Now it is an unassuming brown leather sofa. Mahogany furniture orbits the couch — each piece would qualify as an antique, but neglect has diminished their value. The only change the room has seen in the last thirty years (other than the couch) is the replacement of the wood-paneled Zenith TV (circa 1980) with a twenty-seven-inch flat-screen that my uncle bought after a very rare, but successful, day at the racetrack.

Behind the living room is the kitchen, which extends into a modest dining room with still more neglected antiques. While I'm still downstairs, I should unlock the door to Spellman Investigations.

My family's office sits on the ground level, in a location that would be called the den in any other home. Four secondhand teacher's desks (the beige metal variety) form a perfect rectangle in the center of the office. Thirty years ago there was only one com- puter — an IBM — atop my father's desk. Now there is a PC on each of the four and a communal laptop in the closet. There are half a dozen file cabinets in an assortment of colors (also secondhand) encircling the room. Other than the industrial-size paper shredder and dusty blinds, that's pretty much it. Files are sometimes stacked two feet high on each desk. Scraps from the shredder are scattered about the floor. The room smells of dust and cheap coffee. The door at the far end of the room leads down to the basement, where all interrogations take place. David used to claim that the basement was the best place in the house to do homework, but I wouldn't know about that.

THE FAMILY
BUSINESS

David and I began working for Spellman Investigations when we were fourteen and twelve, respectively. While I had already made a name for myself as the difficult child, my status as employee redeemed many of my other less-than qualities. I suppose it surprised no one that, generally speaking, I took well to breaking the rules of society and invading other people's privacy.

We'd always begin in the trash. That was routinely the first job assigned to the Spellman children. Mom or Dad (or the off-duty cop du jour) would pick up refuse from a subject's residence (once the trash is left out for the sanitation department, it is considered public property and legal to appropriate) and drop it at the house.

I'd put on a pair of thick, plastic dishwashing gloves (and occasionally a nose clip) and sift through the garbage, separating the trash from the treasures. My mother gave precisely the same instructions to all of us: bank statements, bills, letters, notes, you keep; anything that was once edible or contains bodily fluids, you trash. I often considered these instructions incomplete. You'd be surprised how many things fall into the *none of the above* category. Garbology often made David violently ill, and by the time he was fifteen, he was pulled off this assignment altogether.

The year I turned thirteen, my mother taught me how to do court record searches in the Bay Area. Most of our work at the time involved background checks, and a criminal record search was the first step. Once again, the instructions were simple: Look for derogatories. Translation: Look for something bad. When we couldn't find a derogatory, the disappointment was palpable. People — the ones we knew by name or Social Security numbers — disappointed us if they were clean.

Background checks were the purest form of grunt work. They often involved traveling throughout the Bay Area to various courthouses, cross-checking names in record books. Before the municipal courts were dissolved in California, this meant visiting the records offices of at least four separate courthouses per county: superior criminal, superior civil, municipal criminal, and municipal civil (and occasionally small claims court).

Later on, our research time was abbreviated when the superior and municipal courts merged and most of the records could be found on microfiche. In the last five years, virtually all courthouse information has been transferred to computerized databases, and unless we were looking for a case more than ten years old, all the research could be done from inside the Spellman offices. What was once a twelve-to-fifteen-hour job turned into four hours or less behind a desk.

Aside from background research, the databases can also be used to locate an individual whose whereabouts are unknown. Acquiring a Social Security number is the key to this task. It is the holy grail of the PI world. But Social Security numbers are not public record. If you are not provided a Social Security number from the client, then a full name and a DOB (date of birth) or at the very minimum a full name (hopefully unusual) and city of residence are required. The next step is plugging a name and DOB into a credit header report. These reports provide some of the information on a complete credit report, such as address history and any bankruptcies and liens against the individual, but not the full report, since credit reports are also not public record. Through a credit header you can often get a partial SSN. Since one database might hide the first four digits of the SSN and another might hide the last four, if you look at enough of them, you can often assemble a full SSN.

Database research requires an attention to detail that my former teachers would not believe I was capable of. However, I liked finding dirt on people. It made all my trespasses seem trivial.

You could say first they tested our stomachs, then our patience, and finally our wits. For the second-generation Spellmans (and maybe even the first), surveillance was what we lived for. It was the part of the job that made you not care that you were working for your parents after school. But it is not without its lows. People aren't on the move all the time. They sleep, they go to work, they have four-hour meetings in office buildings, leaving you waiting in the foyer, your stomach growling and your feet aching. I loved being on the move; David loved the downtime. He used it to catch up on his homework. All I did was smoke.

Age 14: My first surveillance job was on the Feldman case. John Feldman hired my family to keep an eye on his business partner and brother, Sam. John had a feeling that his brother was involved in some shady business dealings and wanted us to tail Sam for a couple of weeks to see if his instincts were correct. While John's instincts were, in fact, correct, his assessment was not. Sam, from my observation, showed little interest in business altogether. He did, however, show great interest in John's wife.

David and I were both surveillance neophytes when we began the Feldman detail. I was an expert by the end. My father would drive the van, my mother the Honda. Both connected with us via radio. When Sam was on foot, David or I took point. We'd jump out of the car, maintain a reasonable distance on foot, and announce our coordinates into the radio so that at least one vehicle would always be ready to pick us up should Sam decide to take a cab, bus, or cable car. Mostly he took a room at the St. Regis.

What we learned on the Feldman job, aside from the fact that Sam was screwing John's wife, was that my years of sneaking around paid off. Simply put, my life to date had ingrained in me a certain natural stealth, had taught me how to test limits, and had disciplined me to know precisely how much I could get away with. I knew how to read people. I knew when I could follow a subject onto public transportation or when I needed to call a cab. I knew how long I could sustain the tail and I knew when it was time to quit. But half of it was that I didn't look like the sort of person who followed people for a living.

At the age of fourteen, I was already about five foot six, just two inches shorter than my current height. I looked a few years older than I was, but still like a student — in wrinkled T-shirts and worn-out denim. There was nothing to notice or not notice about my appearance — long brown hair, brown eyes, no freckles or identifying marks. If I had taken entirely after my mother, I might even be beautiful, but my father's genes have blunted my features and I hear the word *handsome* far more than *pretty.* Still, at my present age of twenty-eight, with the help of a best friend (who is a hairstylist) and a slightly improved fashion sense, I look all right. Let's leave it at that.

Age 15: Uncle Ray asked me what I wanted for my birthday. I told him a bottle of vodka, and when he said no, I suggested he teach me how to pick locks. This is not a common activity in the arsenal of PI skills, but he taught me anyway since he knew how. (When my mother discovered this fact, she gave him the silent treatment for two weeks.) I would never use this skill on the job, but I've found many recreational uses for it since.

Age 16: A pretext call is getting information under false pretenses. This was where my mother was genius. She has acquired SSNs, DOBs, entire credit card bills, bank statements, and employment histories all from a single phone call that might go something like this:

"Good morning. May I speak with Mr. Franklin? Oh, hello, Mr. Franklin. My name is Sarah Baker and I work for ACS, Incorporated. What we do is locate individuals who may have lost track of some of their assets. We have discovered over a thousand shares of a blue-chip stock in the name of one Gary Franklin. I need to verify that you are the same Gary Franklin. If you could give me your date of birth and Social Security number, then I can begin the process of transferring the stock certificates back to you . . ."

While I consider myself talented in the pretext department, my mother is and will always be queen.

Age 17: I drove on my first surveillance. For a year after I got my license, my dad would practice with me on the road. The concept is simple — aggressive but safe driving. Never drop more than two cars back (if you're working alone) and know your subject, anticipate where he/she might be going, so that you do not rely entirely upon sustaining a visual. This was my father's area of expertise. Having worked vice for so many years, he had a feel for the road and an almost psychic ability to predict a subject's next move.

As my dad taught me most of the on-the-road tactics, Uncle Ray taught me the off-the-road shortcuts. For instance, when you're driving at night, it's easier to maintain a visual on a car with only one working taillight. I still remember the day Uncle Ray passed me a hammer and told me to smash out the taillight of Dr. Lieberman's Mercedes-Benz. *That* was a perfect day.

Age 18: the magic year in my employment with Spellman Investigations. Because most of our work relates to legal matters, it is important to have the investigator be of legal age. At eighteen, I could serve court papers, perform interviews, and begin accruing the six thousand hours of fieldwork required for my PI license. The only thing standing between me and my license was a criminal record. A thorough background check is done on all potential PI candidates. Everything that happened before I turned eighteen would be sealed in my juvenile record, but as my father reminded me, I needed to stay out of serious trouble after that.

Age 21: On my birthday, I took the two-hour multiple-choice exam and three months later got my license.

David, on the other hand, ended his career with Spellman Investigations when he was sixteen, citing its interference with his schoolwork. He would never work for my family again, although one day we would work for him. The truth was, the job didn't interest David. He thought people had a right to privacy. The rest of us did not.

Do Not Disturb

It was the nature of the business: snooping, legally and sometimes illegally. Like an executioner, you harden yourself to the truth of your job.

When you know what you and your parents are capable of doing to pry into another person's life, erecting highly structured fortresses to protect your own privacy becomes second nature. You grow accustomed to your mother asking your brother if you have a boyfriend these days and then following you, when you venture out, to get a look at him. You think nothing, when you're sixteen, of taking three buses in opposing directions and killing an hour and a half to lose her. You install deadbolts on your bedroom door and instruct your brother to do the same. You change those locks twice a year. You interrogate strangers and spy on your friends. You've heard so many lies that you never quite believe the truth. You practice your poker face in the mirror so often that your face freezes in that expression.

My parents always had a more than passing interest in the company I kept. My father insisted that the boys in my life were directly responsible for my juvenile-delinquent tendencies. My mother, more accurately, assumed that I was the bad influence. As my parents theorized about my various relationships and their effect on my alcohol consumption and truancy status, Petra theorized about my habit of sabotaging relationships. She said I either chose men who were entirely inappropriate for me, or I tested their patience to the point where they had to break up with me. I told her she was wrong. She suggested I make a list and see for myself.

Like my lists of basement interrogations and unproven crimes, the list of ex-boyfriends[1] is like a cheat sheet of my past. In the interest of brevity, I kept the information to a minimum: number, name, age, occupation, hobby, duration of relationship,

[1] This list does not include one-night stands. That is a separate list, which will not be included in this document.

and last words — i.e., reason given for termination of relationship.

List of Ex-Boyfriends

Ex-boyfriend #1

Name:	Goldstein, Max
Age:	14
Occupation:	Ninth grader, Presidio Middle School
Hobby:	Skateboarding
Duration:	1 month
Last Words:	"Dude, my mom doesn't want me hanging out with you anymore."

Ex-boyfriend #2:

Name:	Slater, Henry
Age:	18
Occupation:	Freshman, UC Berkeley
Hobby:	Poetry
Duration:	7 months
Last Words:	"You've never heard of Robert Pinsky?"

Ex-boyfriend #3:

Name:	Flannagan, Sean
Age:	23
Occupation:	Bartender at O'Reilly's
Hobby:	Being Irish; drinking
Duration:	2.5 months
Last Words:	"Oder dan Guinness, we don' haf much in common."

Ex-boyfriend #4:

Name:	Collier, Professor Michael
Age:	47 (me: 21)
Occupation:	Professor of philosophy
Hobby:	Sleeping with students
Duration:	1 semester
Last Words:	"This is wrong. I need to stop doing this."

Ex-boyfriend #5:

Name:	Fuller, Joshua

Age:	25
Occupation:	Web designer
Hobby:	Alcoholics Anonymous
Duration:	3 months
Last Words:	"Our relationship is a threat to my sobriety."

Ex-boyfriend #7:

Name:	Greenberg, Zack
Age:	29
Occupation:	Owner of web design firm
Hobby:	Soccer
Duration:	1.5 months
Last Words:	"You ran a credit check on my brother?"

Ex-boyfriend #8:

Name:	Martin, Greg
Age:	29
Occupation:	Graphic designer
Hobby:	Triathlons
Duration:	4 months

Last Words:	"If I have to answer one more fucking question, I'm going to kill myself."

As for Ex-boyfriends #6 and #9, I'll get to them later. Some people you simply cannot reduce to the data that will fit on a three-by-five index card. No matter how hard you try.

Sometimes I create a list at the moment of the event. Other times, the list is formed long past its point of origin, when its significance ultimately becomes clear to me. Even if I were to do away with all the other lists, this one must remain, because this is the list that documents the end of my reign of terror in the Spellman household.

The Three Phases of my Quasi-Redemption
- Lost Weekend #3
- The Foyer-Sleeping Incident
- The Missing-Shoe Episode

As you might have gathered, Lost Weekend #3 is part of its own separate list. Eventually, when the scraps of paper that contained my lists were transferred to a password-protected computer file, I created a spreadsheet so one (me) could easily cross-reference data that appeared on more than one list. As for the Lost Weekends, there were twenty-seven total. At least that's the number I came up with. It wouldn't surprise me if there were more that I didn't know about.

OLD UNCLE RAY

I cannot tell you about new Uncle Ray without a fair profile of Uncle Ray before there ever was a Lost Weekend. One Ray means nothing without the other.

Uncle Ray: my father's brother — three years his senior. Also a cop. Or was a cop. He joined the force when he was twenty-one, made homicide inspector by twenty-eight. His moral compass was highly evolved, as were his dietary standards.

He ran five miles a day and drank green tea before anyone ever told you to drink green tea. He ate leafy greens and cruciferous vegetables and read *Prevention* magazine the way Russian lit professors read Dostoyevsky. He drank exactly one whiskey and soda at weddings and wakes. No more.

Uncle Ray met Sophie Lee when he was forty-seven, and while he had always been a serial monogamist, this was the first time he really fell in love. Sophie taught elementary school and happened to be the only witness to a vehicular homicide Ray was investigating.

Six months later they were married in a banquet hall overlooking San Francisco Bay. I have little recollection of the night. What I can say for sure is that, at twelve years old, I drank more at Uncle Ray's wedding than he did.

From all I could tell, Uncle Ray and Sophie were happy. Then shortly after their first anniversary, Uncle Ray, a man who never smoked a cigarette in his life, got cancer. Lung cancer.

Within a month, Uncle Ray went into the hospital, had part of his lung removed, and endured a grueling stint of chemotherapy. He lost all of his hair and twenty pounds. The cancer metastasized. Uncle Ray began another spate of chemo.

The whispers in our house during that time were deafening. There was a constant hum of words, short phrases, and occasionally muffled arguments all unintended for our ears. But David and I are highly trained eavesdroppers. "Surveillance starts at home" we used to say. Over the years we discovered "soft spots" in the house, specific locations where the household acoustics allow you to listen in on conversations in an entirely separate location. David's and my intelligence gathering resulted in yet another list.

- *Uncle Ray's chemo wasn't working*
- *Sophie stopped visiting him in the hospital*
- *Mom was pregnant*

The pregnancy was an accident, David and I concluded upon comparing notes. After thirteen years of raising me, I was sure my parents were ready to call it a day. But new life is the only thing that softens death. And when it became clear that Uncle Ray was going to die, it was then, I suspect, that my mother decided to have the baby. It was a girl and they named her Rae, after the man who would soon be dead. But then Uncle Ray didn't die.

No one could explain it. The doctors said he was within weeks from the end. It was as obvious on his medical chart as it was on his body. This was a dying man. And then he just got better. When the dark circles around his eyes faded and the flesh seemed to return to his cheeks, we still said goodbye. Three months later, after his appetite returned and he gained back thirty of the forty pounds that he lost during the vicious chemotherapy treatments, we still said good-bye. Six months later, when the doctor told Sophie that her husband was going to live, it was Sophie who said good-bye. She left him with no explanation. That is when the new Uncle Ray was born.

He started drinking, really drinking — more than one whiskey and soda at weddings and wakes. For the first time in my life, Ray could hold his liquor better than me. He started gambling, not friendly poker matches among friends, but high-stakes games with minimum bets of five hundred dollars in secret locations delivered through codes on a pager. The racetrack became his second home. The ponies were his new love. The only time I ever saw Uncle Ray run again was during halftime of a 49ers game when he ran out of snacks. His health food days were over. Mostly he ate cheese and crackers and drank piss beer by the case. He was no longer a one-woman kind of man. Uncle Ray would play the field for the rest of his life.

It could be argued that the new Uncle Ray was more fun than the old Uncle Ray. I, however, was the only person doing the arguing. Uncle Ray lived with us for the first year after That Fucking Bitch left him. Then he found a one-bedroom in the Sunset district just around the corner from the

Plough and Stars pub. During football season, you'd find him in our living room watching the games with my dad. Uncle Ray would pile the beer cans next to his chair, forming a perfect pyramid — the base sometimes as wide as eight across. Once, my father commented to Uncle Ray on his new diet and nonexercise regime. Uncle Ray said, "Clean living gave me cancer. I'm not going through that again."

THE THREE PHASES OF MY QUASI-REDEMPTION (AND LOST WEEKEND #3)

I was fifteen the first time Uncle Ray disappeared. He missed Friday night dinner, then Sunday morning football. His phone went unanswered for five days. My father dropped by Ray's apartment and found a week's worth of letters and flyers jutting out of the mailbox. He picked the locks to Ray's apartment and discovered a sink full of moldy dishes, a refrigerator devoid of beer, and three messages on the answering machine. My dad used his more-than-ample tracking skills and located my uncle three days later at an illegal poker game in San Mateo.

Six months after that Uncle Ray disappeared again.

"I think Ray is having another Lost Weekend," my mother said in muffled tones to my dad. This was the second time I had heard my mother refer to Ray's disappearing acts by the title of the 1945 film, a cautionary tale starring Ray Milland. We'd watched the film in English class once. I can't remember why. But I do recall thinking that 1945 debauchery didn't hold a candle to modern-day depravity. That said, my mother's reference stuck, and while I had no idea what truly went on during Uncle Ray's first two Lost Weekends, by the third I was an expert. That brings me back to the list I mentioned earlier:

Phase #1: Lost Weekend #3

It was a weekend that lasted ten days. Not until the fourth day of Ray's absence did we begin our search. The phone numbers, which my father amassed during the first two mysterious disappearances, were now typed, alphabetized, and filed neatly away in his desk drawer. Mom, Dad, David, and I quartered the list and began making inquiries. Several generations of contact numbers later, we learned that Uncle Ray was staying in room 385 of the Excalibur Resort and Casino in Las Vegas. Uncle Ray wasn't like those dogs you hear about that get lost on a camping trip with their family and somehow manage to limp, starving and dehydrated, the three hundred or so miles back to their owners. Uncle Ray would be dehydrated all right, but he never seemed to find his way home.

My father decided to invite me along "for the ride." David wanted to go, but he was in the middle of filling out college applications at the time. Any notions of a fun father-daughter vacation were soon laid to rest. The invitation to accompany my dad was my parents' version of an after-school special on the evils of drug and alcohol abuse.

Dad banged on my door at 5:00 a.m. We were scheduled to be on the road at 6:00. I slept in until 5:45, when my father grew suspicious of my lack of noise and made some more of his own. This time, a deafening series of thumps followed by a guttural *Get your lazy ass out of bed.* I dressed and packed in fifteen minutes and made it to the car as my dad was pulling away. I jumped into the moving vehicle like an action star in a buddy film. The image was lost after I buckled up and my dad told me I narrowly missed the worst grounding of my life.

I slept the first four hours of the drive and then flicked through the dismal radio station options for the next two, until my dad told me that he was going to rip my arm off and beat me over my head with it if I didn't stop. We discussed the open cases on the

Spellman calendar for the final three hours. What we didn't talk about was Uncle Ray, not for even a minute. We stopped for a quick lunch and arrived in Vegas shortly before 4:00 p.m.

Ignoring the DO NOT DISTURB sign, my dad banged on the door to room 385 of the Excalibur, I think even louder than he banged on my door that morning. There was no answer and my father managed to convince the hotel manager to open the room for us. A commingling of scents greeted us at the door — stale cigar smoke, flat day-old beer, and the sour, distinctive odor of vomit. Fortunately, the manager excused himself and allowed my father and me to take in this spectacle privately. Upon viewing the room, with its tacky winks to medieval times, Uncle Ray's debauchery seemed a fitting homage to King Arthur's court.

My father scanned the room, searching for evidence of Ray's present whereabouts. He gathered a few scraps of paper from the nightstand, studied the refuse, checked the closets, and then headed for the door. In the foyer, my father turned and looked back at me.

"I'm going to find Ray," he said. "You

clean this place up while I'm gone."

"What do you mean, clean?" I asked, needing clarification.

My father replied with the dry, even tone of a computerized voice, "To clean. Verb. To rid of dirt. To remove half-empty beer cans from window and dispose of appropriately. To empty overflowing ashtrays. To mop up vomit on bathroom floor. To clean."

That wasn't the definition I was hoping for. "Dad, they have this thing in hotels now. It's called housekeeping," I said in my own instructional tone. But my father didn't like my response. He closed the door behind him and came back into the room.

"Do you have any idea how hard those people work? Can you try to imagine the kind of filth that they see, smell, and touch on a daily basis? Do you have any idea?"

I'm pretty good at not answering rhetorical questions, so I let him continue.

"Uncle Ray is our mess," he said. "We clean up after him, whether we like it or not." With that last sentence, my father stared at me pointedly and then left the room. I knew he was reminding me that my messes, too, had to be cleaned up. I was sixteen at the time, and although his lesson was not without some impact, I didn't change. Not then.

Phase #2: The Foyer-Sleeping Incident

At nineteen, I wasn't much different. Instead of going to college, I went to work for my parents. I moved into an attic apartment in the Spellman home that was refinished as part of my employment contract. While I was still an asset to Spellman Investigations, I continued to be a liability in the Spellman household. My list of misdeeds had lengthened in three years and many of my habits, like staying out long past midnight and returning home too tanked to find my keys, were now out of my parents' control.

I don't remember much about the night of the Foyer-Sleeping Incident other than the fact that I had been at a party and had to be at work at 10:00 the following morning. I walked up the front steps, searched my pockets for the house keys, and came up empty. In the past, when I'd locked myself out — as I mentioned, a common occurrence back then — I'd climb up the fire escape to my bedroom or shimmy up a drainpipe in the back of the house and knock on David's window, which was closest to the ground. However, the fire escape ladder was not extended and David had left for college two years earlier, so his room window was locked. I weighed my options and decided that sleeping on the porch was more reasonable than dealing with my parents at this hour and in my state.

Rae, now five, discovered me the next morning and shouted out my location to our mother. "Isabel's sleeping outside." I slowly came to as my mom stood over me. Her expression was a hybrid of confusion and annoyance.

"You slept out here the whole night?" she asked.

"Not the whole night," I replied. "I didn't get back until three."

I picked up my coat/pillow, casually walked inside the house, and climbed the two flights of stairs to my attic apartment. I slipped into bed and grabbed three more hours of sleep. Added to my porch rest, that was almost seven hours total, which was well above average for me at the time. I woke somewhat refreshed and worked my full shift.

That same night, I arrived home just after 11:00. I had my keys this time and unlocked the front door. It opened just a crack. Apparently the security chain had been attached. I shook the door a couple of times, testing the strength of the chain, wondering if this was some kind of not-so-subtle hint from my parents. Then my mother came to the door, shushed me, shut the door in my face, released the chain, and let me in.

"Be careful," she said as she blocked the door and left only a small triangle for entry. I slipped inside and followed her gaze to the floor. There was Rae, bundled up in her sleeping bag, clutching her teddy bear, sound asleep.

"Why is she sleeping there?" I asked.

"Why do you think?" my mother snapped back.

"I have no idea," I said, trying to keep the brusqueness out of my voice.

"Because she wants to be just like you," my mother said, as if she had a bad taste in her mouth. "I found her on the porch two hours ago and after twenty minutes of coercion I managed to convince her to sleep in the foyer. You're setting an example here, whether you like it or not. So don't drive drunk, don't smoke in the house, cut down on the swearing, and if you're too wrecked to make it up the stairs to your bedroom at night, don't bother coming home. Just do that for me. No, do it for Rae."

My mother, exhausted, turned around and walked up the stairs to her bedroom. I did change that night. I did what I had to do to keep Rae from becoming the mimic of a fuckup like me. But my mother set the bar too low; I was still me and I was still a problem.

Phase #3: The Missing Shoe Episode

Before I opened my eyes, I knew something was amiss. I could feel a breeze overhead and heard the hum of a ceiling fan, which led me to the logical conclusion that I was not in my own bed, since I don't have a ceiling fan. I kept my eyes closed as I tried to piece together the night before. Then I heard ringing and quiet grumbling — the human kind — the male human kind. The ringing, or subtle chirping, was my cell phone. The moan was from a guy I must have met last night, although if pressed, I couldn't tell you where. All I knew was that if I didn't find my phone before it woke him up, awkward small talk would ensue. I knew I wasn't in the mood for small talk, because when I opened my eyes and sat up in bed, my head began throbbing violently. Fighting back nausea, I staggered through the room, which was a dump and I'll leave it at that. I found my phone under a pile of clothes and muted the sound. Then I noticed DAVID SPELLMAN on the screen and I clicked open the receiver and walked into the hallway.

"Hello," I whispered.

"Where are you?" He didn't whisper.

"In a café," I answered, thinking that would make him less suspicious of the whispering.

"Interesting, since you were supposed to be in my office fifteen minutes ago," he fumed. I knew I was forgetting something. Besides the last twelve hours, that is. I had a 9:00 a.m. meeting with Larry Mulberg, head of personnel for Zylor Corp., a drug company that was considering outsourcing their background checks. David occasionally throws business in our direction with clients of his firm. Although I was twenty-three at the time, I still would not have been charged with such a delicate responsibility, but Mulberg had called for the meeting at the last minute, offered no other scheduling option, and Mom and Dad were out of town on business. I suppose they could have asked Uncle Ray to handle it, but generally he refuses to get out of bed before 10:00, and Lost Weekends come on unexpectedly, just like the flu or a skin rash.

While I was more than comfortable committing run-of-the-mill screwups, blowing the chance at bringing in another hundred thousand dollars a year to the family business was not a screwup I or my parents could afford. I tore through random male's apartment, gathering my clothes and dressing as if it were an Olympic sport. I was already contemplating a professional career when I realized that I couldn't find my other shoe — the match to the blue sneaker already on my right foot.

I limped down Mission Street like Ratso Rizzo. As I staggered along, I tried to come up with a plan, one that involved me showing up at the meeting with two shoes and freshly showered. But it's hard to find new footwear before 9:00 a.m. and I was running out of time. I checked my wallet and found a three-dollar BART ticket. I trod carefully down the piss-stained stairs of the Twenty-fourth and Mission station and began rehearsing my apologies to David.

I arrived on the twelfth floor of 311 Sutter Street thirty minutes after my initial conversation with my brother and fifteen minutes late for my meeting with Mulberg. I should mention that David, at this point, was an associate at the law firm of Fincher, Grayson, Stillman & Morris. After high school, he attended Berkeley, graduated magna cum laude with a double major in business and English, and then went on to Stanford Law. I believe it was law school that destroyed David's sympathetic patience. By the time he was recruited by Fincher, Grayson in his second year, David had learned that not all families were like ours and that being perfect was nothing to feel guilty about. In essence, David discovered that I was not his fault and abruptly ceased his habit of compensating for me.

I entered the Fincher offices through a back entrance to avoid detection. I was hoping David had kept Mulberg in the reception area, so I could have a chance to clean myself up before I was seen. I wove through the mazelike hallway, trying to remember precisely where David's office was located. He spotted me first and yanked me into a conference room.

"I can't believe you go to cafés looking like that," David said.

I realized I probably looked worse than I thought and decided to come clean. "I wasn't in a café."

"No kidding. What was his name?"

"Don't remember. Where's Mulberg?"

"He's running late."

"Late enough for me to go home and take a shower?"

"No," David replied, looking down at my feet. He then stated the obvious with sullen disappointment. "You're wearing only one shoe."

"I need a Coke" was my only response.

The nausea was kicking in again.

David was silent.

"Or a Pepsi," I offered.

David grabbed me by the arm and led me down the hallway, through the main corridor, and into the men's restroom.

"I can't go in there," I protested.

"Why not?"

"Because I'm a girl, David."

"At the moment, it's not even clear that you are human," David smartly replied as he dragged me inside. A suited man was standing at the urinal, overhearing the last bit of our conversation as he finished up.

David turned to the suited man, who was zipping his fly. "Excuse the interruption, Mark. I need to teach my twenty-three-year-old sister how to wash her face."

Mark smiled uncomfortably and exited the bathroom. David placed his hands on my shoulders and turned me squarely toward the mirror.

"This is not how you show up for a business meeting."

Finding the courage to look at my reflection, I saw that my eye makeup had migrated halfway down my face and my hair, stringy and tangled, was bunched up on one side. The buttons on my shirt were askew and it looked like I had slept in it. Because

I had. Then there was the problem with my wearing only one shoe.

"Clean yourself up. I'll be right back," David said.

Rather than request a transfer to the women's restroom, I stayed put and did as I was told. Once I finished scrubbing the dirt and makeup off my face and gulped a pint of tap water directly from the spout, I retreated to a stall to avoid any further contact with my brother's colleagues. At least two men entered and urinated while I was waiting for David to return. I began daydreaming that he'd find it in his heart to bring me a Coke on ice.

"Open up," David said, as he banged on my stall. I could tell by the tone of his voice and the timbre of the bang that he was Coke free. I opened the door and David handed me a newly starched men's oxford shirt in a 38 regular, along with a stick of extra-strength deodorant.

"Put these on," he said. "Quickly. Mulberg is waiting in my office."

When I exited the stall, a pair of women's sandals was waiting for me on the floor.

"Size seven, right?" David asked.

"No. Size nine."

"Close enough."

"Where did you get those?"

73

"From my secretary."

"Since you're so good at persuading women to remove their clothes, maybe you could get the rest of her outfit," I suggested.

"I could, but your ass wouldn't fit in it."

We finished assembling my slapdash ensemble and concluded that while I looked remarkably unfashionable and unattractive, I no longer appeared hungover and irresponsible. David sprayed me with his cologne as we left the men's restroom and ventured into our meeting.

"Great. Now I smell like you."

"I wish."

Larry Mulberg was hardly a fashion plate himself and I suspected he would have no comment about my substandard attire. David's secretary entered the office in stocking feet and asked if anyone would like a beverage, and I finally got my Coke. The meeting went well: I explained to Mulberg the financial benefits of outsourcing background checks and gave him a thorough overview of my family's expertise in that area. I'm rather good at talking nonrelatives into things, so Mulberg bought it all, not once noticing the green tinge to my complexion or my bloodshot eyes.

I detached the size-seven sandals and

handed them back to David's secretary, thanking her profusely. Returning to my brother's office, I changed back into my wrinkled shirt and reluctantly tossed my abandoned sneaker in the trash.

"David, can you loan me cab money?" I asked, gesturing at my bare feet, expecting some sympathy. David, already behind his desk hard at work, stared at me coldly. He reached into his back pocket, took out a twenty, and left it on the edge of the desk. He then returned to writing his brief.

"Well, uh, thanks," I said, after I took the bill. "I'll pay you back," I continued, heading for the door. I almost made it out of the office before David finished me off.

"Make sure I *never* see you like that again," he said slowly and deliberately. It was not a piece of advice.

Then he ordered me to leave. And I did. In that moment I realized that the role of the raven-haired golden boy David played to my mousy-brown fuckup was not the plum part I had always imagined. It occurred to me that while I was egging the neighbor's yard, David never had the chance to try it himself. Destruction and rebellion are a natural part of adolescence. But David, always cleaning up after me, compensating for me, lost that essential rite of passage. Instead, he became a textbook son. And his only flaw was that he didn't know how to be imperfect.

I believe that miraculous transformations, the kind that usually involve a preacher smacking you over the head, are rare, so rare that when they do occur, they often cause suspicion. While my change was hardly on the scale of a miracle, it was substantial. Yes, you could still find me in a wrinkled shirt, or downing a few too many, or uttering an inappropriate comment, but you wouldn't find me leaving messes for other people to clean up. That part I stopped cold turkey.

Initially, the wave of distrust precipitated by quasi-responsible Isabel was profound enough to almost cause a relapse. My mother was convinced it was some kind of sinister trick and questioned my motives with the skepticism of a research scientist. For at least two weeks straight, my father said around the clock, "All right, Isabel, what gives?" Uncle Ray, on the other hand, appeared genuinely concerned and suggested that vitamins might help. In fact, for the first few weeks, New Isabel prompted more hostility than Old Isabel. But I knew it was only a matter of time before I would

build the trust, and when it finally happened, I could almost feel the breeze from
the collective sigh of relief.

THE INTERVIEW: CHAPTER 2

The mythology that surrounds my work is impossible to shake. The lore of the gumshoe has had decades to flourish in our culture, but not all myth is based in fact. The truth about the PI is that we don't solve cases. We explore them. We tie up loose threads, perhaps uncover a few surprises. We provide proof of a question for which the answer is already known.

Inspector Stone, on the other hand, does solve mysteries. Not the tidy ones from crime novels, but mysteries nonetheless.

Stone consults his notes in an effort to avoid eye contact. I wonder if it is me or if it's what he does with everyone, in order to shield himself from their pain.

"When was the last time you saw your sister?" Stone asks.

"It was four days ago."

"Can you describe her mood for me? The details of your interaction?"

I remember everything, but it doesn't seem relevant. Stone is asking all the wrong questions.

"Do you have any leads?" I ask.

"We're looking into everything," Stone replies, the standard police response.

"Have you talked to the Snow family?"

"We don't believe they were involved."

"Isn't it worth checking into?"

"Please answer my question, Isabel."

"Why don't you answer mine? My sister has been missing for three days now and you've got nothing."

"We're doing everything we can. But you need to cooperate. You need to answer my questions. Do you understand me, Isabel?"

"Yes."

"We have to talk about Rae," Stone says in an almost hushed tone.

I suppose it is time. I've been postponing it long enough.

Rae Spellman

Born six weeks premature, Rae weighed exactly four pounds when she was brought home from the hospital. Unlike many preemies who grow into normal-size children, Rae would always remain small for her age. I was fourteen at the time of her birth and determined to ignore the fact that a newborn baby was sharing my home. I referred to her as "it" for the first year, pretending that she was a recently acquired object, like a lamp or an alarm clock. Any acknowledgment I made of her presence was along the lines of "Can you move it outside? I'm trying to study," or "Where's the mute button on this thing?" No one found my objectifying remarks amusing, let alone me. I was not amused at all. I was terrified that this child would grow up to be another symbol of perfection like David. I soon discovered that Rae was no David, although she was extraordinary nonetheless.

Rae, Age 4

I told her she was an accident. It was over dinner, after she bombarded me for twenty minutes with questions about my day. I was tired, probably hung over, and in no mood to be interrogated by a four-year-old.

"Rae, did you know you were an accident?"

And Rae started laughing. "I was?" It was her habit back then to laugh whenever she didn't understand something.

My mother gave me her usual cold stare and began damage control, explaining that some children were planned and some were not, et cetera. Rae seemed far more baffled by the concept of planning a child than not planning one and grew bored with my mother's unnecessary discourse.

Rae, Age 6

Rae begged for three days straight to be allowed on a surveillance job. The begging was relentless and inconsolable. It was the on-her-knees, clasped-handed, insistent-whine-of-*pleeeeease* kind of begging that continued for most of her waking hours. Eventually my parents gave in.

She was six. Six, I repeat. When my parents told me that Rae would be joining us the next day on the Peter Youngstrom surveillance, I suggested that they'd *lost their fucking minds.* My mother apparently had, shouting, "You try! You try listening to that begging all day long! I'd rather have a toenail slowly removed than go through that again." My father seconded that with, "Two toenails."

That night I showed Rae how to use a radio. My father hadn't updated the equipment for a few years. While the radios were perfectly utilitarian, they were also the size of Rae's entire arm. I stuck the five-pound electronic device into her Snoopy backpack, along with some fruit roll-ups, packaged cheese and crackers, and a couple of *Highlights* magazines. The mouthpiece I slipped through the opening of the backpack and clipped to the collar of her coat. I showed her how to reach through the zipper opening and adjust the volume on the radio. Then all she had to do was press down the button on the mouthpiece when she wanted to talk.

We began the detail outside the subject's home at approximately six o'clock in the morning. Rae awoke at 5:00 a.m., brushed her teeth, washed her face, and dressed. She sat by the door from 5:15 to 5:45 a.m., until the rest of us were ready to leave. My father told me I could take a lesson. As we waited in the surveillance van three doors down from the subject's residence, Rae and I once again tested and reviewed radio procedures. I reminded her that crossing a street without being given the okay from Mom or Dad would result in a punishment so awful, her young mind could not envision it. Then my mom reiterated the street-crossing rule.

Rae followed every instruction to a T her first day on the job. I usually took point, instructing Rae by example on the general rules of surveillance. You could provide a manual on how to perform an effective surveillance, but those most suited for it follow their instincts. It didn't surprise anyone that Rae was a natural. I suppose we all expected it, just not to the level at which she adapted to the work.

I closed my distance from Youngstrom when the noon lunch traffic cut down on visibility. I was within ten feet of my subject when he made an unexpected one-eighty and shot back down the sidewalk in my direction. He passed me, brushing against my shoulder and offering a quiet "Excuse me." I was made and could no longer take point. Rae was about ten yards behind me and my mother and father were a short distance behind her. Rae saw Youngstrom turn back before my parents did. She quickly ducked under some scaffolding hidden from his view. My parents, focused on their six-year-old daughter, didn't notice the subject until he was practically standing right in front of them. Rae realized that she was the logical person to take point and made the offer into the radio.

"Can I go?" Rae pleaded, watching Youngstrom slowly fade out of view.

I could hear my mother sigh into the radio before she replied. "Yes," she said hesitantly, and Rae took off.

Rae ran down the street to catch up to the brisk walk of a man over two feet taller than she. When the subject turned left, heading west on Montgomery, my mother lost sight of Rae and I could hear the panic in her voice when she called to her through the radio.

"Rae, where are you?"

"I'm waiting for the light to turn green," Rae replied.

"Can you see the subject?" I asked, knowing that Rae was safe.

"He's going into a building," she said.

"Rae, don't cross the street. Wait until Daddy and I catch up," my mother said.

"But he's getting away."

"Stay put," my father said more forcefully.

"What does the building look like?" I asked.

"It's big with lots of windows."

"Can you see an address, Rae?" I asked, then rephrased the question. "Numbers, Rae. Do you see any numbers?"

"I'm not close enough."

"Don't even think of moving," my mother reiterated.

"There's a sign. It's blue," said Rae.

"What does it say?" I asked.

"M-O-M-A," Rae slowly spelled. This was undoubtedly an unnatural situation: My little sister was learning how to perform a surveillance before she could even read.

"Rae, Mommy's going to pick you up at the corner. Don't move. Izzy, I'll meet you at the entrance to MOMA," said my father. And then it occurred to me that, as a family, this was the first time we had gone to a museum together.

After that day, it was not unusual to find Rae on a surveillance job that didn't interfere with school or bedtime.

Rae, Age 8

There was a sixteen-year age difference between Rae and David. He was out of the house by the time she was two, and while he lived nearby, he was not a consistent presence like I was. He distinguished himself by buying her the best birthday and Christmas gifts and by being the only member of the family who didn't boss her around. On one of his rare dinner appearances, Rae asked David the question that had always been on her mind.

"David, why don't you work for Mommy and Daddy?"

"Because I wanted to do something else with my life."

"Why?"

"Because I find the law interesting."

"Is the law fun?"

"I'm not sure I'd use the word 'fun.' But it's compelling."

"Wouldn't you rather do something that is fun than not fun?"

David, unable to honestly explain to Rae why he left the family business without offending my parents, resorted to a different tack. "Rae, do you have any idea how much money I make?"

"No," Rae replied disinterestedly.

"I charge three hundred dollars an hour."

Rae appeared confused and asked what she believed was the next obvious question. "Who would pay that?"

"Lots of people."

"Who?" Rae pushed, probably thinking

she could tap the same spout.

"That's confidential," replied David.

Rae mulled this new information over in her head and continued on suspiciously. "What exactly do you do?"

David contemplated how to answer that question. "I . . . negotiate." When the confusion did not lift from Rae's face, David asked, "Do you know what 'negotiating' is?"

Rae responded with a blank stare.

"Negotiating is something you do on a daily basis. Some negotiations are implied, like when you go to the store and give the clerk a dollar for a candy bar; both parties are essentially agreeing on the exchange. You always have the option of saying to the clerk, 'I'll give you fifty cents for this one-dollar candy bar,' and he can say yes or no. That's negotiating. It's the process of coming up with a solution that different parties can agree upon. Does that make sense?"

"I guess so."

"Do you want to negotiate something right now?"

"Okay."

David considered a negotiable topic. "Let's see," he said. "I would like you to get a haircut."

Since Rae's last professional haircut had occurred well over a year ago, this was not the first time such a request had been made. And yet each appeal was met with the same unsatisfying response: Rae would administer her own haircut. The resulting lopsided ends and jagged bangs were certainly an eyesore, but to the dandy in my brother, Rae's hair was truly offensive.

My sister, tired of the repeated haircut harassment, snapped back, "I. Don't. Need. A. Haircut."

"I'll give you a dollar if you get one."

"I'll give you a dollar to shut up about it."

"Five dollars."

"No."

"Ten."

"No."

"David, I'm not sure this is a good idea," my mother interjected.

But this was David's job and he couldn't stop. "Fifteen dollars."

This time there was a brief pause before Rae said, "No."

David, sensing weakness, went in for the kill. "Twenty dollars. You don't need to cut it all off. Just trim the split ends."

Rae, showing an aptitude for bartering beyond her years, asked, "Who pays for the haircut? That's at least fifteen dollars."

David turned to my mother. "Mom?"

"This is your negotiation," said my mother.

David turned back to Rae, ready for the final settlement.

"Twenty dollars to you. Fifteen for the haircut. Do we have a deal?" David asked, reaching his hand across the table.

Rae turned to me for a nod of approval before the handshake.

"You're forgetting about the tip, Rae."

Rae pulled her hand away and turned to me. "Tip?"

"Yes," I replied. "You have to tip the hairstylist."

"Oh. What about the tip?" Rae said to David.

That is when David shot me an annoyed look and shifted from instructive older brother to ruthless corporate lawyer. "Forty dollars total. Take it now or the offer is off the table."

Rae turned to me again and I knew David's patience had come to an end. "Take it, Rae. He's ready to walk."

Rae held out her hand and they shook on the deal. She turned out her palm and waited for the money. As David paid Rae her forty-dollar bribe, he appeared pleased that he was able to teach his little sister something about his line of work.

The lesson in negotiation stuck with Rae. It stuck hard. She discovered that even simple acts of grooming could be negotiated to her end. In the first half of her tenth year, the only time she would brush her teeth, wash her hair, or take a shower was when money changed hands — more precisely, leaving ours and entering hers. After a brief family meeting my parents and I agreed that we had to cut her off cold turkey and deal with the consequences. It was three weeks before Rae realized that hair washing was not a career.

Rae, Age 12

Sometime in the winter of Rae's seventh-grade year, she made an enemy. His name was Brandon Wheeler. The genesis of their conflict has always remained somewhat fuzzy. Rae likes her privacy as much as I do. What I do know is that Brandon transferred to Rae's school in the fall of that same year. Within weeks he was one of most popular boys in her class. He excelled in sports, possessed a firm grasp of all academic subject matter, and had clear skin.

Rae had no problem with him until one day in class, when Jeremy Shoeman was reading aloud from a passage in *Huckleberry Finn,* Brandon offered a dead-on imitation of Jeremy's stutter. The class laughed up-roariously, which only encouraged Brandon, who added the Shoeman imitation to his regular playlist. Rae never had a problem with Brandon's previous impersonations, which included a red-headed boy with a lisp, a girl with horn-rimmed glasses and a limp, and a teacher with a wandering eye. Rae wasn't even friends with Shoeman. But for whatever reason, this rubbed her the wrong way and she was determined to put an end to it.

Rae's first line of attack was an anonymous typed note that read, *Leave Jeremy alone or you will be very, very sorry.* The next day when Rae caught sight of Wheeler corner-ing Shoeman during the lunch hour, appar-ently thinking the note was from the victim himself, Rae decided to come clean. Wheeler then spread the word around school that Rae and Jeremy Shoeman were a couple. While this infuriated Rae, she kept her cool as she plotted her revenge. I cannot say how my sister acquired this information, but she discovered that Brandon was not twelve, but fourteen, and was repeating seventh grade for the second time. The next time Brandon was flattered for his excellence in academ-ics, Rae made sure her classmates under-stood that it was a matter of practice and not talent.

Some minor verbal sparring between my sister and the fourteen-year-old seventh grader ensued. But Brandon soon learned that talk was Rae's weapon of choice and he resorted to the only weapon he knew. While I have never met a girl as mentally tough as Rae, she favors my mother and, at the age of twelve, was still under four foot ten and barely eighty pounds. She can run fast, but there were times she didn't have the chance. When I saw the unmistakable rash of an Indian burn on her wrist, I asked her if she wanted me to take care of it. Rae said no. When she came home with a black eye from a "dodgeball accident," I asked again. Rae insisted everything was under control. But I got the feeling that the constant bullying was starting to break her.

I had just picked up Petra from her apartment and we were on our way to a movie when my cell phone rang. Petra answered it.

"Hello. No, it's Petra, Rae. Izzy is right here. Uh-huh. What happened to your bike? Yeah. We're not far. Sure. 'Bye." Petra hung up the phone. "We need to pick up your sister at school."

"What happened to her bike?"

"She said it doesn't work."

We were five minutes away. Rae was sitting on the grass outside, her bike in pieces in front of her — the five-hundred-dollar mountain bike that David had given her for her birthday. I saw several boys standing some distance back, laughing at her expense. Rae told me to pop the trunk and Petra helped her gather the spoils of the wreckage and put them inside. Rae jumped into the backseat, took out one of her schoolbooks, and pretended to read. I could see her eyes watering, but I couldn't quite believe it. I hadn't seen Rae cry since she was eight years old and ripped open her arm on a barbed-wire fence. She had bled so much that day that it had been impossible to see the actual wound.

"Rae, please. Let me handle this," I said, dying for a chance to set things straight. We sat in silence for a few minutes, then she looked over at the flock of boys and caught sight of Brandon waving cheerily at her. And that was it.

"Okay," she whispered. I was out of the car.

As I swaggered across the grounds to the pack of future frat boys, I tried to gauge what level of bully I was dealing with. I have a knack for looking menacing (at least for a woman), so I made sure to walk slowly and

93

purposefully, deep down hoping that a few of the boys would scatter before I got too close. Three answered my prayers and took off, leaving four behind. At five foot eight, I had at least three inches and fifteen pounds on Brandon, the tallest. And I *knew* I could take him. But if all four boys decided to stick around, I could not predict the outcome. Petra read my mind and got out of the car. Leaning against the passenger door, she slipped a knife out of her back pocket and started cleaning her fingernails with it. The blade reflected the sun and before I reached Brandon, the rest of the boys decided that it was time to go home. In fact, so did Brandon.

"You. Stop," I said, pointing at my target. Brandon turned around and forced a sneer in my direction. I moved closer, backing him up against a chain-link fence.

"Wipe that dumb-ass smile off your face," I seethed.

The smile disappeared, but not the attitude. "What are you gonna do? Beat me up?"

"That's exactly what I'm going to do. I'm bigger than you, I'm tougher than you, I'm angrier than you, and I fight dirtier than you. Plus, I've got backup. You don't. So if I were to make a wager on how this fight would turn out, I'd bet on me."

"What's the big deal? We were just joking around," Brandon said, his nerves showing through.

"Joking. Interesting. Do you think destruction of property is funny? A black eye is funny? Intimidating a girl half your size is funny? Well, then we are going to have a good time." I grabbed his shirt by the collar, twisted it around, and shoved him against the fence.

"I'm sorry," he whispered nervously.

"Are you?"

"Yes."

"Listen to me very carefully," I whispered back. "If you lay a finger on my sister or her property ever again — if you even look at her the wrong way — I will fuck you up. Got it?"

Brandon nodded his head.

"Say 'I understand.' "

"I understand."

I released my grip and told him to get lost. Brandon ran away, a changed man, I told myself.

When I got back into the car, Petra suggested we go rough up some punks at the preschool around the corner. I looked at Rae through my rearview mirror.

"You okay?"

Rae returned my gaze with dry eyes. Then she asked, "Can we get ice cream?" as if nothing had happened at all.

I wish that were the end of the story, but it isn't. Brandon ran home crying to his father, who in turn called my parents and followed up by filing assault charges against me. When Rae and I arrived at home with our ice cream cones, my mother and father had already received the first threatening phone call from Mr. Wheeler. Their stern expressions offered a flashback of my misspent youth. I'm sure they were wondering whether the Old Isabel was making a comeback. My father suggested we speak privately in the office and told Rae to go watch TV.

Rae, of course, didn't watch TV. She lurked by the door (which my father had locked), eavesdropping on our conversation.

"Isabel, what were you thinking?"

"Believe me, you would have done the same thing."

"You threatened to kill a twelve-year-old boy."

"First of all, he's fourteen —"

"He's a kid —"

"— and I didn't threaten to *kill* him; I threatened to *fuck him up*. There is a difference, you know."

"What is wrong with you?" my mother yelled.

"That is the most reckless, irresponsible thing you've done in years," screamed my father.

Then Rae smacked her hand against the door and shouted at the top of her lungs, "Leave her alone!"

My mother shouted back, "Rae, go watch TV."

Rae banged on the locked door again. The thud was so loud it sounded as if she was throwing her whole body against it. "No. Leave Isabel alone! Open the door."

My father sighed and let Rae in the room. Rae pled my case, which I didn't, because I've got too much attitude. My father was forced to tone down his reprimand to, "In the future, let us handle this sort of thing, Izzy."

There was almost nothing my mother wouldn't do to protect her children, even if it was morally ambiguous. It was Mom who handled the potential assault charges, mostly because she can spot an Achilles' heel with almost X-ray vision. If there is a single unfiltered trait I inherited directly from her, that might be it.

Olivia ran a civil lawsuit check on Mr.

Wheeler and discovered a handful of sexual harassment suits in his wake. The pattern piqued my mother's curiosity and she ran an informal tail on Wheeler over the next week. She caught him with a mistress, snapped some revealing photographs, and then cornered him at the coffee shop on his way to work. My mother suggested he drop the charges. Wheeler said no. My mother showed him the photos and repeated her suggestion, adding that she expected Rae's bike to be replaced within the week. Wheeler called her a bitch, but the charges were dropped by the afternoon and a new bike was delivered on Friday.

Rae never forgot what I did for her that day. However, I should remind you that Rae's brand of loyalty takes an entirely different form than the devotion to which one might be accustomed. While she can readily tell you she loves you, it is entirely void of the sappy heart of a greeting card. She is merely stating a fact for your own edification. There were times it seemed Rae lived to please our parents and sometimes even me. But this often lulled us into a false sense of security. Rae's interest in pleasing ended if it didn't align with her own agenda. Yet there were times she followed instructions with the blind faithfulness of a well-trained dog.

How to Evade Capture

When Rae was about thirteen, the local media began to cover child abductions with the regularity of weather reports. Statistically, there was a decline in abductions compared to previous years; however, the media's alarmist tactics engendered a veritable mass paranoia among parents of school-age children. Even my own mom and dad took the bait.

On the six o'clock news, when retired special agent Charles Manning presented a series of preemptive tactics to ward off child predators, my parents took notes and implemented the only one that was not already in use. Avoid routines. Rae was instructed to lose her habits, to mix up her daily routine, to become a moving target.

To see the difference, you'd have had to be acquainted with her previous morning ritual: She staggered out of bed at 8:00, brushed her teeth, grabbed a Pop-Tart on her way out the door, and rode her bike to school, slipping into the classroom at 8:30 on the dot. On the weekends, she slept until 10:00 and then spent an hour making an enormous sugar-laden breakfast.

She was given her assignment Sunday night and by the next morning, Rae had fully implemented an entirely new routine.

Monday

Rae wakes up at 6:00 a.m. She goes for a twenty-minute jog and takes a shower. Rae doesn't like jogging — or showering, for that matter. She drinks a glass of calcium-fortified orange juice and eats a bowl of cornflakes. She walks to school, arriving thirty-five minutes early.

Tuesday

Rae sets her alarm for 7:30 a.m. and hits the snooze button for the next forty-five minutes. She crawls out of bed at 8:15, meanders downstairs to the kitchen, and begins preparing chocolate-chip pancakes from scratch.

Even though my apartment has a fully functioning kitchen, I usually head downstairs in the morning and drink my parents' coffee and read their paper. I observe Rae's activities and determine that she is in no rush. Then I state the obvious.

"Rae, it is eight twenty-five."

"I know."

"Doesn't school start at eight-thirty?"

"I'm going to be late today," Rae says casually, as she scoops the pancake batter onto the griddle.

Wednesday

I arrive in the kitchen at 8:10 a.m. Rae pours me a cup of coffee and hands me the newspaper.

"Read fast," she says. "You're driving me to school."

"Don't you think you're taking this too far, Rae?"

"No, I don't," she says, as she takes a bite out of an apple.

The last time I saw Rae eat an apple it was pureed and came in a tiny jar with a picture of a baby on it. In fact, produce in general has never been a part of Rae's food pyramid, which is primarily built on ice cream, candy, cheese-flavored snack food, and the occasional beef jerky. I'm so pleased to see her ingest something that fell from a tree that I don't protest when Rae grabs her backpack and tells me she's going to wait in my car, a 1995 Buick Skylark.

Thursday

At 7:45 a.m. my father yells from the bottom of the staircase, "Rae, you still need a ride to school?"

"Yeah!" Rae shouts from a distance.

"Then hurry up," my father bellows back.

Rae rushes to the top of the staircase, jumps onto the banister, and slides down to the bottom. As she and my father head out the door, my father says, "I asked you not to do that anymore."

"But you told me to hurry."

My father tosses Rae a Pop-Tart as they get into the car.

Friday

I enter the kitchen at 8:05 a.m. Rae sits at the table, drinking a glass of milk (another first) and eating a peanut-butter-and-banana sandwich.

"How are you getting to school today?" I ask, praying that she won't hit me up for another ride.

"David's driving me."

"How did you swing that?"

"We negotiated."

I don't bother with a follow-up question. I pour myself a cup of coffee and sit down at the table.

"You've done that five days in a row,

102

Isabel. Drinking coffee and reading the paper."

"No one is going to abduct me, Rae."

"That's what all abductees say."

My Evidence

The sprawl of facts that I am piecing together comes from an assortment of methods. Through direct contact or indirect observation, by questions after the fact, tape recordings, interviews, photographs, and eavesdropping whenever an opportunity presents itself.

I don't pretend that my evidence is flawless. What I am offering is a documentary of my own making. The truth, in the individual facts presented, is reliable. But don't forget that every image I submit is in my own frame and there are countless frames I cannot provide.

Inspector Stone has said that the past is irrelevant, that my treasure hunt of evidence has no real purpose. But he is wrong. Knowing *what* happened to my family is not enough. I need to understand *how* it happened, because maybe then I can convince myself that it could have happened to any family.

ONE YEAR AND EIGHT MONTHS AGO

One year and eight months before my sister disappeared, it was the third week in May and I was three months into Ex-boyfriend #6. Name: Sean Ryan. Occupation: Bartender at the Red Room, a semiswank joint in the Nob Hill area. Hobby: Aspiring novelist. Unfortunately that wasn't his only hobby. But I'll get to that later.

My mother and I had been surveilling Mason Warner for the last five days. Warner was a thirty-eight-year-old restaurateur who ran a successful bistro in North Beach. We were hired by one of his investors, who suspected Warner of skimming cash from the business. While a forensic accountant would have been more suited for this job, our client didn't want to raise any eyebrows. Warner had the effete handsomeness of a modern-day movie star and he wore nice suits; therefore, my mother stood by his innocence. I liked the job because Warner was on the move most of the day, so I wasn't trapped in a car for eight hours listening to my mother say, "Why can't you bring home a guy like that?"

I followed Warner into an office building on Sansome Street. I'd worn a baseball cap and sunglasses, so I decided to join him on the elevator ride to see his ultimate destination. Fortunately it was a crowded elevator. I entered first, hit the button for the twelfth floor (of a twelve-story building), and slipped into the back corner. Mason got off on floor seven. I followed him out of the elevator, removed the cap and glasses, and hung back until Warner turned a corner. He entered the office of a psychoanalyst, Katherine Schoenberg, MD. I returned to the lobby and waited in the foyer. I turned my radio back on and told my mom that we had an approximately fifty-minute wait ahead of us. She decided to get coffee. I sat down on a leather bench and read the paper. Five minutes later, Warner was back in the lobby, heading outside.

"Subject is on the move," I said into the radio.

"Take point. I'm still at the coffee shop," said my mom.

Normally we'd have given Warner a generous head start and let my mom run the tail from the car. However, without a second visual, I needed to keep my eyes on the subject continuously until my mom could provide backup. I dropped the newspaper and shadowed Warner outside. The second I was out the door, Warner turned back around and proceeded straight in my direction. I fished through my purse and pulled out a pack of cigarettes. I quit smoking years earlier, but a cigarette still is the best prop there is in our line of work. As I patted down my pockets, looking for a book of matches, Warner stepped in and gave me a light.

"Stop following me," he said, offering up a charming smile before he casually walked away.

I should have known: Men like that never go to shrinks.

That night, Ex-boyfriend #6 and I were having drinks at the Philosopher's Club, an old man's bar in West Portal. It's too clean to be a dive, but it has just the right amount of wood paneling and dated sports posters to remind you that this is not a place catering to the San Francisco elite. I saw the image of a martini glass adjacent to the words "Philosopher's Club" as Petra and I were riding the L train on the way back from her birthday celebration.[1] There was something about the sign that compelled us into the bar and we stayed the whole night, mostly because of our bartender Milo's bottomless bowls of peanuts and popcorn. That was six years before I arrived that night with Ex #6 and seven years before now. I've been a regular all that time. But the only reason Ex #6 and I were at the bar that night was because I won the coin toss.

"Tell me about your day," Ex #6 said.

"I got burned on a surveillance job."

"That means you got made?" he said, showing off his learned jargon.

"Uh-huh."

"You told me you never got made."

"Rarely. I think I said rarely."

Milo stepped over to us and refilled my whiskey. Milo was then in his midfifties, now (for those lousy at math) in his early sixties. He's an Italian-American male, approximately five foot seven, with thinning brown hair streaked with gray. He wears only pleated trousers, short-sleeved oxford shirts, an apron, and usually the latest in athletic footwear, which provides the only

---

[1] I asked Petra what she wanted to do for her twenty-first birthday and she said, "Get high and go to the San Francisco Zoo."

modern touch to his ensemble. You might imagine that I have only a passing relationship with Milo, but you'd be wrong. I've seen the man at least twice a week for the past seven years. I count him as one of my closest friends.

Ex #6 patted the bar and pointed to his glass. Milo eyed him rudely and refilled his drink at a snail's pace. Ex #6 put some bills on the bar and snapped a thank-you.

"I got to take a leak," Ex #6 said as he strode to the back of the bar. Milo watched him disappear, with the phony smile on his face dropping off as he turned to me.

"I have a bad feeling about that guy," said Milo. I didn't pay attention since Milo has said the same thing about all my boyfriends since I was twenty-one.

"I'm not having this conversation again, Milo."

"It's your life," he said.

Sometimes I get the feeling it isn't.

The following morning, I was in the Spellman offices typing up a surveillance report from a job earlier in the week. My mother was waiting for Jake Hand, a twenty-four-year-old hipster, guitar player, and porn shop clerk we occasionally employ when we're overbooked on surveillance jobs. Dad and Uncle Ray were working a case in Palo Alto. The clock struck 8:00 a.m., and Jake walked in the door sporting his tattoos and an extra spring in his step.

"Mrs. Spell, look at the clock."

My mother glanced up at our classroom-size timekeeper and said, "You're on time. I could kiss you."

Jake thought my mother was serious and offered up his cheek. She gave him a quick peck and then sniffed the air.

"Did you shower, Jake?"

"Only for you, Mrs. Spell."

Jake is secretly in love with my mother, which manifests itself primarily in grooming-related activities. In fact, most of her male acquaintances are secretly in love with her. Mom's blue eyes and ivory skin are perfectly offset by long, dark auburn hair (from a bottle these days). Only the crow's-feet around her eyes give away her age. But Jake can see no flaws through their thirty-year age gap, and Mom enjoys the luxury of having a truly devoted employee. I often wonder what turns their conversations take after eight hours in a car together.

"Isabel, when you're finished with the background, I need you to go shake down your brother," my mother said casually as she gathered her surveillance equipment.

"About?"

"About the twenty grand his firm still owes us on the Kramer job."

"He's going to tell me the same thing he always does. We get paid when they get paid."

"It's been three months. We expended six grand out of pocket and have not seen any return. I can't pay our bills."

My father likes to remind me whenever he hands me my paycheck (and has some time on his hands) that PI work will never make me rich. The fact is the PI bill gets paid last. Rent, office supplies, utilities are necessary for a business to thrive, but you can live without your private investigator. Although my parents have made a decent living for themselves with the business, there are times when we have a serious cash flow problem, which often happens when we do jobs for David.

"Then you talk to him. He's your son," I said. "You can use the whole guilt thing on him."

"Your brother responds more to violence than guilt. Rough him up if you have to. But don't leave that office without a check."

Mom zipped up her bag and headed out the door with Jake in tow. When she was halfway out, she turned back to me. "Oh, and give David a kiss from me."

I decided to drop by David's office at 1:00 p.m., thinking I could get a free lunch out of the visit. When I arrived, his secretary, Linda, who is not-so-secretly in love with him, told me that my sister had already arrived. Linda, like all of David's secretaries, believes that one day he will return her affections. But like so many other alpha males, my brother thinks monogamy is something you do somewhere between the age of forty and retirement. In fact, if I were searching for David's single flaw, this would be it. My brother is a true and unrepentant heartbreaker.

I entered David's office on the offensive. "What are you doing here?" I said, glaring suspiciously at Rae.

"Visiting," Rae replied without a hint of contrition.

"Why aren't you in school?"

"Half day," she said, rolling her eyes.

"Show her the evidence," said David.

Rae handed me a crumpled piece of paper — an official memo from school. Evidently she expected David to ask for documentation. I'd never known Rae to ditch school, but we are related, so it was natural for me to be suspicious.

"Okay, I'm out of here. See you next

Friday, David. Later, Isabel."

After Rae left, I turned to David for an explanation. "Next Friday?"

"She drops by every Friday," David explained.

"Why?"

"To visit . . . mostly."

"What else?"

"Well, she usually asks for spending money."

"David, she makes ten bucks an hour working for Mom and Dad. She doesn't need your money. How long has she been doing this?"

"Almost a year, I guess."

"You give her money every week?"

"Sounds about right."

"How much?"

"Ten dollars usually. Sometimes twenty, but I try to remember to keep the smaller bills on me these days."

"So you've given her about five hundred bucks this year?"

"Do you ever say 'dollar' anymore?"

"That's pathetic."

"Isabel, why are you here?" David asked, desperate to change the subject.

"For money."

"I see," David replied, smirking, the irony of the situation not lost on him. "A collection call."

"I can break a finger or two, bruise a few ribs, but Mom says to leave your pretty face alone. It's twenty grand, David. Pay up."

"You know our policy: We pay when the client pays. I can write you a personal check."

"Mom won't take it."

"I don't know what to tell you, Isabel."

It didn't end there. I plopped myself down on David's couch and refused to move until he let me speak with a superior. David sighed and walked out of the office, returning ten minutes later with Jim Hunter. Hunter had been a partner in Fincher, Grayson for five years and specialized in fraud defense. Hunter is a fit-looking forty-two-year-old divorcé with a boyish haircut and an unsettling way of looking you directly in the eye. Since I couldn't go home without some cash, I had to match his stare.

I thought my intimidation tactics were working when Hunter said he could get the bookkeeper to cut me a check for ten grand before I left.

"Under one condition," he said. "You have dinner with me next Friday."

Caught off guard, I said yes, knowing that if I didn't I wouldn't get paid that week, and if Mom found out I turned down both a date with a lawyer and ten grand, I'd never hear the end of it.

"I'll pick you up at eight," Hunter said, exiting the office.

David stifled a smile and I realized he had planned the whole thing.

"So you're my pimp now?"

While I was trying to squeeze money out of David, my mom was dodging Jake's flirty questions as they sat parked outside Mason Warner's bistro.

"Mrs. Spell, were you always so hot?"

"Jake, give it a rest."

Warner was on the move. He hopped into his Lexus and drove down Larkin Street. He parked on the corner of Larkin and Geary and entered the New Century Theatre, a strip club. After Warner entered the establishment, Jake unbuckled his seat belt and turned to my mom for instructions.

"Dream on," my mother said, unbuckling her own seat belt and hopping out of the van.

Inside the New Century, my mother sat at a booth and ordered a club soda. Warner seemed decidedly uninterested in the floor show, studying paperwork provided by a gray-haired patron in a black turtleneck and designer jeans. There was a smattering of customers throughout the sea of maroon velvet.

However, it was not Warner who caught my mother's eye. Seated in the front row, regarding the auburn-haired stripper with the focus of a religious zealot, was Sean Ryan, (soon-to-be) Ex-boyfriend #6. My mother is a woman who has seen everything, and so finding her daughter's boyfriend in a strip club did not in itself raise a red flag. What troubled her was that the entire staff knew his name.

Warner left after a half-hour meeting with the turtleneck guy. Their conversation was lost under what sounded like the soundtrack from *Shaft.* My mother reluctantly exited the club on Warner's heels and finished the job with Jake.

However, the next day, my mom pawned off the Warner detail on Dad and Uncle Ray, and returned to the New Century Theatre, wearing a shoulder-length blonde wig and sunglasses. She didn't expect to see Sean there again, but he returned at precisely the same time and sat in precisely the same spot. Two days in a row at a strip club spurred my mother's suspicion and she extended her tail on Ex-boyfriend #6 for the next week. He returned to the New Century twice more and frequented a number of sex shops in the neighborhood during the daytime. At night, Mom dropped her tail, knowing that Sean was either with me or at work.

My mother asked me when Sean's birthday is. I fell for that trick since she was reading the horoscopes and had gone through every member of the family and a few of our seasonal employees first. When she asked about Ex #6, it was so casual, I didn't catch on. I just assumed she was showing some interest, since Sean and I had been seeing each other for over three months — which, I should remind you, was some kind of record for me.

However, the birth date was not so Mom could buy him a present, but to acquire a Social Security number and run a credit check. (I never fell for that again.) From the credit check my mom used her sources at one of the credit card companies to access his recent charges. The ethics and legality of this move are beyond questionable, but my mom had a question that she needed answered.

Thursday morning, after my mother determined that her investigation was complete, she called me into the office for a debriefing.

"Sweetie, your boyfriend is a porn addict."

"Jesus Christ," I said, thinking if she really loved me, she'd have waited until I'd had my coffee. "And you know this how?"

My mother itemized Sean's behavior during the prior week and then presented me with several credit card bills, as well as his rental history at Leather Tongue Video. I skimmed the titles, trying to keep my expression steady, but it was hard when the list included *Tits of Fury; Dude, Where's My Dildo?; Double-D Inspector;* and *Sperms of Endearment,* among less derivative, but equally X-rated, titles.

"Honey, I got no problem with anyone who wants to give their sex life some spark with an adult video now and again. However, what I have observed points to a compulsive tendency."

"What do you expect me to do with this information?" I asked.

"It's up to you, sweetheart. I'm not suggesting you break up with him. All I'm saying is, if you plan on staying with Sean, you might want to learn how to give a first-rate lap dance."

I made my exit without a sound. I couldn't give my mother the satisfaction of any response. While I had no previous suspicions of what she had told me, I knew my mother and I knew that she didn't misinterpret evidence. But I had to see it for myself. I had to assemble my own proof. That same night, I waited until Ex-boyfriend #6 was in a dead sleep and I turned on his computer. If a man's not careful, you can learn an awful lot about him that way.

I broke up with #6 the next morning. But this time I got to utter the last words: *I don't think we have enough in common.*

Lawyer #3

Friday night, an hour before my date with the fraud defense attorney, David called me up and told me to be on my best behavior or there would be repercussions. As I raced out of my apartment to meet Hunter on the street (in an attempt to avoid any parent-lawyer introductions), my mother shouted out the window at me, "Just be yourself, honey." Contradictions like this have made my family life so difficult.

I knew immediately that this was not going to work out. Hunter is the kind of guy who dates women who wear high heels and a cocktail dress on a first date. I can't even walk in heels, and I generally believe that someone has to earn the right to see my legs. Besides, I had just broken up with #6 that morning. And while I was not actively grieving over the demise of that relationship, I was still feeling the sting over how it had ended. I had no real romantic interest in Lawyer #3, but I didn't see any point in wasting an opportunity to study the opposite sex. I decided to come up with a series of questions that would subtly weed out the potential porn addicts in my future and I practiced on Hunter.

1. Do you like movies?
2. How important is a film's plot to you?
3. Approximately how many videos do you rent a month?
4. If stranded on a deserted island, would you rather have:
   a) *The Complete Works of Shakespeare*
   b) The Led Zeppelin boxed set
   c) The entire *Debbie Does* oeuvre
5. Who's your favorite actress?
   a) Meryl Streep
   b) Nicole Kidman
   c) Dame Judi Dench
   d) Jenna Jameson
6. What is your favorite genre of film?
   a) Action-adventure
   b) Drama
   c) Romantic comedy
   d) Pornography

David phoned me the next morning with

empty threats. He then called my mother to tattle on me. At breakfast, Mom railed against my lack of breeding and suggested that if I ever wanted to date a man who didn't serve drinks for a living, I might have to take an etiquette class. My dad asked me what I ordered for dinner.

To review: Ex-boyfriend #7:

Name:	Greenberg, Zack
Age:	29
Occupation:	Owner of web design firm
Hobby:	Soccer
Duration:	1.5 months
Last Words:	"You ran a credit check on my brother?"

Because of my job, not in spite of it, I have always held a solid reverence for individual privacy and tried to respect it whenever I could — or whenever it didn't interfere with my work. I used to, that is. Before Ex #6. Before my mother invaded our privacy and told me secrets I should have figured out on my own. After him, I began questioning my own instincts, wondering whether fifteen years on the job had taught me nothing about human behavior.

Three weeks later, Petra called me, insisting on setting me up with her newest client. For the last five years, Petra had been working as a stylist at a trendy salon on Lower Haight. It never occurred to me that going to beauty school could one day pay off with a salary in the six figures, but in Petra's case it had. Having a way with scissors and a physique that attracted the moneyed metrosexuals of San Francisco, Petra charged over one hundred dollars a head. Her clientele was eighty percent male and no one pretended that the repeat business was purely for the cut. Her leather pants paid for themselves, she used to say. More like the leather pants paid her mortgage.

Petra was on the prowl to find me a date — specifically, a non-porn-addicted date. That was when Petra met Zack Greenberg, a walk-in who just happened to arrive during an unusual lull in business. He was polite, soft-spoken, and conditioned his hair regularly.

Petra, without realizing what I would do with the information, provided me with Zack's home address and birth date. From that, I acquired a Social Security number and was able to run a credit check, criminal history (only in the state of California), and property search. On paper Zack Greenberg was clean and impressive. I pulled his birth record and ran further checks on his parents, two brothers, and one sister. Aside from his youngest brother's Chapter 11 filing in 1996, the entire family was like a fifties sitcom. It was not until Petra told me that Zack didn't own a TV that I agreed to the date. The equation seemed simple. No TV = No Porn. Sure, he could have a solid magazine collection and an Internet habit, but a real addict would be a film buff, too.

Our first few dates were a bit dull, possibly because he was going over material I already knew. His parents ran a bakery in Carmel. His sister was a homemaker with 1.8 children (pregnant). His older brother owned a successful family restaurant in Eugene, Oregon. His younger brother owned an unsuccessful used-book store in Portland. By all the evidence presented to me, Ex-boyfriend #7 was a Boy Scout from a long line of Boy Scouts (who occasionally earned the bankruptcy badge). Having never dated a man who had the courage to order wine coolers at happy hour, I was initially intrigued by his milquetoast ways.

On our first date we went to the Castro Theatre and saw a revival of *The Philadelphia Story,* followed by cappuccinos and a stroll through Dolores Park, where a number of youngsters offered us drugs. Zack responded to the solicitations with a polite "No, thank you," as if he were turning down the product from a makeshift lemonade stand. Our second date consisted of an hour of arcade games (mostly skeeball), ice cream, and a brief soccer lesson, which ended with Zack on my couch, his shin packed in ice and me apologizing profusely. The relationship continued on in its quasi–Norman Rockwell fashion until I mentioned his brother's bankruptcy (don't ask) and Zack realized that he had never mentioned it.

Petra told me she would never set me up with anyone again until I "learned to use my powers for good and not evil." My mother, who had met Zack and promptly begun daydreaming about a wedding, didn't speak to me for three days. My father offered to pay for a video dating service, then laughed himself silly at that prospect. I, not so politely, declined.

Camp Winnemancha

Last fall, when Rae returned to school after summer break, she was assigned the customary five-hundred-word What I Did on My Summer Vacation paper for Mrs. Clyde's eighth grade English class. Instead of writing an essay, Rae (now twelve and a half) turned in a copy of the Merck Investments surveillance report with all the sensitive information redacted. Upon receipt of Rae's assignment, Mrs. Clyde without delay invited my mother and father for a parent-teacher conference and firmly suggested that next summer Rae go to sleepaway camp.

The following spring, when Rae was thirteen years old, Mrs. Clyde reinvited my parents for a follow-up parent-teacher conference and repeated her original suggestion with as much influence as she could marshal. My mother countered with an offer of swimming lessons and a dance class, but Mrs. Clyde held her ground, insisting that Rae needed to begin socializing more with her peers and participating in activities suitable for a girl her age. My mother made all the CAMP (said in a whisper) arrangements surreptitiously. She chose the setting, paid the tuition, and purchased most of the packing list, all the while remaining undetected. She and my father decided to wait until just one week before Rae's departure date to reveal her summer plans.

Mom broke the news to my sister Saturday morning at exactly 7:15. I know this because Rae's Greek-tragedy wails woke me out of a much-needed slumber. Her desperate protests continued throughout the morning and into the early afternoon, when she began phoning relatives in a quest to find allies in her camp-avoidance campaign. She even threatened to contact Child Services.

Of course she turned to me at one point. My response was, "David went to sleepaway camp. I went to sleepaway camp. Why shouldn't you?" Then she turned on me, pointing out that I went to camp because it was ordered by the court.[1]

[1] This is true: Shortly before my fifteenth birthday, Petra and I decided to teach ourselves how to hotwire a car. We checked out a book from the library

My mother sent Rae to her bedroom with a box of Cocoa Puffs and suggested she take some time to digest the shocking news. Then Mom sent me to the store to buy more sugared goods to bribe her younger daughter. While I was debating whether to purchase the generic or name-brand Nutter Butters, my cell phone rang.

"Hello?"

"Izzy, it's Milo at the Philosopher's Club."

"Is everything all right?"

"No emergencies. But your sister is in my bar and I can't get her to leave. Could you come and pick her up?"

"My sister?"

"Yeah. Rae, right?"

"I'll be right there."

I arrived at Milo's twenty minutes later, stopping in the foyer to overhear the continuation of my sister's hopeless appeals.

"I have a B-minus average. And that's not,

---

called *Preventing Car Theft* (which, surprisingly, detailed exactly how to steal a car) and roamed the neighborhood (book in hand) for a car with a cracked window or unlocked door. We were caught shortly after midnight when the owner of the vehicle looked out his window, noticed the glow of a flashlight (reading light) coming from inside his car, and called the cops.

like, an A in PE and a C in math. That's a B-minus across the board. I said I was willing to negotiate. I said I'd be flexible with my negotiations. I even suggested we go to a mediator to work this out. But nothing. Nothing. They wouldn't budge an inch."

I tapped Rae on the shoulder. "Come on. Time to go."

"I'm not done with my drink yet," she coldly replied. I looked down at the amber-hued beverage and turned to Milo.

"Ginger ale," he said, reading my mind.

I finished Rae's drink for her.

"Now you're done. Let's go." I grabbed her by the back of her shirt and yanked her off the barstool.

In the car, Rae was suddenly silent — hopelessly and pathetically silent.

"I'm going to camp, aren't I?"

"Yes."

"And there's nothing I can do about it?"

"Nothing."

Rae calmly and suspiciously accepted her fate. She did not utter another word of protest for the rest of the week. She made casual small talk during the two-hour drive through the wine country and up the gravelly dirt road to Camp Winnemancha. My mother always taught Rae to choose her battles and her opponents wisely. It would

127

take some time to realize, but Rae had learned this lesson all too well.

It began with phone calls — hourly messages, uncalculated and desperate. "Get me out of here or you'll blow my college fund on mental health care." "I'm serious, if you know what's good for you, you won't make me spend another day in this pit of hell." Then Rae's emergency cell phone was confiscated, which gave her some time to regroup and develop new tactics.

The letter-writing campaign was next. In the evening my dad would unwind while drinking a beer and reading aloud from Rae's epistolary pleas:

My Dearest Family,
    In theory, I'm sure that camp is an excellent idea. But frankly, I don't think it is right for me. Why don't we cut our losses and call it a day?
    I look forward to seeing you when you pick me up tomorrow.
                    I love you all very much,
                                        Rae

Rae's second letter arrived on the same day as her first:

My Dearest Family,

I have skillfully negotiated with the camp director, Mr. Dutton, who assures me that if you pick me up from camp tomorrow, he will refund half of your investment. If you are still more concerned with the money than my mental well-being, I am willing to repay the remainder by working the rest of the summer for free. I look forward to seeing you tomorrow when you come get me out of here.

Love always,
Rae

P.S. I've enclosed a map and a $20 bill (gas money).

A second wave of phone messages began with a decidedly different flavor. Tuesday, 5:45 a.m.:

Hi, it's me again. Thanks for the candy, but I'm on a hunger strike, so it's useless to me. If you get this message in the next ten minutes, call me at . . .

My father skips to the next message. Tuesday, 7:15 a.m.:

I think they're running a white slavery

ring out of this place. Use that information however you see fit. Uh-oh, I better run —

The next message didn't arrive until Tuesday, 3:42 p.m.:

Hi, it's Rae. I changed my mind. This place isn't so bad. I just snorted a line of cocaine and things are looking much brighter. I could use some more money — like a grand. And maybe some cigarettes.

The last message made my dad laugh so hard, he choked on his coffee and then spent the next ten minutes recovering from a coughing fit. He said the messages alone were worth the cost of camp. But then the phone calls to Spellman Investigations halted abruptly.

When I arrived early, for an 11:00 a.m. meeting at David's office, Rae was already into her fourth phone call of the day to our brother. It was the first time that I noticed David spoke to all his family members as if we were well-funded but extremely difficult clients.

"Listen to me very carefully, Rae," my brother said. "I'm going to have my secretary send you a care package today — let me finish. In it will be all the crap you like. You're going to eat it. You're going to share it. And you will write me a letter — one letter only — thanking me for my thoughtful gift and informing me of at least one friend you've made. If I receive the letter and you refrain from making any more phone calls to me during the duration of your stay, then I'll have a nice fifty-dollar bill for you when you return. Got it? I will not accept any more phone calls from a Rae Spellman."

David hung up the phone, satisfied that he had made his point.

"For fifty bucks and some candy, I'll stop calling you, too," I said.

Five minutes later, David got another phone call. The interim receptionist buzzed through.

"Mr. Spellman, your sister Isabel is on the phone."

David replied, "My sister Isabel is sitting right in front of me."

"Excuse me, sir?"

"Put her through." David paused before he picked up the phone, still deciding what tack to take, presumably.

"That's it, Rae. No candy and no money," David said in his most hardball lawyerly manner and slammed the phone into the receiver.

"It's hard to believe I'm related to her," David said. Then, after he thought about it, continued, "Or you, for that matter."

What I found hard to believe was that Rae never called David back. I didn't realize until much later that Rae had chosen a new opponent and an entirely different battle.

Weeks later, Rae told me precisely when the tables had turned for her, when she knew that "this was a matter of life or death."

"At no point was it a matter of life or death, Rae," I said. To which she replied, "If that's what you have to tell yourself."

Semantics aside, the turning point was the Camp Winnemancha talent show.

Kathryn Stewart, age twelve, was singing that annoying song from *Titanic.* Haley Granger and Darcy Spiegelman had just performed a tap dance duet to some crappy showtune. Tiffany Schmidt lip-synched and pranced around to a Britney Spears song. And Jamie Gerber and Brian Hall performed an original hip-hop number "so embarrassing it hurt." Rae claimed that the talent show was the first thing that had made her cry in over two years. She responded with a talent act of her own: nicking one of the camp director's cell phones and stealing out of the auditorium undetected.

While the rest of the camp was distracted by the parade of future *American Idol* contestants, my sister roamed the woods draining the battery on Director Webber's mobile phone. This time she didn't call my brother, my mother, or my father. Rae had a plan and she was only interested in talking to one person: me. There were three messages on my cell phone, one at the office, and five on my home phone when I finally decided to pick up the latest call from a 707 area code. It was my plan to put an end to this once and for all.

"Rae, if you don't stop calling me, I'm going to file harassment charges with the police."

"I don't think you can file those charges against a minor. You might have to file them against Mom or Dad on behalf of me. And I think they'd get mad at you if you did."

"Rae, where are you calling from?"

"A cell phone."

"I thought your phone was confiscated."

"It was."

"So where'd you get the phone?"

"I borrowed it."

"Is 'borrow' in quotes?"

"Remember the Popovsky case?" Rae

asked coolly.

My hand tightened over the phone, wondering where she was going with this. "Yes," I said.

"You told Mom and Dad not to take the case. You said Mrs. Popovsky was a horrible woman and Mr. Popovsky didn't deserve to be hounded by PIs."

"I know what I said, Rae."

"Do you remember calling Mr. Popovsky to warn him that he was going to be under twenty-four-hour surveillance?"

"I remember."

"Do you remember driving Mr. Popovsky to the airport in the middle of the night and telling him that his soon-to-be-ex wife was hiding assets in an offshore account?"

"I said I remember."

"Do you remember giving him the account number?"

"Get to the point, Rae."

"I don't think Mom or Dad would take kindly to this information."

I knew my sister was capable of many things. But this did, in fact, surprise me.

"Are you blackmailing me?" I asked point-blank.

"That's an ugly word," Rae replied, and I wondered what movie she'd gotten that line from.

"Yes, it is."

"I'll see you tomorrow," Rae said and hung up the phone.

My drive through the wine country breezed by. Rage kills monotony better than any book on tape. I screeched to a halt in front of the camp office, a building fashioned after a log cabin. Through the dust that billowed around my car, I spotted Rae sitting on a collection of duffel bags. When she saw the car, her eyes lit up and she raced toward me for a hug.

"Thank you. Thank you. Thank you."

I pried her arms off me and pushed her away. "Do I need to sign you out?" I said as roughly as I could.

She tentatively pointed to the office. I settled the paperwork and returned to the car. I popped the trunk and told her to put her bags inside.

"I'll never forget this, Izzy."

After I slammed the trunk shut, I grabbed Rae by her forest-green Camp Winnemancha T-shirt and twisted the collar into a mild choke hold. Then I slammed Rae against the side of the car. (If you're thinking this is harsh, trust me, she can take it.)

"Now you want to play nice? I don't think so. I will *not* live like this. I will not have my thirteen-year-old sister playing me like a puppet. Blackmail is a crime, Rae. It's not a game. Manipulating people is wrong. Sometimes life isn't perfect and you just have to suck it up and deal. Can you do that? Or do you want to keep playing games with me? If you do, we're on. But I should warn you: Fucking with me is an extremely bad idea. So what's it gonna be, Rae? Are we gonna play nice, or do you want to see how dirty I can fight?"

Sometimes you can just feel eyes upon you. Two camp counselors and two campers were frozen in their tracks, internally debating whether they should call the authorities. I released my hold on Rae and walked around to the driver's-side door. Rae turned to our audience and broke the tension with a shrug of the shoulders.

"We're actors," she said, and then hopped in the car.

Rae remained silent for the first seven minutes of the drive, breaking her previous record by five-and-a-half minutes. I wasn't surprised when she finally spoke.

"I love you, Isabel. I really, really love you."

"No talking," I answered, wondering how long I could realistically enjoy the quiet.

Five minutes later, Rae asked, "Can we

get ice cream?" as if nothing had happened at all.

Lawyer #4

When David learned that I had retrieved Rae from camp, he immediately grew suspicious and invited me out to lunch. Over mussels and *pommes frites* at Café Claude, David asked a question that would have been obvious only to him.

"Does Rae have dirt on you?"

"Excuse me?" I replied, playing innocent.

"You wanted her to go to camp more than anyone else and then out of the blue you change your mind and bring her home. She's got something on you. That's the only logical explanation."

"You're wrong —"

"Deny it all you want, but since Rae has got dirt on you, I in theory have dirt on you, since I could reveal Rae's dirt to Mom and Dad without actually knowing what the specific dirt is. Then it would only be a matter of time before they got it out of Rae. And I have a feeling you really don't want them to know. Therefore, whatever power Rae wields over you, I do, as well."

"Where are you going with this?" I asked nervously.

"Saturday you're going on a date with my

friend Jack. You don't get a last name. He'll pick you up at seven. Please wear something clean and brush your hair."

I slowly gathered my belongings and headed for the door. At the last moment I turned back and said, "This is not normal."

"That's what I've been saying for years," David replied.

Jack Weaver, Lawyer #4, arrived at 6:55 p.m., which rendered the parent-lawyer introductions inescapable. My mother gushed over the cashmere-clad attorney with the transparent tact of a campaigning politician. I checked my watch every minute or so and suggested it was time to go, until my mother snapped, "Give it a rest, Izzy." My father gave Jack his cell phone number and told him to call should I give him any trouble and then laughed himself silly over his little joke.

By 7:45 p.m. we were on the 101, heading south to Bay Meadows Racetrack. Apparently Jack liked to gamble with more than just his time.

I became suspicious immediately. Jack was clearly not a man in need of a matchmaker. He had a clean-scrubbed messiness about him that I associate with men who try to downplay their looks. His clothes were just a bit untucked and his hair a touch un-coiffed, yet nothing seemed calculated for that effect. I became certain that there was no way in hell Jack willingly submitted to this date. Coercion was involved, yet there was no logic I could impose on David's ar-ranging this date. The only person who benefited was my mother.

It is an uncommon condition, but my mother has a true and unwavering love for lawyers. I can cite only a few possibilities for why this is the case. Perhaps because her perfect son is a lawyer, or because we get most of our business from lawyers, or maybe it's the nice suits they wear, or maybe she's just a sucker for higher educa-tion. I am less concerned with the founda-tion for this fact than the fact itself. The fact cuts into my quality of life.

As the evening wore on, my suspicion mingled more and more with attraction. What I discovered beneath the surface of this well-groomed attorney was a man with a serious gambling problem. It was his care-ful study of the morning line followed by outrageously inappropriate betting that gave it away. This would turn off most women, but not me. I've always preferred men with flaws; it's simply easier for me to relate to them. But what made this discovery particularly sweet was that my mother had unwittingly sanctioned a date between me and a man who probably had a bookie on his payroll.

While Jack placed yet another five-hundred-dollar bet on a two-year-old gelding that he had a good feeling about, my attention shifted to a suspicious male roaming the upper tier of the racetrack bleachers. I watched Suspicious Male from a distance at first and noticed that none of his movements indicated any real interest in the horse races themselves. When a race was on, Suspicious Male rarely looked at the track, just at the patrons. When I observed Suspicious Male bump into a man eating an ice cream cone by the concession stand, I approached the man eating the ice cream cone after the fact and asked him if he still had his wallet. He did not.

I ran after Suspicious Male, who was now descending the bleachers in the direction of the men's restroom. Jack caught up with me and asked me what I was up to. I explained I was following a potential pickpocket.

I caught up with Suspicious Male and blocked his passage into the restroom.

"Hey, asshole, hand it over."

Suspicious Male visibly paled and said,

"Excuse me, ma'am?"

"Don't call me 'ma'am.' Just give me the fucking wallet," I said, shoving Suspicious Male against the graffiti-coated wall. He eyed Jack and then me and decided it wasn't worth the fight. Suspicious Male handed me the wallet and then raced into the bathroom.

My sting operation distracted Lawyer #4 from race #7. His horse lost, which was statistically predictable since it was a long shot, but Jack was still disappointed at missing the race. Like many gamblers or habitual sporting-event watchers, he was convinced that his observation of an event could alter its ultimate outcome. After we returned the wallet to its rightful owner and offered a description of the perpetrator to the head of security, I asked Jack if he wanted to bet on another race, but he said no. He was no longer feeling lucky.

The following Monday I dropped by David's office to discuss an upcoming surveillance job and Lawyer #4. The fact was, this lawyer I could like.

"What did he say about me?" I subtly inquired.

"Who?"

"Lawyer Number #4."

"You will never be in a normal relationship if you keep bar-coding your dates."

"I know he said something."

Struggling to control a smirk, David said, "He described you as a cross between Dirty Harry and Nancy Drew."

"Is that a compliment?" I asked.

"I don't think so."

Lost Weekend #22

Uncle Ray disappeared again. It had been twelve days since anyone in the city had seen him. My father tracked Ray's credit card charges to a Caesars Palace in Lake Tahoe. Neither of my parents was able to break away for a trip to collect him. The responsibility then fell on me. I didn't want to go alone, so I called David, thinking it was a long shot.

"Will I have time to ski?" he asked.

"Sure, while I'm prying the bottle of bourbon out of Uncle Ray's hands and paying off his hookers, you have a ball."

"Okay, I'll go," David replied, ignoring my sarcasm.

I saw the drive as an opportunity to find out what dirt my mother had over my brother.

"Admit it, David, I embarrass you."

"I'll admit that freely."

"There is no logical reason why you would want to set me up with your friends."

"I'm hoping some of their manners will rub off on you. Think of it as cheap charm school."

"This is all part of Mom's master plan. And I know you. You wouldn't do this just to please her. She's got dirt."

"Are you suggesting that Mom has blackmailed me into setting you up with my colleagues?"

"Can anyone in our family answer a straight question?"

"Uncle Ray is pretty good at it."

Seven hours later, I found my uncle playing Caribbean poker in the Tahoe Harrah's casino. I asked him what he'd been up to for the past two weeks and he replied, "Let's see. I went on a five-day bender, sobered up during a forty-eight-hour poker game. Had a few dates in Reno. Another poker game. Three days, for the life of me, I can't remember. And the last four days or so, I've been trying my luck at the tables. How are you, sweetie?"

David was right. Uncle Ray was the only straight shooter in the family. On occasion my sister would come close, but she used deception when necessary. For my uncle, there was no stealth in his debauchery. He wore it like a crown.

It had taken four hours of casino hopping to locate Uncle Ray. David, true to his word, went skiing and left the dirty work to me. In the last fortnight it turned out that Uncle Ray had lost everything — in fact, more than everything — his entire savings, his pension for the next six months, his fifty-dollar watch, a gold money clip my mother had given him for his last birthday, and a pair of shoes (I think), since he was wearing dime-store flip-flops. I tried to pry him away from the tables, but he refused to leave until he won something.

"Something, Izzy. I can't end it on a streak like this. It's bad for my karma."

"What about your bank account?"

"Izzy, there are more important things in life than money."

"You have to say that, since you don't have any left."

"Sweetheart, I'd really like you to work on that negativity problem."

Ray played another hand and lost. But there were still chips on the table and I could think of only one way to disengage him.

"Uncle Ray, how about we go to the bar and I buy you a drink."

"You got it, Izzy. But you'll be buying me more than one."

Uncle Ray passed out the second we put him in the backseat of David's car. We buckled in his chest and his legs and kept him sideways, should he decide to vomit.

On the drive back to the city, David and I reverted to our adolescent pastime of ranking Ray's Lost Weekends.

"If that wasn't a five-star weekend, I don't know what is," I said.

"This may sound naïve," David said, "but I always believed this was a phase. That one day old Uncle Ray would return."

"He's gone forever," I said with complete conviction. "And I should warn you, there's a good chance he's going to piss himself."

David sighed and answered with ease, "Yes, I know."

Uncle Ray's Brush with Rehab

Lost Weekend #22 was, fiscally speaking, more devastating than the rest. Uncle Ray really had lost it all. My father, at his wit's end, arranged for Ray to go to a thirty-day rehab program that specialized in multiple addictions, called Green Leaf Recovery Center (David and I laughed convulsively for fifteen minutes when we heard the name), in Petaluma. Ray went along for the drive, but as they approached the verdant road lined with A-frame houses, Uncle Ray turned to my father and said, "It's not gonna stick, you know."

"Will you try?" asked my dad.

"Anything for you, Al. But it's not gonna stick."

"How do you know?"

"I know myself. At least now I do."

"Tell me what to do, Ray."

"Keep your money."

"You can't keep disappearing like that."

Uncle Ray had been waiting for the opportunity to ask the next question.

"So maybe I can move in with you guys until I get on my feet? Pay off my debt. That sort of thing."

"You want to move in?"

"I thought maybe I could have David's old room. You don't think he'd mind?"

"No," my father said laconically. The last thing in the world David would want was his old room back.

Dad started up the car and then turned to Uncle Ray to solidify the deal. "No hookers, drugs, or poker games in the house."

"You got it, Al."

And that is when Uncle Ray moved in to 1799 Clay Street.

THE INTERVIEW: CHAPTER 3

"Do you think it was wise," Inspector Stone asks, "for your parents to allow an admitted drug- /gambling- /sex-addicted alcoholic into the home of an impressionable adolescent girl?"

"I don't think Uncle Ray was a sex addict. He liked hookers — sure — but it wasn't like a regular thing for him."

"Do I need to repeat the question?"

"Uncle Ray was a disaster, but he wasn't interested in taking anyone down with him. You couldn't count on him to mow the lawn or do the dishes, but you could trust he wouldn't hurt anyone."

"According to all sources, your sister's reaction to his arrival was quite volatile. Do you care to elaborate?"

"They were at war."

"So tell me about the war."

What Inspector Stone doesn't realize is that there was not just one war, there was a series of wars, battles, and melees simmering constantly. It was endless. I could draw a diagram of all the family members on a piece of paper and map the conflicts until the page resembled a spiderweb. It is not just one war that is responsible for the one that we will all remember. Like a house of cards, if you remove one piece, the structure topples.

■ ■ ■ ■

Part Two:
The Spellman Wars

■ ■ ■ ■

THE SUGAR WAR

The wave of familial discord, precipitated by Rae's camp ordeal, soon settled into an eerie calm. A few weeks later, Rae was still feeling the gratitude of having been sprung and strived to be on her best behavior. I, however, was still feeling the sting from her shady tactics and needed a modicum of revenge. Since Rae is usually aboveboard in her activities, I had a single offense: to take away her one and only vice — junk food. I began noticing that her Pop-Tart breakfasts bled into Frito and Twinkie lunches. At family dinners, she picked at the main course, ate her vegetables under extreme duress, and then devoured dessert like a wild animal. I was irked by the fact that I was the only one who noticed this. But it was my fault, wasn't it? I raised the bar on acceptable behavior in that house and Rae always managed to stay well under it.

However, just because her habits went unnoticed did not mean that I couldn't persuade my parents to attend to them. I brought home articles on the effects of large sugar consumption on adolescents and its relationship with low scores on aptitude tests in school. I showed documentation on the correlation between old-age diabetes and sugar consumption in youth. I suggested that precautionary measures be enforced. My mother suspiciously agreed: Sugar on the weekends only. No exceptions.

Rae ran upstairs and banged on my apartment door when she heard the news. "How could you?" she asked, almost teary-eyed.

"I'm concerned for your health."

"Yeah, right."

"You want to call a truce?"

"Fine."

Rae reluctantly held out her hand and we shook on it. However, a truce with me would eventually seem trivial, as Rae was about to begin a battle I didn't know she had in her.

THE RA(E/Y) WARS

I locked my apartment door and tiptoed down the staircase, hoping to avoid chitchat with any family member. In particular, I was trying to avoid my mother, who had found another lawyer she wanted me to drink coffee with. I tried explaining to her that I was capable of drinking coffee without legal help, but she did not follow my logic.

Instead of running into my mother, I found Rae (with binoculars) peering out the window on the second landing. I checked the view and saw that Uncle Ray was moving in. Instead of a large orange-and-white truck outside, his moving vehicle was a Yellow Cab. It was a heartbreaking sight, and I turned to Rae, hoping that she might have seen the same thing.

"What are you doing?" I asked.

"Nothing," she replied sharply, and I knew she didn't see a tragic old man. She saw her archenemy.

"Don't you think it's time to let this thing go?"

I could tell from the look on Rae's face that she didn't.

Let me explain: My sister Rae and my uncle Ray had been at odds for about six years. It began when Rae was eight and discovered that her uncle had dipped into her well-catalogued Halloween stash. The tension mounted when she turned ten and Uncle Ray bought her a pink dress for her birthday and not the walkie-talkies she had so pointedly demanded. And then it escalated into a full-grown battle when my uncle fell asleep on a surveillance job they were working together and could not be woken with even the most violent kicking. Between all the aforementioned events, their strife was peppered with TV hogging, appropriations of favorite cereals, and the constant sharp tongue of my grudge-holding sibling.

Still, I repeated my question: "Don't you think it's time to let this thing go?"

"No, I don't," Rae replied. So I left her alone on the staircase to spy on her uncle.

I met Uncle Ray as he was walking up the steps into the foyer, lugging a badly packed duffel bag. I took the bag off his shoulder and questioned its contents.

"Let's see. I got a winter coat, a couple pairs of shoes, a bowling ball, and I think some sandwiches I made this morning with what was left in the fridge."

"Next time, ask Mom to help you pack." I carried the bag inside and put it on David's — now Uncle Ray's — bed. "Good to have you here, Uncle Ray."

Ray pinched my cheek and said, "You were always my favorite designated driver."

I leaned against the windowsill as Ray proceeded to unpack. He pulled items from the lumpy bag and placed them throughout the room without any hint of order or purpose. There was only one article that he had packed with a sense of care. Wrapped in towels of increasing size was a tastefully framed photograph of the Spellman clan. Uncle Ray laid the picture on his dresser and then adjusted its placement just so. While there are dozens of photographs throughout my parents' house, there is not a single one of all the family members. The image merely reminded me of how incongruous we appeared together.

My mother's long hair and athletically petite frame have erased at least a decade off her fifty-four years. Her sharp, even features stood up well to the hazards of time. But Dad's thinning hair and growing gut have added some years, and only his wrinkles provided unity to his mismatched features. Uncle Ray shared a single feature with Albert — the broad, slightly flattened nose. Ray was leaner, handsomer, and blonder than my father. And then there was David's fashion-model perfection, which appeared utterly alien next to Rae, who was ultimately a tiny, cuter version of her uncle. She was the fairest of the Spellman children, dirty blonde with gray-blue eyes and a pattern of freckles across her often tanned face. I towered over Rae, appearing like a clumsier version of my mother.

Uncle Ray dusted off the photograph and decided that he needed a break after the arduous five minutes of unpacking. He offered to make me a sandwich. I declined, thinking it might be a good idea to give my father a warning message.

I caught my dad at his desk.

"Trouble is brewing with the short one. I'd get on it if I were you," I said.

"How bad?" my dad asked.

"Five stars, if you ask me. But only time will tell."

That afternoon, I dropped by David's office to deliver a surveillance report on the Mercer case (stock analyst suspected of insider trading).

I was able to deliver the report early because the subject did the same exact thing seven days in a row. Gym. Work. Home. Sleep. Repeat. I adore creatures of habit. They make my job so much easier.

When I announced myself to Linda, she explained that he was in the middle of a haircut. I strode into David's office and discovered that the haircut was being administered by my best friend, Petra.

"What are you doing here?" Petra casually asked.

"Delivering a surveillance report. Why are you cutting my brother's hair?"

"I can give you two hundred and fifty reasons why," Petra, now in a new tax bracket, replied.

I feigned shock at my brother's intemperance, but really, it didn't surprise me at all.

"Did you have to tell her how much I pay you?" David asked.

"There is no such thing as client-stylist confidentiality."

"How long has this been going on?" I inquired.

They turned to each other to calculate a response. I was disappointed. Any relative or friend of mine should have a better concept of stealth.

I offered up an exaggerated sigh and said, "Forget it." I tossed the surveillance report on David's desk and headed for the door. "Why you feel the need to keep a fucking haircut from me, I will never understand."

"See you tonight, Isabel" was David's only response, that night being Uncle Ray's welcome-home dinner.

I had forgotten about the dinner until David reminded me. Had I remembered, I would have tried to weasel my way out of it. The Ra(e/y) Wars were brewing and I was determined to stay out of them. However, their impact, as I correctly anticipated, could not be outrun.

I returned home early that evening and found Rae on the living room floor obliterating a gift-wrapped box from the local electronics store. It was the newest, top-of-the-line digital video recorder. In fact, Spellman Investigations still had not updated their equipment to this level. Somehow my parents deemed it reasonable to bestow this enormous gift on a teenage girl when birthday and Christmas were either long gone or far away.

As Rae sat as an island amid a sea of Styrofoam, plastic wrap, and cardboard, I eyed my parents with the superior skepticism of an IRS agent and waited patiently for them to catch my stare. True to form, they avoided eye contact, knowing full well what I was thinking. I casually walked over to my father.

"Not one word, Isabel."

"Are you willing to pay for my silence?"

My father's posture sagged as he imagined an endless stream of payoffs and buyouts. I was joking, of course, but I let the threat hang in the air.

"I suppose it's only fair. What do you want?"

"Relax, Dad. I don't want to shake you down. But I would like to say —"

"I am begging you, Isabel, don't say anything."

Finding the prospect of holding my tongue almost unbearable, I grabbed a beer and then plopped down on the couch in the den next to Uncle Ray, who thoughtfully handed me his plate of cheese and crackers as he channel surfed. When he hit upon an episode of *Get Smart* from the first season, I said, "Stop."

Max[1] and Agent 99, disguised as a doctor and nurse, roamed the halls of Harvey

---

[1] Aka Secret Agent 86.

Satan's sanitarium.[2]

"Can you bring me up to speed?" asked Uncle Ray, who sadly does not have a catalogue of episodes imprinted in his brain.

"KAOS[3] agents have kidnapped the chief and are holding him for ransom. Oh, and there's this scene that you just missed where Max uses seven different kinds of phones. A shoe phone, wallet phone, eyeglasses phone, tie phone, handkerchief phone, and . . . I can't remember the last one.[4]"

"What is the chief doing in the closet?" asked my uncle.

"It's not a closet. It's a freezer."

"Why are they freezing him?"

"They need to lower his body temperature for mind-control surgery."

"Okay. That makes sense," said Ray, who took back his plate of cheese and crackers.

A commercial came on the TV and Uncle Ray pretended to be engrossed in the latest acne remedy.

"You think the kid will get used to me after a while?"

"Yeah, Uncle Ray, I think she'll come

[2] Called "Satan Place."
[3] The International Organization of Evil (pronounced "chaos").
[4] Sock garter phone.

around. Eventually."

"I hope so. Been wearing my lucky shirt."

"I noticed."

The lucky shirt: a threadbare, short-sleeved, Hawaiian-print number that had been in circulation nearing two decades. It used to surface only on special occasions — the Super Bowl, the playoffs, the World Series. Eventually it made its way into a smattering of poker games and casual weddings, but lately it was rare to see him in anything else.

At dinner my sister's pointed glares across the table discomfited all. David and my father made dull small talk about work, but it was my mother who briefly eased the tension, by redirecting it.

"Don't you think that's enough red meat for one day?" she asked as my father reached for a second helping of roast beef.

Dad served himself two more slices and said, "Yes, now it is."

"I thought Dr. Schneider put you on a diet."

"He did," Dad replied.

"How's it going?" my mom asked.

"Great."

"Have you lost any weight?"

"As a matter of fact, I have."

"How much?" she asked.

"A pound," my father replied proudly.

"You were supposed to start that diet one month ago. You've lost only one pound so far?" asked my mom.

"All the experts say it's better to lose it slow and steady."

"That's good. So you'll be thin somewhere around the time you're eligible for Social Security benefits," said Mom, holding her glare.

"You're not the boss of me, Olivia."

"The hell I'm not."

Since some variety of this conversation was a staple of most Spellman family meals, the rest of table continued eating without much notice. Then Uncle Ray made the fatal mistake of speaking to my sister.

"Rae-Rae, pass the potatoes, will ya?" said my uncle.

My sister continued eating, deliberately not responding to the request. My mother waited a moment, hoping, probably praying. When her younger daughter still refused to move, she intervened.

"Sweetie, Uncle Ray wants you to pass the potatoes."

"No, he wants 'Rae-Rae' to pass him the potatoes. I don't know who 'Rae-Rae' is," my sister snapped.

I reached across the table, elbowing Rae,

picked up the potatoes, and handed them to my uncle.

"My name is Rae. Just one Rae. Not two. Just one." Rae spelled it out like the rudest member of the debate team.

"How long are you going to hold this grudge?" my uncle asked.

"How long are you going to wear that shirt?"

"Don't talk about the shirt."

"Why, can it hear me?"

"Just don't talk about it. We don't need the negative energy."

My brother, the lawyer, the corporate dealmaker, the man who bills four hundred dollars an hour, believes he can negotiate anything. He is foolish enough to think that he can negotiate peace through mutual understanding. At times like this, I believe it is very possible that David was swapped with the real Spellman boy at the hospital.

"Uncle Ray, tell her about the shirt. Maybe she'll understand," said David.

"No way."

"Either you tell her or I'll tell her," my brother said, knowing the effect of his words.

"You won't tell it right, David."

"Go on, tell me about the shirt," Rae said, folding her arms across her chest.

Uncle Ray contemplated his delivery, cleared his throat, and offered a dramatic pause.

"January twenty-second, 1989. Superbowl Twenty-three, score sixteen to thirteen Bengals, with three minutes, twenty seconds left on the clock. Montana makes five consecutive passes to move the ball to the Bengals' thirty-five. A holding penalty. The ball goes back ten yards. Yet Montana comes up with a twenty-seven-yard completion to Rice. A time-out and he connects with Taylor in the middle of the end zone. I'm wearing the shirt. June second, 1991. Oak Tree. I put one hundred on Blue Lady. Who knows why? I'm in the mood for a long shot. Blue Lady noses Silver Arrow in the final stretch. Payoff: thirty-six to one. I'm wearing the shirt. September third, 1993. I go into Sal's Deli and Liquor to buy some lottery tickets. I walk in on a two-eleven in progress, surprising the perp. He fires five rounds in my direction before I can pull out my piece and take him down. Not a scratch on me. No one dies that day, and the perp has only a flesh wound. I'm wearing the shirt."

Uncle Ray clears his throat and continues devouring his plate of potatoes.

Rae puts a worn blue high-top sneaker on the table. I smack her foot off, but she puts it up again.

"February, this year," she says, "I take third place in the eighth grade tetherball tournament. I'm wearing the shoes. June, same year. I score eighty-three percent on my algebra final without cracking the book. I'm wearing the shoes. Last Thursday, I narrowly miss running my bike into a squad car. I'm wearing the shoes. But still, I rotate!"

"Get your feet off the table," my mother snaps. Rae retires her shoe to the floor and glares, once again, at Uncle Ray. I decide to remind my sister of some recent events and their implications.

"In case you didn't notice, Rae, today you were bribed. That high-tech, digital surveillance camera you received is not a free gift. Do not be mistaken. The gift is intended to persuade you to be at least moderately polite to your uncle during his stay here."

Rae doesn't believe me. She sustains a half grin, waiting for the punch line. When none is offered, she looks around the table, eventually turning to my dad.

"Is it true?" she asks.

"Yes, pumpkin. It's true."

THE WAR ON RECREATIONAL SURVEILLANCE: CHAPTER 1

It had started when Rae was thirteen and I ignored it. We all ignored it for a while. She did it after school, on weekends and holidays, when the sun was shining and she felt like a bike ride or a stroll. But then Uncle Ray moved in and with his presence came another able-bodied workhorse. Not that he worked hard — on the contrary, but hiring Uncle Ray over Rae, whether that was a conscious or unconscious decision, made sense. Billing out for the work of a fourteen-year-old girl brought in twenty-five dollars an hour, plus expenses. However, billing out for the services of a retired SFPD inspector, we could charge fifty dollars an hour. Besides, Ray could drive and pee in a jar (a gender-specific talent that should not be underestimated). There were four sound reasons to use Uncle Ray over Rae and, generally speaking, you could rely on Ray staying out of the bars until the end of his ten-hour shift. It was only Rae who noticed that her assignments had waned over the last few months. Only I noticed how Rae was compensating for this loss.

Now, at age fourteen, my sister's curfew had been set at 10:00 p.m. on weekends and 8:00 p.m. on school nights. Until recently she had never tested those boundaries. Rae has only two friends in school — Arie Watt and Lori Freeman — both of whom have curfews well before Rae's. That said, on a typical school day, Rae came home at 5:00 p.m., sometimes 7:00 when she was studying with Arie or Lori, and on the weekends, she never left the house unless she was on the job, going to a movie, or had a specific plan with one of her two friends. There were rare sleepovers (at Lori's) and even rarer supervised parties. But for the most part, Rae's home was her castle and she couldn't wait to be safely ensconced within it or at least within the surveillance van.

So when she began testing the limits of her curfew, when she would arrive home flushed and clammy from running the last distance before the clock struck eight, I knew she was hiding something. I could have asked Rae what she was up to, but that is not our way. Instead, I followed her.

Rae had mastered the B-minus average

that my parents mandated. She had mastered the B-minus while doing virtually no work beyond school walls. I picked up the tail at the end of her school day. Rae hopped on her bike and rode up to Polk Street. She carefully wove her lock from the front wheel through the base of the bike, as my father had taught her, sat on a bench, and pulled out a schoolbook. An uninformed observer would tell you that she was studying while waiting for a bus — the book, her school uniform, and the bus bench would evidence that assessment. But I knew she was prowling for someone to tail. A few minutes later a woman in her early thirties, carrying an oversize purse, exited the bookstore a few doors down. She pulled some papers from her inelegant bag, ripped them in quarters, and tossed them fervently into the garbage can that was sitting next to Rae.

The woman's jittery hands and nervous bearing piqued Rae's interest. My sister closed her book as the woman took her leave, waited the requisite twenty seconds, and then followed her. I was still parked around the corner at the other end of the block. I quickly started the car and turned onto Polk Street, driving as slowly as I could until I caught up with Rae. I made a quick turn in front of my sister as she was crossing the street.

"Can I give you a lift?" I offered as I rolled down the window. She knew that I had followed her. She knew that I knew what she was doing. I could have written out the math equation she was internally calculating. Defiance was typically not Rae's method. Unlike me, she acquiesced whenever her heart allowed for it. She knew enough to avoid raising further suspicion.

"Thanks. I didn't feel like walking," she said, getting in.

I said nothing, thinking this might be a one-time deal and so what if, after school, my sister on occasion shadows complete strangers? It *is* exercise, isn't it?

I let it slide for a few weeks, as she tested her curfew more and more. Then it appeared that she had scaled back her recreational surveillance. She was suddenly returning home before dinner and staying in her room most of the night. My parents attributed the solitude to Uncle Ray avoidance. I, on the other hand, was not so ready to trust someone who shared my DNA.

My attic apartment sits just above Rae's bedroom on the second floor. An outside fire escape connects the two rooms. When Rae was five, she caught me sneaking out one night and discovered an alternate passage into my bedroom. I quickly disabused her of this habit, not just because it was dangerous, but also because my bed sat just below the window and her late-night entrances usually involved leaving size-three tread marks on my face.

Six Months Ago

I heard the slow creak of the fire escape ladder shortly before 7:00 p.m. I was about to look out my window when the telephone rang.

"Hello."

"Hello, is this Isabel?" a male voice asked.

Generally I don't answer questions like that, but this was my private line.

"Yes. Who is this?"

"Hi. My name is Benjamin McDonald. I met your mother at the library."

"The library?"

"Yes."

"Which library?"

"The main library. Downtown."

"What was she doing there?"

"I assume checking out books."

"Did you see her with any books?"

"I think so."

"Do you remember which ones?"

"No."

"Not even one?"

"No. Anyway, the reason I'm calling —"

"What were you doing there?"

"Where?"

"At the library?"

"Oh, I had some research to do."

"Legal research?"

"Yes, as a matter of fact."

"So you're a lawyer?"

"Yes. So I was thinking that maybe we could —"

"Have coffee?"

"Yes. Coffee."

"No. I'm no longer having coffee with lawyers. But could I ask you a question before we hang up?"

"All you've been doing is asking me questions."

"Good point. What did my mother tell you about me?"

"Not much."

"So why did you agree to this?"

"She offered me a twenty percent discount on investigative work."

I hung up the phone and raced downstairs.

"Mom, we need to call in the white coats and have you hauled off just like Blanche DuBois."

My mother clapped her hands together

enthusiastically. "Benjamin called, didn't he?"

"Yes. And I can guarantee he won't call again."

"Well, Isabel, there goes your raise."

"You weren't going to give me a raise."

"Yes, I was. If you went out with Benjamin. But now, nothing."

"I can get my own dates, Mom."

My mother rolled her eyes and said, "Of course you can," then switched subjects, since she knew nothing was going to change. She would continue fixing me up with lawyers and I would continue dating men who could comp my drinks.

"I'm taking you off the Spark Industries background work tomorrow and giving you a surveillance job," Mom said.

"New client?"

"Yes. Mrs. Peters. Called last week. She suspects her husband, Jake, might be gay."

"Did you suggest she ask him?"

Mom laughed. "Of course not. Business is slow."

I returned to my apartment and reviewed the materials for the following day's surveillance.

At 10:15 that night, I heard rattling on the fire escape. I turned the lights off in my bedroom and carefully peered through the curtains. I caught sight of Rae's legs wiggling through the window into her room. I quickly slipped on a pair of sneakers, defenestrated myself, and climbed down the fire escape. I crawled through Rae's window before she had a chance to take off her shoes.

"I have a door, Isabel."

"Then why aren't you using it?"

"Cut to the chase," she said like a cowboy in an old Western.

"Surveillance isn't a hobby."

"What's your point?"

"You have to stop following complete strangers."

"Why? You do it all the time."

"I follow people when I'm paid to do it. Get the distinction?"

"I like it enough to do it for free."

"We give you as much work as we can."

"Not as much as I used to get."

"You could get hurt, Rae."

"I could get hurt playing squash."

"You don't play squash."

"Not the point."

"You could follow the wrong person and get kidnapped or murdered."

"Unlikely."

"But not impossible."

"If you're talking about me quitting cold

turkey, it is not going to happen," Rae said as she slipped into a chair behind her desk.

I sat down across from her. "How about you cut back?"

Ray scribbled on a square notepad, folded the paper into quarters, and slid it across the desk. "How does this number work for you?"

"You need to spend less time with David," I said, commenting on her technique. When I unfolded the paper, I practically shouted, "Ten percent?"

"The point of writing it down is so you don't say it out loud."

"Yeah? Well, ten percent does not work for me."

Rae pushed a pen and notepad across the table. "I'm willing to negotiate."

I chose to play it her way, since I knew we'd be negotiating the method for hours if I didn't. I wrote down my number, folded the paper, and slid it back to her.

Rae laughed incredulously. "Not in this lifetime." She jotted down her own number and slipped it back to me. "Let's see how this works for you."

"Fifteen percent? You can't be serious."

"You're doing it wrong! Don't say it out loud."

I wrote down my own number again and

held it up for her to see: forty percent. "Rae, I'm not leaving this room until you agree to that."

Rae mulled it over and figured there had to be a way she could make that work.

"If I trim my recreational surveillance by this number, then I'll need to compensate for it in other ways."

"Where are you going with this?"

"At least one day a week, you take me on one of your jobs."

"If that's how you want to spend your weekends."

"And holidays and administrative half days."

"It's a deal."

After we shook on it, Rae confidently suggested, "How does tomorrow work for you?"

According to Mrs. Peters, Jake Peters was playing tennis the next morning with an unidentified male whom she believed to be his lover. The job would begin at the San Francisco Tennis Club. Mrs. Peters had already followed her husband to that site on a number of occasions and there was no need to risk getting burned for a ten-minute drive from the Peterses' home to the club.

In the morning, I drank coffee with my

mom and went over the case file on Mr. Peters, which included the schedule Mrs. Peters provided for her husband. Between my second and third cup, and right after my mom said, "Maybe you'd be less snippy if you cut down on that stuff" and I replied with, "Please don't use the word 'snippy,' it doesn't suit you," Rae hopped downstairs wearing white shorts, a pink Izod shirt, and socks with pom-poms, carrying a Wilson aluminum tennis racket.

"Mom, do I look okay?" asked Rae.

My mother glowed with approval. "Perfect," she said.

"Rae, you're wearing a pink shirt," I observed, praying for a logical explanation.

"I'm not blind," she replied, reaching for the Froot Loops. I was about to protest, but remembered it was Saturday. Rae shook the box, hearing the weak resonance of powdered sugar. She poured the leftovers into the bowl, which offered up not even one solid loop.

"Bastard!" Rae shouted.

"Rae, Grandma was married when she had your uncle," my mother corrected.

"Sorry," Rae said, then replaced the prior insult with "big fat jerk."

"Thank you," my mom said, as if a lesson had really been learned here. "Sweetie, look on the bottom shelf in the storeroom behind the paper towels."

Rae burrowed in the nether regions of our pantry and surfaced with a box each of Cap'n Crunch and Lucky Charms. My mother, brilliant at anticipating potential conflict, had bought a secret stash. Sometimes she amazed me.

"I love you," Rae said more sincerely than you might imagine.

"I thought you wanted Froot Loops," I said.

"I didn't know I had options," Rae replied, pouring herself two separate bowls of sugar.

I knew the answer to the question as I was asking it. "So what's up with the outfit, Rae?"

Rae turned to our mother before she answered. My mom nodded the *go ahead, you can talk* nod.

"Mom's invoking section five, clause d."

Rae was speaking of the Spellman Investigations Employment Contract. All employees (full-time or seasonal) are required to sign it. Like my family itself, the contract alternates between reasonable employer dictums and wildly unabated whims. Section 5, clause (d) falls into the latter category. Essentially, the clause in debate states that Albert and Olivia have random wardrobe control whenever a case requires some element of camouflage. A tennis club falls into that category. When I reached maturity and was required to sign the contract, once again, I negotiated an addendum stipulating that section 5, clause (d) could be invoked no more than three times in a twelve-month period. My parents added another stipulation, which specified that if I breached this clause, they could fine me five hundred dollars. (This was added when the threat of firing me proved ineffectual.) The contract has been drafted and redrafted throughout the years by my brother. Therefore, it is legally binding and my mother insists that should any part of it be breached, she will enforce the fines.

Even so, I had to protest. "No. No," I said, tossing my coffee into the sink and running upstairs to my apartment.

"If I were you, I'd shave my legs," my mother shouted after me. I could feel a lump forming in my throat.

I found the outfit hanging on my front door. All crisp and white and painfully short. I'd never worn a tennis dress before — mostly because I've never played tennis. But if I did play tennis, I can guarantee I would never willingly wear the dress. I showered and shaved my legs (for the first time in two months). For about ten minutes, I stared in the mirror, trying to stretch the skirt out and diminish my posture so it would appear longer. Nothing worked. I pulled an extra-large gray sweatshirt out of my drawer and headed downstairs.

David was waiting in the foyer when I reached the bottom landing. At first he emitted only a hearty chuckle, but when my father joined him and doubled over, the two lost complete control and began laughing so convulsively it occurred to me they might need medical attention.

I walked into the kitchen and poured more coffee. My father and David remained in the foyer, apparently still paralyzed with hysteria. Uncle Ray entered the kitchen and looked me over inquisitively. He kindly remained nonreactive. He simply observed, "Section five, clause d?"

I nodded my head and told my sister to get her stuff. My mother stood in the corner, sipping her coffee with a satisfied grin. David and my father finally learned how to walk again and met us in the kitchen.

David turned to my mom and said, "You were right, Mom. It was totally worth it." Then he handed me his tennis bag and suggested I not lose it.

"You need to get a life. All of you," I

snapped as I headed outside.

Rae quickly ran after me, racket in hand. I stopped in my tracks and looked over my shoulder at her.

"Tell me the truth," I said. "How much is my ass hanging out?"

"How much is it supposed to?" Rae asked.

I tied the sweatshirt around my waist and got in the car.

THE TENNIS WAR
(TENNIS 101)

Rae and I entered the San Francisco Tennis Club minus the snobbish questioning we had anticipated. I suppose, in our crisp, white outfits, we passed for the country club set. Based on David's brief floor-plan tutorial, Rae and I headed up to the second level. A clean, wood-floored hallway encircled the building, offering a glassed-in overhead view of the four courts below. The airy space between the concrete floor and the wood beams above offered an odd mix of echo and silence. The *pings* of the balls bubbled through the building, but voices, conversations, the things you really wanted to hear, remained mute and impenetrable.

I showed Rae the picture of Jake Peters and she spotted him immediately on the bottom middle court. We returned to the main level and found our way to the four-tiered bleachers dividing the courts. We sat to the left of center, pretending to observe two middle-aged women in outfits more immodest than mine.

But it was Jake we were really watching as he performed a slow but legal serve. His opponent responded with an even slower backhand.

"Who's the other guy?" Rae asked, pointing at Jake's weak but remarkably handsome opponent. While there were many things to notice about this man, it was his legs that were hardest to ignore. They were the color of cocoa, brilliantly set off by his white shorts. His sinewy muscles subtly contoured his long, elegant limbs, which were almost feminine, but never crossing that subjective line. The man was dark, but not swarthy, with a strong brow that highlighted a pronounced Roman nose.

"What are you staring at, Isabel?" Rae said, snapping me out of my daze.

"Nothing. Can you tell who is winning?"

Rae and I continued watching the painfully slow rally, accompanied by Olympian efforts and awkward stumbles.

"When you play as bad as this, who cares?" Rae said.

Something about this game seemed all wrong — suspicious, in fact. When we finally heard the score after the first set, it was Jake who was ahead four games to three.

In the realm of all things possible in this world, Jake beating his dark, handsome opponent was possible. However, Jake was a forty-eight-year-old man who — by his wife's own admission — had only started playing tennis three months ago. His legs were scrawny, his belly was not. His arms, especially the serving arm, revealed no identifiable muscle category. So the idea that he was beating a man at tennis who was ten years his junior and had evidently exercised in recent years seemed off.

That said, we were not here to observe Jake's tennis game. We were here to observe whether Jake seemed in love with his tennis opponent. He did not. He seemed eager to beat him, eager to shout out forty-love, but he in no way seemed eager to hop into the sack with him. And I can personally guarantee that if he were gay, that would be the foremost thing on his mind.

"Why do you keep staring at that guy? Do you know him?"

"No."

"Do you want to?"

"What are you talking about?"

"You know," she said in her annoyingly knowing way.

183

"Shut up, Rae."

For forty-five minutes, Rae and I watched what would have gone down in history as the dullest tennis game ever if more people had witnessed it. We observed underhand serves and lobs so slow the ball appeared frozen in midair. We watched full-grown men beat themselves with their own tennis rackets and trip on their own shoelaces. When the game mercifully ended with Jake Peters a two-set victor, he leapt over the net and fell flat on his face.

His cocoa-legged opponent shook Jake's hand as he helped him to his feet. He said, "Nice game," without even a hint of bad sportsmanship.

Jake patted his opponent on the back and offered a compliment, trying to cultivate the easy confidence of a winner. The act seemed as unnatural as walking on water.

The mismatched men parted ways without a hint of longing on either side. I began to wonder what had garnered Mrs. Peters's distrust. We could tell her that, simply, she was wrong, that she should look within herself for her own suspicions. But that would leave both her heart and pocketbook empty. She wanted more information, and for what she was paying, I was willing to give it to her.

Rae and I lagged behind our subject as he exited the court and passed through the hallway into the men's locker room. I told Rae to sit in the foyer and keep her eyes peeled for Mr. Peters. She adjusted the volume on her radio and pulled out a newspaper. I turned back and looked at my sister briefly. She had been using the "reading the newspaper" foil for years. It always struck me as being silly, almost a parody — especially when she was eight or nine and would choose the business section of the *Chronicle.* But this was the first time I looked at her, newspaper folded in half, eyes darting between the pages and her environment, and it somehow appeared legitimate.

As I walked toward the hallway to the locker rooms, I saw the cocoa-legged opponent in the hallway talking with a preppy gentleman wearing a royal-blue shirt and powder-blue wristbands. His pricey cologne floated above the sweaty air. I quickly bent before the water fountain, trying to remain unnoticed.

"Daniel, you got time for another game?" said Preppy Gentleman. "Frank got called into surgery and had to cancel. I have the court."

Daniel. Daniel. I had a name now for Cocoa Legs.

"I was heading back to the office," Daniel said.

Now I knew Daniel had an office. You see how this whole PI thing works?

"Come on, you killed me the last time. Let me redeem myself."

Perhaps I am stating the obvious, but this conversation was very wrong. Daniel couldn't beat Jake Peters, but he could beat a preppy guy who gave the impression that he came out of the womb with a tennis racket? Since my water consumption was brimming on ridiculous, I walked over to the pay phone as the men finished their conversation.

"All right," Daniel said. "You have one hour for payback. That's it."

I don't imagine that I am the only person to notice the details. But I am the only one I know who would forgo her responsibilities to discover an explanation for an errant one.

I returned to my sister in the foyer and told her to keep her eyes peeled for Jake and to stay off the radios. They were too awkward in the club.

"Call my cell when he comes out of the shower."

"Where are you going?"

"I have to check on something," I said as I grabbed a section of her newspaper.

186

I returned to the courts and once again sat down on the adjoining bleachers.

Daniel served and the preppy lunged for the ball but couldn't make the return: 15-love. Daniel served again. This time Preppy returned the serve and a sharp manic volley followed, which ended with Preppy landing an out-of-bounds shot: 30-love. I was, without a doubt, observing an entirely different tennis player. I couldn't tear my eyes away from the game. It was as compelling as the previous game was dull. I kept watching, hoping to construct a logical explanation, but there was none. This was simply schizophrenic tennis playing.

My phone was set to vibrate and I picked up.

"Subject is on the move," Rae said.

I knew I couldn't break away.

"Can you handle him on your own?" I asked, knowing this was irresponsible.

"Of course," Rae said, already out the door. "Mom gave me cab money just in case."

I briefly reconsidered what I was doing, but instead I said, "Keep your cell phone on, stay in public, and don't do anything that is going to piss me off. Got it, Rae?"

"I got it."

■ ■ ■ ■

I began to feel too conspicuous sitting down on the bleachers for so long. So I returned to the upper level and entered the bar, sitting by the window and observing the rest of the game. I could no longer hear the scorekeeping, but the result of the match was obvious and I was more confused than ever.

I returned to the bottom level and waited for Daniel to exit the locker room. I called Rae on her cell phone.

"Rae, where are you?"

"I'm outside the Mitchell Brothers O'Farrell Theatre in the Tenderloin. Subject entered the establishment approximately ten minutes ago. I tried to go inside, but they didn't buy my fake ID."

"That's because you are fourteen."

"But my ID says I'm twenty-one."

"Stay put, don't talk to strangers, and I'll be there as soon as I can."

"Izzy, I think this is a strip club, with women strippers."

"It is," I replied.

"You know what I'm thinking?" asked Rae.

"No."

"I don't think Mr. Peters is gay."

"Yes. I would agree."

Daniel, freshly showered and wearing blue jeans, a worn T-shirt, and flip-flops, exited the locker room and headed upstairs. I should have returned to my sister, but I needed an explanation and followed him instead.

Daniel sat down at the bar and ordered a beer. Not wasting any time, I sat down next to him. He turned to me slightly and smiled. Not the smile of a pickup artist, but the friendly open smile of one person acknowledging another's presence. Up close I could see that his heavy-lidded eyes were the lightest shade of brown. His almost black hair, still damp and fragrant from some fantastic shampoo, formed a perfect cowlick over his forehead. His teeth were straight and unstained, but without the glare and perfection of your average talk show host. Suddenly I realized I had been staring way too long.

When the bartender served Daniel his drink, I woke myself from this daze and laid some bills on the counter.

"I'm buying," I said.

Daniel turned to me. "Do I know you?" he asked without a hint of suspicion.

"Definitely not."

"But you want to buy me a drink?"

"It's not exactly free."

"How do you mean?"

"I'm offering a simple exchange. I buy you a beer, you answer a question. How does that sound?"

"I'd like to hear the question first," he said, not touching his beer.

"You played two tennis matches this morning. The first one was against a man in his late forties who was substantially out of shape. Neither of you appeared to be skilled at the sport. I found this odd, since this is an exclusive tennis club, which implies that it caters to people who know how to play the game. Had one or the other of you been a capable opponent, that would have eased my curiosity."

"Of course."

"You lose the match against the inept opponent and you demolish the capable one."

" 'Demolish.' I like the sound of that."

"So now it's time for you to explain."

"Some people need to win and some people need to lose," Daniel said, taking a sip of his beer.

The simplicity of the answer took me aback. The fact that a man would use tennis as a leveler of the universe struck me as, well, beautiful. I am unaccustomed to immediate and unabated crushes. But I was experiencing one at that moment.

"That's it?" I asked, preparing for my getaway.

"That's it."

"What's your name?" I asked, still planning on moving from the bar stool.

"Daniel Castillo."

"What do you do?"

"I'm a dentist." It was like a punch in the stomach, like I was being punished for everything I had ever done wrong.

"Day off?" I asked, certain that the color had drained from my face.

"Yes. Saturday and Sunday, just like everybody else."

"Well, have a nice day," I said as I was halfway out the door.

Daniel caught up with me outside, just as I'd reached my car.

"What was that back there?" he asked.

"Is there a problem?"

"What is *your* name?"

"Isabel."

"How about a last name?"

"I don't give out that kind of information."

"What do you do?"

"What do you mean?"

"For a living. What do you do?"

From the moment that I said it and since, I have regretted and paid for the following response.

"I'm a teacher."

I said it because, well, men like teachers. I said it because if I told him what I really did, he would be uncomfortable. He would be concerned that I had been tailing him. He would want to know what I was doing at the tennis club and I would not be able to tell him. So saying "teacher" seemed so much easier at the time.

"You don't seem like a teacher."

"Why is that?" I said, somewhat offended.

"I don't think you have the patience for it."

"You're quick to judge."

"Can I interest you in a game of tennis?"

"No. I don't play." Since I was wearing a tennis dress, had been previously observed in a tennis club, and was carrying a racket, this was not the smartest response. I had to change the subject fast.

"I'll see you around, Doc," I said and quickly got into the car.

Daniel slowly turned and walked away. I watched him until he disappeared through the entrance of the club. The entire time all

I was thinking was, Could this be Ex-boyfriend #9?

Rae was talking to a couple of prostitutes when I pulled up outside the Mitchell Brothers O'Farrell Theatre. She said good-bye to Tiffani and Dawn when she got into the car. I sent Rae into a liquor store and let her stock up on candy for our stakeout. We ate bridge mix, licorice, and cheese puffs as we watched men of varying ages, sizes, and colors enter and exit the establishment, like waves lapping against the sand.

"The cheese puffs are too messy for the car, Rae."

"But we needed some substantial food."

"There is nothing substantial about a cheese puff," I said as I tossed a chocolate-covered filbert out the window.

"That's so wasteful, Isabel."

"Nobody eats the filberts."

"I would."

"When?"

"In an emergency."

"What kind of emergency are you talking about?"

"The kind where you run out of the almonds and the cashews and the peanuts and everything but the filberts."

"And how would that happen?"

"Uncle Ray moves in and eats everything

but the filberts."

"Wouldn't you prefer that he just eat the whole bridge mix rather than everything but the filberts? I mean, the filberts sitting there alone, don't they just remind you of what you're missing?"

"No. I'd still want the filberts for an emergency."

"What planet are you from?"

"Earth."

"That was a rhetorical question, Rae."

"So what?"

"So you're not supposed to answer them."

"No. You don't *have* to answer them, but you can if you want."

This argument could have gone on indefinitely, but the subject was moving, and so were we.

That evening Rae and I worked on the surveillance report together, demolishing the entire bag of bridge mix (filberts included). Our mother phoned Mrs. Peters and explained to her that Mr. Peters was definitely of the heterosexual persuasion and suggested couples counseling. I remained in the office until midnight, finishing some paperwork.

I told myself I wasn't going to do it, but I did. Daniel Castillo is a fairly common name, but not so common when you can tie him to a dental practice. By 1:00 a.m., I had a Social Security number, date of birth, marital status (single), as well as his business and home addresses. I promised myself that this was a thing of the past. This thing I did. This thing my mother did to me. But I had to know more about Daniel Castillo and learning about him the ordinary way was both unreliable and time-consuming.

Petra was giving me one of her quarterly *I can no longer be seen in public with you* haircuts when I asked the question I was planning on asking her all week.

"When's the last time you went to the dentist?"

"I don't know. About a year, maybe."

"Don't you think it's time you had your teeth cleaned?"

"I could ask you the same question."

"I can't go to this dentist."

"What are we talking about here?"

"I met a dentist," I blurted out before I was really ready to say it.

"A dentist? Are you crazy?"

"I like him. I just have to make sure he's worth it."

Staged Dental Appointment #1

Petra made a 3:00 p.m. appointment for the following Monday at the offices of Daniel

Castillo, DDS. The deal was that I would pay for the cleaning and she would carefully integrate nine previously prepared questions into casual conversation. The criterion for my questions was to cover ground that I could not uncover through background research and short-term surveillance. I expected some protest when I handed her the neatly typed sheet of paper, but Petra didn't balk. She memorized the nine questions, then headed inside.

Two hours later, we met at the Philosopher's Club and ordered drinks. I had insisted Petra bring a recorder into the examination room, so I could listen to the proceedings without the filter of her shoddy memory.

"Are you ready?" she said, one eyebrow held aloft in wicked anticipation. She turned on the tape recorder.

[click of recorder]

P. Clark: This is Petra Clark speaking. It is a foggy Thursday afternoon and I am about to visit the offices of Daniel Castillo, DDS, for the purposes of spying on him for one Isabel Spellman.

Dr. Castillo: Hello, Ms. Clark. I am Dr. Castillo.

P. Clark: Nice to meet you, Doctor.

Dr. Castillo: This is your first time here, I see. Can I ask how you were referred?

P. Clark: Who remembers those things?

Dr. Castillo: Okay. How is your memory on your last cleaning?

P. Clark: I've had better.

Dr. Castillo: I meant, do you recall when you had your last cleaning?

P. Clark: About a year ago. I remember because it was right after my divorce. Have you been divorced, Doctor? [Question #3]

Dr. Castillo: (clearing his throat) Um, no. I have not. Shall we get started?

P. Clark: Are you married? [Question #2 — single status already established, question asked to gauge reaction.]

Dr. Castillo: No. Please open wide.

[Dr. Castillo puts on a pair of latex gloves and examines patient's mouth.]

P. Clark: [indistinguishable grunting noises]

Dr. Castillo: Did you say something?

P. Clark: Do you prefer local or general anesthesia? [Question #5]

Dr. Castillo: Ms. Clark —

P. Clark: I insist you call me Petra.

Dr. Castillo: Petra, no anesthesia should be necessary for this procedure.

P. Clark: Oh, I know. I just mean, generally speaking, which do you prefer?

Dr. Castillo: It depends on the individual situation. However, I prefer to use a local whenever possible. I can't clean your teeth unless you open your mouth.

[thirty seconds of teeth cleaning]

Dr. Castillo: Please rinse.

[sound of spitting]

P. Clark: But isn't there something to be said for having a patient totally knocked out? [follow-up to Question #5]

Dr. Castillo: Yes, there is.

P. Clark: Have you always lived in the Bay Area, Doctor? [variation on Question #6 — Where are you from?]

Dr. Castillo: I was born in Guatemala. My parents and I moved here when I was nine. I need you to open your mouth again.

[thirty seconds of teeth cleaning]

Dr. Castillo: Please rinse.

[sound of spitting]

P. Clark: So you're bilingual? [Petra Question #1]

Dr. Castillo: Yes. Tell me about your flossing regime.

P. Clark: Often.

Dr. Castillo: Is that every day?

P. Clark: No. But it seems like it. Are you depressed? [Petra Question #2]

Dr. Castillo: No. Why do you ask?

P. Clark: I heard dentists have emotional problems.

Dr. Castillo: I'm fine, thanks. But I appreciate your concern.

P. Clark: It was my pleasure.

[sound of teeth cleaning]

Dr. Castillo: Please rinse.

[sound of spitting]

P. Clark: Have you ever had a problem with drugs or alcohol? [Question #7]

Dr. Castillo: Do you work for the *Chronicle* or something?

P. Clark: No. I'm a hairstylist. Here's my card. So — drugs, alcohol?

Dr. Castillo: No thank you. I'm good for now, Ms. Clark. You know, this would go a lot faster if I didn't have to keep telling you to open your mouth.

[sound of cleaning]

Dr. Castillo: Please rinse.

[sound of spitting]

P. Clark: So, Doctor, what do you do for fun? [Question #4]
[sound of sighing]

Dr. Castillo: I play tennis.
P. Clark: Other than tennis?
Dr. Castillo: I'm a dentist. What more fun do I need?
P. Clark: So you like inflicting pain? [Petra Question #3]
Dr. Castillo: Your questions are making me uncomfortable.
P. Clark: Forgive me, Doctor, I'm just a very curious person. Are you Catholic? [variation on Question #9 — Religious orientation]
Dr. Castillo: Yes.
P. Clark: Do you believe in a woman's right to choose? [Petra Question #4]
Dr. Castillo: I beg of you, please open your mouth.
P. Clark: That sounded a little naughty, don't you think?
[sound of sighing]

Dr. Castillo: Do you want to have your teeth cleaned or not?
P. Clark: Why else would I be here?

Dr. Castillo: Frankly, I don't know.
[long pause]

Dr. Castillo: Are you going to keep it open?
[inaudible grunting noises; sound of teeth cleaning]

Dr. Castillo: Please rinse and don't speak afterward.
[sound of spitting]

P. Clark: So are you aggressive or conservative?
Dr. Castillo: Excuse me?
P. Clark: With your taxes. Do you file aggressively or conservatively? [Question #8]
Dr. Castillo: [flat-out annoyed tone] I don't see how that is any of your concern.
P. Clark: You've had your fingers in my mouth for the last twenty minutes. I think I'm entitled to a little bit of personal information.
Dr. Castillo: I'm conservative. We're in the final stretch here, Ms. Clark. Open wide.
[sound of teeth cleaning]

Dr. Castillo: Rinse.
[sound of spitting]

Ms. Clark: Do you ever date your patients? [Question #1]

Dr. Castillo: No. Absolutely not. Never. [long pause] Don't make me tell you again.

[inaudible grunting noises, indicating that patient has opened her mouth and will keep it open; sound of teeth cleaning]

Dr. Castillo: Rinse.

P. Clark: You seem tense, Doctor.

Dr. Castillo: It's been a long day.

P. Clark: Some people use porn to unwind. [noninterrogative version of scrapped Question #10: Do you like porn?]

Dr. Castillo: Thank you for coming in, Ms. Clark. Please check out at the front desk with Mrs. Sanchez.

[sound of door opening and closing]

P. Clark: This is Petra Clark signing off from the offices of Daniel Castillo, DDS. [end of tape]

"I thought we decided not to ask about the porn?"

"It felt right, so I thought I'd go for it."

"It didn't sound right."

"He is so out of your league," Petra said, popping another pretzel.

"I know," I replied, without taking any offense. I've never been the kind of girl to let that sort of thing get in the way. I credit my years of rejection to hardening me to the word "no." I just don't hear it the way other women do.

"You're going to have to try to act normal," she said.

"Already working on it."

"Any relationship you had with him would be based on a lie."

"But other than that, it could work out, right?"

Within two weeks, I had reduced Daniel's life to a single-page reference sheet:

Monday:	Office	(8:00 am to 4:00 pm)
	Tennis	(5:30 pm to 7:30 pm)
	Home	(8:00 pm to 7:00 am)
Tuesday:	Office	(8:00 am to 3:00 pm)
	Varying activities with 11 year old boy[1]	(4:00 pm to 8:00 pm)
Wednesday:	Office	(8:00 am to 4:00 pm)
	Tennis	(5:30 pm to 7:30 pm)
	Home	(8:00 pm to 7:00 am)
Thursday:	Office	(8:00 am to 4:00 pm)
	Dinner with assorted males	(6:00 pm to 7:30 pm)
	Poker with assorted males[2]	(7:30 pm to 12:00 am)
Friday:	Office	(8:00 am to 4:00 pm)
	Tennis	(5:30 pm to 7:30 pm)
	Drinks/dinner with friends	(9:00 pm to 11:00 pm)

Saturday:	Tennis	(10:00 am to 12:00 pm)
	Miscellaneous activities[3]	(1:00 pm to 12:00 am)
Sunday:	Lunch with mother[4]	(11:00 am to 2:00 pm)
	Miscellaneous activities[5]	(3:00 pm to 7:00 pm)
	Home	(8:00 pm to 7:00 am)

Two things became unmistakably clear after my two-week surveillance on Daniel Castillo: He was definitely going to be Ex-boyfriend #9 and I had to learn tennis.

I promptly began lessons with a Swede whose advertisement I found in a trendy café across the street from Dolores Park. Stefan said I was a natural, but I'm unclear whether that was his flirty style of instruction or simply an observation. What I know is that I practiced hard and learned to keep score and bought dark blue shorts and a white top that made me feel like an imposter but not, thankfully, an exhibitionist. Within a month I was as good as Daniel had been when he played Jake Peters. I determined it was time to return to the San Francisco

[1] Big Brothers of America–sanctioned activities.

[2] Same assorted males.

[3] Cannot establish a trend.

[4] Or woman with whom he shares a resemblance and appears to be his mother.

[5] Cannot establish a trend.

Tennis Club. There was only one glitch: David.

My brother put his feet up on his desk and leaned back, getting comfortable for what he believed was going to be a long, amusing conversation at my expense.

"Can we go over this one more time?" he said.

"I don't see what the big deal is. I just want you to meet me at the San Francisco Tennis Club on Saturday at ten a.m. sharp. We'll play a game of tennis. I'll buy you lunch. Why can't you just say 'I'd love to, Isabel' like a normal brother would?"

"Since when do you even play tennis?"

"I took it up about a month ago."

"He must be something."

"I don't know what you're talking about."

"I'm sorry, Izzy, I'm busy Saturday morning."

"Next Saturday?"

"Still busy."

"He's not a bartender, I swear."

My brother's secretary buzzed the office: "David, your sister Rae is here to see you."

"Send her in."

Rae entered the office and promptly demanded an explanation for my presence. I, in turn, demanded an explanation for hers, knowing full well she was here for her weekly shakedown. Rae hopped up on the corner of David's desk and handed him a typewritten sheet of paper. David reviewed the sheet, crossed out a line, and reached for his wallet. "I'm not paying for the snacks. You never buy anything healthy."

"What if I can provide you with a receipt?"

"No deal. You'll just trade receipts. On this point, I defer to your sister. We've got to get you off the candy."

David offered Rae a twenty-dollar bill and demanded three dollars in change.

"Does Izzy want money, too?" Rae asked David.

"No, Izzy wants me to help her snag a guy, except I don't approve of her methods."

"What methods?" Rae asked innocently.

"She stalks them first. Finds out every detail of their life and insinuates herself into it until they have no choice but to ask her out."

"Why don't we use the word 'investigating,' " I offered.

"What's wrong with that?" said Rae. "She's just trying to find out something about them first before she gets involved."

A stunned David turned to me for a response.

"Don't defend me, Rae."

"Why not? It makes total sense," she said

more casually than I can bear to describe.

"You should never do that. Ever."

"Do as I say, not as I do," mocked David.

I leaned back on his couch, withered from the conversation, flattened by the prospect that I am, once again and always, setting an example.

"David, tell her how it's supposed to be done," I mumbled.

"Rae, women — other than your sister — when they are attracted to a member of the opposite sex — or the same sex, depending on preference — introduce themselves in some capacity. They smile, they wave, they offer up their business card, or a scrap of paper with their phone number on it, or they ask for a phone number. They make their intentions known and hope that the other party responds. They don't follow the person around for a couple of weeks, learning said person's schedule, assessing his moral character, ensuring that no surprises will arise should they ever begin dating. Relationships entail some element of the unknown. You cannot escape that, no matter how hard you try."

A bored Rae responded, "David, Mom has already given me the 'Don't be like Isabel' speech. And while yours focused more on dating than marijuana abuse, it's all the same. Thanks for the cash. I love you."

She kissed him on the cheek, having learned when she was young that he was the man with the deep pockets. In an act of parity, she walked over to the couch, lifted the pillow off my face, and did the same.

" 'Bye, Izzy. I'll see you later," she said and left me alone, once again, with my judgmental older sibling.

I slowly sat upright on the couch, suddenly feeling as though I weighed three hundred pounds. I got to my feet and put on my coat.

"See you later, David," I said sluggishly.

"Saturday, ten a.m. sharp at the club," he replied, and some of that extra weight lifted.

The debriefing, required on both sides prior to entering the tennis club, consumed approximately twenty minutes. My instructions involved David not speaking unless being spoken to, David not revealing any information regarding family, career, or previous relationships. He was not allowed to correct information I gave or offer information to another party about me. David's only rule was that if he observed any illegal behavior, he would call the police.

We flipped a coin and I served first. It was a legal serve, but David refused to return it.

He motioned with his racket for me to meet him at the net.

"You said you've been playing about a month."

"Right."

"That was quite a serve."

"Thanks. Do you want to play or what?"

"Let's go."

"Fifteen-love."

I served again. David returned with a moderate lob, which gave me enough time to land a powerful backhand that cut diagonally across the court, which David decided to miss. We rallied for a few more minutes and then David called me to the net again.

"What's the deal, Izzy? Remember, I've actually seen you in PE class. Your hand-eye coordination was average at best."

"Well, Stefan would disagree with you."

"Nobody gets this good in one month."

"It's probably been more like five weeks now. But I have taken several lessons and I practice on my days off."

"How many lessons?"

"About twenty-five or so."

"In a month?"

"Yes. Give or take."

David shook his head and returned to the edge of the court. Before he served, he had to put his two cents in. "There is something very, very wrong with you."

While it is true that I had become quite the tennis player in one month's time, I was still no match for David, especially when he was determined to humiliate me.

David won two straight sets, 6-0, 6-0, barely breaking a sweat. I, on the other hand, looked like a tornado victim by the time we reached the bar on the top level. I had a few minutes to reiterate the rules to David before I knew, based on historical evidence, that Daniel would arrive.

"This is important, David. Please don't use this time for payback."

Daniel entered the Match Point Bar and Café as David was ordering our drinks. It occurred to me that consuming alcoholic beverages before noon might come off as suspect, but it was too late. Daniel spotted me on his way to the bar.

I was trying to conjure the appropriate expression under the circumstances. A double-take, perhaps, a look that says, *Don't I know you from somewhere?* not *Statistically speaking, I have been expecting to see you, but now that I have, I'm not sure what to say.* I had not yet managed to plant any safe expression on my face when Daniel sauntered over.

"I was wondering if I'd see you here again."

"Oh, hello" was my clever response. I could feel myself freezing up, words jumbling in my head, my heel tapping uncontrollably on the floor. Then David arrived, handed me a beer, and saved me from certain humiliation.

"Hi, I'm David. Are you a friend of Izzy's?"

"Izzy?"

"Isabel. This one sitting right here."

"We met some time ago."

"Would you like to join us?" David asked.

Daniel was about to say no, automatically assuming that David was my boyfriend and not my brother. Our resemblance being so meager, that is a common misconception. Although, with women, the misconception is often accompanied by audible remarks such as *Wow, she must have done something right in a past life.*

"Oh, no, thank you. I don't want to intrude."

"Sit down," insisted David. "I've talked to my sister enough for one day."

I often record conversations that involve my family to evidence disparaging remarks. Sure, David was doing me a favor, but favors in my family are often a recipe for disaster. I turned on my palm-size digital recorder, just in case.

The transcript reads as follows:

Daniel: Let me get a drink. I'll be right back. You both good?

David: I'm fine. Although, Izzy drinks fast, so you might get her another beer. Ouch.

Isabel: No. I'm fine. Thanks.

[Daniel goes to the bar]

David: He's not your type.

Isabel: I like him. Therefore, he is my type.

David: Let me rephrase. You're not his type.

Isabel: How do you know?

David: I know.

Isabel: How?

David: Men like that like women who pluck their eyebrows.

Isabel: I pluck.

David: Biannually doesn't count.

Isabel: I pluck plenty and you'd have to look really close to notice when I don't.

David: I just don't see you two together.

Isabel: David, if you sabotage this, I swear to you —

David: Isabel, you've invaded this man's privacy for two weeks straight. I'd say you're well on the way to sabotaging this all by yourself.

[Daniel returns with two beers]

Daniel: I got an extra, just in case.

David: Smart man. So, Daniel, how do you know my sister?

Daniel: We met a few weeks ago, was it?

Isabel: Something like that.

David: Are you sure it wasn't more like five weeks?

Daniel: Perhaps.

Isabel: I borrowed his pass. David's pretty good at remembering details.

David: I remember because that's when Izzy decided to take up tennis.

Daniel: Do you prefer to be called Izzy or Isabel?

David: Just call her Izzy. Why waste your time with the extra syllable?

Isabel: Either one is fine.

David: So how did you and Izzy end up talking that day, approximately five weeks ago?

Daniel: Your sister had a question regarding a tennis match I played.

David: What kind of question?

Daniel: Let's just say Isabel is very observant.

David: You have no idea. Ouch.

Isabel: I'm sorry. Was that your leg?

David: You know damn well it was.

Isabel: I apologize. So, Daniel, what brings you here today?

Daniel: I play in a dentists' league, so I had a few matches this morning.

David: You're a dentist?

Isabel: I thought we weren't going to talk about work.

David: You're a dentist?

Daniel: Yes, I'm a dentist.

David: Did you know that, Isabel?

Isabel: Yes, I did, David.

Daniel: So, David, what do you do?

David: I'm a lawyer. Corporate. Mergers and acquisitions. That sort of thing. Did my sister tell you her profession?

Daniel: Yes, she did. When we first met.

David: So you know? Ouch.

Daniel: Yes. I know.

Isabel: I'm a teacher, David. Why would I keep that a secret?

David: A teacher? I had no idea. I mean, I have no idea why you'd keep that a secret.

Isabel: Actually, I'm a substitute. But once I get my credentials, then I'll probably look for a full-time position.

David: Or you could join the family business. Ouch. Isabel, do you understand that when you share a table with others that also implies sharing the space beneath the table?

Isabel: I'm sorry. Was that you?

Daniel: What is the family business?

Isabel: Teaching. We're all in the business of education.

David: Not me. I think I'll have that beer, if you don't mind.

Isabel: No, that's my beer. Go get your own.

David: You know, I think I'll call Mom and ask her how her teaching career is going. Ouch. You should have the tic in your leg looked at. You might have a neurological disorder.

Isabel: David, there's a pay phone over there. Go.

[David limps over to the pay phone]

Daniel: Your brother doesn't have a cell phone?

Isabel: He does. I was just trying to get rid of him.

Daniel: Are you two always like that?

Isabel: Like what?

Daniel: I believe you were kicking him quite a bit.

Isabel: David has a tendency to say inappropriate things. I was simply trying to keep him in check.

Daniel: I see.

Isabel: It's really quite exhausting.

Daniel: So why do you do it?

Isabel: He is my brother.

Daniel: That doesn't mean you have to play tennis with him.

Isabel: I suppose not. But I do like this club and he has a membership.

Daniel: So do I.

Isabel: Yes, you do.

[David returns to the table]

David: Mom says hi.

Isabel: How is she?

David: She's thinking of retiring. They don't make kids like they used to. Speaking of kids, do you have any?

Daniel: Ouch. No.

Isabel: I'm sorry. I thought that was David.

Daniel: I assumed as much. [removes card from his wallet] Here's my card. Call me if you'd like to play tennis sometime. That is, if you don't mind, David.

David: You can have her. Ouch.

Isabel: That wasn't me.

David: *I know that.* I bumped my knee.

Daniel: Good-bye.

[Daniel is out of earshot]

Isabel: Could you be more of an ass?

David: Sure. I could have told him the truth.

Tennis Dates #1 to 3;
Normal Dates #1 to 3

After the disastrous introduction at the club, I phoned Daniel under the guise of wanting to play tennis with him. The only problem with that plan was the tennis part. Each match ended with a calculated but seemingly random result. Daniel won two straight sets, each win was either 6-2, or 6-1 if he got sloppy, and occasionally 6-3, if Daniel was feeling particularly generous. While I found his sliding scale of competitiveness intriguing from afar, it annoyed me when I was its recipient. The truth was, tennis meant nothing to me. Sure, I loved watching his cocoa-colored legs bound across the court, but I came for the beer, pretzels, and stilted conversation that followed. I don't mind losing. Losing is like breathing to me.

Sometime during the fourth game of the second set of my third tennis "match" with Daniel, I walked over to the net after he made a particularly clumsy and badly performed sloppy forehand. He met me at the net and complimented my last return.

"I've kept my mouth shut long enough," I said.

"Excuse me?"

"Unless you're planning on turning this

Jerry Lewis impression into a paying act, how about we just play a normal game of tennis?"

"You want me to play normal?"

"I'm not sure you know what that is anymore."

"But then I will win."

"You've *been* winning."

"I will win faster."

"Agreed. Your serve."

Seven minutes later, Daniel and I were in the bar, halfway through our first beer.

"So how was that?" he asked.

"Maybe next time you could scale it back a bit."

Daniel stared pensively at his pretzel. I got the feeling the phrase *next time* didn't agree with him. I prepared for the brush-off.

"Must we play tennis?" he asked.

"No," I replied.

"Could we do something else?"

"You mean like bowling?"

"No," he answered, louder than usual.

"I take it you're not much of a bowler."

"I'd like to avoid all competitive activities."

"Because there's no fun in winning all the time?"

"Isabel, the polite thing to do would be

for you to make this easier on me," he whispered.

"Sure. What are you trying to do?" I whispered back.

"Are you playing dumb?"

"No," I said, not whispering at all.

"Do you like me?"

"Yes."

"Then what do you say about us going on a normal date?"

"Sure," I said. But then I had to ask the obvious question. "What is a normal date?"

For Daniel, a normal date was pretty much defined by a home-cooked meal followed or preceded by another activity such as a movie, happy hour, or tennis. But I came to the conclusion that playing tennis should only be a normal date activity for people who actually enjoy tennis. I was still undecided in that regard and grateful for the respite. We would play one last time, but I'll get to that later.

Normal Date #1

Three days after Daniel asked me out at the tennis club, we met for drinks at a wine bar in Hayes Valley. A hovering sommelier with a few too many "suggestions" prompted us to leave. Then Daniel had a suggestion of his own: I come back to his place for a "home-cooked meal." Eventually those words — home-cooked meal — would carry an air of doom with them, but on that very first night, Daniel and his home-cooked meal seemed almost perfect.

Dr. Castillo resides on the first level of a three-story apartment building. Two bedrooms, one bath, clean — but not obsessively so — and tastefully decorated without even a hint of a professional's touch. It was far too modest a space for a man whose name is followed by the letters DDS.

Daniel defrosted a plate of enchiladas from his freezer collection. I questioned whether defrosting really qualified as a home-cooked meal, but Daniel explained that he had indeed made the dish (from his mother's recipe) and therefore it counts. I didn't argue once the food was served. I'll give Daniel this: He sure knows how to make a good enchilada. Unfortunately, that was the only thing he could make.

Normal Date #2 (five days later)
After a walk in Golden Gate Park, Daniel invited me over for another home-cooked meal. This time he tried a chicken cacciatore recipe that he found in a *Gourmet* magazine sitting in the reception area of his office. The dish might have been edible, but

when Daniel failed to locate a spice, he would substitute it with one that was similar in color or name, but not necessarily flavor. So instead of oregano, he used thyme. Instead of black pepper, he used cayenne.

The charming thing about Daniel was he didn't seem to notice that the failure of the meal was his own failure. He simply thought that the recipe wasn't properly tested. With each bite came a comment along the lines of, "Interesting combination of flavors." Then a few bites later, "I probably won't be making this again," and lastly, "But I do enjoy experimenting."

Still, I have fond memories of Normal Date #2. After Daniel cleared the table, he pulled a six-pack of beer out of the refrigerator.

"Let's go up to the roof and look at the stars."

There were no stars that night, but I didn't say a word, since rooftop drinking is one of my favorite activities.

We sat on plastic lounge chairs under the dark, foggy sky, mostly in silence, but there was nothing awkward about it. Just two people quietly enjoying each other's company. I was fairly certain he'd brought me to the rooftop to make his first move, but three hours later, when it got too cold to sit there any longer, I realized I was wrong.

Normal Date #3 (three days later)

Once again, Daniel insisted on making me a home-cooked meal. Nothing could prepare my stomach for the sweet-and-sour stuffed cabbage that was presented to me. Daniel, of course, blamed the recipe: "Don't they test these things out?" he said. "I'm definitely not making that again."

"I kind of liked it," I replied.

That entire statement was a complete untruth. But I figured since I was lying about my entire biography, the least I could do was lie about his cooking.

While Daniel washed dishes, I roamed his living room, scanning his bookshelves. It was then that I made the discovery that would change everything — at least it would change our range of activities. I pulled one of the DVD box sets off the shelf and walked into the kitchen.

"Daniel, I noticed you have —"

"Speak up. I can't hear you over the water."

I moved next to him and showed him the DVD. "I noticed you have the entire *Get Smart* collection on DVD. I didn't even think this was available."

"It's a bootleg copy," he replied.

"Was it a gift?" I asked.

"Yes," he said. "A gift to myself. I love *Get Smart.*"

"No, I love it," I said enthusiastically. "My best friend [censored][6] and I used to [censored][7] watch this show all the time."

Daniel turned off the water and dried his hands. "What do you say to a marathon?"

Ten episodes and an inestimable number of shoe phone calls later, Daniel yawned and I realized that I had to be up at seven the next morning to be at school by eight.[8] It was time to go.

Daniel turned off the DVD and said, "When I was a child, I thought for sure I would grow up and work for CONTROL.[9]"

"Me, too," I replied, although what I really thought was that I'd work for KAOS.[10]

Normal Date #3 ended much on the same note as Normal Dates #1 and #2. Daniel walked me to my car, followed by a hand-

---

[6] Petra (must not mention her in case he remembers Staged Dental Appointment #1).

[7] get high and

[8] Untrue.

[9] A top-secret counterespionage organization (the good guys).

[10] The International Organization of Evil.

shake (on #1) and a brief hug (on #2). It was the pat on the head (on #3) that ultimately shattered my patience. After three tennis dates and three normal dates, I still had not gotten my first kiss.

I sat in my car as Daniel disappeared into the foyer of his building. I started the engine, prepared to leave, prepared to accept yet another night of dentist rejection. But then I changed my mind. I had waited long enough.

The window of Daniel's living room is only six feet aboveground and readily accessible if you use the drainpipe that runs horizontally along the front of the building. When I saw the lights go on in Daniel's apartment and his shadow moving about, I got out of my car and knocked on his window.

People don't respond to window knocking as they do to doorbells or door knocking, but they do respond eventually. Daniel opened the window just as I was losing my grip on the dusty sill.

"Hello, Isabel. Is my buzzer broken?"

"No," I said, not understanding the question.

"What are you doing out here?"

"I wanted to talk to you."

"Okay. Would you like to come in?"

"Sure," I said, pushing the window up another notch with the palm of my hand.

"Why don't you go around to the front and I'll buzz you in?" Daniel said.

I'm not sure when doors became the single mode of entry and exit in our domesticated world, but something about that hard and inflexible rule struck me as unscientific. Daniel wanted me to jump off the drainpipe, walk ten yards to the front door, wait for a buzzer, and pass a security gate and two doors to reach the same destination that a pull-up and leg throw could accomplish.

"I'll just use the window, if you don't mind," I said.

Daniel stepped back as I threw my left leg over the window and straddled the sill. I swung my other leg inside and dusted off my hands.

"You might want to clean that," I said.

Daniel remained unresponsive to my suggestion.

"Is everything all right, Isabel?"

"No."

"Care to elaborate?"

"What am I? A golden retriever?"

"Of course not," Daniel replied, confused.

"Three games of tennis, one happy hour, a stroll in the park, twelve beers, one glass of wine, and three home-cooked meals. What does it take?"

Daniel leaned back on the arm of his couch.

"What does it take?" he repeated.

"Four handshakes, a businessman's hug, and a pat on the head?"

"Isabel, I need you to spell it out for me," Daniel replied.

And so I did. I reached for his tie and pulled him close. After seven weeks, twenty-five tennis lessons, two weeks of short-term surveillance, three tennis dates and three normal dates, and ten episodes of my favorite television show of all time, I finally got my first kiss.

"You get it now?" I said as I pulled away.

"I get it," Daniel replied as he put his arm around my waist and kissed me back.

Hiding Daniel from my parents and hiding my parents from Daniel required a more aggressive regimen than my previous exercises in stealth could prepare me for. The easiest part was keeping Daniel from my home. I explained that any unannounced visit could result in the accidental meeting of the parental unit. I explained to him that if he met the unit at this point in our relationship, he would undoubtedly break up with me. Daniel wrestled with the concept that people who sacrificed their lives to become educators could be the kind of lunatics their daughter portrayed, but he accepted it as truth.

My parents would have found nothing unusual in my behavior had it not been for the sudden sartorial changes. I don't dress like a schoolteacher and for Daniel to believe a lie, which I believed was so observably untrue, I figured the only way to sell it was to dress the part.

THE SKIRT WARS

Initially I'd rush home after work, shower, change into a tailored dress or a tweed skirt and a somewhat ironed shirt, and try to slip out of the house unnoticed. But nothing goes unnoticed in that house. If it rained, I could hide my attire with a long overcoat. On the rare occasions when I was expected to meet with a client, the outfits were essentially interchangeable. But mostly I did my best to remain unnoticed. Defenestration became my coming-and-going method of choice, but it's hard to say what is more suspicious: a sudden, drastic change in wardrobe or not using doors.

However, the greatest challenge would occur in the middle of the day, when Daniel would want to meet for a "surprise" lunch. A patient canceled. He's suddenly free. I'm astounded by the number of people who don't think twice about canceling a dentist's appointment. I railed against every cancelation, wanting to call each and every patient and shout, "Do you know what this is doing to me?!" or "Don't you care about dental hygiene?!" Instead, I learned to change in the car. I would park down the street from the school du jour — Mission High School, Presidio Middle School, Jefferson Elementary School, etc. — change my clothes, and wait for Daniel on the street. Occasionally I'd wave to a complete stranger who had that weary haze of an educator and say, "See you next week, Suzie" or "Take care of that cold, Jim." Daniel never noticed the awkward stare I'd receive as a response. He bought it all, and why shouldn't he have? This particular truth was much stranger than any fiction.

It became such a routine — car changes adjacent to public schools — that I began viewing these sessions as amateur sporting events rather than a by-product of deceit. My best time was three minutes and twenty-five seconds for a full wardrobe change. My worst time was eight minutes and fifty seconds, when I caught the zipper of my wool skirt on the tail of my linen shirt. A week after Daniel and I began our Normal Dates, Petra commented that my dress seemed over the top, as if I were performing the part of a schoolteacher in a play. But I found that I needed the clothes to remind me of the act. In my case, the clothes didn't make the woman, they made the lie. And while I should have found my own behavior disturbing, I did not. Not until one day when I caught a glimpse of myself in the rearview mirror. The arm of my sweater had twisted into a secure knot and I writhed in the backseat of my car, besieged by my own clothing.

It was time to put an end to Daniel's surprise lunch dates. To satisfy Daniel's desire for spontaneity and mine for restaurant food, I started dropping by Daniel's office whenever I was in the vicinity and appropriately dressed. Since substitute teachers have a notoriously flexible schedule, Daniel was none the wiser.

The first time I was introduced to Mrs. Sanchez, Daniel's sixty-year-old hygienist, office manager, and all-around saint, she looked me up and down and smiled politely. Then she mumbled something to Daniel in Spanish.

On my second "spontaneous" visit, approximately six weeks after Daniel and I started dating, Mrs. Sanchez told me to take a seat, that Daniel was with a patient and should be finished in fifteen minutes or so. Then I made the mistake of engaging in small talk.

"Daniel tells me you're a substitute teacher," Mrs. Sanchez said.

"He did? I don't know where he got that idea from."

Silence.

"Sorry, that was a joke," I said, although it wasn't much of one and it's always a bad sign when you don't even get polite laughter. "Yes, I'm a teacher. A substitute teacher. Aren't kids great?"

"Yes," she replied. "I have three grandchildren of my own."

"That's wonderful," I said. "I hope you have some regular children, too."

Silence.

"I meant that you would need to have your own kids first and then the grandchildren follow."

"I have three children," she replied with a polite but unsettling smile.

"Congratulations," I said because I was losing steam.

"So Isabel, where do you teach usually?"

"Oh, everywhere."

"Don't you have some schools where you're a regular."

"Not really. I like to mix it up. Keep things interesting."

"Well, where did you teach last week, for instance?"

Last week had been one of Daniel's surprise lunch visits, and I'd changed my clothes outside of Presidio Middle School. It's important to maintain consistency in lies — I learned that at a very early age.

"I was at Presidio Middle School last Tuesday and Wednesday, if my memory serves me."

"My grandson Juan goes to Presidio. Then you must know Leslie Granville, the vice principal."

"Oh, I don't know her[1] very well."

Silence.

"Him, you mean. Leslie is a man, last I checked."

"Right," I said, feeling the blood drain from my face. "Him. Yes, of course. I have that thing where you swap pronouns. There's a word for it. An actual condition. Anyway. Yes, Leslie is a man."

An act of God — the telephone ringing — saved me from any further embarrassment, but after that day, Mrs. Sanchez always looked at me like I was a person with a

[1] Statistically speaking, there are far more women than men working in education, so this was not an entirely reckless assumption.

secret. Can't blame her. I was.

By the time Daniel and I had been dating for six weeks, there were too many acts of deceit occupying my everyday life. It was time to come out of the closet, so to speak. I could hide my real self from Daniel, but I would no longer make heroic efforts to hide my fake self from my family. I was aware that my priorities were faulty, but I did see this evolution as an improvement. The next day, I wore a tweed skirt and sweater set and walked right out the front door. Then I did it the following day and the day after that, albeit different outfits.

On the fourth day, my father intercepted my path out the front door. Since it was only 7:00 a.m. and my father routinely crawls out of bed no earlier than 9:00, I was already on guard.

"Good morning, Isabel."

"Dad, what are you doing up so early?"

"I thought I'd watch the sun rise."

"How'd it go?"

"I missed it by a half hour. Who knew it was so early?"

"Are you deliberately blocking my path out the door?"

"Yes."

"Why?"

"What's new?"

"Nothing much."

"Your clothes say otherwise."

"I wasn't aware that my clothes were on speaking terms with you."

"Oh, they are."

"What are my clothes saying?"

"They're telling me that you're up to something."

"Harsh words from fabric, wouldn't you say?"

"The dresses, Izzy, they're suspicious," my father said, slowly raising his voice.

"Dad, I have to be across town in ten minutes," I replied as I slipped past him and opened the door. "I'm going to instruct my clothes not to speak to you anymore. I hope you understand."

THE INTERVIEW:
CHAPTER 4

I notice that Stone has jotted down my habit of window entry and exit in his notebook. His scribble is borderline illegible and difficult to read upside down. Usually I'm pretty good at that sort of thing, subtle upside-down reading, but I stare just a little too long.

"Isabel, would you stop trying to read my notes?"

"I wasn't."

"Yes, you were."

"No, I was not."

Stone puts down his pen and stares at me sternly. "How old are you?"

"You know how old I am. It's in your notes."

"Answer the question."

"Twenty-eight."

"Last I heard, twenty-eight was an adult. You can legally drive, drink, vote, marry, sue people, go to prison —"

"What is your point, Inspector?"

"I'd like you to act your age."

"What is that supposed to mean?"

"It means it's time to grow up, Isabel."

His reprimand strikes me harder than it should. I want to believe that his remarks are a product of endless hours of parental brainwashing, but I know that's not the case. Stone's made his assessment of me all on his own.

I look down at some etchings on the wooden table that I made during my childhood-through-adolescent interrogations. I try to forget about why I am here. I try to avoid thinking about all the words that must have transpired against me in this very room. I try to forget that he has already interviewed every other member of my family. Well, almost every member. I try to think about anything else, but Stone brings me back to reality.

THE WAR ON RECREATIONAL SURVEILLANCE: CHAPTER 2

I returned home that night prepared for a second wave of wardrobe-related interrogations, but another conflict was brewing that distracted everyone from my comparatively benign outfits. I found Rae standing alone in the hallway, staring myopically at her bedroom door.

"Rae?"

My voice shook her out of a daze and she turned to me. "Have you been in my room?" she asked.

"No. Why?"

"Somebody has," she replied and tapped the door with her index finger. It creaked open and she turned to me for confirmation of some sort.

"Rae, don't jump to conclusions," I called out to her, but I knew it was to no avail. Rae has had a deadbolt on her door since she learned how to install deadbolts two years ago. We all have deadbolts on our doors and, with the exception of the two-year period of time when mine was removed for drug-related offenses, this is standard fare in the family. We're really into privacy, especially since we have no respect for it.

I continued up the stairs to my apartment. A few moments later, I heard a door slam and the stomping of the feet of a one-hundred-pound person. I exited my apartment and followed the footsteps into the living room.

"You old hack, what gives you the right to steal my stuff?" Rae shouted upon entering the room.

Uncle Ray barely looked up from the television when he replied, "Kid, I had a job to do and the batteries on my camera were dead, so I borrowed your digital. I was in a jam. What's the big deal?"

"You picked three locks, entered a room with a sign that says NO TRESPASSING, searched premises for a camera that was hidden under my bed in a lockbox, and then took it. I DON'T KNOW WHAT YOU CALL IT IN THE OLD COUNTRY, BUT WHERE I COME FROM THAT'S CALLED STEALING!"

Rae rushed past me as she stormed out of the room. I could hear her mutter under her breath, "This means war."

As she would later describe, Rae snuck out that night to "blow off some steam." I sat in my apartment, proofreading a surveillance report that David refused to accept until I located the five typos on my own, because, he said, "I wouldn't learn otherwise." I heard a familiar creak on the fire escape and caught sight of Rae, dangling from the final rung on the ladder as she made the three-foot leap to the ground. I checked the clock and it read 9:30 p.m. I decide that on the off chance Rae missed curfew, someone would be there to prove it.

I exit through the front door, unnoticed, and head up the block in Rae's direction. I hang back until she reaches Polk Street. As much as she likes to mix up her routine, there are certain habits I can trust. Polk Street is only a few short blocks from our house and she requires a public place to choose her target and practice her technique.

She enters a café and leaves shortly thereafter, eating what I believe to be a brownie. I decide the trip is worth it, since I've already caught her on one offense: sugar on a school night. Rae weaves her way down the street and I realize she's already chosen her prey. I close the gap between us, confident that I'll remain unnoticed.

Rae shadows a man in his mid twenties, with creative facial hair and a standard assortment of tattoos, into the Polk Street Bookstore. Rae is fourteen but she looks thirteen and she is roaming solo nearing ten o'clock on a school night; she is not as incognito as she imagines she is. I wait outside for the right opportunity to reveal myself, instead of entering the bookstore and spoiling her fun.

The tattooed guy leaves, without any books, which doesn't surprise me. I step away from the doorway and wait for my sister to follow. She exits at an appropriately timed pace and follows the man down the street in the direction of the Tenderloin. I remain on their tails, still unnoticed.

Rae's subject turns left onto Eddy Street and she follows. My anger is brimming as I realize that she has no intention of turning back. After years of drilling into Rae's head all the dangers that lurk around the corner, it's shocking to watch her actually turn that corner.

The tattooed guy makes another left turn at the end of the block. Rae rushes to the corner to avoid losing a visual. Once my sister rounds the bend, I do the same. The tattooed guy turns left one more time, finishing the final segment of a complete loop. I want to scream at Rae a litany of *Are you an idiot?*–related comments, but I am still convinced there is a lesson to be learned and I hold my tongue until I reach the corner.

This time I hear voices, and when I peer around the bend, I see Rae and her subject in the shadows of an office building under construction. The tattooed guy cages Rae between his arms as he leans against the red brick.

"Sweetheart, what are you doing?" he says in an affected whisper.

"Nothing. Just going for a walk," Rae replies.

"At this time of night?"

"I needed some fresh air."

"You know what I think?" he says.

"How would I know that?" she answers.

"I think you were following me."

"I wasn't," she snaps back nervously.

"You like older men, is that it?"

"That's definitely not it, definitely not."

"I could teach you a few things."

"Izzy? Can you please help me now!" Rae shouts.

I take out my knife and flick it open. Tattooed Guy recognizes the sound and turns to me as I round the corner.

"Get the hell away from my sister," I say calmly, while trying to invoke the spirit of Lee Van Cleef.

"Take it easy, ladies, there is enough of me to go around."

I pick up my phone and pretend to dial 911. "I hope that line works for you in prison."

The tattooed guy considers that possibility and decides to call it a night. He offers Rae a suggestive wink. "See you around, kid."

I watch him until he disappears into an alley down the street. Then I shove Rae against the wall and remind her that we had a deal.

"I agreed to trim my recreational surveillance significantly, but not entirely."

"You were loitering in the red-light district after curfew. Do I need to remind you that you're fourteen years old?"

"I am allowed to stay out after curfew when accompanied by a family member. You were with me, so I figured it was okay."

"When did you spot me?"

"At the bookstore. I wouldn't have followed him if I didn't know you were there."

I shake my head, unable to respond. I grab

Rae by the arm and drag her down the street. "Let's go home now. I'll deal with you later."

We walk up Polk Street in silence, until Rae predictably breaks it.

"Did you see the way he winked?" she asks.

"I did."

"I hate it when people wink."

"I know. You're not getting away with it anymore. I hope you understand," I tell Rae.

"Can we negotiate?" she asks.

"I'm afraid this one is nonnegotiable."

In the interrogation room later that night, my parents — using a tag-team method — lectured Rae for two straight hours on the potential dangers of recreational surveillance. My parents have a gift for seeing the negative in things. I can assure you, if a danger existed, Rae learned about it that night.

THE DENTIST WAR

My father eventually gave up trying to decode my fashion U-turn. My mother, however, did not. After her initial stream of random interrogatories, like "Are you doing this to piss me off?" "Who do you think you're fooling?" and "When is the last time you went to the doctor?" Mom refined her focus.

Initially she railed against my prior sartorial rut.

"For two decades straight, it was denim and leather, denim and leather, denim and leather, it was just like living with one of the Hell's Angels — especially with that mouth you have on you."

"You never told me you lived with a Hell's Angel," I replied.

"I would beg you to wear a dress. Beg. Remember Aunt Mary's funeral? And now it is skirts and dresses all the time. I want to know why."

"No reason, Mom. Just mixing it up."

"What's his name?" she said, finally getting to her point.

Every time she asked that question, she got precisely the same answer: "John Smith." By offering my mother the common name, it was understood that she would have to fight me for this secret.

"How long do you think you can sustain this, Isabel?"

I didn't have an answer for her at the time, but most questions eventually have an answer, and three months was the answer to that one.

While I continued to foil Daniel and my parents, other deceptions lined our family tree. Believing myself to be the master of all forms of trickery, I was surprised to learn that one sleight of hand was arranged entirely for my benefit, or lack thereof.

I don't make a habit of dropping by David's house unannounced, mostly because he told me not to make a habit of it. However, there was an occasion when I happened to be in the neighborhood because when I was driving not far from that neighborhood, I got a flat tire. I parked in my brother's driveway and rang the bell. It was seven o'clock on a Saturday night and I considered that the chances of finding him home were slim.

David opens the door on the third ring. When he sees me, his face drops as if he were smiling at the prospect of who he thought would be there and disappointed by the reality of it.

"Isabel."

"Good. You remember me."

"I thought we talked about this."

"I assumed there was some flexibility in that rule."

"Is 'flexible' a word you'd use to describe me?"

"No. But I got a flat tire — in the neighborhood. So I don't care."

"You really have a flat tire?"

"My car is in your driveway. Would you like to inspect it?"

"No. What do you need?"

"Well, I'd like to use your phone and relax in your luxurious home while I wait for the tow truck."

"Don't you have a cell phone?"

"I left it at home. I was just running a quick errand."

David turns back into his foyer and leaves the door ajar, silently and impolitely allowing my entrance.

"Make it quick, Izzy. I got plans tonight."

"What kind of plans?"

"I'm not in the mood for an interrogation."

"You never are."

"Shall I draw you a map to the telephone?" David says, more snappish than usual, which on a scale of snappish is about a ten.

Just as I reach out to pick up the cordless phone on the kitchen counter, it rings. I remove the phone from the cradle and David charges toward me, quickly prying it out of my hands.

"Hello," he says breathlessly. "Yes. I know. My sister is here right now and I have to wait until the tow truck arrives, so maybe we can move it back about a half hour? Okay, an hour. I'll see you then."

David hangs up and offers me the phone. I watch him carefully, but remain silent. I make the car-related phone calls while David primps impatiently in the mirror. I ask to use his bathroom and predictably itemize his medicine cabinet. Usually I discover the latest in age-defying propaganda and mock David relentlessly for his vanity. Sometimes I think if he weren't my brother, I'd despise him. However, what I do discover alongside the alpha-hydroxy lotion is a box of tampons and I interpret this evidence to mean only one thing: David has a serious girlfriend.

You might think I'm jumping to conclusions, but I'm basing my leap of logic on history and I'm already feeling resentful that he wants to hide this from me.

I lean out the bathroom door. "Where are you going tonight, David?"

"Out to dinner."

"With a date?"

"A friend."

"What's her name?"

"None of your business."

"That can't possibly be her name."

"Give it a rest, Isabel."

I hold out the box of tampons. "I'm onto you."

The War on Recreational Surveillance: Chapter 3

A few weeks later, after Rae was pulled off a surveillance job for receiving a C-plus on an algebra exam, she snuck out again. This time she returned home in the company of two uniformed police officers. My father answered the door in his pajamas, surprised to find Rae outside and not inside.

Officer Glenn introduced himself and his partner, Officer Jackson, then offered my father a warm handshake and said, "Good evening, sir. Is this your daughter?"

"That depends. What did she do?"

"We received an anonymous tip that a young woman matching your daughter's description was following random people around in the vicinity of Polk Street. Shortly thereafter, we found Emily following an elderly couple on Nob Hill. While that is not a crime, we consider it a somewhat unusual activity for a young lady at this time of night."

"Honey," said my father, "you don't give officers of the law a fake name. I apologize for my daughter, Rae Spellman. Will you be filing a report?"

"No, I don't think that will be necessary," said Officer Glenn, and the two cops took their leave.

Rae stepped inside and my father slammed the door behind her.

"How many times do we have to have this conversation?" he asked.

Still not grasping the rhetorical question, Rae answered, "You want a number?"

"There's a lot of bad shit out there. You know that."

"That's why I was following old people!"

Fortunately my father did not accept her rationale. In a quiet, threatening whisper, he said, "You're gonna pay for this, pumpkin," and sent her to bed.

Rae passed her uncle's room just as he shut the door. She knew he had been eavesdropping on the conversation and she knew he was the one who called the cops on her. And while she accepted that her punishment was inevitable, she also vowed that she would take Uncle Ray down with her.

THE BAR WAR

For the infraction of following a couple whose combined age was approximately one hundred and sixty, Rae's punishment was epic. At least it was by comparison to her previous résumé of punishments. She was grounded for three months, which was unprecedented, but the kicker was that she was forbidden to participate in any sanctioned surveillance activities during that time, as well. Before settling into the doldrums of the average life of a grounded child, Rae decided to drown her sorrows in a glass of ginger ale at the Philosopher's Club.

While Milo tried unsuccessfully to convince my sister to depart on her own, Daniel was cooking me yet another meal in which he took far too many liberties with the recipe.

During the green onion chopping (they were supposed to be leeks), Daniel said,

"I'm thinking of having a dinner party."

"Are you sure that's wise?" I replied before my internal censor kicked in.

"Yes," he insisted. "I think it will be fun."

"Who will you invite?" I asked.

"Some friends. Maybe my mother."

Uh-oh, I thought to myself, but then I decided that as long as he didn't want to meet my mother, I was on easy street. So I decided to be accommodating and maybe help the situation.

"That sounds like a great idea. You should make enchiladas."

"No, I'm thinking of something fancier."

"I think enchiladas are very fancy," I said, praying he would come around. Then my phone rang. Normally I wouldn't have answered my cell phone, but the number looked familiar, but not familiar enough to be a family member — my usual criterion for answering my phone.

"Izzy, it's Milo. Your sister is here again."

"At the bar? But she's grounded."

"I know that. I know everything. Could you come and get her?"

"Yeah, I'm leaving now."

The moment I got off the phone, Daniel asked me who was grounded, which guided my lie in a different direction than I was planning. I told him that my sister, Rae, missed the bus home from school (there is no bus) while at ballet practice (in case he heard me mention "the barre"), but that if she wasn't home before 7:00 p.m., she would be grounded.

Daniel asked if he could come with me because he wanted to meet my sister, but I reminded him that the sauce hadn't reduced yet, and he relented.

When I arrived at Milo's, Rae was in mid-speech and Milo, like the good bartender he is, was lending a sympathetic ear.

"They were old, Milo. Old. And it was in Nob Hill. Drug dealers and prostitutes don't hang out there."

"You've got a point, kid."

"I said let's negotiate. Mom said it's non-negotiable. Right. Everything's negotiable. I'm not hurting anyone, am I?"

"I think the concern is that you might hurt yourself."

"I offered to cut back sixty percent. Nothing. Then eighty percent. Eighty percent! But Dad said no and on top of that, no more work. He took away my livelihood."

Rae knew I was watching her and spoke purely for my benefit. But I'd heard enough. I sat down on the adjacent barstool and once again finished off her ginger ale.

"You're grounded, Rae."

"I know."

"So what are you doing here?"

"The rules say that I'm not allowed to be out after school without the supervision of an adult."

"And your point is?"

"Milo's an adult."

I yanked Rae off the bar stool and dragged her to the car. I redefined the fine print in her punishment and we agreed to keep this incident secret if she would behave herself thereafter.

That night I used *Get Smart* to distract Daniel from my sister's interruption. We watched four episodes, culminating in one from 1966 in which KAOS[1] uses the literal-minded[2] robot Hymie[3] to infiltrate CONTROL and kidnap Dr. Shotwire, an important scientist who is being guarded by Max. But Max's kindness turns the sensitive robot from evil to good and in the end Hymie[4] saves the

[1] The International Organization of Evil.

[2] For instance, if you ask Hymie to "give you a hand," he starts unscrewing his hand.

[3] Named after the father of the evil scientist who created him.

[4] Hymie looks human.

lives of Max, 99, and Dr. Shotwire and shoots his own creator. The chief asks Hymie to join CONTROL, but Hymie says he'd rather work for IBM to meet some intelligent machines. This was supposed to be Hymie's only episode, but he was so popular, he was brought back several more times.

"I love Hymie," said Daniel.

"How can you not?" I replied, thinking I had sufficiently gotten him off the subject of my sister and my family. But I was mistaken.

Daniel pressed the pause button and said, "I want to see where you live."

Demands were made, followed by negotiations on the demands, which resulted in Daniel and me sneaking into my apartment via the fire escape at 2:30 in the morning. The novelty of the high school–level caper distracted Daniel from the blunt fact that his girlfriend wasn't in high school anymore. He stayed the night — well, four hours — until I woke him and sent him out the fire escape again.

My mother's impatience grew commensurately with Daniel's, but I held firm with both of them. The teacher ruse was hard to maintain, but I did eventually begin to infuse my own personal wardrobe and vocabulary into the person I presented to Daniel until I could eventually say that I was being myself with him — other than the lying about what my family and I did for a living.

On the weekends of her incarceration, Rae would roam the house in a quiet rage, unable to find an outlet for her ample energy. My mother finally suggested she take a bike ride and reiterated the rules of her temporary freedom. Rae rode her bike to Milo's and this time Milo called my dad. My parents discussed the situation and came to a conclusion befitting only them.

Note: (While I was not a direct witness to the following encounter, I have interviewed all the parties involved and consider my research within the ballpark of the truth.)

When my parents finally picked Rae up at the Philosopher's Club, the rain was already in full force. Rae secured her bike to the rack on the bumper of my mom's Honda and got into the backseat. My father and my mother turned to Rae and offered up stern expressions. Rae immediately went on the defensive.

"You're asking me to stop doing the one thing that I love the most," Rae said.

"Don't be dramatic," said my mother.

"Frankly, I don't know if I can stop."

"You will stop if we tell you to stop," said my father.

"Your expectations are unrealistic."

My mother turned to my father for the go-ahead. My father nodded and my mother said, "We have a job for you. This should keep you busy for a while and out of trouble. Please understand that this is sanctioned surveillance, Rae. If I find out you're freelancing again, you won't be on the job another day until you're eighteen. Got it?"

"Got it. What's the job?"

"We want you to follow your sister," said my father.

"I need an ID on that man she's seeing," said my mother.

Rae was silent as my dad laid out the ground rules. "The job cannot interfere with your schoolwork. And your curfew sticks. No matter where Isabel is or what she is doing, you make it home by eight p.m."

"But my curfew is nine," said Rae.

"Not anymore," said my mother. "Are you interested?"

"Let's talk money," said Rae.

After Rae got a dollar-an-hour bonus for the extra risk of surveilling me, plus over-time and expenses, they shook on the deal.

Rae followed me for three straight days

until I caught on. The slap to my ego when I learned this fact was nothing compared to my mother's reaction when Rae laid out the photos and the truth in front of her. My mother reviewed the pictures of me and Daniel together and even commented to my father that he was a handsome, well-groomed man, and seemed somewhat relieved until my sister handed her the final photograph.

"Mom, try to stay calm," Rae said as she proffered her last offering.

My mother snatched the final picture out of Rae's hands. It was a photograph of the DANIEL CASTILLO, DDS signpost.

"He's a dentist?" my mom asked.

"Yes," said Rae. "But he seems really nice."

Exactly three months after Normal Date #1, Daniel's patience had come to an end. He gave me an ultimatum that spared no room for negotiation.

"I want to meet your family," he said.

"Why? They're not that exciting."

"No. I demand to meet your parents."

"Or?"

"What do you mean, 'or'?"

"Well, usually when someone makes a demand, there are consequences if the demand isn't met."

"Yes. Of course."

"So what are the consequences?" I asked, because I thought maybe they would be something like *Or I will never cook another meal for you again.*

"If I don't meet your family within one week, this relationship *is* over."

"If you meet my family, this relationship *is* over."

Daniel rolled his eyes and offered an exaggerated sigh. "They've dedicated their lives to educating our youth. How bad can they be?"

"Have you ever met a teacher?"

"Isabel, this is an ultimatum. I meet your folks or we're done."

Ultimatums must have been in the air, because the next day my mom gave me her own.

"Sweetie, if I don't meet your new guy within a week, I'm going to track him down myself and arrange my own introduction. Got it?"

When I arrived in the Spellman kitchen the following morning, Rae was making her standard Saturday breakfast — chocolate-chip pancakes, heavy on the chocolate chips. In fact, my dad had to pry the bag out of her hands. Then my mom had to pry the bag out of my dad's. Rae gave me a plate from the first batch. I told her I wasn't paying for them, which was a common scam she played after a seemingly generous offer. This time she said they were on the house and smiled guiltily.

I turned to my mother, who was still waiting for a response from the previous day's ultimatum. I gave it to her.

"You can meet him. But under my conditions."

"I'm listening," she said.

"He thinks I'm a teacher."

"Where'd he get that idea?" asked my dad.

"I told him I was a teacher."

"That's a believable lie," he muttered sarcastically.

"I might become one. Who knows?"

"You're not going to become a teacher," said my mom.

"How do you know?" I snapped in reply.

"How about we get back to the meeting?" interrupted my dad, and I clarified my expectations for the event.

"I'm not ready to tell him the truth."

"Does he know about us?" asked my mom.

"No. And I'd like to keep it that way."

Uncle Ray entered the kitchen, bare-chested, wearing only his standard blue jeans and sneakers.

"Hey, anybody see my shirt?"

Three nos followed and my mother asked, "Where did you see it last?"

"I was doing laundry last night."

"Retrace your steps."

"I've been retracing my friggin' steps for the past two hours. Jesus Christ." Uncle Ray directed this at no one as he marched out of the kitchen.

My mom turned the conversation back to important matters. "When will this meeting happen?"

"Friday night."

"What's our cover?" my dad asked reluctantly.

"Mom, you're a seventh grade math teacher. Dad, you're a retired principal for the Alameda school district."

"Am I a teacher, too?" asked Rae.

"No," I said.

"Why not?"

"Because you're in the ninth grade."

"So what's my cover?"

"You're in the ninth grade," I said as forcefully as I could.

My mother stared down at her coffee and mumbled, almost inaudibly, "What are you so ashamed of?"

Later that night, Rae knocked on my apartment door.

"I need a dark past," she said when I answered it.

"Excuse me?"

"Friday, when we meet the dentist. The whole being-in-the-ninth-grade thing isn't enough for me to work with. Let's say I had a heroin habit, but I kicked it about six months ago and now I'm doing fine."

"That's not funny," I said.

"No, it isn't," she replied, playing the part. "It was the hardest thing I ever had to do. Now I just take it one day at a time."

I grabbed her by the collar and shoved her against the door, prepared to squash whatever determination she had. I spoke slowly and clearly to drill in every word. "Your father is a retired principal. Your mother is a math teacher. Your sister is a sub. End of story. You get that down."

"But I've got that down," she said with whatever air she had left.

I threw her into the hallway and reminded her of the level of retribution I was capable of. But I knew she wouldn't be able to control herself. I braced myself for what I knew would be a disastrous night, although I never could have anticipated how disastrous.

Petra met me for drinks the following day. I briefed her on all the Spellman news, hoping for some sympathy.

"You should tell the dentist the truth before it's too late," Petra said.

"I'm waiting for the right moment."

"That would require time travel."

"Very funny."

"You're jumping through a lot of hoops just for some guy."

"That's because I like this one."

"But what's the attraction? I mean, falling for a handsome doctor is, frankly, a bit clichéd for you."

I had to think about it: "He's everything I'm not."

"Guatemalan with a medical degree? True."

"How about highly educated, bilingual, and capable of tanning," I replied.

"Do you have anything in common?"

"As a matter of fact, we have lots of things in common."

"Like what?"

"*Get Smart.* He's a fanatic. Has seen every episode at least three times."

"I'm not sure a thirty-five-year-old sitcom is enough of a foundation to build a relationship on."

"It worked for you and me."

"Anything else?"

"He has the entire series on DVD. Bootleg, no less."

"And?"

"As you are aware, there are one hundred and thirty-eight episodes."

"I repeat the question: Do you have anything else in common?"

"We both like drinking on rooftops."

"Who doesn't?" Petra replied, not buying any of it. "The fact remains that he is a dentist and you know what that will do to your mother. So it still kind of feels like teenage rebellion. You know what I mean?"

"No, I don't," I said. But I did.

Petra shrugged her shoulders dismissively and took off her jacket to rack the balls. I noticed a large bandage on her bicep.

"What happened?"

"Nothing. I just got a tattoo removed," she casually replied.

I gasped dramatically and said, "No, not Puff?" already in mourning.

Petra got Puff the Magic Dragon one foggy night after drinking nine shots of whiskey in two hours. She claimed to have wanted a fire-breathing dragon — the meanest you could find — but in the morning, when she woke, it was the upside-down, child-friendly smile of Puff that stared back at her. She returned to the parlor the following day, a hangover firing her sloppy speech, and demanded an explanation for the inexplicable, yet permanent, artwork on her shoulder. The owner of the establishment remembered Petra, mostly because she tried to order French fries from him on three separate occasions, but also because she provided her own artwork for the tattoo.

The owner showed Petra the bar napkin with the picture of Puff and Petra's initials by its side. Petra, confused by her drunken rendering, accepted fault for the previous night's misstep and left the tattoo parlor without another word. Eventually, Puff grew on her and was often mentioned fondly, like a distant cousin or a long-deceased pet.

"I'm going to miss Puff," I said.

"Well, I'm not going to miss a daily reminder of the worst hangover I ever had."

"I asked you ages ago if you ever considered removing it and you said no."

"A girl can change her mind, can't she?"

"Sure, but you usually don't."

Petra made a clean break without sinking

any balls.

After I cleared two stripes, I turned to her and asked, "Are you seeing anyone?"

"No," she answered unconvincingly.

"Are you sure?"

"Izzy, are we playing pool or what?"

The Dentist War, the Shirt War (and Car Chase #1)

I greet Daniel outside as he walks up the driveway to 1799 Clay Street. "No matter what happens tonight, you can't break up with me."

"They can't possibly be that bad."

"Promise."

Daniel kisses me and promises that he won't break up with me tonight, although he tacks on a friendly reminder that the moratorium will end in twenty-four hours. He is joking. I am not.

We enter the house and my parents descend upon us. I use the brief introductory phase to leave Daniel and get him the drink I know he will require. My mom invites him into the living room, while I pour double shots of whiskey into two glasses. Then I consider the fact that if the meeting goes as badly as it has potential to, I might require evidence of my parents' indiscretions. So I rush into the office, grab my digital recorder, slip it into my pocket, and join the others in the living room.

But I don't need a voice recording to remember the events of that night. They are as clear as yesterday to me.

I hand Daniel his drink as he sits down on the couch. "You'll need this," I say.

My mother, ignoring me, gushes, "I'm just so happy to finally meet you, Daniel. Or should I call you 'Doctor'?"

"No. Daniel is fine, Mrs. Spellman," Daniel politely replies.

"Please, call me Livy. Everybody calls me Livy."

"I don't," I remind her.

"Behave yourself, Isabel," Daniel reminds me.

"Thank you, Daniel," my mother says with a healthy grin forming on her face. "So, Daniel, tell me, were you born in California?"

"No. Guatemala. My family moved here when I was nine."

"Where do your parents live?"

"San Jose."

"Do they go by Castillo, as well?"

Not even minutes have passed and the investigation has begun.

"Don't answer that question," I interrupt, like a public defender.

But Daniel ignores me. "Yes, they do."

"Same spelling?" asks my dad.

"Of course," Daniel replies, his eyebrow rising, along with his suspicion.

"That's wonderful," my father chimes in.

When Rae enters the room, I'm almost pleased to see her, which indicates how far my spirits have dropped. She walks right up to Daniel and holds out her hand.

"Hi. I'm Rae, Izzy's sister. Should I call you Dr. Castillo?"

"Nice to meet you, Rae. Please call me Daniel." Daniel smiles at Rae and I can tell that briefly, at least, he's bought her charming schoolgirl act.

Then Uncle Ray lumbers downstairs, shouting, "Kid, I got your little note."

I had a feeling it would come to this, but I had hoped that it would wait one more day.

My uncle hands my father a folded piece of charcoal-gray craft paper.

"Al, look at this," he says, then turns to Rae and continues, "If you think I'm gonna be your patsy, you got another think coming."

I watch my father as he unfolds the paper. Superhuman efforts are required to stifle the laugh he so desperately wants to release.

Rae replies to her uncle, "I have no idea what you're talking about," with impressive acting skills.

"You're going down for this. Mark my words," Uncle Ray says with a force that would have scared even me.

My mother chooses to ignore the entire episode, which comes off as even more absurd than her pointed interrogatives.

"So, Daniel, how old are you?"

"That's none of your business," I tell her.

"It's okay. I'm thirty-seven."

I sigh, frustrated.

"That's a nice age," says my mom. "So you were born in, what? 1970?"

"Mom." I say it as a threat.

"What is your birthday, Daniel?"

"Don't answer that question."

"February fifteenth," Daniel says, probably wanting to flip a coin to decide which one, my mother or me, is the most unbalanced.

"I told you not to answer her," I say, frustrated.

"Relax, Isabel."

My mother jots down the results from her investigation. "February fifteenth, nineteen-seventy. I hate to forget a birthday."

Meanwhile, my dad is mediating the conflict on the other side of the room.

"Rae, give your uncle his shirt back," he

says, handing me the craft paper for my own perusal.

"What makes you think I have it?" Rae protests.

"The ransom note, pumpkin."

I unfold the paper, while Daniel looks over my shoulder. In letters cut out and glued from newspaper and magazine print, the note reads:

**I HaVe yOUr ShIRt.
iF YoU eveR WaNt 2 SeE it AgaIN,
YoU wILL meET mY DeMaNDS.**

Rae persists with her "anyone could have written that note" defense.

"Rae, give him the damn shirt," I say, offering up my most threatening stare.

"Dust it for prints if you want," she confidently replies, then walks up to Daniel to finish pleading her case. "They suspect me immediately because I had a drug habit a while back. I've been clean for six months now, but that doesn't matter. You have to rebuild the trust."

I was expecting that part and, frankly, it was the least of my worries. Uncle Ray approaches Daniel, genuinely apologetic.

"Sorry to interrupt. I'm Ray, Izzy's uncle."

"Two Rays. That could get confusing."

"She was named after me. When Olivia was pregnant with the kid, I had cancer. It didn't look like I was gonna make it, so they decided to give her my name."

"But then he didn't die like he was supposed to," Rae says, as if she's revealing the surprise ending to a whodunit.

"Rae, five bucks if you get out of here now," I offer.

"Make it ten and you've got a deal."

Money exchanges hands and I realize that we better make our escape before it is too late.

"Nice meeting you, Daniel. You're nothing like I expected," Rae says upon leaving the room.

Uncle Ray stays close on her heels. "This isn't over, kid."

I try to explain. "They're in the middle of a thing."

"They're at war," says my mother, still with that awful grin.

"So you're a dentist?" my father says, trying to hide the edge in his voice.

"Yes," Daniel replies cheerily.

"How is that?" Dad asks.

"I like it. My father's a dentist, so was my grandfather. It runs in the family, you could say."

"Isn't that nice," my mother says in a

voice that doesn't match her statement.

"So how long have you been a teacher?" Daniel inquires.

"Twenty years or something," Mom tosses out.

"You must be very dedicated."

"Not really."

"We should be going," I say, feeling the barometer in the room dip.

"It wasn't really our calling," my dad, continuing the act, says. "Frankly, we don't like children," he whispers as if he's revealing a dark secret.

"Okay. We are leaving," I say and stand to bring the point home. But it's too late.

"Do you find it difficult staying off the drugs?" my mother asks, the friendly grin dropping from her face.

"Excuse me?" Daniel replies, his grin fading as well.

"You people do seem to have drug problems more than most," she continues.

I take Daniel's arm, but he's already on his feet. "I cannot speak for all of 'my' people, but I have never had a drug problem."

"She didn't mean it the way it came out," I say.

"I'm glad to hear that Daniel is clean," my mother says.

"This is unbelievable," Daniel says directly to my mother.

"Would you look at the time," is my only response.

"Nice meeting you, Daniel," my dad says, still hanging on to his "nothing is unusual here" smile.

"Come again," adds my mom in the same tone in which one might say, *I'll see you in hell.*

Daniel walks out. I turn to my parents, betrayed. "You said you'd behave."

"Have a nice evening, sweetie," my dad shouts to me as I chase Daniel outside.

"I told you they were weird," I say, hoping for a sympathetic response. I mean, I had to be raised by them. All he had to endure was ten minutes of conversation.

"Forgive me, but I'd like to take a rain check on dinner tonight," Daniel says.

I watch Daniel get into his car and start the engine. I'm about to let him leave, thinking that it's taken me years to process having those people as family, so why not give him a night? But then I change my mind and jump into my Buick.

I catch up with Daniel's BMW as he turns north on Van Ness Avenue. I remain on his tail for two blocks before my cell phone rings.

"Isabel, is that you behind me?"

"Daniel, please stop the car." I notice that he's speeding up. "You want to put your foot on the left pedal, not the right."

"I know how to drive, Isabel."

"I just need five minutes to explain. Actually, it will take about fifteen, maybe twenty minutes. But that's all."

Daniel makes a sharp right on Broadway.

"I should warn you, Daniel, if you're trying to shake me, that is not going to happen."

"But my car is faster than your car."

"Trust me. It's not that simple."

Daniel disconnects the call and speeds through a yellow light. I speed through a red light. I want to call him back and explain that what we are doing now is simply a ritual. Daniel is a responsible citizen. He is a man who obeys the laws of society and the laws of traffic. I obey neither, which means there's no way he can lose me in a car chase.

Daniel cuts a maze through the city, driving with no discernible design or direction, at thirty-five mph or less. I consistently maintain a distance short enough to remind him that I'm there, but not close enough to frighten him. I'm not going to lose him, is all I can think.

Daniel takes Franklin Street down the hill to Bay, makes a left, and continues on until he hits Fillmore, where he makes a sharp right and then a left on Marina Boulevard. He speeds up a bit, but still with the pace of traffic, and pulls onto the Golden Gate Bridge. I can see him looking for me in his rearview mirror and then shaking his head in disappointment. He turns on his right blinker and slows at the end of the bridge, looking for a place to pull off the road. The chase is about to come to an end.

Daniel slows to a halt at the first turn-around off the bridge. He gets out of his car and waits for me to park.

"Are you trying to kill me?" he asks as he approaches my car.

I ignore the hyperbolic response to the slowest car chase known to man.

"Daniel, you misunderstood."

"Did I? You're dating a 'spic' to rebel against your parents."

"I had a feeling you'd take it the wrong way."

"Did you hear what she said to me? 'You people.' "

"Yes. Dentists. My mother hates dentists."

"People may not like going to the dentist, but generally, they don't hate us as a people."

"Daniel, it's a long story, but I have too many others to tell you right now to focus on that one. Keep in mind that a lot of what was said tonight was not true."

"Were those your parents?"

"Yes."

"Too bad."

"I'm not a teacher. My parents aren't teachers."

"Finally, some good news."

"They're private investigators. So am I. It's the family business. The day I met you, I was surveilling your tennis partner, Jake Peters. His wife was under the impression that he was gay and you were his lover."

"That's absurd."

"Yeah, I know. When I saw you play that second game I got suspicious, so I waited for you in the bar. I would have told you the truth then, but it sounded so strange and I couldn't divulge any client information."

"You told me you were a teacher."

"Right."

"Why?"

"Because it sounded normal. I just wanted to pretend for a while. See how the other half lives. Something like that. Later, there never seemed to be a good time to come clean, although I probably should have done that before you met my family."

Daniel stares back at me with an expression of betrayal that I've seen only a handful of times from my parents. It's interesting how the same emotions on different people often have a photographic similarity.

"I want to go home now," he says. "I don't want to be chased. I want to quietly get into my car and drive away. Can I do that?"

"Yes," I say quietly and let him go. But as I watch him get into his car and drive off, I've already decided that I'm going to get him back no matter what it takes.

But first, I have a score to settle.

I get out of bed after a sleepless night, walk down two flights of stairs into my parents' kitchen, pour myself a cup of coffee, cross the hall to the Spellman offices, and break the news.

"I quit."

"Quit what, dear?" asks my mother.

"Quit this job."

"You can't just quit," says my dad.

"Yes, I can."

"No. You can't. Ask your mother."

"Your father is right," says my mom. "It's not that simple."

"I'll just stop coming to work."

"And we'll stop paying you," says my dad.

"Fine."

"Fine."

"Fine," says my mother. "Except that eventually you'll need to get another job, and since this is the only job you've ever had, you'll need some kind of reference."

"What are you saying?" I ask.

"Yes, what are you saying?" repeats my father.

"You'll take one last job and then you can leave. I'll write you a letter of recommendation and everything."

"One last job. That's it?"

"And then you're free," says my mom.

Free. That had a nice ring to it. After sixteen years of working for the family business, it was time to learn whether life would be easier on the outside.

It's as if they planned for this day . . .

■ ■ ■ ■

Part Three:
Negotiating Peace

■ ■ ■ ■

ONE LAST JOB

My parents took a full twenty-four hours to discuss the details of my final assignment. I imagined they spent the night laboring over the open files, wrestling with the decision of which was the most impossible. Which case would keep me in their grasp the longest? I braced myself for the worst, but I don't believe anything could have prepared me for what would come, that morning or over the following weeks.

I met them in the office at 9:00 a.m. My mother handed me a thick case file, yellowed with age and ringed with coffee stains. She went over the brushstrokes of the case.

"On July 18, 1995, Andrew Snow disappeared while on a camping trip in Lake Tahoe with his brother, Martin Snow. The boys were raised in Mill Valley, California, by their parents, Joseph and Abigail Snow. The police conducted an all-out search for

Andrew during the month following his disappearance, but found no trace of him. Nor was there anything in his behavior that could explain his disappearance. He simply vanished. We originally got the case twelve years ago, worked on it for about a year until the client's funds ran out, then intermittently for the next year, pro bono. We let the case drop in 1997 when all our leads dried up and we didn't have the manpower to continue the investigation."

"You're giving me a missing persons case from twelve years ago?" I asked.

"We want you to see if we left any stones unturned," my father said casually.

"You and I both know that those stones are endless."

"What's your point?" said my mother.

"You're giving me a case that can't be solved."

"Are you refusing to take it?" she asked.

I should have refused, but I didn't. I figured if I could come up with a single new piece of information, I would have done my job and would have felt justified in leaving. I didn't believe I could solve the case, I didn't believe for a second that I could find Andrew Snow — neither did they — but I did believe I could shelve that file once and for all.

"I'll work the case for two months," I said. "After that, I'm done."

"Four months," countered my mom. As you might imagine, I've negotiated with her before. She's worse than Rae. I had to give in just a bit.

"Three months," I said, "and that's my final offer."

When Rae got the news of my impending departure, she felt compelled to offer her studied assessment of the situation to Milo, *my* bartender. Milo shook his head at Rae when she arrived at the Philosopher's Club just after opening.

"I don't want any trouble today, Rae."

My sister sat down in the center of the row of empty barstools, ordered a double on the rocks, and told Milo not to water it down. Milo reminded Rae that she would be drinking ginger ale and poured her a whiskey-size glass over ice. Rae tossed a few bills onto the bar, which Milo slid back to her.

Milo picked up the telephone and said, "You want to call your sister or should I do it?"

"I'm having a rough week, Milo. Can't I just sit here for a while? I won't bother anyone."

Rae took a sip of her soda and followed it

with a hard-liquor grimace.

Milo shook his head. "So I'll make the call."

Rae, as expected, was in mid-discourse when I arrived.

"It would be bad enough if I had only my rat Uncle Ray to worry about, but with Izzy deciding to get out of the business, I'm a wreck, Milo. A wreck. That leaves only me. What am I gonna do? I can't run Spellman Investigations on my own. Who's gonna buy the staples and the files? We use a lot of files. Who's gonna do the books? I don't want to do that stuff. It's boring. Oh, and who is gonna drive the surveillance van? Who? I guess I'll have a license by the time they will me the business. But my point is, who will do the boring stuff? Don't get me wrong, I'll do it on my own if I have to, but —"

"Izzy, it's about time," Milo said, smiling to hide the edge in his voice.

"This is *my* bar, Rae. You've got to stop coming here," I said.

"It's a free country."

"Not that free. You could get Milo in a lot of trouble."

"I'm drinking ginger ale."

"It doesn't matter."

"How could you do this to me?"

"Do what?"

"Quit."

"Most people don't spy on each other. Most people don't run background checks on their friends. Most people aren't suspicious of everyone they meet. Most people aren't like us."

"What's happening to you?"

"I'm seeing things clearly, that's all."

"Well, I hope it doesn't happen to me," she said as I grabbed the back of her shirt and marched her out of the bar. Rae was silent the entire drive home, breaking her previous record by thirteen minutes.

MISSING PERSONS

Missing persons cases are rare in our business. It is the police who have the tools, the manpower, and the legal authority to exhaust the possibilities, all of which are necessary to find someone who is lost. But the police can only look for so long, and when they stop, families occasionally turn to PIs to continue the investigation, because as long as the search continues, hope is not lost.

As cruel as the discovery of a body can be, it allows those connected to it to grieve and move on. And with the strides made in forensic science, now it is as if the dead were pointing to the killer — whether it is man, nature, or human error. But the absence of a body leaves an unlimited number of possibilities. Without any cohesive leads, you're left with nothing. A person cannot literally vanish before your eyes, but, as the pictures on the milk cartons suggest, people disappear all the time.

I phoned Abigail Snow, Andrew's mother, that evening and made an appointment to meet with her the following day. I knew that any contact at all would offer her a false sense of hope, but I convinced myself that I had no choice.

I had only two things on my mind after the last meeting with my parents: 1) Get Daniel back; 2) Work the Snow case.

I gave Daniel a week after Car Chase #1 before I knocked on his window. It was around 10:00 p.m. and I realized as soon as I knocked that I had no further speech planned in my defense. But still, I knocked again.

Daniel opened the window and said, "No."

"Maybe in Guatemala 'no' is in fact a greeting, but here we use 'hello' or 'nice to see you again,' or even 'hey there.' "

"Do you think making wisecracks right now is smart?"

"No, but I already tried 'I'm sorry' and that didn't work."

"Isabel, I have a door."

"Actually you have three doors."

"And your point is?"

"Three doors or one window. You do the math."

"Your math doesn't interest me. Use the front door in the future."

"So there is going to be a future?"

"It was a figure of speech."

"Can I come in for a minute? I'll even use the door."

"I don't want to see you, Isabel."

"But I have much more explaining to do."

"What did I just say?"

" 'I don't want to see you, Isabel.' See, I was listening."

"What does that mean?"

"What you just said?"

"Yes."

"It means you don't want to see me."

"Right."

"Can I ask why?"

"Am I really having this conversation?"

"I'm not sure where you stand on the answering of rhetorical questions."

"I'm angry, Isabel."

"I understand that. I just want to know which thing you're most angry about, so that I can fix it."

"You lied about everything."

"Not everything."

"Good night, Isabel," he said as he shut the window.

THE RANSOM

The following morning, my sister woke up at exactly 6:30 a.m. on her first day of winter break, which coincided with her first day of freedom after the three-month grounding (a grounding, by the way, that allowed for surveillance and blackmail). It had been two weeks since Uncle Ray received the ransom note. Two weeks for my sister to plan her attack.

She woke, brushed her teeth, washed her face, threw on a pair of jeans, one long- and one short-sleeved cotton T-shirt, white and red, respectively, put a comb through her hair exactly five times, picked up the phone, covered the receiver with a dishrag, and made the call.

Uncle Ray, a notoriously late sleeper — so late, in fact, on occasion it became his nickname — picked up on the fourth ring.

"Hello?"

"Listen carefully to my instructions," said

the less-high-than-usual, muffled voice on the other end. "Any deviation from the rules will result in the destruction of your shirt. Do you understand?"

The mere mention of Uncle Ray's lucky shirt jarred him out of whatever soporific fog still remained. The shirt had been out of his possession nearing two weeks at this point and its absence was felt around the house. Uncle Ray stubbed his toe and it was because he wasn't wearing the shirt. Uncle Ray got a parking ticket, spilled a glass of water, gained two pounds, had his latest poker game broken up by the cops, and it was because his lucky shirt had been hijacked.

"I'm gonna tell your dad," threatened Uncle Ray.

"And you'll never see your shirt again. Is that what you want?"

Ray was cornered and he knew it. "Tell me your demands," he mumbled reluctantly.

"Take the bus to the Wells Fargo Bank on Montgomery and Market and withdraw one hundred dollars."

"This is extortion, you know."

"You have forty-five minutes."

Per the voice's instructions, Ray entered the Wells Fargo Bank on Montgomery and Market streets and withdrew exactly one hundred dollars. As he exited the bank, a young male, approximately fourteen years of age, riding a skateboard, approached the older man.

"Uncle Ray?" asked the young male.

Ray spun around in a circle, trying to find his niece, but she was nowhere in sight. He turned back to the skateboarder and eyed him cruelly. "What?"

The young male handed Ray a disposable cell phone. "You have a phone call."

Ray took the phone and the young male skated off.

"Hello?"

"Be at the pay phone in front of the Wax Museum on Fisherman's Wharf at eight-fifteen on the dot."

"When will I get my shirt?"

"You have twenty-five minutes. Lose the phone."

Uncle Ray tossed the phone in the trash, genuinely believing that he was being watched. He hailed a cab and arrived in front of the Wax Museum with time to spare. He waited outside the phone booth until he saw a young woman approach, fishing through her purse, presumably for coins. He entered the booth, picked up the phone, and slyly held down the receiver while he pretended to talk. Had anyone been in the booth with him, they would have heard a random series of curse words, which served no narrative function. Eventually the phone rang.

"Yeah," Ray answered in his best tough-guy voice.

"Buy a ticket and enjoy the show," the slightly less disguised voice said.

"That's thirteen bucks a pop!" said my uncle, who wouldn't have stepped foot in a wax museum if it was free and served booze.

"I think you qualify for the senior discount. So it's only ten-fifty."

"And what if I don't do it?"

"I'll throw the shirt in the bay right now."

"What did I ever do to you?"

"You want a list?"

"I'm going."

THE SNOW CASE: CHAPTER 1

As Uncle Ray bit his tongue and entered the Wax Museum, I knocked on the door of Joseph and Abigail Snow's house on Myrtle Avenue in Marin County. When Mrs. Snow opened the door, I was blasted by an overwhelming fragrance that emanated from the home. I would later learn that the scent was potpourri, but there were too many other effects offending my sensibilities at that moment for me to investigate the odor.

Abigail Snow, now in her early sixties, was wearing an outdated floral dress that looked like it came from the wardrobe of a 1950s sitcom star. Her hair, as well, was trapped in the past and in half a can of hair spray. She was probably about five foot six, but her stocky build, which was more sturdy than plump, made her seem taller and oddly intimidating. While her attire was (in my estimation) unflattering, it was kept in immaculate condition. When I entered the house, I would discover that this was a theme for Mrs. Snow — tasteless, but immaculate.

I walked across plastic runners into the Snows' living room, which was, coincidentally, a vision in white. Other than the cherrywood furniture and collection of collectible plates, that is. And, I should add, I had never seen so many doilies in my entire life. I scanned the walls for photographs of her sons, but there were only two eight-by-ten photographs above the fireplace. The boys, in their preteen perfection — bow ties, unblemished skin, forced smiles — could tell me nothing about the men they would become. I got the feeling Mrs. Snow wanted to keep them frozen in time, just like everything else in her house.

My hostess gave me a stern looking-over before she offered me a seat on her plastic-covered white couch. I had recently ceased wearing my schoolteacher get-ups, so I was back in jeans, leather boots, and a frayed wool peacoat from an army surplus store, since it was a fifty-degree day. I thought I looked perfectly presentable, but the expression on my hostess's face said otherwise.

"My, my," Mrs. Snow said, "the girls today dress just like the boys."

"I know. Isn't it great?" I replied, having

already decided that I didn't like Mrs. Snow one bit.

"Would you like some tea and cookies?" Mrs. Snow asked, not wanting to engage in a discussion of the benefits of menswear.

Since I had been avoiding my parents' kitchen (to avoid them) and was therefore starving, I said yes. I stayed put on the squeaky couch since the plastic runners offered little freedom to move in this painstakingly sanitized room. I was afraid if Mrs. Snow caught my boots on exposed carpet, I would be promptly evicted and no interview would transpire. I reminded myself to behave politely, but then I forgot about that a few minutes later.

My hostess returned with a shiny silver tray that held a teapot, two teacups, cream and sugar, and a plate of vanilla sandwich cookies. She asked how I liked my tea and I told her with cream and sugar (but really, I like my tea to be coffee), and she prepared the weak brew with careful precision.

"Cookie?" Mrs. Snow asked, holding a set of silver tongs.

The sandwich cookies were fanned across the plate in a semicircle, like fallen dominoes. I grabbed one from the middle, knowing it would peeve my hostess, but I couldn't help myself. When faced with a controlling personality, it is in my nature to rebel.

Mrs. Snow held up the tongs and said, "That's what these are for, dear."

I apologized and split my cookie in two. Then I ate the cream filling out of the middle and dunked the sides into my tea. Mrs. Snow frowned in disgust. As I began the interview, I reminded myself that Mrs. Snow's brand of truth must be weighed against her pathological need for order.

"You're probably wondering what I'm doing here," I said.

"It crossed my mind. I believe the last time I spoke to your mother was about ten years ago."

"On occasion we revisit old cases. Sometimes fresh eyes reveal a new detail."

Mrs. Snow realigned the cookies on the plate, filling in the gap from the middle where I had served myself. "Ms. Spellman. Don't do this for me or my family. My son is gone. I have accepted it."

"Sometimes people like answers."

"I have all the answers I need. Andrew is in a better place now."

I couldn't help but agree with her. Anyplace was better than this. I took another cookie from the center of the fan, just to test Mrs. Snow's patience.

"Dear, you're supposed to take the cookies from the end and please use the tongs."

"I apologize," I said politely. "I must have missed cookie-eating day in charm school."

"I think you missed more than that," she said. What was odd about the insult was that it came out so naturally, as if it were reasonable to talk to a complete stranger this way. While I would have liked to challenge Mrs. Snow in a wicked debate on the merits of modern-day living, I had work to do.

"I know this must be hard for you, Mrs. Snow, and I can't imagine what you're going through," I said, summoning my most sympathetic voice. "But I would really appreciate it if I could ask you just a few questions."

"You drove all this way. I suppose a few questions would be all right."

"Thank you. Can I ask where Mr. Snow is?"

"He's playing golf."

"I was hoping to talk to him, as well."

"Why would you need to talk to him?" she asked. An air of defensiveness was lending itself to her voice.

"Different people have different perspectives," I replied. "Sometimes one person remembers something that another person doesn't."

"I assure you, my husband's and my

perspective are exactly the same."

"How convenient," I said, wanting to bolt. There was something terrifying about this woman. I couldn't put my finger on it, and yet it was impossible to keep my general suspicion of her at bay.

"Is that all, Ms. Spellman?" she asked, brushing away the crumbs next to my teacup.

"What is Martin up to these days?"

"Martin?"

"Yes. Your other son."

"Martin is an attorney for one of those environmental organizations," she said, rolling her eyes.

"You must be proud of him," I said, just to stick the knife in deeper.

"After all the money we spent on his education, he gets a job at a nonprofit. If I'd known that our hundred thousand dollars would go to saving trees, I would have let him take out student loans."

"Can I have his address and phone number?"

"You want to talk to him?"

"If that's all right with you."

"It's not up to me," she replied. "Martin is a grown man."

Mrs. Snow's fake smile was losing some of its conviction. She would draw this interview to a close shortly, so I had to scramble for any last bits of information. I picked up the tongs and grabbed one more cookie from the center of the fan.

"Oops," I said, shoving it back in. "I forgot." Then I grabbed a cookie from the side. The fan was now a squiggle and I passed the tongs to Mrs. Snow.

"You probably want to fix that."

"You must have been a handful as a child," Mrs. Snow said coldly.

"You have no idea," I replied. I'm not sure if it was the cookies on an empty stomach mixed with the overwhelming smell of potpourri or my unsettling hostess, but I was growing nauseous and knew that it was time to finish the interview.

"Did your sons go camping together often?" I asked.

"Not that often, but on occasion."

"Did they always go alone, or with friends?"

"They usually went with Greg," she replied.

"Greg Larson. I remember his name from the file. But there was no indication that he was camping with your sons at the time of Andrew's disappearance."

"He didn't go with them that weekend."

"But he went with them almost every

other time?"

"I think so, but I wasn't keeping track."

"Do you know how I could get in touch with Mr. Larson?"

"I don't have his number, but he's with the Marin County Sheriff's Office."

"He's a sheriff?"

"Yes," Mrs. Snow said as she got to her feet. "Now if that will be all, I have quite a bit of cleaning to do today."

I scanned the room and decided that any dirt Mrs. Snow found would be imaginary, but I was anxious for some fresh air and followed my hostess to the door.

The Ransom — Continued

As I was driving back across the bridge into the city, Uncle Ray sat on a bench seat in the center of the Wax Museum next to the Last Supper exhibit. Never having been a religious man, he found nothing in the colorful, nonsecular display to hold his interest. He took deep, quasimeditative breaths, read the sports page, and reminded himself that eventually he would get his shirt back and this whole nightmare would come to a close. Another unidentified young male approached Uncle Ray and handed him a piece of paper.

Uncle Ray huffed and puffed his way the three blocks to the ringing pay phone.

"I have a cell phone, you know," he shouted breathlessly into the receiver.

"I like to mix it up. Hail a cab —"

"I'm hungry! I didn't have breakfast. My blood sugar is getting low," Uncle Ray said, truly at his wit's end.

"What do you feel like?" said the voice.

"I wouldn't say no to one of those clam chowders in a bread bowl."

"You can get the clam chowder, but be at the Sutro Baths by one o'clock sharp," said the voice that was sounding more and more like a fourteen-year-old girl.

"Make it one-thirty. I don't like to rush my digestion."

The voice hesitated before responding. One must not give too much in a standoff or one risks losing power and respect. The pause was just long enough to make clear that any further demands would be met with a stony resolve.

"One-fifteen. Don't be late."

Uncle Ray ate his creamy clam chowder in a sourdough bowl and wondered why he didn't do this sort of thing more often —

the eating of clam chowder in a sourdough bowl, not the running from pay phone to pay phone at the mercy of a teenage girl. Then several loud tourists passed by, families arguing, flashbulbs piercing the gray sky, music blasting, rampant break-dancing, and he remembered why he consistently avoided this tourist trap, even though it served one of his top five meals of all time.

Uncle Ray hopped into a cab and arrived at the Sutro Baths fifteen minutes early — the time originally marked by the voice. He sat on a bench and enjoyed the view and the calm, rubbing his hands together to keep warm. He even thought about packing it in. Could this twenty-year-old, one-hundred-percent-cotton-weave shirt really hold the powers of good fortune that he believed? Was it not the grown man's equivalent of a security blanket? Was it not time to accept that he was alive and maybe going to stay alive for a while? He remembered Sophie Lee at that very moment and recalled the time she told him to throw the shirt away. The time she said that she couldn't be with a man who felt such attachment to a piece of fabric. She gave him a fabled ultimatum — either the shirt goes or she goes. He had done everything for her and would have sacrificed anything for her, but not the shirt. He didn't dispose of it then. He couldn't. He had simply packed it away and didn't look at it for two years. When those two years ended and both Sophie and the cancer were gone, Ray swore he would never part with the shirt again. It didn't matter that it defied logic. Ray simply loved that shirt.

A young female tourist approached Uncle Ray and handed him an envelope.

GOLDEN GATE BRIDGE. ONE HOUR.

Ray decided he could use the exercise and took a leisurely walk to the bridge. He was late. Rae was on her bicycle at the entrance to the walkway, impatiently riding in circles. She had to be home by four o'clock or risk another grounding and shortening of curfew.

Uncle Ray approached her with a slow, lumbering swagger. His years as a cop made him no stranger to negotiation. He, too, was aware that giving in too quickly destroys whatever edge you might have. He waited for his niece to speak first.

"Did you bring the money?"

"Yes. Did you bring my shirt?"

"Yes."

"Hand it over, kid. It's been a long day."

Rae and Uncle Ray swapped packages. Ray removed the shirt and immediately put it on over his hooded sweatshirt. He brushed out the wrinkles and straightened the collar. He exhaled a sigh of deep, overwhelming relief.

Rae counted the money in the envelope. "Sixty-three bucks? I said one hundred."

"Two bus rides. The Wax Museum. Cab fare. Clam chowder. It adds up."

"I'm gonna let it slide," my sister generously offered, figuring that fighting Ray for the shirt was a winless prospect.

"Are we done here?" he asked.

"We're done."

Uncle Ray turned around and walked off the bridge. But Rae wasn't done. She had to ask him the question that had been on her mind for months.

"Why?" she said. "Why'd you come back?"

Uncle Ray turned around and carefully considered how to answer the question. He didn't believe she deserved his honesty, but he gave it to her anyway.

"I was lonely."

It seemed odd to me, the ease with which Rae and Uncle Ray resolved their conflict. My sister had never experienced loneliness, yet she understood how powerful that feeling could be. Her own cruelty stung her with regret and she ended her war that very moment. Uncle Ray would later tell me that being enemies with Rae was easier than being friends with her. I don't think he ever said anything so completely on the nose.

That same afternoon, I returned home and reviewed the Snow file yet again. I studied the photographs of Andrew and Martin that I found slipped in an envelope inside the file. Unlike the framed portraits in Mrs. Snow's home, these pictures must have been taken not long before Andrew's disappearance when he was seventeen. The brothers shared certain common features and coloring. Both were brown-haired and -eyed. But Martin's square-jawed handsomeness made him appear older than the one year he had on his brother. Andrew was leaner than Martin, with softer features. I wondered what Andrew might look like twelve years later; as for Martin, I would eventually find out.

When my mother entered the Spellman offices, she sniffed the air and said, "Isabel, are you wearing perfume?"

"No," I snapped at her, knowing the potpourri was still lingering on my clothes.

"What is that smell?" my mother asked, enjoying her fun.

"Don't play dumb, Mom."

"Oh, right," my mom said as if a lightbulb had flashed on over her head. "Abigail Snow does like the smell of dead flowers, doesn't she?"

"Now I know why you gave me this case."

"Because Andrew Snow has been missing for twelve years?"

"No, because Mrs. Snow is the most annoying woman on the entire planet."

"Unless you've met every woman, you can't say for sure."

"What's Mr. Snow like?" I asked, changing the subject.

"He wasn't there?"

"No, he was playing golf."

"Hmm. I wouldn't have pegged him as a golf man. Isabel, are you on a hunger strike?"

"No. Why do you ask?"

"Because you appear to be boycotting the kitchen."

"I have a kitchen in my apartment."

"Is there food in it?" she asked, eerily on the nose.

"I know how to buy food, Mom."

"I'm sure you know how, but you usually don't. My point is: If you're hungry, there's food in our kitchen and you're welcome to it as usual, even though you are ashamed of our family and what we do for a living."

"Thanks, Mom," I said as I disappeared upstairs with the Snow file.

My mom was, in fact, right. I had been boycotting the kitchen to avoid further jabs at my quest for independence. And like a silly teenager, I went hungry to prove a point.

Later that evening, Rae knocked on my apartment door, offering me food. I found it interesting that she was perceptive enough to know I was hungry, yet not perceptive enough to realize that what I craved could not be served from a cardboard box. There was something so endearing about the way she set my table, poured me a heaping bowl of Froot Loops with a quarter cup of milk, placed the napkin on my lap, and handed me a spoon that I ate it anyway. Rae pulled a chair across from me and snacked from the box. I gave her the eye that reminded her of the sugar rule and then she gave me the eye back that said *it's Saturday.*

I could tell Rae had something on her mind because, in between devouring fistfuls of Froot Loops, she sorted my giant stack of mail in order of size, then re-sorted it according to color. I didn't rush her, since I wasn't anxious to hear what was on her mind. But eventually she spoke, as I knew she would. My sister doesn't like to stress her nervous system by holding things back.

"Mom says there's only one difference between you and me."

"Really," I said. "Would that be the fourteen years?"

"No."

"How about the six inches I've got over you?"

"No."

"Hair color?"

"No."

"I've got three things already, so clearly there's more than one difference between you and me."

"Don't you want to hear what it is?"

"Not really."

"I don't hate myself. That's the difference," said Rae.

I picked up the box of Froot Loops and tossed it into the hallway. Then I picked up Rae, literally, and did the same.

"Give it time. You will," I replied.

Rae landed on her feet and said, "You don't know how to do anything else."

I kicked the door shut, without offering any response. There was no response, because she was right: I don't know how to do anything else. She might have been right about the other thing, too.

Rae's words lingered, preventing me from sleeping. I tried to think about my future, a future without Spellman Investigations, but it was impossible. At twenty-eight, I had lived under the same roof and worked for my parents almost my entire life. I had no other plans. I had no other skills. I needed an escape, but there was no exit. Not a door, not even a window. So I stopped thinking about myself and began thinking about Andrew Snow. I put on my bathrobe and went down to the office to review the case file once again.

I was still awake at 2:30 in the morning when my father came into the office with a plate of cheese and crackers, which he placed on my desk in front of me.

"Rae told me you ate Froot Loops. You don't eat Froot Loops. I assume that meant you were hungry."

"Thanks," I said and devoured the snack shamelessly.

My father pretended to work, but he wasn't there for work. He wanted to have one of those awkward yet ambitious father-daughter chats that he breezed through with Rae but could barely approach with me.

"If you need to talk about anything, I'm here."

"I know," I said, politely dismissive, not wanting to hurt the man who had served me a plate of cheese and crackers.

"You know there is nothing I wouldn't do for you," my father said in his most heartfelt tone.

"Would you rob a bank for me?" I asked.

Sigh. "No."

"So there is that *one* thing."

My father walked over to my desk, patted me on the head, and said, "I love you, too." Then he left me alone in the office to obsess about Andrew Snow. My mother had picked the case because she knew that the concept of someone being gone without explanation would be impossible for me to resist. I grew up in a home where explanations were required for everything. If someone left an empty jug of milk in the refrigerator, interrogations ensued until the truth was uncovered. Uncle Ray left the empty milk jug in the refrigerator because that's what he always does. But not all truths can be unearthed as simply as Uncle Ray's finishing off the milk. And sometimes the truths that you have grown accustomed to suddenly change.

Monday morning as I was heading out the door, I overheard what sounded like an amicable conversation between my uncle and my sister.

"You see what I'm doing here, kid?"

"I'm not blind."

"Milk and salt and you beat those eggs to death."

"The onions are burning."

"That's good. You want to burn 'em a bit."

"The fire alarm will go off."

"I know what I'm doing."

I entered the kitchen to the sound and smell of eggs sizzling in a sauté pan. Uneducated eyes would have told you that Uncle Ray was teaching Rae how to make his favorite omelet. But my eyes were educated and never imagined in a million years they would see such a thing, and so I asked what might have seemed like an obvious question.

"What is going on in here?"

"I'm teaching the kid how to cook eggs."

"He gave me five dollars to have an open mind," said Rae, who last ate an egg when her vocabulary was still under one hundred words.

"Time for the cheese, kid. Hurry up," said Uncle Ray, who then added more cheese and more cheese.

"Great. So instead of diabetes, you can have a cholesterol problem," I said to my sister.

"You want some?" asked Uncle Ray.

"Yes," I said, and a plate of cheese and eggs was served.

My mother entered the kitchen as I was finishing my last bite.

"Isabel is eating!" she shouted to no one in particular.

"Your observational skills are uncanny," I said.

"I'm glad. That's all. What are you up to today?"

"Driving to Tahoe to speak to the detective who was originally in charge of the Snow case."

"Is he still on the job?"

"Three years until retirement. Runs the department now."

"Can't you just interview him over the phone?"

"I could. But I want to get a copy of the file —"

"There's this thing now called the United States Postal Service. Shall I explain how it works?"

"No. I'm driving to Tahoe. I don't like interviewing people on the phone. You can't see what they're doing with their hands."

"Well, one hand is probably holding the phone."

"It's the other hand I'm worried about."

"Where did you get that sense of humor?" my mother asked, genuinely baffled.

"Mom, you gave me the case. I'm going to work it. See you later."

THE SNOW CASE:
CHAPTER 2

I had called Abigail Snow earlier that morning and asked if she had saved any of Andrew's high school yearbooks. She had kept them in storage, and after much persuading and a promise that this would be the last time I would contact her, she agreed to locate them for me. Mill Valley was hardly on the way to Tahoe, but I thought I'd better get the yearbooks before she changed her mind.

Mrs. Snow opened the door in a dress that was a different pattern from the first but precisely the same otherwise. She handed me the yearbooks without inviting me inside.

"Is Mr. Snow around?" I asked.

"I'm afraid he's not."

"Playing golf again?"

"Yes, as a matter of fact."

"Sounds like you're a golf widow."

"Excuse me?" Mrs. Snow said, sounding offended.

" 'Golf widow.' It's a term for the wife of someone who plays a lot of golf. Because golf is a very long game and so it seems like the husbands are, well —"

"I see." Mrs. Snow cut me off without any real expression.

"Thanks for the yearbooks," I said, but my mind was still on Mr. Snow and his golf habit.

I hadn't checked the weather report before I started the drive and found myself buying chains on the side of the road to make it the final twenty miles. What should have been a three-hour drive took five and a half hours through a blinding snowstorm and unrelenting wind. My mother, however, did check the weather report and called me three times during the trip to make sure I hadn't careened off the road to my death. All three phone calls followed a similar pattern:

"Hello."

"How fast are you driving?"

"Thirty-five miles an hour."

"That's too fast."

"I'm moving with traffic."

"Isabel, if you die before me, I will *never* recover."

"I'm slowing down, Mom."

I phoned Daniel during the drive and attempted my pretend-nothing-is-wrong method of easing out of a fight. I left a message on his answering machine that went something like this:

"Hi, Daniel, it's Isabel. I was thinking maybe I could come over tonight or tomorrow or maybe early next week, whatever works for you. Oh, and I'll cook. There's this *Get Smart* episode that I really need to see again. It's the one where that doctor slips something in Max's wine, which turns out to be the map to the Melnick uranium mine. But the map won't work unless Max remains vertical for forty-eight hours. After that it will show up as a rash on his chest. Unfortunately this is the day before Max and 99 are supposed to get married and so nobody believes Max's story when he tries to postpone the wedding and they think he just has cold feet. Then Max is held hostage by KAOS[1] agents, who plan to read the map when it's ready, then fake Max's suicide. It's a classic. Call me."

I caught Captain Meyers on his way to lunch. He picked up the Snow file and

[1] The International Organization of Evil.

invited me to join him. We ate in one of those unambiguously male restaurants. Wood paneling covered the walls, a rich fire burned in the corner, and various dead animals peered down at you from their final resting place. The lighting was dim for lunch, and with the candlelight and Meyers holding the chair for me and all, it felt oddly like a date. Except that Captain Meyers had no interest in me. Once again, oddly like a date.

Captain Meyers couldn't provide very much new information for me. We spent some time discussing the Snow family and agreed that the mother was odd and slightly controlling. But Meyers didn't just find the mother suspicious, he found the whole family odd. Abigail, he said, seemed genuinely unconcerned the first few days of Andrew's disappearance, insisting that he would show up any minute. It was almost as if she thought Andrew had run away. At least that was Captain Meyers's assessment. As for Andrew's brother, he said that Martin participated in the search party activities but without a sense of commitment. Meyers also said that Martin didn't seem to blame himself for his younger brother's disappearance, even though that would have been a natural response to the situation.

But still, Meyers said, "There was no reason to suspect foul play."

"What can you tell me about the camp-site?" I asked, hoping the captain wouldn't notice that my investigation had no focus.

"Good place to pitch a tent. During the right season, that is."

"Good place to get lost?" I asked.

"If you're asking me what I think the odds are that Andrew wandered off, couldn't find his way back, and something in the wild took him, I'd say they were good. The landscape is vast, with plenty of deep water and sharp rocks, and enough foliage to hide a body until there's almost nothing left. Some people, when they lose their way, keep going. They think they can find their way back. Instead, they get themselves more lost. He could have made it a long way overnight. Based on what we know about the boy, it's the most logical explanation."

"Or he could have run away," I suggested.

"Anything could have happened," he replied.

"Do you think this investigation is a waste of time?"

"Honestly? Yes," the captain said good-naturedly.

"Maybe you could call my mom and tell her that."

Captain Meyers said he had already talked to my mom a number of times during their original investigation and didn't care to repeat the experience. Meyers drank a whiskey with his lunch of lamb chops and garlic potatoes. In spite of his old-school ways — e.g., his habit of calling me "sweetheart" — Meyers was hardly the equivalent of a small-town sheriff. Reno had enough big-city problems to turn the unassuming man into a seasoned investigator. I believe he did a sound job with the Snow investigation. I wasn't certain he did a great job.

On the drive home, amid my mother's telephone calls (four) suggesting I find a motel and wait out the storm, two details in the file were nagging at me. A witness at the campsite claimed he saw two brothers the morning following Andrew's alleged disappearance. That morning, Martin claimed to be alone at the campsite, searching for his brother. Meyers attributed this discrepancy to the witness being faulty on the dates. He would have seen two brothers together the day before and the day before that. It was an easily explained error, except for the fact that the witness was a history professor. They're usually pretty good with details. And then there was the statement written by Martin when he first went to the police station to file a missing persons report. It was one line that you could skim over or attribute to the shock of the event. It could have been the equivalent of a handwritten typo; it read, "We searched for Andrew all morning." It was possible that someone helped Martin with his search, but when asked to clarify his statement, Martin said that he was alone all morning while searching for Andrew.

I had left three messages for Martin Snow since the day I began the investigation. He still had not returned any of my calls.

Staged Dental Appointment #2

My mother made the mistake of telling my sister that I was quitting the business because "the dentist," as he would forever be known, had broken up with me. Even Rae knew this was simply untrue, that my decision was far more complicated than being spurned by a man. But Rae is a fixer at heart and decided to fix what she could. She promptly made an appointment at Daniel's office under an assumed name.

Mrs. Sanchez handed him a thin file. "Last patient of the day. Room three. If you don't mind, I think I'll go home now."

"Mary Anne Carmichael?" asked Daniel.

"She's new. Uninsured. Promises to pay

cash. Wouldn't let me near her teeth. Insisted on seeing a 'real dentist.' "

"Have a nice evening, Mrs. Sanchez."

Daniel entered the examination room and spotted my sister sifting through drawers and cabinets. He did not require a second introduction.

"Rae, what are you doing here?"

"There's something wrong with my teeth," replied my sister, simultaneously spinning around and leaning her weight against the open drawer.

"Snooping is impolite, young lady."

"You're right. I'll stop."

"Sit down."

Rae sat in the chair and folded her hands politely.

"What is the reason for this visit?"

"My teeth hurt."

"All of them?"

"Just one or two."

"Open up."

Daniel pulled on a pair of latex gloves and began examining Rae's teeth.

"Haf chonching inhaha —"

"Please don't talk."

"Inhaha. Aaahhhh."

Daniel removed the scaler and mirror from her mouth.

"I have something important to tell you,"

she said.

"Does it relate to your teeth?"

"It's more important than my teeth."

"Rae, my relationship with your sister is not any of your concern."

"Four years ago, my mother investigated a dentist accused of molesting his patients after he had put them out. She made an appointment for a root canal, was given general anesthesia, and while she was unconscious, he did things to her. My parents wouldn't tell me anything about it, so I snuck into the file room, picked the lock, and read the file about a year ago. They still believe I don't know about it, so if you could keep this between us, I'd appreciate it."

"Okay."

"Anyway, I'm not sure that she would have been so mad about what happened except that when they brought the case to the DA he refused to press charges. Said there wasn't enough evidence to prosecute. We had two cases involving dentists after that: an oral surgeon who was performing root canals while on crack and another who was filling cavities that didn't exist."

"Those are unfortunate and disturbing occurrences."

"So maybe you can understand why my

mother said those things to you."

"Yes, Rae, I can. But your sister lied to me — a lot. That part, I cannot understand."

"She lies to everyone she likes. She lies to me all the time. She told me Froot Loops give you diabetes."

"There is a link between high sugar consumption and diabetes."

"But it's not like I eat a box of Froot Loops and twenty-four hours later, I have to start on insulin injections."

"Do you eat an entire box of Froot Loops in one sitting?"

"Not unless it's Saturday."

"You shouldn't be eating Froot Loops at all."

"I didn't come here to talk about my diet."

"You're right. You came here to talk about your teeth."

"Not really."

"When's the last time you had them cleaned?"

"By a dentist?"

"Yes."

"I don't know. The last time we went to Chicago. Like two years ago."

"I think I know the answer to this question, but what the hell. Why Chicago?"

"Because that's where Dr. Farr moved."

"And who is Dr. Farr?"

"My mom's dentist. She went to him as a kid."

"You need to have your teeth cleaned."

"You need to get back together with my sister."

"That's not going to happen."

"She really likes you. I know this because guys break up with her all the time and she's fine. But she's sad now and that's not a good emotion for her. I've seen her angry a lot, but I don't see her sad all that often. You like her. I know you do, or you would have kicked me out of here ages ago."

"Let's take care of your teeth right now."

"I'm willing to negotiate."

Rae endured an hour-long cleaning and X-rays in exchange for Daniel promising to call me, which he did two days later. It went something like this:

Daniel: May I speak to Jacqueline Moss-Gregory?

Me: Daniel?

Daniel: Stop making appointments at my office under assumed names.

Me: Okay. I'll stop.

Daniel: Meet me at the club. Noon. Tomorrow.

Me: The tennis club?

Daniel: No, the Friar's Club. Yes, the tennis club. Noon. Don't be late.

THE LAST TENNIS MATCH

I assumed Daniel wanted to play tennis, so I brought my racket. It occurred to me that it would be difficult to talk in between rallies. Later I realized that was part of his plan. Not talking.

Daniel silently stepped onto the court, tossed me a ball, and ordered me to serve. I served and had to jump out of the way to miss the return. When Daniel served, I would awkwardly leap for the ball, but never quite make it. I counted three diagnosable muscle pulls for the match. The rest of the first game followed the same pattern — dodging oversize yellow bullets or chasing after bullets I couldn't return.

Daniel's sliding scale was no longer in effect. The second game went much like the first and the third game went much like the second. I won two points off Daniel's foul balls and made only three returns in the entire two sets. By match point I had stopped playing and was merely dodging yellow ammunition. Soon exhaustion dulled my reflexes and with that came the sting from the ball making contact with my skin.

Daniel didn't notice that a crowd had begun to form. Frankly, I enjoyed this modern country-club version of a medieval punishment. Each yellow bullet that left a red blotch on my skin meant that he cared, and I liked Daniel even more for it. I think he half expected me to become outraged and react, but I figured that once he got it all out of his system we could start again.

Daniel took a breather and noticed all the incriminating eyes upon him. He knew they thought him a monster and it would be impossible to explain to the crowd that I deserved each and every bruise. I am not a masochist, but sometimes you want to punish yourself and you don't know how. Sometimes you have this feeling that you're doing something wrong, but you're so used to doing something wrong that you're not sure what it is anymore. Daniel seemed like the kind of person I would want to know, I just figured I wasn't the kind of person *he* would want to know. Hence, all the lies. The only difference between me and other people was that I wasn't going to let the simple fact that Daniel might not want to know me get in the way of me getting to know him.

"Is there any point in playing another set?" he asked.

"I'll leave that decision up to you," I replied with a smile.

Daniel picked up his bag and walked off the court. I followed him outside into the gray, rain-soaked air.

"Well, that was fun," I said with unnatural enthusiasm.

"You are tough, I'll give you that."

"I'm sorry. I'm really sorry. I don't know why I do things like that."

"I would imagine it has something to do with your family."

"Yes! It does!"

"What do you want from me?"

"Your DVD collection."

"Seriously, Isabel. What do you want from me?"

"Your soul, of course."

"I'm going now. When you manage to piece together a sincere sentence, I'll think about it. Until then, good-bye."

THE SNOW CASE:
CHAPTER 3

I switched into street clothes inside my car
— a talent I had grown all too good at —
and drove to Marin County, where I scheduled a couple of afternoon interviews with
onetime acquaintances of Andrew Snow. I
pulled the names from the few people who
had signed Andrew's yearbook.

None of the people I interviewed could
recall too many details of the missing boy
twelve years later. All the descriptions were
vague and delivered through memory's
unreliable filter. Audrey Gale, who was in
Andrew's homeroom for three years and occasionally studied with him, described the
younger Snow brother as polite, unassuming, and sensitive. Susan Hayes, who had
English class with him all through high
school, described him as easy to talk to,
sensitive, but also a serious pothead. Sharon
Kramer, who lived down the street from the
Snow boys and used to date Martin, de-

scribed Andrew as thoughtful and kind of sad. I asked her what he was sad about and she said that he seemed uncomfortable in his own skin, like he just didn't fit in. Almost everyone I interviewed had seen Andrew smoke pot on more than one occasion, but none could tell me whether he was into harder stuff. I asked if he'd ever been bullied and the response was a resounding no.

No one messed with Andrew unless they wanted to answer to Martin — maybe the most popular boy in school. He was class president, a member of the track team, the debate team, and the football team. I asked about Martin's known acquaintances and Greg Larson's name came up yet again.

But Larson had ignored my first three phone calls. It was time to try a different tack. I called Sheriff Larson at the precinct, used a phony name, and finally managed to make contact. Once I got Larson on the line, I explained my ruse and asked for a meeting. He reluctantly agreed and I met him the following day at the station house.

Sheriff Larson greeted me in the foyer and shook my hand with a firm grip. He was well over six feet and lanky, with a pronounced bone structure that looked stressed against his thin skin. The uniform didn't make him more attractive, just more severe. Larson invited me back to a tiny cubicle at the far end of the main corridor. He put his feet on his desk and pulled a toothpick out of his pocket. I didn't waste time with pleasantries.

"How did you know the Snow brothers?" I asked.

Larson had a disconcerting stillness about him. His movements, speech, and expressions appeared to happen in slow motion, although I suspect that if I timed them with a stopwatch, I would find nothing out of the ordinary. All the same, his iciness piqued my suspicion from the start.

"We were neighbors," Larson casually replied.

"Did you often go over to the Snow house?"

"Nope."

"Right. The Snow house probably wasn't ideal for playing."

"Nope."

"So your mother had no problem with the Snow boys?"

"Nope."

"Was Andrew gay?"

"Excuse me?" the sheriff asked without a hint of a change in his expression.

"People keep describing him as sensitive.

Sometimes that's a code word for gay."

"Couldn't tell you."

"Maybe something was troubling him. Maybe his disappearance wasn't that, maybe it was a suicide."

"Maybe."

"Did Andrew take drugs?"

"Maybe he smoked a joint here and there."

"Anything harder than that?"

"Maybe."

"Where did Andrew get his drugs?"

"Couldn't tell you."

"If you do remember, let me know."

"Sure thing."

"Don't you care what happened to Andrew?" I asked, growing tired of Larson's monosyllabic disinterest.

"Yes, I do."

"How often did you go camping with the Snow brothers?"

"Often."

"But not the time Andrew disappeared?"

"Nope."

"What were you doing?"

"When?"

"The weekend of Andrew's disappearance."

"Visiting my uncle."

"Where?"

"In the city."

"Do you ever see Martin anymore?" I asked, knowing that if I pushed for an alibi the conversation would end.

"Every now and again."

"He won't return any of my calls."

"He probably thinks you're wasting your time. Or his."

"Is that what you think, Sheriff?"

"Yes. That's what I think."

"Well, I'll take that into consideration," I said casually as I stood to leave. "One more thing, Sheriff."

He gave me the lift of an eyebrow that said I could keep talking.

"Does Joseph Snow golf?"

"That's the first I've heard of it."

After a couple of hours of sleep, I returned to the office early the next morning. My mother was already at her desk, toiling away at a series of banal background checks for one of our major corporate clients. The silence lasted only as long as it took me to turn on my computer.

"How is the Snow case going?" she casually asked.

"As good as can be expected."

"What does that mean?"

"I'm not going to find him, Mom."

"I don't expect you to."

The case file contained Social Security numbers for every member of the Snow family. I decide to run a credit header on Joseph Snow. Within a few short seconds the report surfaced on the screen and I sent it to the printer.

"Mom, do you think it's possible that Andrew was a runaway?"

"Why do you ask?"

"Because if Mrs. Snow were my mother, I'd run away."

"I think if Mrs. Snow were your mother, *she'd* run away," said my mom.

I picked up the report off the printer and within a second I had the answer to at least one of the questions that had been nagging at me.

"Joseph Snow doesn't live with Abigail," I said.

"Where does he live?" asked my mom.

"I have an address in Pacifica for him."

"That's odd," said my mother. "Didn't she tell you he was playing golf?"

Before I left for my unannounced meeting with Joseph Snow, I checked the Marin County Civil Court for a divorce filing. I couldn't find anything on the Snows, but that didn't mean a thing. There's no national divorce registry, so you have to go county by county, and people can get divorced anywhere.

I would check the rest of the Bay Area later, if Mr. Snow proved as reticent as the rest of his family.

Driving down Highway 1, I caught a partial view of the ocean through the thick fog. I parked in front of a rambler on Seaside Drive, just a few short steps from the ocean. There's a certain casual quality that all California coastal towns seem to possess. The salty air causes paint to chip faster and the wood to bend more frequently. Its state of disrepair seemed the perfect antithesis to Abigail Snow's picket-fenced perfection.

An attractive woman in her mid forties opened the door. She was wearing wrinkled linen pants and a light blue man's oxford shirt with a gray sweater over it. Her skin was tanned and creased, but you could tell she had been striking in her youth.

"Can I help you?" she asked, in the guarded way you speak to someone who you think might start in on a sales pitch or religious propaganda.

I asked the woman if this was the home of Joseph Snow. She said yes. I asked her if Joseph Snow was her husband. She said no. Then she asked a few questions of her own.

I briefly mentioned the reopening of the case, and the woman, whose name I learned was Jennifer Banks, walked me around the house to a workroom in the garage. Joseph Snow, a fit but weathered-looking man in his midsixties, was staining a bookshelf that he had recently completed. The workshop floor was carpeted with sawdust, an assemblage of tools was scattered about, and sheets of wood leaned against the walls. After the initial pleasantries and a brief summary of my purpose there, Jennifer left us alone.

Joseph played with a nail in his hand, but answered my questions with the most forthrightness I had yet to come across on this case.

"Are you still married to Abigail?"

"Yes."

"Why?"

"I tried to get a divorce. She refused to sign the papers."

"She won't even acknowledge that you don't live there. She told me you were playing golf."

"I hate golf."

"Mr. Snow, do you have any idea what happened to your son?"

"No. I don't think I ever will."

There was nothing about my meeting with

Joseph Snow that would have raised any suspicion. Everything he said was in line with what was already in the case file. I wanted to return to Abigail's home and ask her what she was hiding, but it was late and I needed a break from this family and my own.

I stopped by Milo's for a couple of games of pool, killing a few hours before I returned home. I wasn't in the mood for an interrogation, so I walked around to the back of the house to use the fire escape entrance. But Mom had locked the ladder with a padlock, I assume to prevent Rae's escape, which had the unfortunate side effect of preventing my preferred mode of entry.

I returned to my car and figured I'd nap for a few hours until I was certain my parents would be in bed. Of course, I always had the option of using the front door. But front doors are fraught with loaded pleasantries like *Hello* and *Where the hell have you been?* Doors have never been my friend.

It turned out that the backseat of my car was more comfortable than I imagined. I didn't wake until morning, when Rae knocked on my window and asked me for a ride to school. I agreed because my exhaustion weakened all rational thought. Rae took the opportunity of the short drive to ask a series of desultory questions, chosen to throw me off the point of her inquisition.

"So how's the case going?"

"Fine."

"Care to elaborate?"

"No."

"So have you seen the dentist recently?"

"No."

"Are you sure?"

"Yes."

"Can I have ten dollars?"

"No."

"So when's the last time you saw him?"

"Who?"

"The dentist."

"The night you gave Uncle Ray the ransom note."

"That's the last time you saw him?"

"Yes."

"Why can't I have ten dollars?"

"Because you have more money than I do."

"Has he called you?"

"Who?"

"The dentist."

"No."

"Are you sure?"

"Rae, why are you asking these questions?"

"Did you eat breakfast this morning?" she asked in a feeble attempt to deflect my suspicion.

"I fell asleep in my car. What do you think?"

"You don't keep snacks in your car?"

"No."

"You should have emergency snacks."

I pulled the car in front of Rae's school. I grabbed the sleeve of her shirt before she could reach the door.

"What did you do?" I asked.

"Nothing."

"Did you go see him?"

"I'm going to be late."

"Tell me the truth."

"Truthfully, I'm going to be late. And the principal is standing over there right now watching you, and if you recall the last time you dropped me off at school, you man-handled me then, as well. So I'd let go, unless you want Child Services to call you."

I released my grip, made eye contact with the principal, smiled, patted Rae on the head, and threatened to kill her. She had the audacity to ask me if I would pick her up from school. I declined.

I drove directly to Daniel's office to make another valiant attempt at winning him back and to get evidence on my sister. He was with a patient when I arrived and Mrs. Sanchez suggested I make an appointment and then cutely asked what name I would be using today. I smiled politely, gave her my real name, and said I would wait.

An hour later, Mrs. Sanchez asked me if I wouldn't mind sleeping in one of the empty examination chairs instead of the couch in the waiting room. I obliged and got another two hours of much-needed sleep. Daniel, convinced that I would never leave, came into the office and woke me.

"Open your mouth," he said, putting on a pair of plastic gloves.

"I don't want an exam."

"When is the last time you went to a dentist?"

"Chicago."

He didn't seem surprised and said, "I take it that was a while ago."

"Not that long."

"Your family has no respect for dental hygiene."

"Did she come to see you?"

"Who?"

"My sister."

"Doctor-patient privilege applies to dentists, as well."

"But it doesn't apply to minors."

"Are you her guardian?"

"You can talk to me or my mother. Take your pick."

"She has three cavities."

"Cavities don't matter when you're dead."

Daniel told me that he never would have called me had it not been for Rae and insisted that I leave her be, even tacking on to that comment that he thought she was an odd but fascinating girl. He made me promise that no bodily harm would come to her as a result of her actions.

I managed snippets of conversation with Daniel as he cleaned my teeth. But the window was short — somewhere between "rinse" and Daniel sticking his fingers back in my mouth.

"Rinse."

I'd rinse and spit and say, "Is it possible for you to forgive me?"

He'd resume cleaning my teeth and reply, "It is within the realm of possibility. You don't floss, do you?"

I'd offer an inaudible response.

"Rinse."

I'd rinse and spit and continue, "So could you give me some kind of timeline for this forgiveness?"

Twenty more minutes of teeth cleaning, spitting, and unanswered questions passed;

Daniel removed the bib and said, "We're done."

"Are *we* done?" I asked, needing the answer.

Daniel pulled his chair in close and put his hand on my knee.

"I knew you were lying. I knew you couldn't be a teacher. I even knew the clothes were all wrong. The way you always pulled at your skirt and stared at your legs as if you had never seen them before."

"It had been a while."

"Since I have a medical degree and am moderately attractive, women tend to like me."

"That must be hard for you."

"Isabel," he said in that "this is your first warning" tone.

"I can't help it. I swear."

"I got the feeling you liked me, not because I was a dentist, but in spite of it. You seemed to like me for different reasons."

"It was the tennis game with the guy who is not gay, your bad cooking, and the fact that you know KAOS[1] is spelled K-A-O-S."

"My cooking is not that bad."

"Sure. Whatever."

"I miss you, too. But if you lie to me again,

[1] The International Organization of Evil.

we're done."

Then he kissed me and I figured I had him for good. In my mind, he was forever off all my lists.

The Snow Case:
Chapter 4

Two weeks after I first telephoned Martin Snow, he still had not returned any of my calls. It was time to let him know I was serious. I dropped by his office the following morning.

"Wendy Miller from the C-A-T-N-A-P [not a real organization] to see Martin Snow."

"Do you have an appointment?" his secretary asked.

"No. But it's urgent."

"Can I ask what it's regarding?"

"It would be better if I could speak to him privately. Is he in?"

"Yes. But —"

Too late. I entered Martin's office and shut the door behind me. Through the intercom his secretary said, "Wendy Miller from the CTA —"

"CATNAP," I corrected her. "Thanks," I shouted back through the intercom. "I've got it from here."

"Who are you?" Martin asked, still in a somewhat polite mode. "What is the CA—"

"Forget it," I said. "I'm Isabel Spellman. You know, the woman you refuse to call back."

"What are doing here?" he asked.

I couldn't help but notice that beneath the look of fear on Martin Snow's face was virtually the same man from the photograph in my file. Often the ten post–high school years wreak the worst havoc on men's looks, but Martin, if anything, was handsomer. The only noticeable difference was that his look of confidence seemed to vanish the moment I said my name.

"I have some questions that only you can answer."

"The police fully investigated the matter and then your family continued the investigation for another year. What can you possibly learn twelve years later?"

"Maybe nothing. But I have to admit that the lack of cooperation I've been getting is making me suspicious."

"Suspicious of what?"

"Why haven't you returned my phone calls?"

"Because I thought if I ignored them, you'd stop calling."

"Now that was dumb."

"I don't want to go through this again, Ms. Spellman. It was hard enough twelve years ago."

"If you answer a few of my questions, I'll go."

"If I call security, then you'll go."

"Maybe. But I'll keep calling you," I replied. "And I can be very persistent."

"Three questions. That's it."

"Why didn't Greg Larson go camping with you that weekend?"

"He was visiting his uncle in the city."

"Did Greg often visit his uncle?"

"Why are you so interested in Greg? Are you looking for an alibi?"

"Not really. Can you answer the question?"

"No. He didn't visit his uncle very often. I think there was a concert he wanted to see. That was two questions. You've got one more."

"When I spoke to your mother a couple of weeks ago, she mentioned that they spent almost a hundred thousand dollars on your education."

"What's the question, Ms. Spellman? I'm a very busy man."

"The question is, if they gave you all that money for college, why do you have a hundred-and-fifty-thousand-dollar loan with the U.S. Department of Education? According to my calculations, those numbers do not add up."

I could tell that Martin was scrambling for a logical answer, formulating a lie right in front of me. I stood to leave and saved him the trouble.

"Save your energy, Martin. I'm not interested in exposing your college tuition scam. But something is not right here and if you think I'm going to let it slide, you're mistaken."

The holes in the Snow case kept me awake that night. The number of questions grew disproportionately to the number of answers. Sleep was getting harder and harder to come by. The following morning I staggered out of bed and decided to chance it in my parents' kitchen since I was desperate for coffee. The pot was full and the kitchen empty — the ultimate oasis. I poured an enormous cup, which drained half the pot. I sat down and hoped that the silence would last. Then David entered the kitchen, all suited up for work, and sat down at the table.

"What are you doing here?"

"Hello, Isabel, how are you this morning?"

"How do you think I am?"

"Based purely on appearances: not good."

"Thanks. Why are you here?"

"I'm going to school with Rae. Career day. I'm giving a talk."

"Why wouldn't she ask Mom or Dad?"

"Something about not wanting any of her classmates to be encouraged to go into the business. Says she doesn't need any competition in the future."

"The foresight is impressive."

"I thought so."

"She's got dirt on you, doesn't she?"

"Where did that come from?"

"You work eighty hours a week. You have a mystery girlfriend. You supplement her allowance for no apparent reason. You have time to kill half a day talking to a bunch of ninth-graders about the law, especially when you know that there will be a dozen lawyers there already?"

"You've got it all worked out, don't you?"

"A few months ago, Mom had something on you. Now Rae has something. I think it's the same thing. And I think you are going to great lengths to maintain their silence for the sole purpose of keeping it from me."

"Rae, get your ass down here now!" David yelled nervously and I knew I had it on the nose.

"ONE MINUTE!" Rae shouted back as loudly as she could.

"She wouldn't talk to you like that if you were graciously doing her a favor. Why don't you just tell me your little secret and then you can stop being her patsy."

"I will. As soon as you tell me what your next job is going to be."

" 'Bye," I said and headed upstairs.

After a few steps, I tripped on my robe and spilled some coffee. I sat down on the stairs, removed my sock, and sopped up the spill. I inadvertently sat down in a "soft spot." The fourth stair from the second landing was the best place in the house to eavesdrop on kitchen conversations. It was as good as if you were right there. A few steps up or down you had nothing, but on the fourth stair you could hear it all. It was purely an accident that I happened to be sitting on it and happened to hear my mother say, "Was that Isabel?"

"I think so. So hard to tell these days," said my brother.

"Did she eat anything?"

"Coffee only. Can I make a suggestion?"

"You're going to anyway, aren't you?"

"Tell her to drop the case. Let her quit. Let her go and she'll come back. What you're doing now is just going to drive her away, and I'm surprised that after all these years, after all you know about her, you haven't figured that out."

"Sweetie, I know what I'm doing."

"Do you?"

"If she works the case long enough, she'll forget why she wanted to quit in the first place."

"Why not let her quit and decide to come back on her own?"

"Because I need to keep an eye on her, David."

"Why?"

"Old Isabel is making a comeback. I can't go through that again. I can't."

"That isn't Old Isabel, Mom. It's a completely new mutation."

My mother ignored his comment and said, "Do you remember what she was like? Because I sure do. I never saw a person so ready to self-destruct. It was terrifying. Every time she didn't come home, every time I found her passed out in the car, on the porch, in the bathtub, I thought she was gone. I've let her go too many times. I won't do it anymore."

"Did it ever occur to you that maybe this job wasn't for her?" David asked.

"Without this job, she's Uncle Ray wait-ing to happen."

THE SNOW CASE: CHAPTER 5

The coffee hit me later that morning as I stared at the Snow file for the third hour.

I phoned Sheriff Larson to arrange another meeting. I could tell he was disappointed that I contacted him so soon after our first encounter, but he agreed. More precisely, he told me where he would be drinking that night and said that if I had a question or two, he might answer them.

Later that afternoon, as I was sitting in the Spellman office running a statewide criminal record check on all the individuals I had interviewed on the Snow case (by the way, coming up dry), my parents entered the office and handed me an envelope.

"What is this?"

"Severance pay," said my dad.

"You're off the job," said my mom.

"Why?"

"Martin Snow called. He wants you to quit working the case. Says it is too upsetting for his mother."

"Do you honestly think he cares how his mother feels?"

"If you want to do something else, go ahead and do it. The money should keep you for a while," said my mom.

I slid the envelope back across the desk and told them to keep their money, told them that I still had work to do. They told me that the case was over. And I told them it was over when I said it was over, and left.

I arrived at McCall's tavern shortly before Sheriff Larson. It was good to get out of the house and into a place that served booze. I drank a beer and soaked up the atmosphere. It was an establishment on the edge of a dive bar. The decor gave it an elegance that its clientele took away, but still, it was a safe place for a woman to sit alone, drink, and contemplate the end of a man's life.

Sheriff Larson's off-duty attire consisted of faded blue jeans, a wrinkled long-sleeve T-shirt, and a hooded wool jacket. Without the clean lines of the uniform emphasizing his overly structured face, Larson looked like someone I would look twice at. In fact, if it weren't for the toothpick hanging out of his mouth and my nagging suspicion about him, he would be just my type. I found his unfettered coolness somewhat compelling, the way he barely raised an eyebrow in recognition when he spotted me, the manner in which he slowly walked over to the bar, nodded his head once, and sat down.

In what appeared to be a telepathic exchange between Larson and the bartender, a pint of beer was placed in front of him.

I put five dollars on the bar, but Larson slid my money back to me. "I never let a woman buy me a drink."

As a chivalric stance, I found his edict amusing, but let it slide.

"Come here often?" I said, trying to ease into the conversation.

"Isabel."

"Sheriff."

"You can call me Greg," he said without sounding friendly at all.

"Greg."

"Isabel, what is this all really about?"

"It's complicated. Can we leave it at that?"

"I think people are entitled to a few secrets."

"I wish my mom thought like you."

"So what do you want from me?" Larson asked, his guard dropping just a bit.

"I'd like you to tell me what happened to Andrew Snow."

"I don't know what happened."

"I had a feeling you'd say that. Now, I can buy that maybe you don't know exactly what happened to him, but you know more than you're telling me."

Larson gave me a half smile, but no response. Unlike Martin Snow, Larson put on less of a show to convince me of his ignorance. I knew he would be impossible to crack. This was a man born with a poker face. But I had to try.

"I have some theories about what might have happened to Andrew and I'd like to run them by you. Would that be okay?"

"Why not?" Larson replied.

"Theory number one," I said, consulting my notes. "Andrew took some hallucinogens and wandered off on the camping trip, got lost, and fell victim to the elements."

"The elements?"

"You know, like sunstroke, or drowning, or getting eaten by a bear."

"I don't think animals count as 'the elements.' "

"I'm using a more open definition. The point is," I said, "something in the environment, not foul play, took him. What do you think?"

"I think that's a fine theory."

"Thank you, but it's not. It has some

problems. First of all, most accounts of Andrew claim that he was a pot smoker; no hallucinogens or narcotics are mentioned. Now, if you're smoking pot on a camping trip, you're not going to want to go on a ten-mile hike in the middle of the night. You're going to want to eat s'mores and stare at the campfire."

"You seem to be an expert," Larson responded.

"I don't think it fits. So it would be helpful for you to get me the name of his marijuana source. Maybe then I can find out if Andrew was into any harder stuff."

"How am I supposed to know that?"

"You could ask around," I offered with a cheerful smile. "Are you ready for theory number two?"

"Sure."

"Andrew and Martin got in a fight on the camping trip. Martin killed his brother, either accidentally or not accidentally, panicked, and hid the body."

"Huh" was Larson's only response. I scanned his face for a hint of recognition, but there was nothing.

"Theory number three," I said.

"I can't wait to hear this one."

"Mrs. Snow murdered her son after he accidentally tracked dirt onto her carpet.

The camping trip was a cover-up. She's hiding the body somewhere in the house."

Larson simply stared at me, trying to decide if I was serious.

"That would explain all the potpourri," I said.

Then Larson did something I didn't even think he was capable of: he laughed.

I had only a brief window while Larson's defenses were down to ask the next question: "What is Hank's last name?"

"Who?" he asked, easing back into his poker face.

"Uncle Hank. The man you were staying with the night Andrew went missing. What's his last name? I'd like to talk to him."

I can't say for sure, but I think I spotted a glitch in Larson's even stillness. It was kind of like a skip in an otherwise perfect record. If you weren't paying attention, you might not even hear it.

"Why do you want to talk to him?"

"He's your alibi, isn't he? You can give me his name or I'll find out on my own. It's up to you."

"Farber," he said, taking out a pen. "Here's his address. You might consider bringing a chaperone. Uncle Hank's got a bit of a reputation. Is that all, Isabel?"

"One more question: Are you and Martin

still friends?"

"We're not enemies."

"When was the last time you saw him?"

"Had to be over six months ago."

"Thank you for your time, Sheriff." I finished my drink and left the bar.

The following night, Daniel threatened to cook for me. Now that our relationship was in the full-disclosure phase, I decided it was time to break the news to him.

"You're a terrible cook, Daniel."

"I know," he replied. "But it's the effort that counts."

"I hope that's not the slogan for your dental practice."

"Very funny."

"How about we do something different tonight?" I suggested.

"I thought you were desperate to see the episode where Max tries to get recruited as a double agent."

"Later," I said. "I thought maybe you'd like to come with me on a surveillance."

"We're going on a stakeout?" Daniel asked. The excitement in his voice was like all first-timers who could never imagine the depths of boredom that awaited them.

An hour later, Daniel and I were parked in his car down the street from Martin

Snow's house in Sausalito.

"I'm hungry," Daniel said.

I anticipated the need for snacks and offered Daniel a bag of bridge mix. Daniel rifled through the bag.

"There are only filberts in here," he said, disappointed.

"I really need to have a talk with Uncle Ray."

More silence passed as I trained my eye on the front door of Martin's home.

"I'm bored," said Daniel.

"We've only been here an hour."

"But nothing's happening."

"Nothing happens most of the time, I've discovered."

Daniel sighed. More silence.

"I have to pee," he said.

"At least you're a man," I replied.

"What does that mean?"

"The world is your toilet."

"You want me to pee outside?"

"Most of our guys pee in jars. But I don't imagine you keep a pee jar inside your recently detailed BMW."

"In jars? That's disgusting," Daniel said as he exited the car.

While Daniel searched for a place to relieve himself, I spotted Sheriff Larson parking his black Jeep in the driveway of

Martin's home. Larson knocked on the front door and a moment later Martin greeted him.

Daniel returned to the car. "Did anything happen while I was gone?"

"One guy dropped by another guy's house."

"That's suspicious," Daniel said sarcastically.

It was suspicious. I just couldn't say why.

As the year came to a close, I took a brief respite from the Snow case, mostly because I didn't want to trouble anyone during the holiday season. But once the dried-up fir trees began making their way onto the sidewalks, I began making inquiries once again. Against my parents' wishes, I phoned Martin Snow to arrange another interview. However, it was not Martin who called me back.

It was Abigail who called. Four days after the new year. I remember the date because earlier that night I had gotten a phone call from a bartender at Edinburgh Castle, a pub in the Tenderloin. Uncle Ray had fallen asleep in the booth, and when they briefly woke him, Ray handed them a card he kept in his breast pocket.

FOR REMOVAL, PLEASE CALL ISABEL SPELLMAN, or Spellman Investigations, 1-415-287-3772.

After I drove Ray home and my dad helped me bring him inside, my cell phone rang. The screen said "blocked number." I let the phone ring a few more times as I unlocked the door to my apartment. Once inside, I answered it.

"Hello."

"Ms. Spellman, this is Abigail Snow." Her voice had grown rougher in the weeks since we'd met and I hardly recognized it.

"What can I do for you, Mrs. Snow?"

"You can stop pursuing my son's case."

"I've tried to be respectful of your privacy," I said.

"Listen to me carefully. My son is an attorney. If I discover that you've made any more inquiries into Andrew's disappearance, we will file harassment charges against you and your family. Have I made myself clear?"

"Yes," I replied. "Mrs. Snow, I promise the case is closed now." And the line went dead.

That very moment, as I hung up the phone, I truly believed that the Snow case was over, that I would soon retire from my career with Spellman Investigations. However, I had little time to consider what that would mean, because what happened next changed everything. Instead of driving me away from the case, it brought me back.

Months later, when I had time to reflect on the events that had transpired, I tried to find that precise moment in time that altered all future events, as if having this knowledge after the fact could have prevented us from making the same mistake again. I may have long since passed it, but for me this is the surest dot in my timeline.

THE DOT

A few days after Mrs. Snow called me, as I was leaving the house (through the front door), my mother asked me if I was going to see the dentist. Since I had given her no evidence that the dentist was back in my life, my suspicion turned in the obvious direction.

I waited in Rae's bedroom for her to return from school. I opted against snooping and simply flopped down on her bed and picked up her worn-out copy of *The Catcher in the Rye.* I wondered for how many years that novel would remain a staple of adolescent bedrooms and wondered why Rae's teenage malaise had not yet kicked in. Then my eye caught a camera case by her desk and I unzipped the charcoal-gray canvas bag and studied the brand-new digital still camera that rested inside.

A moment later, Rae entered her room.

"How did you get in here?" she asked.

"You're not the only one who can pick locks," I said as I zipped up the bag.

"You have other business here?"

"Just a few questions."

"Let's have 'em."

"Have you been following me, Rae?"

"I stopped that a long time ago."

"Does Mom know that you went to see Daniel?"

"Don't tell her. She won't like it."

"Does she know I've been seeing him again?"

"A week ago I heard her tell Dad that she was sure it was over."

"Who is David's new girlfriend?" I asked quickly, hoping to throw her off and get an unfiltered response.

"I'm not falling for that," Rae said as she kicked off her shoes.

"How much did that camera and the equipment cost you?"

"I'd have to look up the receipts and do some calculations."

"Give me a rough estimate."

"Five hundred dollars — give or take."

"Give or take what?"

"A hundred dollars."

"Were you raised by La Cosa Nostra?"

"I don't know. Were you?"

"It's blackmail, Rae. Blackmail is bad.

Why don't you get that?"

"I'm glad this case is over."

"Who says it's over?"

"Mom says. The missing boy's mother called and told you to stop."

"Did she?"

"You know she did."

"How do you know?"

"I got ears."

I grabbed Rae by the collar, twisted it three hundred and sixty degrees, and shoved her against the wall.

"If you are lying to me and I find out, I will make your life a living hell."

"You already are!" she shouted.

"HOW DO YOU KNOW HIS MOTHER CALLED ME?! ARE YOU SPYING ON ME?! WERE YOU LISTENING AT MY DOOR?! WHAT WERE YOU DOING?!"

"I overheard Dad tell Mom that the guy's mother called you and ended it."

"Dad said this?"

"Yes."

"When?"

"Yesterday."

"What time?"

"I don't remember."

"Try."

"At night."

"You sure?"

"I wouldn't testify under oath —"

I tightened my grip and said, "Are you pretty sure?"

"Yes. I'd like you to leave now."

She didn't need to tell me, I was already out the door.

I returned to my apartment and looked for the bug. In all my twenty-eight years, I never thought my parents capable of sinking this low. Even when I was Old Isabel, they refrained from breaching basic laws of privacy. In California it is illegal to record someone without at least one party's consent. I began wishing I had dated those lawyers my mother set me up with, so I could use one of them to help me file a complaint against her. It seemed almost inevitable that one day we would see this poetic caption: *Spellman v. Spellman.*

The original conversation that my parents appeared to have knowledge of had occured on my cell phone. They don't have the technology to tap a cell line. However, I do recall mentioning, at a later date, my conversation with Mrs. Snow to Petra, on my land line. Tapping a regular phone is a piece of cake. Even though phone taps are illegal, they are not a recreational drug, and therefore I am not an expert on them. But to pull apart a room inch by inch, you just need patience, not expertise, which I have when I know for a fact that I will find something to incriminate my parents. I followed the phone line to the jack and tracked the same line along the wall and outside. I climbed out the window and crawled down the fire escape, visually tracing the trail to the base of the house. Simple telephone monitoring devices can be attached at any point on the phone line and, when used in a conjunction with a voice-activated recorder, prove to be an excellent choice for monitoring a single phone line. I concluded, based on the information Rae presented to me, that my father had overheard my phone conversation and that is how he was privy to that information. However, reaching back, it appeared possible that he simply overheard one side of the conversation. Mine.

When I couldn't find any device attached to the phone line, I began looking for a bug somewhere in my apartment. At seven hundred and fifty square feet, wall-to-wall furniture, and seven years of accumulated clutter, finding a device that might fit inside your nostril wasn't easy.

I needed help. I needed the help of a neutral party. I thought about calling Daniel, but I couldn't imagine in what universe "Wanna come over to my apartment and help me look for a bug?" would sound normal and I was working really hard at trying to be normal with him. I called Petra, but she wasn't home. The only person who was home was Uncle Ray. He was always home, unless he was at a poker game or a bar. I asked Ray if he wanted to help me look for an audio surveillance device. Uncle Ray asked me if I had any beer. I did. It is rare that my universe presents me with such perfect symbiosis.

Since Uncle Ray lives with my parents, I often forget that he has a beautiful sense of detachment. Unless the fight turns him into one of the warring parties, he stays out of it. Usually one potato-chip-munching line like "I'm watching the game here" says it all. Petty disputes between individuals mean nothing when teams of men have decade-long scores to settle. The only thing Uncle Ray knew was that he was looking for a bug. It never would have occurred to him that his brother had planted it.

I tore apart the apartment in an unfocused, unsystematic search. Uncle Ray sat on my bed and drank three beers. Then he walked over to an outlet next to my bed, unplugged a lamp, then an alarm clock, pulled a three-way adapter out of the socket, and handed it to me.

"Thanks for the beer," he said and left the room.

My instinct was to rage, to contact attorneys — maybe the ACLU — but my intellect told me to play it cool, to calculate my response. As it turns out, neither my instinct nor my intellect is really all that reliable. I took the adapter and relocated it to the file room. They'd figure it out eventually, but it bought me some time. I needed to get out of the house to clear my head. I needed to be in non-Spellman territory. I got in the car and drove to Petra's.

Petra met me at the door, wearing a strapless black satin evening gown with a lace shawl. Her hair was tied up conservatively and several of her extraneous piercings had been removed.

She was taken aback by my presence. "What are you doing here?"

"I just found an audio surveillance device in my room. Are you going to the opera?"

"No. Just a function."

"With whom?"

"Oh, this guy I met recently."

"What does he do?"

"He's a . . . doctor."

"Really?"

"Well, I haven't verified it with the AMA, but I'm assuming he's told me the truth."

"What's his name?"

"What's with all the questions?"

"Usually you mention when you're seeing someone new."

"Don Sternberg."

"Excuse me?"

"That's his name."

"If you insist."

"Do you need anything?"

"No. I'm good. Have fun with the lawyer."

"Doctor," Petra corrected me.

"Doctors, lawyers. They're really all the same, aren't they?"

"Not if you're in the emergency room."

The conversation was going nowhere, at least nowhere near the truth. I looked at her arm and noticed another void where a tattoo used to reside. I believe it was the gravesite with "Jimi Hendrix, RIP" written on the tombstone.

"Why'd you get rid of Jimi?"

"People change."

"They do? I had no idea."

I left Petra's apartment and drove to the one place where I knew I could get answers. I didn't have to knock on his door. I didn't have to ask any questions. All I had to do was wait outside David's home and see if he left wearing a tuxedo and then I would know for sure: My brother was not only dating my best friend, he was buying the silence of a fourteen-year-old girl and catering to the whims of his fifty-four-year-old mother just to keep this one fact from me.

I felt a surge of self-righteousness, a powerful need to prove that the measures they took against or because of me were wrong — or at least unnecessary. As I predicted, David exited his home in formal wear. I drove away before he could spot me. I would deal with the two of them later.

Staged Dental Appointment #3

My parents and I agreed on a temporary reprieve. The warring had taken its toll on both sides. However, the reprieve didn't include Rae. After convincing my mother, I broke the news to my sister.

"You have three cavities. Daniel will see you tomorrow at four o'clock sharp. Don't be late."

"Do you really think that's necessary?" she asked.

"You make that appointment or you will be very sorry."

Later that night, I walked into the living

room and caught Rae and Uncle Ray watching television together. On the screen Laurence Olivier washed his hands in the sink and asked Dustin Hoffman, who was tied to the chair, "Is it safe?"

I stepped behind the couch and stared at the screen.

"Is it safe?" Olivier asked again as he unrolled a collection of dental tools.

I turned to Uncle Ray, betrayed. "Do you think this is helpful? Watching *Marathon Man* the night before her dental appointment?"

My sister shushed me and stared attentively at the television. Uncle Ray played innocent.

"What?" he said. "It's a good movie."

"Is it safe?" Olivier asked one more time, as I made my exit.

The following afternoon, Rae sat in examination room #2, nervously awaiting Daniel. She could hear him saying his good-byes to Mrs. Sanchez, who was done for the day, and remembered at the last second to turn on her tape recorder. He was still a dentist, wasn't he? Months later, I would discover the following transcripts with Rae's visual commentary:

[Daniel enters the room.]

Rae: Dr. Castillo?

Daniel: I told you, it's Daniel, please.

Rae: Are you positive I have three cavities?

Daniel: Positive. In fact, I've never been this sure of anything.

[Daniel washes his hands.]

Rae: Could I see the X-rays?

[Daniel stares at Rae for an uncomfortably long time.]

Daniel: Don't you trust me, Rae?

Rae: Sure, I'd just like to see the X-rays.

[Daniel picks up a set of X-rays, puts them up on a back light, and turns it on. He points to specific areas on her teeth.]

Daniel: One and two in your lower right second bicuspid and first molar. The third in your upper left lateral incisor.

[Daniel takes out a syringe.]

Rae: Don't you need your nurse to assist you or something?

Daniel: She's gone for the day. We're all alone. Now open wide.

[Rae doesn't open wide.]

Rae: How can I be sure those are *my* X-rays?

Daniel: You're stalling, sweetheart. Now be a good girl and open your mouth.
Rae: I asked you a question.
[Daniel leans in close.]

Daniel: Are you afraid of me, Rae?
Rae: I'm afraid of having unnecessary dental work.
Daniel: A little pain never hurt anyone. Personally, I think it builds character.
Rae: Isabel said this wouldn't hurt.
Daniel: Do you believe everything your sister tells you?
Rae: No, I don't.
[Daniel prepares the novocaine.]

Daniel: Is it safe?
[Daniel says the last line with a stab at a German accent. Then he winks suggestively. Rae leaps out of the chair and races out of the office, discarding her paper bib just outside the front door.]

In a fitting homage to the previous night's film, Rae ran the entire two miles from the Market and Van Ness Muni stop to 1799 Clay Street. Her shaky hands unlocked the front door and she maintained her speed as she raced into the Spellman office. She stood before my parents, huffing and puffing, trying to catch her breath. My parents looked up.

When Rae was finally able to speak, she said, "Daniel Castillo is evil."

My parents listened to an hour's worth of thesaurus entry descriptions of her encounter. He was creepy, weird, sinister, eerie, unsettling. "And he winked," she reminded them. "An evil wink." But Mom and Dad were accustomed to Rae's occasional bouts of hyperbole and took her rant with a grain of salt. The fact is, after acquiring Daniel's statistics during their first meeting, Albert and Olivia conducted a background check that would have done the government proud. They still didn't like him, but they had to admit that on paper he was as clean as they come.

The parental unit came to the logical conclusion that Rae was merely frightened of the needle and a victim of the years of dentist mythology that circulated in our house. For maybe the first time in her life, my parents didn't believe Rae. And so, alone, Rae knew that she had to save me from the dentist.

As predicted, Rae began following me again sometime after her derailed dental appointment. Although for the first two days, all she ever saw was me sitting behind my computer, running criminal checks on every member of the Snow family.

My mother, noticing the paperwork atop my desk, tried, yet again, to dissuade me from this endeavor.

"Isabel, the job is over," she said. "You're free to work elsewhere. Be a waitress, a secretary, a bartender. I don't care."

"We had a deal, Mom. I'm sticking to it."

"Sweetie, Martin Snow is an attorney. Do you understand what that means?"

"You want me to ask him out on a date?" I replied, still staring at my computer screen.

"No. It means if you continue harassing his family, he will consider a lawsuit."

"I wouldn't worry about it if I were you," I said casually.

"How can you say that? Even the cost of defending a lawsuit could destroy us."

"Mom, listen. He's hiding something. People who have a secret that they don't want out don't generate attention for themselves. They try to keep a low profile. His threats are just that."

I suspect my parents knew that I had found the listening device. Nothing was said on the subject, as I was still calculating my revenge. Rae's teeth became a secondary concern over the next few days, which I recall with the grainy clarity of an old movie.

I should have slept off my anger. I should have thought about what I was doing. I should have given myself and everyone else a chance to breathe, to slow down, to stop. But I could not bring the momentum to a halt. My parents had given me a case that they believed could not be solved and three weeks later I was thinking maybe it could be.

"How do you feel about buying some drugs with me?" I asked Daniel over the phone the following afternoon.

"Sure," he said as if I had asked him if he wanted milk in his coffee.

"I'll pick you up tomorrow at seven."

THE DRUG DEAL

I couldn't believe what I was about to do, even as I was doing it. I pulled up outside Daniel's house just after 7:00 p.m. and honked the horn. He exited his building wearing a well-tailored suit with a pink shirt open at the collar.

"Nice duds," I said as Daniel put his briefcase on the floor and slid into the car.

"Thanks. This is my drug-buying outfit," Daniel said dryly.

"Did you bring the money?" I asked.

"Yes, I brought the drug money," he said.

"You can just say 'money'; you don't have to say 'drug money.'"

"Yes, I brought the money."

Silence.

"Eh-hem," I said to Daniel, cuing him for his next line.

"You need a lozenge?"

"Eh-hem," I said again. I had instructed Daniel to say only one line. How hard could that be? I coughed, loudly, and gave him a sharp glare.

"If all you wanted was some blow, I could get that for you," he said as if he were reading a script off a TelePrompTer.

"We're meeting Martin Snow's dealer, Jerome Franklin. He won't talk to me unless I'm buying. Just stay cool and everything will be fine."

"This isn't the first time I've bought drugs."

"Laughing gas doesn't count."

"I know my drugs, Isabel."

"Why don't you be the silent partner?" I said.

"Good idea. I'll just sit here and look menacing."

Daniel was in a bad mood, so I let him stew in his flashy suit. The weekend brought even more traffic than usual on the bridge. Daniel and I ran out of safe things to say and made the rest of the trip in silence. When we reached our destination, along a patch of unfinished warehouses in West Oakland, Daniel said, "I think I've been here before." I shot him a look that told him not to improvise.

We knocked on the third door from the end and "Jerome Franklin" answered. He wore a Pittsburgh Steelers jersey and hat, baggy jeans that hung just below the hip, and an array of gold jewelry that matched his gold tooth. I wanted to say something about the tooth, like, *Please, isn't that a bit much?* but I wasn't sure how he'd take it.

"Are you a cop?" Jerome asked me as he led us inside.

"No. I already told you that," I said as I took in my surroundings.

"Is he a cop?" Jerome asked, coldly eyeing Daniel.

"No. I'm a dentist," Daniel said proudly.

Jerome pulled a gun he had stuck in the front of his jeans and jabbed it against Daniel's rib cage. "I hate dentists."

"I would, too, if I had your teeth," Daniel replied.

Jerome shoved him onto the couch and told him to shut up. I seconded that.

Chris, another young black male, wearing suit pants, a buttoned-up vest minus a shirt, and a black do-rag, entered the room.

"Everything cool, bro?"

"Ai'ight."

"Who the bitch?" he asked, I assume referring to me.

"She used to be down with Snow."

"Snow? I remember that dude. Dead, right?"

"Missing. But probably dead."

"What does she want?"

"What do they all want?"

I didn't plan properly where I was going to strategically work in questions about Andrew Snow. Pleasantries and drug buys were taking up enough of my time as it was. I should have written a script. That was a mistake. I tried to ease my nerves by taking in the surroundings. What was noticeable about the warehouse was the absence of things: pictures had clearly been removed from the walls, shadows of the frames hanging in their place, old folding chairs scattered about the room haphazardly in place of more permanent furniture. Ashtrays with weeks-old cigarette butts punctuated every surface. It was an odd contrast to the spotless kitchen sink, but I skimmed over it.

My attention returned to Jerome, who dropped a satchel on a vintage blue diner table, revealing several Baggies full of white powder. "You want a taste?"

Jerome took a vial out of his pocket, shook it onto a mirror, sliced the powder into a perfect line with a razor blade, and handed me a straw.

I paused for a moment, making sure that all eyes were on me. Then I took the straw and leaned over the line.

That was when I heard the all-too-familiar

voice shout, "No, Izzy!"

I looked up and saw Rae standing in front of the bathroom door. She must have climbed through an open window in back.

Everyone froze. The room was unnaturally still, as if no one could decide what to do next. Rae saw the gun on the bureau. I saw her calculate that she could reach it first and make a run for it.

My mind was on a time delay until the gun was in her hand and aimed at Jerome. This was not how it was supposed to go down.

"Get away from my sister," Rae shouted.

Jerome looked to me for instruction.

"Drop the blade," she continued, aiming at Jerome, who had forgotten about the shiny razor's edge in his hand.

Jerome dropped the blade on the table.

"Come on, Izzy. Let's get out of here. Now," she said, and then turned to Daniel and continued, "You stay here."

My shock was quickly replaced with an astounding rage. "What is wrong with you?" I asked.

"I'm saving you. Let's go."

I smiled at Jerome, whose real name is Leonard Williams (remember? my high school "source"), and said, "Cut!," slicing my finger through the air in front of my throat. Then I turned to Rae.

"The gun is not loaded. Daniel is not evil. This is not cocaine. It's powdered sugar.[1] Meet Len and his friend Christopher. They are actors — MFA candidates at the Academy of Dramatic Arts. I went to high school with Len. He owed me a favor and I finally cashed it in over a decade later. Unfortunately, I had to play off negative racial stereotypes because you watch way too many movies."

Rae remained speechless. A first, as far back as I can remember.

"I don't know about any of you, but I am dying for a cup of tea," Christopher said with his natural British accent. "Who's in?"

Daniel raised his hand and said, "Earl Grey."

Len said, "Some chamomile, please."

Christopher turned to my sister and said, "And you, pet?"

Rae stared at him as if he were speaking another language.

"If you have any hot chocolate," I said. "And nothing for me."

Christopher left the room and put the kettle on. Len cleaned up the fake cocaine

---

[1] Baking powder looks more authentic but is much harder to snort.

and turned to me. "I need the truth. How were we?"

"Perfect," I said.

"I can't believe that guy is English. Wow. His accent was amazing," Daniel said cheerily.

"Did you hear that, Christopher?" shouted Len.

From the kitchen, Christopher replied, "You are a dear."

"Sit down, Rae," I said, pulling a chair for her. "Let me tell you how this was supposed to play out."

Rae slowly sat down, but she held on to the gun and kept her eye on every suspicious male in the room.

"I needed you to start following me again. I needed you to document my activity. I needed you to witness something that you would have to record. I knew that if you went to Daniel's office and believed he was a bad guy, you'd follow me even if nobody told you to. It was an act, Rae, the creepy demeanor, the wink, the quote from *Marathon Man*. It was an act."

"Although I was not acting when I said you had three cavities," Daniel interjected.

Rae swirled around in the chair, pointed the gun at Daniel, and shouted, "I Don't Have Any Cavities!"

I took the gun from Rae's hands and continued. "I had a feeling if you thought I was up to something, you'd follow me. But you can't drive. I gambled that you'd hide on the floor of my car. I was willing to do this again and again until I got you to jump through the right hoops. But you hit your mark the first time around. And I'm guessing that your digital camera is in your backpack right now, which you left in the car, right?"

Rae averted her gaze, indicating that I was on the money.

"What I counted on was that you would follow me, that you would watch me through the windows. If you'll notice, they're freshly cleaned and you have a clear shot from the north corner, where the car is parked. I counted on you recording my activities and showing the recording to Mom and Dad. What I didn't count on was you breaking into the home of alleged drug dealers and pulling a gun on everyone in the room. How insane are you?"

"That's a rhetorical question, right?" she replied.

"What you just did, Rae. It was crazy."

"What *I* did was crazy?" Rae repeated incredulously. "I'm going to tell Mom and Dad."

"You're right, you *are* going to tell Mom and Dad. And you are going to tell them exactly what I want you to tell them."

Rae stared down at the table and mumbled, "I can't believe I tried to save your life."

"Tea," chirped Christopher as he carted in a tray of assorted beverages and scones.

Daniel was delighted by Christopher's antique china set and commented on how civilized he felt. He seemed relieved to finally drop the "evil" act. It had taken hours to persuade him to participate in this ruse. It was not only the fake drug deal that slowed up the negotiation, but also including a minor in a charade involving scare tactics, white powder, and empty firearms. After three long hours of convincing Daniel that this was the only way to get proper revenge on my parents, he reluctantly agreed.

Len's and Christopher's performances outshone their sets by a long shot. Even with the absence of the pricey leather-and-mahogany couch, antique coffee table, and the impeccable throw rugs, the hand of a professional decorator was all over the warehouse — the hand being that of Christopher's generous and wealthy mother. Had Rae's suspicion been jarred, had she been looking for clues to a setup, she might have noticed the DVD collection, constructed almost entirely of 1940s screwball comedies and cinema vérité. She might have found the tastefully framed collector's edition poster of the Sidney Poitier classic *They Call Me Mister Tibbs!* something of a giveaway, but Rae wouldn't know what to look for. She is not a sheltered child, but she does not know the drug world. She saw white powder and black men in the sartorial gear common to rap videos and made an uneducated guess.

"I want to go home," said Rae.

But my plan was not complete. I needed Rae to return home with evidence on me.

"Drink your cocoa and then we'll start filming."

On the drive home, Rae studied the footage while Daniel had a minor nervous breakdown, as if his actions had only just come into his consciousness.

After reminding Rae that he really wasn't evil and that she really did have cavities, Daniel said to me, "That was the most juvenile thing I've ever done."

"Are you counting even when you were a juvenile?" I replied, annoyed. "If you agree to participate in a fake drug deal, don't complain about it later."

Rae then interrupted, "I still don't understand why you were pretending to buy drugs."

"Mom and Dad bugged my room. That's a line you don't cross. If they're going to invade my privacy, I want them to find the kind of thing worthy of invading my privacy. Listen to me carefully, Rae. You better do exactly as you're told. I got enough dirt on you to keep you grounded for a year. Got it?"

Rae remained silent all the way back to the city, breaking her previous record by six minutes.

Isabel Snorts Cocaine: The Movie

The following night Rae screened her debut feature for my parents. She passed around popcorn and invited Uncle Ray to join them in the living room. My sister popped the homemade DVD into the player and took a formal stance in front of her audience. She introduced the film by describing a suspicious telephone conversation she overheard me have with Daniel — a conversation on the topic of making a drug buy. She explained that she hid in the back of my car under a blanket and once we were inside the "crack house," she found an angle through the window and started filming.

Rae pressed play and sat down on the floor in front of the coffee table. She grabbed the popcorn from Uncle Ray and told him to stop hogging it.

My mother sat frozen, not even a breath passed her lips, as she watched Rae's silent film on the twenty-inch screen. She watched me lean into the frame, slice the white powder with a razor blade, pick up a straw, and . . .

"That is Izzy snorting cocaine," Rae said as if she were narrating to a room full of blind people.

My mother's knee-jerk reaction was to protect her younger daughter from witnessing such a transgression.

"Rae, I don't want you watching this," said my mom.

"But I recorded it," my sister replied.

The fake drug deal was purely a retaliatory measure against my parents' room-bugging. Unfortunately, I failed to anticipate their response. Immediately after Rae's film night, my parents commenced a twenty-four-hour surveillance on me that did not let up until I became the last thing on their minds.

The Interview: Chapter 5

Stone's calculated detachment gives way to visible scorn. His jaw clenches as he catches up on his notes.

"I know what you're thinking," I say.

Stone takes a sip of coffee and avoids eye contact.

"I don't believe you do."

It's true. I can read almost anyone, but not him, and it unnerves me. I need to assert some element of control.

"Are you married, Inspector?"

"No."

"Divorced?"

"I'm not the subject of this investigation."

"Why did your wife leave you?"

"That trick is older than you, Isabel."

"So she didn't leave you?"

"Isabel, please stop," Stone says. The sincerity of the request takes me aback, and I do. I stop. But then I ask the question that has been in the back of my mind since we started this interview.

"What did they tell you about me?"

"Does it matter now?"

"Yes. It does."

Stone, consulting his notes, says, "I know you used to knock over trash cans with your car on garbage night. I know about the drugs, I know about the drinking, I know that you can't keep a boyfriend, I know about the Neighborhood Watch meetings in your honor, I know about a string of unproven cases of vandalism that all occurred during your school years. Shall I go on?"

"You got anything good in there?"

"I hear you're much better now," he says, doing his best to avoid a condescending tone.

"Do you think this is my fault?"

"How could I? I don't even know what's happened yet."

THE SNOW CASE:
CHAPTER 6

As it was, I didn't pull the name Jerome Franklin out of thin air. According to Audrey Gale, one of the three people who signed Andrew's yearbook, he was the main drug source for most of the Marin high school students. The real Jerome Franklin's life of crime ended in high school. He is currently a financial advisor, living in San Diego, California. Once I explained the purpose of my call to Jerome and further explained that I was uninterested in exposing his youthful indiscretions (as he called them), he was cooperative, although he provided no more insight into Andrew Snow's life than anyone else: Andrew liked smoking weed. That's all he could tell me.

Since I could find no leads beyond the Snow family and Sheriff Larson, I refocused my efforts on that particular cast of suspicious characters. It was time to visit Hank Farber, Larson's uncle and only alibi for the night of Andrew's disappearance. I phoned Hank (never Henry) and arranged a meeting for the following day.

My mother tailed me halfway across the city until I lost her by making an illegal U-turn that I knew she wouldn't duplicate.

I knocked on apartment 4C of the aging Tenderloin building at exactly 10:45 a.m. The man who answered the door was a slightly more pickled, R-rated version of your average grandpa type. The kind you see at racetracks and strip clubs chain-smoking cigars. Although cigarettes were Hank's poison — among other things — I suspect.

"Well, well, well, what have we here?" Hank said after he opened the door and looked me up and down. My grimy host then guided me to a thirty-year-old plaid couch that could exfoliate your skin through your clothes. He sat down across from me, lit a cigarette, and smiled with anticipation, as if being interviewed about a missing adolescent was kind of like the Q&A session of the Miss America pageant.

"Mr. Farber . . ."

"Call me Hank," Mr. Farber said with a wink.

"Do you remember the weekend of July 18, 1995?"

"Boy, that was a while ago."

"Yes, it was. Do you remember that weekend?"

"Can you give me a refresher?" Hank asked.

"Yes. That was the weekend that Andrew Snow went missing."

"Right," said Hank. "I remember. That was very sad."

"Do you recall what you were doing that weekend?"

"I think my nephew Greg was visiting me. Must have been about seventeen at the time."

"Do you remember anything unusual about the visit?"

"No. Greg went to a concert."

"Do you remember what concert?"

"No. I don't keep up with what the kids are listening to these days."

"Do you remember what time Greg got home?"

"Around eleven p.m."

"How did Greg get to the concert?"

"I think he took the car."

"Whose car? Your car or his car?"

"It was my car, but then he bought it from me."

"When?" I asked.

"Sometime around then."

"He bought your car the weekend of Andrew Snow's disappearance."

"Not that weekend. But a few weeks later. He drove it, though. At least I think he did."

"What kind of car was it?"

"A Toyota Camry."

"Do you remember the color and year?"

"White. Nineteen-eighty-eight."

I left Hank in a cloud of his own cigarette smoke and drove directly to Abigail Snow's house. She looked disappointed when she saw me standing on her doorstep.

"Ms. Spellman, what can I do for you today?"

"I know I'm the last person you wanted to see, but —"

"What would give you that idea, dear?" Mrs. Snow said in her painfully polite tone.

"Well, you called me and firmly suggested I stop looking into your son's case. So I figured —"

"Ms. Spellman, I never called you."

"You didn't?"

"No. Are you sure it was me? Perhaps it was another client."

The conversation was going too quickly for me to fully process what she was saying. If Abigail Snow hadn't called, then who had? And maybe she had called and was now denying it because, well, I couldn't begin to imagine how this woman's mind worked.

"Can I come in for a minute?" I asked.

Mrs. Snow looked down at my boots and was, I suspect, calculating how much dirt I would track into her home.

"I'll take them off," I offered.

"And your coat, too, dear. It's a bit grungy," Mrs. Snow replied.

I removed my boots and left my coat outside on a porch swing. Mrs. Snow allowed my entrance — reluctantly, I suspect.

"Can I use your phone?" I asked as I turned off the ringer on my cell phone.

"Go ahead," she replied, waving in the direction of the phone.

I called my cell phone. When I received the first call from Abigail Snow, the caller ID said "blocked number." This time a 415 phone number showed up on the screen. The easy answer was that my mother made the phone call to get me off the case.

Just to cover all bases, I asked, "Do you have a cell phone?"

"Of course not," she replied, casually wiping down the phone with a rag.

I had only a few more questions for her and then I could make my escape. The smell of the potpourri was starting to give me a headache.

"This may sound like an odd question," I said, "but do you recall what kind of car Greg Larson used to drive?"

"Yes. It was a red Camaro. Late-seventies model."

"Are you sure you don't mean Camry?"

"Yes, I'm sure," Mrs. Snow replied sharply.

"And it was definitely red, not white?"

"Dear, I know the difference between red and white."

"I can't argue with you there," I said, and quickly made my way to the door. "So you don't remember Greg ever having a white Camry?"

"No," she replied flatly.

"According to my parents' file, Martin and Andrew shared a 1985 Datsun hatchback in blue. Is that correct?"

"Yes."

"They didn't have any other cars, did they?"

"No."

"Thank you, Mrs. Snow. You've been very helpful."

After I exited the Snow home, I knocked on several doors in the neighborhood. Of the four people who were home, two were living in their current residence twelve years ago. Both of them remembered Greg Larson and his red Camaro. Neither of them recalled ever seeing a white Camry.

When I returned home, I spotted my mother's car parked in the driveway. I smashed the headlight to make it easier to spot her if she was following me. Traditionally I would have planned a more sophisticated counterstrike against my mother for making the counterfeit phone call, but my family's collision course was becoming a traffic jam and I opted for a simpler response. I ran down to the office and ratted her out to my dad.

"Sweetheart, your mother wouldn't do such a thing," responded my father before I even completed my tattle.

"Maybe you don't know her as well as you think."

"We've been married thirty-three years."

"And your point is?"

"Isabel, your mother didn't make that phone call. But let me reiterate: You are off the case. We don't want a lawsuit on our hands."

I might have pursued the conversation, but Uncle Ray interrupted, swinging open the door and shouting, "Al, you have to help me. I can't take it anymore!"

ONE TRUCE (AND A FEW MORE BATTLES)

With all the covert surveillance, room tapping, and generic spying going on, I forgot to mention the kind of peace that Rae and Uncle Ray had cultivated. Now that they were friends, Rae took it upon herself to single-handedly cure Uncle Ray of each and every one of his vices. This meant slipping greeting cards with photographs of diseased livers under his door, "Thinking of you. Love, Rae" scrawled on the inside.

Over dinner she would offer random facts about the evils of alcohol consumption and occasionally throw in dietary advice (which I often reminded her was somewhat hypocritical considering her sugar addiction). She researched drug and alcohol abuse religiously and even consulted an herbalist, who provided an elixir that Rae began slipping into Uncle Ray's food and sometimes his beer. She tried to attend a Gamblers Anonymous meeting, but was tossed out at the door. Dejected, she turned to Al-Anon and routinely shared the saga of Uncle Ray's journey into debauchery. Each retelling was loaded with yet another dramatic flourish, until it barely resembled Uncle Ray at all.

For the most part, my parents overlooked this new obsession of Rae's, since it kept her off the street. She was too busy researching and reporting facts on liver function to randomly surveil strangers. This sort of thing is considered progress in our house, although they maintained no misguided notions that Rae's endeavors would result in any alteration of Uncle Ray's habits. We had tried to fix him years before. Like a porcelain doll, if you drop it once, there is no amount of glue that will restore it to its previous glory.

Uncle Ray plopped down on a swivel chair and dropped his head on the desk. My sister entered right on his tail, carrying an enormous medical book called *Liver Function and Dysfunction.*

"Wait," Rae said. "You haven't looked at the liver after ten years of cirrhosis."

Uncle Ray turned to my father for assistance.

"Pumpkin, give me the book," said my dad.

Rae handed our father the textbook.

"You told me to spend more time at the library," she said.

"I did, didn't I? Meet me in the kitchen. We need to have a talk."

Rae rolled her eyes, offered an exaggerated sigh, and stomped out of the room. My dad turned to Uncle Ray.

"I'll do what I can," he said as he headed after his younger daughter.

I leaned against my desk, trying to figure out my next move. Uncle Ray lifted his head, turned to me, and said, "All I want to do is drink some beer and eat some peanuts in peace. Is that too much to ask?"

I had decided after I found the listening device in my apartment that it was time to move out of my parents' house. However, between fake drug deals and the Snow case, I found it hard to look for a new place. But then I remembered that I had a place to stay and began packing. A few hours later, Rae knocked on my door and asked if she could keep me company. I let her inside, where she began secretly unpacking. Until I caught her, that is, and literally picked her up and tossed her out, carefully securing the deadbolt after her.

Once I got bored with my packing, I

decided to pick up the key to my new place. A moment after I was out the door, my mother was strolling down the steps in her bathrobe and slippers.

"Where are we going, sweetie?" she asked.

"Nowhere," I cleverly replied.

"I love you," she said with an awkward, deadpan delivery. She said it as if she thought I might have forgotten. The truth was, I never doubted for a moment that my parents loved me. But love in my family has a bite to it and sometimes you get tired of icing all those tooth marks.

My mother sat patiently in her car, waiting for me to make my next move. I didn't bother trying to lose her. I had nothing to hide with this trip.

I pulled into David's driveway and left my mom sitting, double parked, in the middle of the street.

I knocked on David's door. He answered.

"Isabel. What are you doing here?"

"Hello. How are you?" I corrected him.

"Hi. Sorry. What's up?"

"Tell me the truth, David. Have you had Botox injections?"

"No."

"Is Petra here?"

"Why do you ask?"

"Because you look nervous."

"She's in the back. Are you looking for her?"

"I'm actually looking for the key to her apartment. She's living here, isn't she?"

"Not exactly."

"How long has this been going on?"

"About three months."

"How did it start?"

"I ran into her at the gym."

"She goes to a gym?" I said in utter disbelief.

"Yes. A lot of people do."

"So you ran into her at the gym and then what happened?"

"Isabel, can we have a conversation instead of an inquest?"

"Sure. As soon as you stop giving Rae hush money."

"Touché."

"So then what happened?"

"I told him he needed a haircut," Petra said as she entered the foyer. "Two days later, he called me for one."

"David," I said, "do you like drinking beer on rooftops?"

"Not particularly," my brother replied.

"See," I said to Petra.

"Anything else you'd like to know?" Petra asked.

"When did you start going to the gym?"

David pushed me aside and stepped onto his porch. "Is that Mom parked out front?"

"Oh yeah. I'm under twenty-four-hour surveillance."

"Why?"

"Because I snorted cocaine."

"What?!"

"Fake cocaine, David," I said and then turned to Petra. "Can I stay in your apartment?"

She handed me her keys and explained that the apartment was empty except for a bed and a case of bottled water. I responded that that was all I required. She further explained that her lease was up in a week and I had to clear out of there by then.

"David, try to stall Mom while I make my escape."

"What is going on, Isabel?" David said as I was halfway out the door.

"I wouldn't know where to begin."

I knocked on the window of my mother's car. "Please tell me the truth, Mom. Did you call me pretending to be Abigail Snow?"

"No," she said, with concern edging over her face.

I knew in that moment that she hadn't made the call and I also knew that I wouldn't stop until I found out who did.

Instead of going directly to Petra's, I

decided to swing by Daniel's place and see whether he had recovered yet from the fake drug deal.

I rang his buzzer, since he had made it clear that window entry was no longer acceptable.

"I was in the neighborhood," I said as I entered Daniel's apartment.

"Doing what?" Daniel asked.

"Just driving around."

"You were driving around my neighborhood?"

"I was driving around all sorts of neighborhoods trying to lose my mom."

"Lose your mom? I don't understand."

"She's following me."

"Your mother is following you, is that what you said?"

"Yes. Do you mind if I turn off your lights?"

I didn't wait for a response; I switched them off and walked over to the window. Peering through the blinds, I could see my mother sitting in her car, reading by a book light. Daniel leaned in next to me; he had to see it for himself.

"How long has she been following you?"

"Only like an hour. But she has a really small bladder, so she can never last that long. Do you have any coffee? Maybe we can speed this up."

"This is not normal, Isabel."

"You're telling me."

As I continued watching my mother, Daniel poured himself a drink and sat down on the couch.

"Isabel, where do you see this relationship going?"

It had been a long day and I was in no mood for the kind of talk Daniel had in mind. I had to get out of his apartment before the conversation progressed further. I peered out of the window again, just for show.

"My mom just nodded off. I have to make a run for it."

I kissed Daniel on the forehead and raced out of the apartment. My mother, of course, had not fallen asleep. I walked up to her car and knocked on the window.

"Go home, Mom," I said. "I'm not doing anything interesting tonight."

"I hope you didn't tell Daniel that."

She didn't go home. She followed me to Petra's and called Jake Hand on his way home after a long night of partying. She suggested he could sober up while making fifteen dollars an hour, and because Jake is still not-so-secretly in love with my mother, he agreed. Jake took a cab from his party and my mother handed him her car keys, explaining that he wasn't allowed to drive it until morning, when he could pass a sobriety test. My mother then took the cab home herself.

Inside Petra's apartment, I phoned Martin Snow one more time. Once again, the call turned over to voice mail. I pleaded with him to call me back and politely suggested that it might be the only way to get me off his back. I didn't mention the unexplained phone call or Greg Larson's extra car or any other aspect of the case. But that was a card I was willing to play.

My mother's fifteen dollars an hour was a waste of cash. The only thing Jake Hand saw through the lit window of Petra's apartment was me, sitting on her bed and reviewing the case file over and over again. At 3:00 a.m., I looked out the window and saw Jake passed out in the front seat of the car. I wished I had somewhere to go, some lead to follow, because it would have been so easy to lose him at that moment. Instead I went to bed. Jake slept through half the morning amidst the traffic on the street. He was still out cold as I made my getaway.

If only I could have made the most of my escape. Instead I went home to finish packing. Jake phoned my mother while I was in transit. I heard her finishing the call as I entered the house.

"Forget it, Jake. She's here. Haven't you heard of coffee? Good-bye."

I went up to my apartment and discovered that all the boxes I had previously packed were now unpacked and the lion's share of my belongings were restored to the wrong place. My parents' tactics are more covert than this blatant attempt to derail my move; Rae was behind this. The loose lock from an amateur pick, the cookie crumbs on the floor, and the way she'd Krazy Glued down a number of items pointed in only one direction.

I spent most of the day repacking what Rae had unpacked and ungluing what Rae had glued down. By the afternoon, I was as packed as I was the night before and hungry for revenge. I drove by Rae's school and waited out front for her. She saw my car first and then saw my father's car on my tail and pretended that she didn't know which car was intended for her.

I rolled down the window and told her not to play dumb. Rae got inside and I drove her home. Then I made her come up to my apartment and forced her to spend the entire night helping me finish packing for real. Her attempts at sabotage were met with empty threats and benign bullying. My packing didn't benefit from her presence, but at least Uncle Ray had a free night and I reminded her that what follows from breaking and entering and gluing is some form of punishment. When I finally told her she could go, Rae said, "You'll come back. I know you will." It sounded less a prediction and more a threat.

LOST WEEKEND #25

Five days later, I woke up in Petra's apartment for the last time. I walked down the street to a local café and ordered a large coffee in a foreign language. As I reached for my wallet, my father appeared from the shadows and threw some bills on the counter.

"It's on me," he said.

I grabbed the coffee and strode out of the shop, still startled by his magic act. My father stayed on my heels and matched my clipped pace.

"What are you doing today?" he asked.

"You don't really think I'm going to answer that question, do you?"

"I meant, are you free? Uncle Ray has gone AWOL again. I could use your help."

I didn't tell him that I had no plans — for the day or the rest of my life. I didn't tell him I was glad to have the distraction of another Lost Weekend.

"Sure. I'll meet you at the house" was all I said.

Uncle Ray had been missing only fourteen hours when Rae began organizing a search party. The day after the first night he didn't return home, she telephoned all of his known acquaintances, told them there was a death in the family, and said that should they come in contact with her uncle, they should drive him home immediately. Uncle Ray was still a no-show, but my parents did receive a number of condolence calls. On day two, Rae took a bus after school to the location of his first poker game, and through interviews and "a Budweiser trail," she discovered that he'd spent the next night at yet another illegal poker game at a Motel 6 in the South Bay.

Typically my father began tracking his brother after a forty-eight-hour absence, the same rule the police apply to missing persons. My sister refused to respond to Uncle Ray's sudden departures and routine debauchery with the same unruffled acceptance adopted by the rest of the family. Fighting Rae on anything always made me question the cost-benefit ratio, But when it came to Uncle Ray, I let her win on all fronts.

A cease-fire was enacted while I helped look for my uncle. I picked my sister up after school and we began an exhaustive search of all the run-down motels in a fifty-mile radius. The poker games, which were illegal in and of themselves, often included illegal substances, prostitution, and a fair amount of cigar smoke damage. Ray and his friends discovered that the individually run economy motels were the most likely to look the other way. The men would pool their money and add an extra two hundred dollars for "cleaning costs" to the bill and were welcome to return at a later, randomly selected, date.

My contribution to the search was acting as Rae's chauffeur. She used study hour at school to map motels on the Internet and planned a three-hour road trip, connecting the dots to twelve different establishments in the Bay Area. Generally, Uncle Ray's poker buddies stuck to motels off Highway 1 or 280, usually staying between Marin County and San Mateo. I'd pull the car into the parking lot, Rae would jump out, go to the front office, show them a photograph of Uncle Ray — keeping a twenty-dollar bill in sight — and ask whether they had seen this man recently.

The first five stops on the motel connect-the-dots were dead ends, but the desk clerk at the sixth motel said that Ray had just checked out. He was with a woman, but the clerk could not offer a description or comment on their future travel plans. We spent the rest of the afternoon hitting the next six motels, to no avail. Instead of doing her math homework that night, my sister re-phoned all of Ray's gambling buddies, asking whether hookers were at the last poker game. It goes without saying that a fourteen-year-old girl querying sixty-something men about illegal prostitution is unlikely to result in a forthright response.

"Kid, your uncle's a grown man. What he does, who he does, is none of my business" was the standard response.

When the phone interviews proved futile, Rae turned to mapping more motel stops for the next day. She tried to convince my parents to let her skip school to continue the "manhunt," but thankfully, they refused. There had been twenty-four Lost Weekends before the twenty-fifth. Each one dulled the impact of the next.

After three days of afternoon searches, after hitting eighty percent of the motels within Uncle Ray's generally agreed-upon travel perimeter, my sister and I found him shacked up with a redhead named Marla in

416

room 3B at the Days Inn in South San Francisco. Uncle Ray borrowed the fifty bucks I had on me, gave it to his new friend, and insisted that we drive her the fifteen miles home to Redwood City.

Uncle Ray walked Marla to her door and they said their good-byes. After we were back on the road, my sister turned to Uncle Ray and asked him if he had practiced safe sex. Uncle Ray told her to mind her own business. Rae then offered a collection of rehab clinic brochures as "reading material" for the ride home. This was not the first time Rae broached the subject of rehab to Uncle Ray and it would not be the last.

Enemies can unite for a common purpose, but when that purpose no longer exists, they are often enemies once again. The lull in my family's discord, precipitated by the search for Uncle Ray, ended immediately upon his return.

Uncle Ray helped me load the last few boxes into my car and asked me where I was planning on staying. I told him I would probably crash at a motel while I apartment-hunted. He told me motels were depressing — an odd statement from a man who considers them his second home — and offered me the keys to an old friend's place in the Richmond district. The friend was out of town at a "convention" (Uncle Ray used finger quotes) for two weeks. I moved into retired lieutenant Bernie Peterson's two-bedroom apartment that afternoon. Based on the decor, one would conclude that Bernie had two loves in his life — golf and women — although women had to be listed second and in the plural.

Bernie's apartment had the sad tidiness of a career bachelor with a regular maid. His decorations lacked taste but not expense, as if he purchased items purely to impress, but without consideration for comfort or design. The result was a crime scene of patterns, every view punctuated by a freshly dusted amateur golf trophy and an expensively framed photograph of a buxom, deceased starlet. Uncle Ray gave me the grand tour, which meant showing me where Bernie kept his liquor and snacks. Opting not to waste an opportunity of freedom from the watchful eye of his younger niece, Uncle Ray opened a jar of peanuts, cracked a beer, and sat down on the couch.

"So what is it about this case that's making you work overtime?"

"It just doesn't add up."

"What have you got so far?"

"Abigail Snow. The mother. She claims

her husband is golfing when he is in fact living twenty-five miles away with another woman and has been for ten years. She cleans obsessively and masks the smell of bleach with potpourri."

"She sounds like a ball of fun."

"Her son, Martin Snow, cheated his parents out of at least a hundred thousand dollars and he's made it clear that he doesn't want me looking for his brother. Isn't that suspicious?"

"Yeah," Uncle Ray concedes. "They usually want you to look. What else?"

"The friend of the brothers, Greg Larson. Even though he went camping with Andrew and Martin almost every other time they went camping, this particular weekend, he went to a concert in the city. And he buys a car from his uncle around the time of Andrew's disappearance, but no one remembers the car."

"Maybe he bought the car for someone else. Maybe he kept it in a garage to fix up and resell."

"A Toyota Camry, Uncle Ray. It's not the kind of car you buy as a restoration project. And one more thing. I got a phone call from a woman claiming to be Abigail Snow, asking me to stop working the case. But Abigail never called me."

"Could it have been your mom?" asked Uncle Ray.

"I don't think so. I asked. She denied it."

Uncle Ray takes a sip of beer and mulls over the information. "What's your next move?" he asked.

"I think I need to revisit Hank Farber," I replied.

I got up from the couch and grabbed my coat and car keys. Uncle Ray also got up and grabbed his coat and car keys.

"Where are we going?" he asked.

" 'We' are not going anywhere."

"Sure we are," he said with an uncompromising grin.

"How much are they paying you?"

"Double overtime."

"Traitor."

"Sorry, kid. I need the cash."

The standoff was brief. I weighed my options and figured that the trip down the stairs was the only chance I had at bridging a gap between me and Uncle Ray. Once we were on the road, there was no way I could lose him.

So I made a run for it. A move that I thought would prompt my uncle into his first aerobic activity in years. Instead, he leisurely shut and locked the door behind him and sauntered down the stairs. I raced down two flights and out the door.

Ray was still on the top landing as I reached my car. I was breathing relief until I looked down and discovered a piece of well-chewed gum over the keyhole. As I peeled the sticky substance out of the lock and off the key, Uncle Ray had time to casually reach his car, unlock the door, start the engine, and adjust the radio station before I was even inside mine.

"Disgusting, Uncle Ray," I shouted over to him.

He rolled down the window, shrugged his shoulders apologetically, and said, "You run fast, kid."

The Snow Case: Chapter 7

Rather than risk a car accident or test Ray's more-than-ample skills, I drove to Hank Farber's apartment well under the speed limit and without any creative use of turn signals. I parked in front of Farber's building, waited for Uncle Ray to pull into a space down the block, and knocked on Ray's window.

"I need to rattle this guy. See if he's lying. Can you help me out?"

"Love to," said my uncle and we entered the foyer of the cheap Tenderloin building.

Judging from the spacing between apartments, the entire structure was made up of equally small studio apartments. The carpet in the hallway was holding twenty years of human dander and coffee stains. I hoped that Hank would crack a window, but he seemed more interested in making a stew of his own cigarette smoke and body odor.

It was 3:00 p.m. when Uncle Ray and I

arrived at Hank Farber's home. According to my uncle's calculations based on the empties on the kitchen counter and Farber's lazy speech, Hank was probably on his third beer. Like a good host, Hank offered refreshments and my uncle gratefully accepted. They chatted briefly about Sunday's 49ers game and then contemplated the future of baseball. Uncle Ray asked Hank if he had any snacks. Hank cracked open a bag of potato chips and prepared a plate of sandwich cookies.

I asked Hank once again what he remembered about the weekend Andrew Snow went missing. In less than a minute, Hank delivered, almost verbatim, the same details he offered up on our previous meeting: His nephew Greg was visiting; he went to a concert of one of those loud rock bands; he came home around 11:00 p.m.

We left after Uncle Ray finished off his second beer. On the short, stuffy elevator ride to the lobby, Uncle Ray said, "He starts early."

"What? The drinking?" I asked.

"Yeah. He starts early," Uncle Ray repeated, lost in thought.

"What are you thinking?" I asked.

"I'm thinking he was probably asleep by

11:00 p.m., if he drank anywhere near that much."

"It was years ago, Uncle Ray. Maybe he wasn't so bad back then."

"He's been at it a while," said my uncle, and I was inclined to believe him.

"Do you think he was coached?" I asked.

"That would be my guess," said my uncle. "There's no way he'd remember that week-end, let alone the exact time his nephew came home, after twelve years. There's no way."

I drove back to my parents' house with Uncle Ray in tow. The driveway was empty, so I knew my parents were out. I decided to do some research in the office and was surprised to discover that the locks had not been changed. Uncle Ray followed me in and looked over my shoulder as I ran a criminal, civil, and bankruptcy search on Hank Farber through our databases. Out of the corner of my eye, I could see Uncle Ray jotting down notes on a square pad of paper.

"What are you doing?" I asked.

"I got to put this in the report."

"What report?"

"The surveillance report."

"On me?"

"I don't get paid unless there's a report."

If I were still employed or even employable, I would have offered to match their price to get him off the job. But standing between Ray and money is the same as standing between Ray and a beer. There ain't no mountain high enough.

As predicted, Hank Farber had a record. No history of violent crimes, but a series of public drunkenness arrests and DUIs as far back as fifteen years. It didn't come as a complete shock that his driver's license had been revoked, but the timing was interesting since it happened just two months before Andrew Snow's disappearance.

I showed the report to my uncle since he was going to look at it anyway.

"What do you make of it?" he asked.

"I think if he was staying off the road as he was supposed to, Greg could have taken the car at any time. Just gave him the money for it a few weeks later. It would be easy to fool a guy who spends that much time intoxicated."

"He doesn't know how to pace himself. That's his problem," said my uncle.

"Yeah, that's his problem," I replied sarcastically.

I phoned the Marin County Sheriff's Office and left a message for Sheriff Larson.

Uncle Ray jotted that down in his notes, too. I got up to leave; Uncle Ray shadowed my every move.

"I can't take much more of this, Uncle Ray."

"Sorry, kid. I'm just doing my job."

"I can't go anywhere without a tail. Do you have any idea what that feels like?"

"As it turns out, I do. A few years before the cancer, the IAB was investigating me for some missing heroin at a drug bust. I couldn't take a whiz without some guy in a coat watching me. It was rough, I tell you."

Uncle Ray and I, like two pathetic mimes, were in the middle of a game of mirror when my parents entered the office. Ray threw up his hands and said, "I'm done for the day." He raced into the kitchen and made himself a pastrami sandwich.

I looked at my mom and dad and debated whether I should make a run for it. I'm faster on my feet, but if they pulled anything like Uncle Ray's gum trick, I wouldn't have a chance. As I weighed my options, I inched closer to the door, hoping to casually afford myself a clear exit.

My mother kicked the door shut with her foot. "We need to talk," she said in that voice she used to intimidate.

It was then that I noticed the open window. The Spellman office is on the first floor. The window is just a five-foot drop to the ground, and the cement path along the side of the house leads directly to the driveway, where my car was parked unobstructed, I believe. I could kick open the window screen and make a run for it. My parents, being adults, wouldn't take the window. They would have to go through three doors and a flight of stairs to meet me out front. My confidence grew. I could escape. Avoid a talk. Have a day of freedom.

"What do you want to talk about?" I asked, shuffling toward the window.

"If you want to be out of the business, then be out of the business," said my mother.

"What does that mean?"

"Stop working the Snow case."

"But that was our deal — one last job. Remember?"

"Consider yourself fired," said my dad.

"He's threatening to sue us," said my mother.

"I told you not to worry about Martin Snow. He's bluffing," I said.

"We can't take that chance, Isabel," said my mother. "You have to stop this now. I mean it. Now."

I would have stopped, had this been an

ordinary unsolvable case. But it wasn't. Opening the Snow case only brought about more questions, more suspicions. Not a single answer. Three people were lying to me, a car had vanished, and a hundred thousand dollars was unaccounted for. This was almost a real mystery. We never have those in my line of work. I couldn't stop. Not then. I had to get out of that house. It was the only thing I was sure of.

I pushed open the window, kicked out the screen, and jumped feet-first to the gravelly path alongside the house. I ran to my car and opened the door. The lock, thankfully, was unobstructed. I could hear my father call out to me but couldn't decipher the words. I put the key into the ignition and . . . the car was completely dead.

I sat for a moment listening to the breeze of my quick breath. My mother stood at the front door, watching me. I popped the hood of my car and checked the engine. There was no art to what I found. The wires hung uselessly in the air and an empty space where the battery should have been stared back at me with smug silence.

"Where's the battery?" I asked my mother.

She shrugged her shoulders and said, "I don't know, sweetie. Where did you see it last?" Then she returned to the house.

I sat down in my car and tried to come up with a plan, a plan that would include getting a battery and driving off undetected. An impossible plan, I realized, as I sat there, reluctantly accepting that my parents had outwitted me once again. I stopped thinking about the consequences or reason or what was inherently right; I just wanted to win, just this once. I left Martin Snow yet another telephone message, calling his bluff. I made it clear that his threats didn't scare me. I also suggested it was time for us to have another talk.

Rae opened my car door and asked where I was going and if she could come. I said sure, since I was going inside. I stormed through the house, into the office, through the kitchen, and circled around the living room. Rae followed me along the entire path until I spun around and grabbed her by the shoulders.

"Wanna make fifty bucks?" I asked.

"Is that a rhetorical question?"

"A car battery is hidden somewhere in this house. Find it."

I set Rae loose to search for the battery while I combed the house for my parents. I caught them on their way downstairs to the office.

I was ready for a fight. I was ready to end

this once and for all.

"Unless you want to spend the rest of your life looking at me through a set of binoculars, you will stop. No more tails, no more bugs, no more lies, and no more threats. Just. Let. Me. Go."

I turned to leave and found Rae standing behind me, holding the battery. Her hands and shirt were covered with auto grease. I reached for the battery and she stepped back.

"Where are you going?" she asked.

"I don't know," I replied.

"Are you coming back?"

I turned and looked at my parents, then back to Rae. "Not anytime soon."

Rae stepped back and I could see her small fingers clutching the battery with a death grip. I could see she was prepared to fight me for it.

"I'm doing this for you," I said.

"No, you're not."

"I'm doing this so that one day you won't wake up and realize that you don't know how to behave like a normal human being."

"Rae, give your sister the battery," my mother said.

"No!" Rae shouted back.

Uncle Ray walked into the hallway, disengaged Rae's greasy fingers, and handed me the battery. He then turned to my parents and said, "Give her a fifteen-minute head start. Let's all take a breather, shall we?"

I left the house, attached the battery, and drove off without a family member tailing me. I wasn't sure how long or if it would last, but Uncle Ray had given me the one thing I really needed — a chance to breathe.

I decided to drive over to Daniel's, hoping to figure out which episode it was where Max crosses a street by climbing in and out of a series of cabs. But then my phone rang. It was David.

He asked me to meet him in the Haight. Now. I asked why and he told me I would find out soon enough. Before we hung up, he asked, "Is Mom still tailing you?"

"I'm not sure," I replied.

"Don't come unless you're sure you're alone," he said and quickly hung up.

Puff #2

Twenty minutes later I was sitting with my brother in a tattoo parlor, reviewing a portfolio of potential body art.

"I never asked her to get rid of the tattoos," David said.

I believed him. What I still couldn't believe was that my brother was dating, no, cohabitating with my best friend. My brother —

the square, perfect lawyer in thousand-dollar suits — with a woman who has pierced or permanently dyed half of her body. My best friend since eighth grade, a woman he has known for over fifteen years. Petra had removed three pieces of body art since she began seeing David — Puff the magic dragon, Jimi Hendrix's RIP, and a heart and arrow with "Brandon" in calligraphy over it.

I had automatically assumed that David had initiated the body-art removal through comments subtly designed to undermine her confidence. Instead, David used subtly designed questions to find out where she'd had the body art done. He needed me to identify the missing pieces. His plan was to tattoo his arm with one of the tattoos she had removed, in an effort to convince her to stop. We opted for Puff, since David was never a big Hendrix fan and "Brandon" was just too gay.

David began to sweat as Clive coated his upper arm with alcohol.

"Is this going to hurt?" asked David.

"This will hurt me more than it'll hurt you," said Clive as he turned on the motor. I decided I liked Clive. A lot.

David sustained his wince for the next three hours. Other than the accompanying moans of pain, I did all of the talking:

"You better hope your face doesn't freeze like that."

"Tell me you're not crying."

"Oh, buck up, will you?"

"You know tattoos are permanent, right?"

"This is fun. Thanks for inviting me."

David was pale and nauseous by the end of the session. We walked down the Haight to a local brewery and ordered a round. I had to ask the obvious question.

"Have you recently had a near-death experience?"

"Excuse me?" David responded grumpily. His wince had reduced to a mild tic.

"Last I heard, you were commitment phobic," I clarified.

"People change."

"Not that again."

"I thought you'd be happy for me."

"I am happy for you. For her, not so much."

"I love her, Isabel."

"Why?"

"Because she doesn't think I'm perfect."

"I can't begin to imagine what it is like to be you."

David adjusted the bandage on his tattoo. "If she asks, tell her I was brave."

"Sure," I said. "What's another lie?"

THE SNOW CASE:
CHAPTER 8

On my way back to Bernie's apartment, my cell phone rang.

"Is this Isabel?"

"Yes. Who is this?"

"Martin Snow."

"Finally."

"What do you want?"

"I need you to meet me," I said.

"Then the phone calls have to stop."

"Meet me just once and they will."

"Where?"

"The San Francisco Public Library."

"I can be there in an hour," he said.

I promptly drove to the library and found a seat in the history section. I phoned Daniel, trying to make plans for later, but he wasn't home. Then I tapped compulsively for the next thirty minutes. Occasionally I'd try to pick up a book and read it, but my mind couldn't focus and I went back to tapping until Martin Snow arrived.

"This is the last time I'm going to do this," Martin said sternly.

"Go to the library? That's too bad. They say people don't read like they used to."

"Why am I here?" he asked point-blank. I decided my pleasantries were wasted on him.

"I just have a few questions. Then you can go."

"Shoot."

"Who called me pretending to be your mother?"

"Are you sure it wasn't my mother?"

"Positive."

"I don't know," he said without a hint of curiosity. "Next question."

"What happened to the Toyota Camry that Greg bought from his uncle?" I asked.

Martin swallowed and pretended to scan the bookshelf in thought. "I think he bought it for a friend."

"What friend?" I asked.

"I don't know."

"What did you do with the hundred thousand dollars your parents supposedly spent on your education?"

"I went to school for seven years, Ms. Spellman. Higher education is extremely expensive. I'm sure you wouldn't know about that."

I smiled at the dig. My brother has given me harsher insults over brunch.

"You shouldn't have come here," I said. "Your friend the sheriff is a better liar than you. At least he doesn't break a sweat. I think you know exactly what happened to your brother. If you ever want me off your back, you'll tell me the truth."

Martin got to his feet and tried to conjure a threatening stare. "You'll be hearing from my attorney," he said and quickly made his exit.

I left the library and went back to Bernie's place. Jake Hand was parked out front — once again, asleep. I would have loved to rat him out to my mom, but Jake's lack of work ethic served me well.

Just as I was about to go to bed, Daniel called.

"Isabel, where are you?"

"At Bernie's place."

"Who is Bernie?"

"An old friend of my uncle's."

"Why are you staying with him?"

"I'm not. He's out of town."

"Oh," Daniel replied. "Guess who just called me?"

"The police?"

"Your mother."

"That was my second guess," I replied.

"This isn't funny," he said, clearly losing his patience.

"I'm sorry. Why did she call?"

"To ask for help. She wants you to stop bothering the Snow family. She told me they are going to file a TRO. What's a TRO?"

"A temporary restraining order."

"Are you serious?"

"He's bluffing, Daniel. Don't worry about it."

"I'm starting to find your behavior disturbing."

"That's my mother talking. Listen, once this case is over, everything will get back to normal."

"That's the problem, Isabel! I don't think you know what that is."

I managed to convince Daniel that I knew what normal was, although I didn't convince myself. The phone call ended with a plan to visit him at the office the following day. He wasn't as much in the mood for hours of dated television as I was. I got off the phone and went directly to bed. I put in a pair of earplugs, which drowned out the sounds of traffic and the exodus of drunken patrons leaving the pubs on the street below. They also drowned out the sound of Bernie coming home and getting into bed with me.

I screamed when I felt the hand on my ass. Bernie screamed when I screamed and he grabbed his heart. I quickly explained that I was Ray Spellman's niece and I needed a place to stay. I sat Bernie down on the bed and checked his pulse. After his heartbeat returned to normal, I made him a cup of tea. Bernie explained that he thought I was a welcome-home gift from his poker buddies.

"Do I look like a welcome-home gift?" I asked, wrapped in my best blue-and-green flannel pajamas.

"Not the best gift I ever had. But not the worst," he replied.

Bernie apologized in that men-will-be-men kind of way and kindly offered me his bed for the night.

"I'll take the couch," he said, followed by a wink. I checked Bernie's pulse one last time and gathered my things. Jake Hand was still asleep in his car and I managed to make my getaway undetected.

I drove two blocks away and slept until dawn in the backseat of my car. In the morning, I changed into street clothes and drove to the Marin County Sheriff's Office. Greg Larson kept me waiting two hours before he would see me. When I was finally guided back to his desk, he casually looked up from some paperwork and said, "Isabel, so good to see you again," in his carefully guarded fashion.

"What happened to your uncle's Toyota Camry?"

"I sold it to a used-car dealer a week after I bought it," he replied without a flinch. I got the feeling he came prepared for my questions.

"Why would you buy a car and sell it a week later?"

"If you looked up my uncle's record, which I assume you did, you'd have noticed the DUIs. All I wanted to do was get that car away from him so he couldn't hurt himself or anybody else."

"How noble. Do you have any paperwork on that?"

"It was twelve years ago, Isabel. You don't have to keep financial records past seven years. You know that."

"Do you remember the license plate number on that car?"

"No. I hear you haven't been sleeping, Isabel."

"Where did you hear that?"

"From your mother."

"When?"

"I called her this morning. When you got here," Larson said, still only breathing and blinking. His fractional expressions were starting to really get on my nerves.

"Did you tell her I was here?"

"Yes. That's why I kept you waiting two hours. To give her time to take a shower and make it over the bridge. She's really quite charming."

I stood up and looked out of Larson's window. My mother was parked in the spot next to mine.

"I don't believe this," I said, slowly losing my breath.

"She's worried. She says you're obsessed with this case and you won't stop."

Through the window my mother waved at me. When Sheriff Larson seated himself behind his desk, his back facing the window, she smashed my left taillight and quickly returned to her car.

"Did you see that?" I said.

"See what?" Larson casually asked as he turned around.

I pointed to my car. "She just smashed my taillight."

"Are you sure?"

"Yes. It wasn't like that before."

"That is unfortunate."

"I want to file vandalism charges."

"Against your mother?"

"Who else?"

"Isabel, you are free to file a report, but without any witnesses —"

"*I* am a witness."

"Not the most reliable one."

"*You* are a witness."

"I didn't see anything, Isabel."

"Let's see. You look out the window. My taillight is intact. Then you look again and it's smashed. The only person in the vicinity is my mother. What the hell did they teach you in the police academy, how to chew on toothpicks?"

"Among other things," said the sheriff, refusing, yet again, to give me any kind of reaction.

I knew I was getting nowhere with him, but I had to end our meeting with a threat.

"I'm onto you."

Weak, I know.

I walked outside and knocked on my mother's window. She casually laid down her newspaper, started her car, and rolled down the window.

"Isabel, what are you doing here?" my mother said, feigning pleasant surprise.

"You're paying for that," I said and got into my car.

I had only one thing on my agenda that day: Lose Mom. I drove to Petra's hair salon. I parked two blocks away and entered through the back door. She was going over her schedule for the next day and was free to talk. Free to do the talking, that is.

"I hated that damn tattoo. Every time I looked at it, it reminded me of dry heaving for four hours straight."

"That's what all your tattoos remind you of," I said.

"You were with him the entire time. You could have stopped him. Now I have to look at that damn thing on his shoulder the rest of my life."

"The rest of your life?" I asked.

"However long it lasts. You should have stopped him."

"I don't get to see my brother in pain all that often."

"He refuses to get rid of it."

"He just got it."

"Is this your version of revenge, Izzy?"

"No. My version is an awful lot like plain old revenge. I didn't stop him because a) my mother will go into hysterics when she sees it, and b) it meant he loved you. He could say it all he wanted, but he's the kind of guy who's said it before. I figured once you saw Puff on his arm, you'd believe him."

Petra wanted to stay angry. She really hated that tattoo. But I was right, and rather than acknowledge that, we changed subjects.

"Your mother still tailing you?" she asked.

"Twenty-four/seven. I need to borrow your car."

"I don't have it."

"Where is it?"

"David has it."

"Why?"

"Because your father is using David's car."

"Why?"

"Because you smashed out every single light on your dad's car."

I exited the front entrance of Petra's salon wearing a blonde wig and an oversize army jacket that I nicked from the lost and found. I might as well have worn a bull's-eye on my back. There was no losing my mother. She heckled me as I strolled to my car. Without a foolproof plan, all I could do was wear her out. And I figured, as I tested her ability to stay awake, I might as well take a nap myself. I had planned to drop by Daniel's office anyway, which was coincidentally the last place I had had a decent rest.

Mrs. Sanchez, Daniel's trusted employee, was not pleased to see me. But she was more than happy to have me out of the waiting room and asleep in a chair. She kindly informed me that I didn't have the personality to carry off blonde hair. I was so tired, I didn't think about what that meant. I simply leaned back in the dental chair and slept.

Daniel woke me approximately two hours later.

"We need to talk," he said.

Even in my postnap fog, my instinctual response to those words — words I'd heard far too many times — kicked in. Daniel didn't just want to have a chat about our relationship, he wanted to end it.

"Oh no," I said, jumping to my feet.

"Oh no, what?" he replied.

"I got to go."

"Where?"

"Anywhere."

"Isabel, we need to talk."

"I don't need to talk."

"Well, I need to talk."

"No, you don't."

"Yes, I do."

"You just think you do. But really, you don't."

"Sit down."

"No."

"Yes."

"Never."

"We need to talk."

"I just took a nap."

"What's your point?"

"You can't break up with me right after I take a nap."

"Why not?"

"Because if you do, I will forever associate naps with being broken up with."

In truth, I knew the breakup was inevitable ever since the fake drug deal. It made him wonder how many more fake drug deals or their equivalent would be in our future. If I could do this to my own family, I could do it to him, too. For the Castillos, love meant trust and respect; for the Spellmans, the definition was far messier.

Daniel followed me out of the office, mumbling something about how I couldn't always use the napping excuse.

My father leaned against David's shiny black Mercedes and struck the pose of a middle-aged man who doesn't care that he's getting old because he's got an unbelievable piece of machinery to drive. At least that's how it would have appeared to a complete stranger. The sadder truth is that my father's sense of pride was merely in the fact that he had a son who owned an amazing piece of machinery and was willing to lend it to him at the last minute because his older daughter had smashed out the lights on two of the three family-owned vehicles. The even sadder truth was that the father thought that if he drove the son's expensive, impressive, and hard-to-repair car, his daughter would leave it unharmed. That was the saddest part.

My father waved at Daniel in a friendly, denying-everything-that-had-previously-occurred kind of way. Daniel had still not forgiven him for their first encounter, and so he nodded and smiled weakly in return. He then noticed my smashed taillight and asked the obvious question.

"Isabel, did you know your taillight is broken?"

"Yes."

"How did that happen?"

I popped the trunk of my car and pulled out a hammer I keep in a toolbox. Before my father could react, I smashed the front right headlight on David's car.

"Just like that," I said.

My father shook his head, disappointed in me and himself. Daniel turned to me, horrified.

"Why did you do that, Isabel?" Daniel asked.

"Because he smashed *my* taillight."

"And why did he do that?"

My father stepped closer to Daniel and explained, "When you're following someone at night, it's easier to keep a tail on a car with one working taillight rather than two."

"Why did she smash your headlight, then?"

"Two reasons," replied my dad. "One, because she's mad and wants payback, and two, because it will be easier for her to tell whether she was able to lose me or not."

"How long is this going to go on?" Daniel asked my father.

"As long as it takes," said my dad as he got back into David's car.

Car Chase #2

I couldn't see the detached expression on Daniel's face because my brain was already plotting my escape. I got into my car and started the engine. I hoped that the nap had sharpened my reflexes, but I knew deep in my heart that losing my father would require a superhuman effort, an effort I didn't truly believe I was capable of.

I zigzagged through the heavy traffic of West Portal Avenue, then turned left onto

Ocean Avenue, which cleared soon after San Francisco State. My father stayed on my bumper the entire ride. He had six months of police academy and twenty years on the job to perfect his technique. He's outrun people far more skilled or more indifferent to death than I. He knows I won't risk my or his safety and so this chase is more of a conversation than actual pursuit. He phoned me on my cell phone and everything that had not been said was.

"I could do this all day, sweetheart."

"So could I," I replied.

"Tell me how to end this, Isabel."

"Stop following me."

"Stop running."

"You first."

"No, *you* first."

"It appears we have a stalemate," I said, and hung up the phone.

I wove my way back to Geary Boulevard and along a series of residential streets in the Richmond district — San Francisco's sophisticated version of tract housing glided through my peripheral vision. My father sustained his unrelenting tail, not realizing that I was no longer interested in losing him, at least not this way, when there was an easier way.

I parked off Geary Boulevard on one of

those impossible-to-park-on side streets that house a dense collection of two- and three-family homes. I parked in a legal space two blocks from the pub, checked the street cleaning signs, locked my car, and passed my father on the way to the bar. He rolled down his window.

"Where are you going?"

"The Pig and Whistle."

"What are you gonna do there?"

"Get drunk."

I walked off knowing that he'd take the bait. My father parked illegally, tossed his old badge on the dashboard, and followed me into the bar.

Dad bought the first round and the next round and the round after that. I bought the fourth round against great protest. While my father and I got good and tanked, we took a brief respite from our game of cat and mouse.

"So how are things with you and the dentist?"

"He has a name."

"How are things with you and Daniel Castillo, DDS?"

"Fine."

"When can we have a real conversation, Izzy?"

"As soon as you stop gathering intelligence."

"Okay, I'll start. There's a chance Ray will go into rehab."

"What kind of chance?"

"I'd say ten percent or so."

"What are the chances it will stick?"

"About ten percent."

"So there's a one percent chance that Uncle Ray will get clean," I said.

"That sounds about right," Dad replied, his words finally starting to slur.

"Has anyone explained the odds to Rae? I mean, if she's going to be a walking after-school special, someone should discuss the cost-benefit ratio with her."

"We've had the cost-benefit talk."

"Still, it's impressive that he's considering it."

"We know you faked the drug deal."

"What gave it away?"

"The dentist can't act, for one thing, and I sat Rae down with a batch of Rice Krispies Treats midweek. Told her she could eat them all if she talked. She talked."

"Is there no low you won't sink to?"

"I gave my kid Rice Krispies Treats. You pretended to snort cocaine in front of her."

"I pretended to snort cocaine because you bugged my apartment."

"We bugged your apartment because you

were becoming obsessed with a case. A case that is over, by the way."

"A case that you gave me."

"It was a mistake."

"What?"

"Giving you the case."

"It wasn't your only mistake."

My dad picked up another basket of pretzels from the bar and returned to the table.

"The first few times I found you passed out on the front lawn, I thought you were dead."

"That was a long time ago, Dad. I haven't passed out in years."

"So Old Isabel isn't making a comeback?"

"If Old Isabel were back, she wouldn't be having drinks with her dad."

"What would she be doing?"

"Picking up one of those nice Irish boys at the bar or trying to score a dime bag in Dolores Park."

"So where do we go from here?" he asked.

"I leave. You don't follow me."

"Not going to happen."

"I think it is," I said as I slowly put on my coat and left a tip on the table.

"What makes you so confident?" he asked.

"You're too drunk to drive and I can outrun you," I replied, grinning wildly. I'd had very few knock-'em-out-of-the-park wins in the past few weeks and I was enjoying this moment. I slowly backed away to the exit. Then I swung the door open and booked out of the bar.

I could hear the rattling from the door as my father made his clumsy exit. There was no point in turning back to see his location. I just ran as fast and as hard as I could. Three blocks later I made a right turn on Fillmore Street and caught a cab. I ducked down in the backseat just in case. The driver found me suspicious and was more than happy when he dropped me off and received payment for his services. I ducked into an overdone tourist-trap café in the Marina. Amid wealthy Midwesterners and their furs on vacation, I drank coffee and sobered up.

A few hours later, as I simultaneously walked off the beer buzz and the coffee jitters, I got another phone call.

"Isabel?"

"Yes. Who is this?"

"Meet me at the West Oakland BART station in one hour," said an unrecognizable voice on the other end. It could have been a man or a woman, impossible to say.

"Nah, I'm busy."

"Don't you want some answers, Isabel?"

"Yes. For instance, I'd like to know who

I'm talking to."

"Not over the phone."

"I'm not crossing the bridge without a good reason. You know what traffic is like at this hour?"

"I can answer all of your questions about Andrew Snow."

"Who is this?"

"Like I said, meet me and you'll find out."

"I'll think about it. Which BART station, did you say?"

"West Oakland. Southeast exit. Two hours."

"Make it three. I'm still drunk."

I couldn't return to my car; my father would have removed a vital part of the engine, like the carburetor. I hopped on the Fillmore bus and phoned Daniel at his office. It took some persuading to get Mrs. Sanchez to release the phone to Daniel, but eventually she did.

"I need to borrow your car."

"Who is this?"

"Isabel."

"You're kidding, right?"

"It's an emergency."

"Isabel."

"Please."

This negotiation was ultimately an unspoken one. I needed something from Daniel — a car — and Daniel needed something from me — an easy breakup. To assuage his guilt, he agreed to lend me his BMW. I waited on the street outside the Folsom and Third Street parking structure. The streetlight flickered for five minutes and went out. Daniel had agreed to meet me after his tennis game. He was late. I grew edgy as I sobered up. Every sound, from footsteps in the distance to aluminum cans traveling with the breeze, made my heart stop.

Then Daniel turned the corner. When he saw me, he averted his gaze. I had seen that look before. It was always followed by "We need to talk." I knew what was about to happen, but I still tried to postpone the inevitable.

"Did you make sure you weren't followed?" I asked.

"Who would follow me?" Daniel replied.

"My mother or my father."

"I don't believe I was followed."

I held out my hand, hoping for a silent gift of the keys.

"This will never work," he said.

"What?"

"You and me."

"Why not?"

"What would we tell our kids?"

"What kids?"

"If we had kids, how would we explain how Mommy and Daddy met?"

"We'd lie, of course."

"It's over. I can't do this."

I won't bore you with the rest of the conversation. I'll simply provide Daniel's epitaph.

Ex-boyfriend #9:

Name:	Castillo, Daniel
Age:	38
Occupation:	Dentist
Hobby:	Tennis
Duration:	3 months
Last Words:	"It was over after the fake drug deal."

. . . The Ford screeches to a halt about ten feet behind the BMW. I turn off the ignition and take a few deep breaths. I casually get out of the car and walk over to the sedan. I knock on the driver's-side window. A moment passes and the window rolls down. I put my hand on the hood of the car and lean in just a bit.

"Mom. Dad. This has to stop."

Before they can compose a sentence that would properly convey their disappointment in me, I slip my hand behind my back, pull out my pocket knife, and slash their front left tire. They gave me no choice. It was the only way to end the chase. They're not as shocked as you might expect. My father whispers my name, shaking his head. My mother turns away, hiding her rage. I stick the knife in my pocket and back away, shrugging my shoulders.

"It doesn't have to be like this."

I drive away, satisfied that I've bought myself some time. I turn onto Mission Street, heading for the entrance to the Bay Bridge. An accident on South Van Ness has stalled traffic to a standstill and the rush of elation from my newfound freedom is dulled by the blasting of horns and the ticking of the clock on the dashboard. The chance of me making it across the bridge and to the West Oakland BART station within the next twenty minutes is a near-impossible task.

I'm about to veer onto the Thirteenth Street on-ramp when my phone rings.

"Hello?"

"Izzy, Milo here."

"What can I do for you?"

"You can get your sister out of my bar before the cops shut me down."

"Milo, I'm busy. Have you tried Uncle Ray?"

"Yeah, he doesn't answer. And I just called your dad and he told me you slashed his tire. I'm not even going to ask. All I'm saying is that it's Saturday night and I got a fourteen-year-old girl in my bar and I want her out of here."

"Let me talk to her."

Rae took the phone and said, "I wouldn't have a drinking problem if things were better at home."

"I'll be there in ten minutes. Stay put."

My phone rings again just after I disconnect the call.

"Isabel."

"Yes."

"You're late," says the unidentifiable voice.

"Seriously, who is this?"

"I thought you wanted to solve this case."

"I need another hour. My sister's drinking again."

"You've got forty-five minutes and then I'm gone."

I'm two blocks from the Philosopher's Club and the phone rings one more time.

"Izzy, it's Milo. Tell Rae she left her scarf here."

"Tell her yourself."

"Didn't you pick her up already?"

"No, I didn't."

"But she's gone."

GONE

My foot was on the floor all the way to Milo's. I slammed on the brakes and double-parked in front of the bar. I threw open the door and raced inside. It was the look on Milo's face that shook me. Fear is more a lack of expression than an expression. Fear pulls all the blood from the extremities to concentrate on the activities that sustain life, like keeping your heart pumping. Milo visibly paled. I could see his lips moving, but could not make out the words over the hum of the bar crowd and the sound of my own breath. I walked through to the back of the bar, pushing aside patrons blocking my path. I checked the restroom and the exit into the alley.

Milo pointed toward the front of the bar and led me outside. He showed me the spot on the stoop where she'd been waiting. We circled the block and questioned all the sidewalk traffic. We got in my car and covered every side street within a three-mile radius. We phoned the house three times and her cell phone twice. We returned to the bar and I tried her cell phone again as we circled the perimeter. And then I heard it. Her phone ringing. Milo pulled the lid off the trash can and the phone was sitting on top. I picked up the phone and turned to Milo.

"There has to be some explanation, Izzy. Maybe she lost the phone and somebody else tossed it."

I drove home breaking every traffic law in the book. I drove home knowing that something horrible had happened that could not be undone. I drove home trying to remember the last time I saw my sister, wondering whether it would be the last time.

Rae had been gone only an hour and yet I was certain her absence was much more than a miscommunication. Rae doesn't disappear. That's not her MO. She telephones. She communicates. She prefers chauffeuring to public transportation. She lets you know everything that is going on in her mind. She doesn't run off when you've told her to stay put. She doesn't do that.

It seemed like minutes had passed before I could steady my hand enough to open the front door of my family's home. So long, it briefly occurred to me, that the locks might have been changed. When the door finally flew open, I ran through the house shouting my sister's name.

I banged on every closed door in the hallway until I came upon Rae's bedroom door. I tried the knob, but it was locked. My hands were too shaky to attempt a pick. I kicked it twice, but it wouldn't budge. You can't kick open locked doors; that is a myth. I ran down to the storage room, grabbed an axe, and returned upstairs. I swung the axe against the lock until the wood around the deadbolt was splintered to pieces. Then I laid one final kick and the door swung open.

Uncle Ray watched me from the other end of the hallway.

"I had a spare key," he said, then picked up the phone and called my parents.

The stillness of her room felt unnatural, but the chill I felt was very real. Her bed was unmade — as usual. Clothes were strewn across the floor in her typical adolescent nonchalance. It was a room waiting for someone to return to it, and yet she hadn't returned.

I searched her desk until I came across her address book. I phoned all two of her friends, neither of whom knew where she was or where she could be. Uncle Ray telephoned his buddies at the police station, who agreed to file an early report.

I passed my parents in the hallway as I exited the room. Avoiding eye contact, I told them that I would comb the neighborhood. I said that so I could leave. I had hoped that the misty air outside would cure my nausea, but once I exited the house, I began vomiting in my mother's flower bed (not for the first time, I might add). In between violent heaving, my phone rang again.

"Isabel, where are you?" said that god-damn voice.

"Did you take her?" I asked. My breath was so weak I could barely get the question out.

"Take who?"

"My sister. Do you have her?"

"What are you talking about?"

"If you've done something to her, your life is over. It's over. Do you understand? They will kill you."

"Who?"

"My father will kill you. Or my mother, maybe. Or they might have a little competition to see who can do it first. Do you have her?"

"Who?"

"If you have her, give her back," I said and the line went dead.

THE INTERVIEW:
CHAPTER 6

Stone gathers his file, aligning each sheet in a perfect stack. He smacks the pages against the wood table to square the edges. He then slides his finger along the side, searching for the flat line. His finger touches on an errant edge and he smacks the stack again and then again. He slides the papers into a crisp file folder and dusts off the top, smoothing the already flat cover.

"They've got medication for that sort of thing," I say.

"I think that is all, Isabel. If you think of anything else, please call me."

"You need to speak to the Snow family."

"As I told you before, we don't think it's related to this case."

"But there's nothing else."

"There are countless possibilities."

"She's not a runaway. She knows how to fight."

"It could be a random abduction."

"Is that what you think? Because I know the statistics."

"That's all I need. Why don't you get some sleep now, Isabel."

Inspector Stone stands. I grab his arm and he freezes uncomfortably.

"Tell me the truth. Is she dead? Do you think she's dead?"

Just saying those words flattened me. Suddenly I wished he wouldn't answer. But he did.

"I hope not."

MISSING

Rae's disappearance was too impossible to explain. No family member could conjure a happily-ever-after scenario. There was an unsettling quiet to the house, a mixture of Rae's absent chatter mingled with stunned silence. An inability to speak that bordered on pathology. At times it seemed that we could not look at one another. Our war was too fresh to offer a soft shoulder to cry on. There was still the us-versus-them mentality. I returned home, sleeping in Rae's bedroom to catch any phone calls that might come her way. But my presence was hardly a consolation prize.

Within the first six hours of my sister's disappearance, her bedroom was searched by the police and then ransacked by every single member of the Spellman family. No relevant evidence was discovered, but the police did find a hollowed-out algebra book holding almost two thousand dollars in cash, which led to further questions and a lengthy discussion between David and my parents.

Within twelve hours of Rae's disappearance, Milo and Jake Hand had plastered the city with missing-person signs. My mother and I spent four hours each on the road, just looking for that blue-striped shirt. As always, we remembered such things. My father called in favors with every PI he ever swapped cards with. The police, despite my father's protests, insisted on investigating every family member, and followed up with schoolmates and any other known acquaintances. Each quest was met with a dead end. David offered a two-hundred-thousand-dollar reward. Uncle Ray made a deal with God. If his niece came back home alive, he would go into rehab.

By day three, I had been awake for eighty-two straight hours. I managed a catnap or two, but nothing significant, nothing that could transform me into anything more than a jumbled set of nerves in two-day-old clothes.

When my interview with Inspector Stone was finished, I drove to the Philosopher's Club and sat down at the bar. Milo poured me a cup of coffee. When he wasn't looking, I added a shot of whiskey. I could tell from his own sallow coloring that he hadn't slept much himself. I could tell that he blamed himself for Rae's disappearance and the guilt was hitting him hard.

"Go home, Izzy," he said. "You look like shit."

"I look better than you do," I said.

"That's just 'cause you're prettier than me."

One hour and three stolen Irish whiskies later, Daniel entered the bar.

"Let's go, Isabel."

I noticed the conspiratorial head nod that transpired between the two men. I turned on Milo.

"You called him?"

"I was worried."

Daniel took my arm. "Time to sleep, Isabel."

Daniel took me back to his place, gave me a sleeping pill, and prepared the bed in the guest room. As I was about to fall asleep, I heard him on the phone to my mother, telling her I was okay.

I slept eight hours straight and awoke in an empty apartment. Daniel had left me a series of notes — arrows mostly — which directed me into the kitchen, where a breakfast of eggs, bacon, and toast was waiting for me. I ate the toast and shoved the rest of the food down the disposal. The narcotics-induced full night's rest had the agreeable effect of clearing my mind. It had been weeks since I had been able to confidently operate a motor vehicle. It was time to go back to work. It had now been four days since my sister disappeared.

THE SNOW CASE: CHAPTER 9

I needed to impose logic on Rae's disappearance. So far all I had was coincidence. A phone call from someone claiming to have the answers to the Snow case happened at the same time Rae vanished from the Philosopher's Club. The link was tenuous at best, but it was the only link, and my instincts insisted that it was the answer.

A detail that had been nagging at me from the start was the history professor. He claimed to have seen two brothers searching for Andrew the morning of his disappearance. I tossed it into the back of my head because there was a logical explanation: Memories are generally unreliable. In the absence of any other leads, I decided to check it out. I took the train back to West Portal, found my car three blocks from the bar, removed the parking ticket, and drove home and picked up the Snow file, which was still locked in my desk drawer. I skimmed the file for the name, which was not unforgettable.

As it conveniently turned out, Horace Greenleaf was a tenured prof at UC Berkeley. I phoned the history department, ascertained the professor's office hours, and made my way across the Bay Bridge. By midmorning the traffic was at a standstill and I couldn't help but wish that more people had day jobs.

I located Professor Greenleaf's office with just ten minutes to spare. I offered the professor an abbreviated explanation for my visit and he kindly offered me a seat.

"According to the police report, you claim to have seen two young males the morning after Andrew Snow's alleged disappearance."

"That is correct."

"You remember making that statement?"

"Yes. And I remember seeing the young men."

"Around what time was this?"

"Maybe six thirty a.m. Sunrise."

"Why were you up so early?"

"Couldn't sleep. I know camping is supposed to be peaceful, but I'd take the sound of traffic over crickets any day."

"Do you remember what the men were doing?"

"Not much. They got into their car and drove off."

"Can you describe them for me?" I asked.

"Both men looked to be between eighteen and twenty. The one who I believe was Andrew's brother, from the pictures I saw in the paper, was maybe five foot ten, one hundred and seventy pounds, fit-looking, broad shoulders."

"You have a good memory."

"I have an extremely good memory," the professor said, correcting me.

"How about the other young male? What did he look like?"

"Taller, lanky, sandy-haired."

"Do you remember anything else about him?" I asked.

"I think he was chewing on a toothpick."

I controlled my urge to jolt out of the office and asked a few more questions to solidify my case.

"Do you remember the car they were driving?"

"A Datsun, I think. A hatchback. Late-eighties model."

"Did either of these men see you?"

"I don't think so. I had just unzipped my tent and was putting on my shoes."

"And you told this to the police?"

"Yeah, about a week or two later when

they tracked me down. I guess they figured I had the dates wrong. But I don't think so. Because the day he disappeared was the day we went home."

I returned to the city and then made my way across the Golden Gate Bridge into Sausalito. I pulled my car over right in front of Martin Snow's house on Spring Street. There was no stealth in this stakeout. Twenty minutes later, Martin peered through his window and spotted me. I could see his fingers part the slats in the blinds every fifteen minutes or so. While I still couldn't tell you what he had done, I was making him nervous, and that confirmed his guilt in my mind. The problem was, I wasn't sure where his guilt ended. Was it possible that he was connected to my sister's disappearance? I had to know for sure.

I got out of the car and knocked on his door. He didn't answer, but I kept knocking. Finally he opened it.

"If you don't leave," he said, "I'm going to call the police."

"You don't want to involve the police."

"Why are you doing this?"

"Do you have my sister?"

"What?"

"Do you know where she is?"

"What are you talking about?"

"She disappeared four days ago."

Martin's face registered confusion. "I'm sorry," he said.

I leaned in close. "If you're holding back on me, if you know anything that might help me find her and you keep it from me — that would be a mistake."

Martin nodded his head and indicated that he understood I was making a threat.

"You need to get off my property. I've already called the police. They're on their way."

I got into my car and left.

Car Chase #4

A few blocks from Martin's home, I spotted a sheriff's vehicle closing in on my car. The lights flashed and I was about to pull over, when I checked my rearview mirror and caught a glimpse of what I believed to be Sheriff Larson's silhouette. My guess was that Martin called him when I left the house. My guess was the sheriff wasn't pulling me over for a burned-out taillight, even though I probably had one of those.

I put my foot to the floor and tried to piece together what I knew. I knew that Martin cheated his parents out of over a hundred thousand dollars. I knew that the sheriff bought a car twelve years ago that no one could account for. I knew he was there when Andrew disappeared. I knew he didn't blink as often as most people.

The sheriff sounded his siren again and motioned for me to pull over. Instead of pulling over, I drove faster, thinking that if I made it into the city, into the jurisdiction of the SFPD, I would be on safe ground. Then I could have the sheriff arrested for, well, whatever it was he'd done wrong.

I wound through the unfamiliar Marin roads in the fading light of dusk. Like my father and uncle, Larson had an edge over me. He was both trained in automobile pursuits and familiar with those roads. The last line of sun disappeared from the horizon. Larson closed the gap to no more than ten yards. I turned onto a mountain road to avoid any streetlights. Larson moved his vehicle alongside my car, shouted for me to pull over, but I didn't. The pounding of my heartbeat was audible. Fear I thought I understood, but this fear — the fear that I might not make it home that night — was an altogether different monster.

I made a right turn onto a side street, which ended up being a dead end. Larson blocked my return path by parking his car at an angle. He quickly got out of his vehicle, pulling his gun.

"Keep your hands on the steering wheel," he said, as if I were a common criminal. Without giving me a chance to react, Larson opened the driver's-side door and pulled me out of the car.

I felt the cuffs unite my hands behind my back. Then a warm hand on the back of my neck guided me toward the squad car. Larson opened the front passenger door, put his hand on my head, and shoved me into the front seat. He slammed the door shut, circled the car, and sat down next to me.

"You won't get away with this," I said.

"Get away with what?" he replied in his annoyingly calm manner.

"You know," I said, not really knowing myself.

"We need to go for a drive, Isabel," he said, pulling his cruiser back onto the road.

"Are you planning on killing me?" I asked, hoping to ease my tension.

"No," he replied flatly.

"Well, of course you're going to say no. That way I won't put up a struggle."

"You're handcuffed. I'm not worried about that."

He had a point. There wasn't much I could do. However, had he frisked me before he put me in the car, he would have found my cell phone. I pulled it out of my pocket and pressed the first number in my speed dial: Albert Spellman. I couldn't bring the phone to my ear or even hear over the sound of traffic whether anyone had answered. So I waited thirty seconds and then spoke as loudly as I could.

"Hi Dad, it's me. If I disappear or something happens to me, a Sheriff Greg Larson, that's L-A-R-S-O-N, is responsible. I'm in his car right now —"

"Who are you talking to?" Larson asked, looking at me as if I were the craziest person he'd ever met.

"My dad," I said smugly. "I just speed-dialed him on my cell phone."

Larson pulled over to the side of the road and grabbed the phone from my hands. He then placed it next to my ear. I could hear my dad shouting into the receiver.

"Izzy, Izzy? Where are you?"

"Hi Dad. I'm in Sheriff Larson's squad car."

"Are you safe?" he asked. I could hear the panic in his voice.

"A minute ago I would have said no, but I think I'm okay. Just in case, his badge number is seven-eight-six-two-two . . ."

Larson leaned in so I could read the last digit.

"Seven," I said.

"What is going on, Isabel?"

"Nothing. I'm fine. Don't worry, Dad," I said, and then Larson spoke into the receiver.

"Mr. Spellman, your daughter is perfectly safe. Martin Snow called the police when she refused to leave his property. That's all, sir. No, we won't be pressing charges today. Thank you, sir."

Larson disconnected the call and got back on the road. He drove onto Highway 101 South and remained silent for the next fifteen minutes. Since I was no longer concerned for my physical safety, I waited for him to speak. But he didn't, so I broke the silence.

"I know you were at the campsite the night of Andrew's disappearance."

"You've managed to figure out a lot of things. In fact, you have most of the pieces to the puzzle, but you still can't put it together. Am I right?"

"Are you going to tell me what's going on?"

"Andrew was an extremely unhappy person. He attempted suicide at least three times before his disappearance."

"Shouldn't that have been in the report?"

"Doctor-patient privilege. Unless the parents provided the information to the police it would not have been known. No one knew it besides the immediate family and me. Even his high school had no idea. Any recovery time was passed off as the flu or strep throat. Mrs. Snow made sure that no one found out."

"Are you telling me you know what happened to him?" I asked.

"I know exactly what happened to him. He escaped from that house, from that woman, from that life that he hated. And Martin and I helped him do it.

"We planned it months in advance. Andrew and Martin drove to Lake Tahoe as planned. I went to my uncle's house and left in the evening for a concert. I knew he'd be out cold by ten p.m. and wouldn't notice my absence until the following morning. I took his car, since the DUI was preventing him from driving. Even if he went looking for it, it wouldn't have raised any suspicion. He could never remember where he parked the thing anyway. I drove to Lake Tahoe that night and gave Andrew the car. He left soon after. Early the next morning, Martin drove me to the Greyhound station so I could get a bus back to the city. There was no reason to be suspicious of us, so the police never really questioned Martin's story."

Larson pulled his car in front of a Tudor-style brick home with a white picket fence. In the yard two preschool-age children were playing with their mother, a tall, dark-haired woman with strong but attractive features.

"Is he still alive? Where did he go?"

Larson pointed at the young mother playing in the yard. "She's right there," he said.

At first I couldn't even register what Larson was saying, but the longer I stared at the woman, the closer I came to understanding the truth.

"Her name is now Andrea Meadows. She is happily married with two adopted children," Larson said.

"That was so not one of my theories."

"If you have any more questions, get them off your chest now."

"So where did Andrew run to?"

"Trinidad, Colorado. There was a doctor there he wanted to talk to."

"So Martin's college money . . . ?"

"Paid for the sex change. Yes."

"Do you know what it would do to Mrs. Snow if she found out?"

Larson couldn't stop the smile from forming on his face. "Yes."

"What about all the phone calls?" I ask.

"That was Andrea. Her brother told her what was going on. Thought she could stop you. Plus, she does a mean imitation of her mother."

"I knew somebody was hiding something," I say.

"I got news for you: Somebody is always hiding something."

I sat in the squad car feeling foolish. All the crimes I had accused the sheriff of in my head were pure fiction. He was just a guy who chewed on toothpicks and didn't blink as often as most people. He was just a man trying to be a friend. That's all.

"She's happy now. If you expose her, everything will change. I took a chance in sharing this secret with you. I hope I haven't made a mistake."

"What about Mr. Snow? Does he know?"

"No."

"He should," I said.

"You're probably right. But that's for the family to decide."

He was right. It was no longer any of my business. Larson asked me if I could close the Snow case for good and I said yes. The Andrew Snow file would never surface again, mostly because I shredded it when I got home.

As for my sister's case, I had nothing. No leads, no theories, not even a long shot. Rae was missing and there was nothing I could do about it. This was a child whose predict-ability is stunning (unless she is deliberately trying to mislead), whose homing instinct was supernatural. It was impossible to ac-cept that if she could contact me, she wouldn't.

Breaking and Entering

It was half past eight when I entered my sister's room, four days after her disappearance. I turned on the reading light above her bed, hoping that the weak illumination wouldn't escape through the crack in the door. Only the discovery of two years of blood money from David confirmed for Stone that Rae wasn't a runaway. Otherwise he still would be following that lead.

Even though the first six searches turned up nothing, I searched again. I wasn't sure what I was looking for, but I had to do something. I opened Rae's closet door and a mass of clothing and junk piled onto the floor. (Oddly, my mother had restored the room to the precise state of disorder in which she found it.) I was too tired to pick anything up, so I left it there and looked under Rae's bed, through her dresser drawers, and even lifted up her mattress. Then I turned to her desk. I opened every drawer and rifled through Rae's collection of surveillance reports, completed homework assignments, and stale candy. I'm not sure how we missed it the first time, but I noticed that one of the drawers on Rae's desk seemed shallow compared to its opposite. I picked up the papers inside and dropped them on the floor. I took out my knife and slid it around the edge, looking for a slot where I could pry up the board. I pulled out the perfectly fitted slab of wood and wondered whether Rae accomplished this project in shop class.

I put the faux bottom on top of the desk and looked into the shallow compartment that remained. Inside was an unfamiliar red leather book. Its shiny cover and crease-free spine indicated that it was a relatively new acquisition. It appeared to be your basic scrapbook. At first glance, there was nothing out of the ordinary — just a collection of candid snapshots of the family. It was the second glance that offered a different opinion. The angles were just too high or low, the image too grainy or obscured — by a chain-link fence or a dirty window. At second glance, one could see this was a collection of surveillance pictures doubling as a family photo album.

The first few pages were dedicated to

Uncle Ray — primarily high-angled shots of him stumbling out of a cab followed by a rigorous test of fine motor skills (putting key into lock) — his average post–2:00 a.m. ritual. Then she moved on to Dad. Hand-in-the-cookie-jar-type photographs — literally. Dad had been claiming to diet for years and secretly snacking late at night. We all knew. I suspect Rae photographed his dietary indiscretions to use as barter at a later date. There were pictures of Mom smoking cigarettes with Jake Hand on the back porch and a long, cloudy shot of David and Petra walking down Market Street, hand in hand. Of course, I wasn't off the hook. Rae covered the first three dates I had with Daniel and managed one embarrassing shot of me, shirtless, in one of my car-changing episodes. There were similar all-too-candid images of her friends and school-teachers; I would have been concerned had my concern not been already occupied.

Nothing compelled me to the end of the book, but I continued turning the pages. It was like everything else I had done in the past month. I did it because it was the only thing I could do. I could have missed the photograph altogether. Nothing stood out. Two men shaking hands, shot through a telephoto lens. I recognized my father's brown-and-green plaid shirt, the frequency of its circulation hinting at lucky status. There was no reason for me to look at the other man, but I did. Then I looked closer and then I pulled out a magnifying glass and studied his grainy but now familiar features.

Inspector Henry Stone.

Inspector Stone shaking hands with my father.

There was no date on the photograph, but my father's recent haircut offered a time-line, and clearly it had been taken prior to Rae's disappearance. There they were to-gether. Inexplicably.

One could argue that I was jumping to conclusions. One could argue that I was not in any condition to think rationally. But I had a sudden, uncontrollable suspicion that Rae's disappearance was a setup. Con-spiracy theories often arise when logical explanations are unsatisfying. This explana-tion worked better than the others. In this explanation my sister did not silently slip away, taken so quickly she couldn't utter a sound. In this explanation my sister was alive and eating Froot Loops, duplicitous in a horrible deceit. In this explanation I had no choice but to expose them all.

I phoned the precinct and asked when

Stone would be off-duty: 8:00 p.m. I parked outside the station and waited. He must have used the gym, as he arrived at his car an hour later, hair wet (all three-quarters of an inch of it) and wearing street clothes. He drove straight home, which didn't surprise me. This was not a man who struck me as having a full social life. I sat in my car four houses down, watching the lights turn on and off in his house. I remained there for two hours with no plan or purpose. I could have walked up to his door, rung the bell, and asked what he had done. But who asks questions these days? Two hours later, I was about to return home and concoct another plan, but then he moved.

Back in a suit, Stone exited his home and got into his police-issued sedan. I could have followed him, but judging from his attire, he was working a case.

Instead, I circled his house, looking for an open window or an unlocked door. There was no easy access, so I picked the deadbolt and barrel lock on the back entrance. I was out of practice, so it took about a half hour. It should have occurred to me that breaking into the home of a police inspector was probably a bad idea, but sleep deprivation trumps common sense.

I justified my lapse into the habits of my

past by convincing myself that, inside this unbearably tidy bachelor pad, I was going to discover that the inspector was merely a pawn in my father's master plan. The truth had to be in here, didn't it? It had to be somewhere. This place was as good as any.

Once my eyes adjusted to the dark, I deciphered the layout of the apartment — your average San Francisco two-bedroom flat. Two entrances. Front. Back. Back door leads from pantry to kitchen. Front door from foyer to living room. The bedrooms and bathroom off to one side. Usually you can guess how long a place has been inhabited based on the accrued clutter. But Stone's space was all clean lines and empty countertops, a place for everything and not a single nonutilitarian item in sight. It was sad, in its way.

I roamed the apartment, searching for the unknown, something that could prove what I knew had to be true. What would this evidence look like? And if I found it, what would I do? Would I go to the police? Would I silently enact further revenge? Would I continue the war?

Stone's bedroom had the warmth and lived-in quality of a high-end hotel. The quilt on his bed was perfectly tucked in and symmetrically aligned.

"You better have one hell of an explanation," Inspector Stone said upon entering the room.

I was too angry to be surprised. "Oh, I do," I responded smugly.

"Sit down," he said.

I didn't at first, but then he shot me a look that I translated into "If you don't sit down immediately, I will arrest you for breaking and entering." So I sat down. Stone paced back and forth, presumably while he formed his reprimand. But I struck first.

"You should be ashamed of yourself," I said.

"Excuse me?"

"You heard me."

"Isabel, you just broke into the home of a police inspector."

"You think I don't know that?"

"Tell me why you're here."

"I had to prove you were in on it."

"In on what?"

"You know."

"In fact, I don't."

"On Rae's disappearance."

I could almost see Stone's indignation deflate. "You think I was involved?" he said.

"You and my parents."

"Have you been drinking?"

"No. But that's a good idea."

"What's going on, Isabel?"

"You tell me."

"Are you serious?"

"I saw the picture of you and my dad."

"What picture?"

"I don't know. Rae took it. Maybe a month or two ago."

Stone appeared unfazed by my discovery. "I don't know why there would be a picture, but I met with your father a few months back to consult on another case. It was unrelated. We can go to the police department and I can show you the file, but you need to listen to me now. I had nothing to do with your sister's disappearance and neither did your parents."

Even in the miasma of sleep deprivation I knew I had been mistaken. It slowly sank in that I had no more answers today than yesterday and the day before that. My sister was missing and there was no logical explanation for it.

I stared down at the floor for what seemed like forever. Stone must have thought I had fallen asleep. He tapped my knee to wake me.

"Isabel, you don't really believe we could do something like that?" Stone spoke calmly and almost sympathetically.

"It's better than the alternative, isn't it?

Anything is better than believing she is dead."

"I suppose so," he said. The fact that he didn't say any more, the fact that he didn't tell me it was going to be all right, that he accepted my statement as a valid point, made me know for certain that he was not my enemy. It would have been so much easier if he was.

"Are you going to arrest me?" I asked.

"I don't think so."

"Thanks," I said. "And sorry for, you know, breaking into your home."

"Apology accepted. But could you promise me you won't do this sort of thing again?"

"I promise I won't break into your home again."

"Not just my home. Any home."

"At the moment, I can't make that promise."

Stone and I sat in silence. I think he expected me to make a run for it, but I had nowhere to go. This place was as good as any.

"Can I get you anything?" Stone asked.

"Got any whiskey?"

Stone silently left the room. He returned some minutes later and handed me a mug. I took a sip of the beverage and spat it out.

"That's the worst whiskey I've ever had."

"It's herbal tea."

"That's why."

"Isabel, why don't you take a nap?"

I'm still not sure why the nap was suggested. Like a child, I was led into the guest room, the covers were pulled back, and Stone shut the door behind him as he left. I removed my shoes and socks, jacket, and watch, and slid under the covers, thinking I'd pretend to sleep since I couldn't think of anything better to do. But the stress of the day exhausted me and sleep took over.

I was jarred awake shortly after midnight by the ringing of a telephone. I slipped out of bed and walked over to the doorway. If I had ever possessed physical grace, it had evolved into stealth. I quietly opened the bedroom door and my bare feet silently passed through the hallway and followed the sound of Stone's voice into the kitchen.

". . . I understand, Mrs. Spellman. But she is fine and she is here. Yes, I'll keep an eye on her . . . no. I don't need to. I don't need to ask her. I assure you, Mrs. Spellman, she had nothing to do with Rae's disappearance . . ."

I returned to the bedroom, slipped on my shoes, grabbed my jacket and watch, and ran out the front door. I could hear Stone chasing after me but couldn't make out the words. His words didn't matter. The fact that my mother thought I was capable of doing something so outrageously cruel stung beyond anything I could measure in my past. It didn't matter that I had mentally accused her of the same.

I got into my car and managed a getaway before Stone had a chance to catch me. I still had the internal map of Uncle Ray's galaxy of motels. Calculating proximity and general cleanliness, I opted for the Flamingo Inn on Seventh Street.

I checked in and got a room on the second level with a view of nothing and a king-size bed. There's something comforting about those cheap, spare rooms with the enormous gold-leaf comforters as the centerpiece. The unfamiliar walls allow you to breathe, to feel like you have escaped. I imagined moving in permanently, wondered what the weekly, monthly, or perhaps yearly rates were. I imagined living in an alternative motel universe, where the past was erased.

But you need money to live in a motel, and it had been three weeks since I had earned a paycheck. The cash in my account was slowly draining and I had never been one for saving. I paid for the room in cash, but I knew that I probably had only two motel nights left in my account.

Once I settled in the room (i.e., threw my bag on the bed and took off my jacket), I ransacked my wallet, pulling credit cards and calling customer service to check my available balances. I would sustain this anonymous lifestyle as long as I could. Between my checking account and two credit cards, I had fifteen hundred dollars to my name, not to mention the emergency card I had stashed in the lining of the wallet. I reached into the worn leather wallet, slipped my finger into a two-inch-wide hole in the lining behind the billfold section. It was empty.

I searched the wallet a half dozen more times, the entire contents of which were eventually splayed across the bed. But the card, the emergency card, was not there. I couldn't call for a replacement, because I didn't have the card number. I had those written down on a slip of paper that I hid on the underside of my desk at the office — the office where I no longer worked. I would have to break into my parents' house the next morning.

I set the alarm for 5:00 a.m. and tried to sleep. I tried to count sheep but discovered that counting the holes in the stucco ceiling was far more satisfying. But neither induced sleep. I was out of bed, showered, and dressed long before the alarm buzzed. Within twenty minutes I had parked around the corner from my parents' house, entered the backyard through the alleyway, climbed the fire escape up to my old bedroom window (which has a pulley on the latch so that I can open it from the outside), and entered my old apartment. In my best imitation of a cat burglar, I worked my way downstairs to the office. The door was locked, but I still had my key and apparently they had not gotten around to changing the locks. I found the sheet of paper with all my identification numbers on it and quickly slid out the office window and made the phone call from my car.

My sister had been missing for five days.

THE FINAL BATTLE

"Isabel Spellman" checked into the Motel 6 by the San Francisco airport five nights ago. It was approximately a half-hour drive from the house, but it seemed like only seconds had passed in transit. When I arrived, I couldn't move from my car. I sat frozen, trying to calculate my next move. What I knew in my heart to be true, I had to see for a fact. And I had to document everything that would follow.

I pulled my digital recorder out of my purse, turned it on, and stuck it in my jacket pocket. I got out of the car and walked across the street toward the motel.

And that is when I saw her. Rae. Crossing the street right in front of me. In her arms was an unruly bundle of snacks (of the sugared variety), which she presumably bought from the convenience store across the street. Within a moment, she saw me approach and the look on her face was like a thousand-word essay of the truth. A package of Ding Dongs fell to the ground, and she didn't try to collect it. Instead, she stared at me, paralyzed, scared, her eyes a slide show of guilt. And I knew then for a fact that my sister's disappearance was not hinged on foul play or any other sinister option. And I knew that she wasn't a runaway. And I knew her memory was fully intact. And I knew that for the last five days she had been safe and sound, consuming vast amounts of sugar.

And what I knew above all else was that she had kidnapped herself. And I knew why. Her intentions were to unite the family. Her intentions were to bring me home. Her intentions were to force the concept of a tragedy so horrific that our family would suddenly become the kind that didn't follow one another, bug one another's rooms, listen in on phone calls, interrogate relentlessly. Our family should only do that to others.

Rae used my credit card so that I would find her. Her disappearance was to leave a mark on everyone. But it was a message to me. I was responsible for everything that happened. It was my fault.

Rae sustained her frozen stare from across the parking lot, her arms still cradling the forbidden stash. The moment I knew that my sister was alive, I said to her, "You're dead." I doubt she heard my words through the hum of traffic, but she got the picture when I sliced my index finger across my throat.

Rae's emergency provisions scattered around her as she made a run for it. With six inches on my sister and the adrenaline of sheer rage on my side, I managed to make up the fifteen yards and caught her just as she reached the front door to room 11.

Her hand grasped the doorknob as I swung my right arm around her waist. I lifted her off her feet and disengaged her grasp. I threw her down on a small grassy section in front of the building, a ten-by-fifteen-foot concrete-enclosed area with a bench and seesaw, impersonating a play-ground.

The transcripts read as follows:

Isabel: You are dead.

[I pinned Rae's arms and legs to the ground as she thrashed about.]

Rae: You gave me no choice.
Isabel: You are so dead.
Rae: I did it for you.

Isabel: Did you hear me? Dead.

Rae: I love you!

Isabel: Don't you dare say that!

Rae: I had a very good reason.

Isabel: I have a very good reason to kill you.

Rae: Let go of me.

Isabel: Never.

Rae: Please.

Isabel: You're going back to camp.

Rae: Let's negotiate.

Isabel: And private school.

Rae: That hurts!

Isabel: Say good-bye to the Froot Loops —

Rae: Ouch!

Isabel: Lucky Charms —

Rae: Help!

Isabel: Cocoa Puffs —

Rae: No!

Isabel: You're going on a macrobiotic diet.
  [Rae's body went slack.]

Rae: Okay, I give up.

I released my grip and rolled off to the side. Rae took that opportunity to attempt another escape. I caught her foot and launched her back to the grass and once again climbed on top of her, trying to pin her like before. But her arms flailed wildly, occasionally making contact with my face, charging my anger.

I rolled her over on her stomach and pulled her arms behind her back.

Isabel: Don't try to escape.

[Just as I got control of Rae, two police officers came up behind me and wrenched me off her.]

Officer #1: Ma'am, I'm going to need you to calm down.

Isabel: Accept your fate.

Rae: You would have done the same thing if you were me.

Isabel: Are you out of your mind? Do you have any idea what you put us through? You're dead.

[I strain against the tight grip of the first officer.]

Officer #2: Ma'am, if you can't control yourself, we're going to have to cuff you and take you in.

Isabel: Cuff *her.* Cuff the kid. She should be arrested.

Officer #1: Ma'am, this is the last time I'm going to ask you to calm down.

Rae: I'm sorry.

Isabel: You will be. Just wait until Mom and Dad hear about this.

Officer #1: Are you two related?

Isabel: Not much longer.

Rae: That's my sister. I think you better let her go.

Officer #2: Not until she learns to control herself.

Isabel: I'm not just going to kill you. I'm going to torture you.

Officer #2: Ma'am, we can't release you if you keep talking like that.

Isabel: You better grow eyes on the back of your head, Rae.

Officer #1: Ma'am, that was your final warning.

[For the second time in two days, I felt the cold metal of handcuffs on my skin and not even an ounce of marijuana to show for it. One of the officers threw me against the trunk of the car. But I couldn't stop.]

Isabel: The rest of your life will be pure hell.

[Rae knew she was in trouble. She knew that whatever happened to me would result in further punishment for her. It was in her best interest to save us both.]

Rae: Please let her go. It was my fault.

Isabel: Of course it was your fault, you lunatic.

Officer #1: Ma'am, stop squirming.

Rae: Let her go. She didn't do anything.

Officer #2: Young lady, can you explain to us what is going on here?

Isabel: I'll explain.

Officer #2: No, let the girl explain.

Rae: She's my sister and she's mad at me.

Officer #1: Did she hurt you, miss?

Rae: Only a little.

Officer #1: Are you afraid of her?

Rae: No. I'm fine.

Isabel: You better be afraid of me.

Rae: If you don't stop saying that, Izzy, they won't let you go.

Officer #1: Young lady, has your sister hurt you?

Rae: If you don't let her go, she will hurt me.

Isabel: You got that right.

Officer #2: We can protect you.

Isabel: They can't protect you.

Officer #2: That's enough, ma'am.

Isabel: Stop calling me ma'am!

[Officer #2 pulled me off the car by the chain on the cuffs, nearly dislocating my arms from their sockets. The back door of the black-and-white was opened, and Officer #1 put his hand over my head and pushed me onto the seat.]

Isabel: You won't go to just any old camp, Rae.

[The second officer shut the door and walked around to the driver's side.]

Isabel: How does music camp sound to you?

Rae: No!

[The first officer kneeled down and spoke sympathetically to Rae.]

Officer #1: What's your name, sweetheart?

Rae: Rae Spellman.

Officer #1: Is that your sister?

Rae: Yes.

Officer #1: What is her name?

Rae: Isabel Spellman.

Officer #1: Okay, Rae, this is what we're going to do. I'm going to stay here with you and call your parents and another squad car will come and take you home.

Rae: I have to go with Izzy.

Officer #1: We have to book your sister.

Rae: Book me, too. I have to go, too.

Officer #1: No. That's not how it works.

Rae: You need to put handcuffs on me, too.

Officer #1: But sweetheart, you didn't do anything wrong.

Rae: I will.

Officer #1: Let's just relax here. Take a deep breath.

[Rae kicked the police officer in the shin, an act she figured would not require lethal retaliation, but would sting enough to force a harsh response. Perhaps one that involved handcuffs and, if she were lucky, an assault charge.]

Officer #1: Ouch!

Rae: Please put the cuffs on me and stuff me in the back of the car next to Izzy.

Officer #1: Rae, I do not think that is necessary.

[Rae kicked him again, harder this time, then silently turned around, reaching her arms behind her back.]

Rae: I'll do it again, if you don't cuff me.

[The officer had no choice. He put the cuffs on Rae and sat her next to me in the backseat of the squad car.]

Isabel: I thought you were dead.

Rae: I'm sorry.

Nothing more was said until we arrived at the police station, met by Inspector Stone. Against protocol, he insisted that my sister and I be placed in the same holding cell.

The officers were about to remove my cuffs when Stone stopped them.

"You better leave them on for now," he said.

"What about the kid?" the officer asked.

Parity was his only move and Rae agreed. Her punishment must match mine or the retaliation would be unbearable.

"Please leave them on," Rae said, referring to the handcuffs.

Before Inspector Stone shut the door on us, I shouted, "Hey, get me out of here!"

"I'm afraid I can't."

"What did I do?"

"Resisting arrest. You know better, Isabel," Stone said, disappointed.

"Did you tell them? Did you tell them what she did?"

"I'll take care of it," he said and then shifted his attention to Rae, sharpening his stare. "What you did," he said, "it was not clever or inspired. It was inexcusable and cruel. For five days your family believed that their life was over. Young lady, I am going to make it my business that you get way more than a slap on the wrist."

Stone latched the door and I could see Rae's complexion whiten. Through the iron bars of the cell, I watched Inspector Stone disappear down the hallway. Oddly, that very moment, the one thing I thought was: Could this be Ex-boyfriend #10?

Our silence extended a good thirty minutes. Rae was too frightened to speak. I believe it broke all her previous records. But curiosity finally got the best of me and I ended the silence.

"So you just stayed in that motel room the entire four days?" I asked.

"I went out for food."

"Oh, right. For Ding Dongs and Snickers."

"I had Slim Jims and Pringles, too."

"Did you brush your teeth?"

"Twice a day. I even flossed once."

"So what did you do all day long?"

"They have cable. All the channels. You wouldn't believe some of the programs."

"You did this to make me come back?"

"We were all happy once. I just wanted things to be the way they used to be. I thought you needed to reevaluate your priorities."

"That is so fucked up."

Rae thought about it for a moment. "It wasn't the right move. I can admit that now."

Our parents' approach, from the end of the hall, seemed to take an eternity. Their expressions were a complicated disarray of unreadable emotions. Stone unlocked the cell door and guided their entry.

My mother's face was ruddy from crying, but she had sopped up all the tears and was glaring with an undercurrent of fury I had never seen.

Stone unlocked my cuffs, then Rae's. My sister's instinct was to run and hug her parents. She had missed them, too, in her absence. But their body language was not entirely receptive.

Rae bowed her head and in her most submissive voice said, "I'm so sorry. I swear I won't do anything bad ever again."

My mother took Rae in her arms and let herself cry one more time. Then she released Rae into my father's embrace. He hugged her hard, forcing her to gasp for breath.

"You're going to pay for this, pumpkin," he said.

It was only in that moment that I knew everything would be all right.

EPILOGUE:
CRIME AND
PUNISHMENT

My father encouraged the court to "throw the book" at Rae, but Rae's compelling and persuasive plea to the bench, which included a cheesy passage regarding how all her actions were done out of love (and which ended with the line "Look at me. I won't stand a chance in juvenile hall") managed to persuade the judge, who, frankly, happened to find Rae the most sympathetic person in my family.

But what she did required more than a slap on the wrist. Judge Stevens gave her nine months' probation, which included a 7:00 p.m. curfew and one hundred hours of community service at Oak Tree Convalescent Home. My parents chose that punishment believing that the lack of excitement would sting Rae the most and remind her that actions have consequences. But Rae had once watched a segment on *60 Minutes* regarding elder abuse in nursing homes and took the opportunity to investigate all the employees at Oak Tree. She found one member of the staff who stole from the clients and another responsible for criminal neglect. She snuck in a camera and managed to get incriminating footage on both employees. She brought the tape to Inspector Stone, the only police officer she knew, and he passed it on to the appropriate departments.

Green Leaf Recovery Center

When Rae returned home, Uncle Ray unfortunately had to grapple with the deal he had made with God. He had promised he would go to rehab if Rae were returned safe and sound. But his deal implied that foul play had caused her disappearance. The fact that Rae had disappeared by her own hand complicated matters. Uncle Ray, having some degree of superstition, had to come up with a compromise that would alleviate any further guilt but not alter his essential lifestyle.

He sat Rae down to explain his decision to her.

"Listen, kid, when you went missing, I made a promise to the Big Guy that if you came back, I'd go to rehab."

Rae responded by throwing her arms

around him. He disengaged her embrace and continued. "But you see, you weren't really missing in the way I thought you were missing. And had I known that you had kidnapped yourself and were gonna show up five days later with those twenty-four-hour-television eyes and not a scratch on you, I wouldn't have made the deal."

"So you're not going to rehab?"

"I've been agonizing over this decision and the fact remains that, semantically, I owe God a trip to rehab. I promised him if you came back I'd go. So I'm going."

Rae threw her arms around him once again and he pried her off.

"Listen. I'm going to rehab semantically, too. Do you understand?"

"Sure, you're going to rehab," Rae said, trying to figure out the definition of "semantically" and whether that was a bad thing.

"No. I'm *going* to rehab. But I'm not *going* to rehab."

"I don't understand."

"I'm gonna spend thirty days at Green Leaf Recovery Center. But it won't stick. When I get out I'm going to be the same old Uncle Ray."

"So you're gonna be Old Uncle Ray, like they told me about."

"No. I'm going to be new Uncle Ray,

which is old Uncle Ray to you. Kid, I'm not changing."

Rae simply got up from the couch and walked away, finally realizing that some people you can't control even with the best-laid plans.

In her first act of defiance since her probation started, Rae took the bus to Milo's for happy hour.

Milo telephoned me when his pleas for Rae to leave went unanswered.

"Your sister is off the wagon again."

"I'll be right there."

When I arrived, Rae was on her third ginger ale on the rocks. Instead of the usual protest and refusal to move, Rae took one look at me and said, "All right, all right. I'm leaving." She left Milo a generous tip and casually mentioned that he wouldn't be seeing her for a very long time.

"Like seven years?" asked Milo.

"Not that long," Rae replied.

I drove Rae directly from the bar to Daniel's office, having made a last-minute appointment for her to get those three cavities filled. I figured that if she connected going to a bar with a dental appointment, it might subliminally force a negative association.

Daniel remained Ex-boyfriend #9 and showed no signs that he wanted to change that status. Mrs. Sanchez told me he was dating a schoolteacher — a real one — who also played tennis. I asked Daniel about her outfits for future reference, but he refused to answer the question.

One month into Rae's probation, my mother got a toothache that she couldn't quell with her emergency stash of Vicodin. All planes to O'Hare airport were grounded because of a bitter storm in the Midwest. Unable to cope with the mounting pain, and per my insistence, my mother made an appointment with Daniel. He performed an emergency root canal — with my father present, of course.

My father made an appointment for a cleaning a few days later. Daniel recommended a colleague of his who was located in our neighborhood, but my mother refused, and, reluctantly, Daniel became the family dentist. With our appointments staggered throughout the year, to his great discomfort, Daniel could rarely go longer than two months at a time without seeing at least one member of the Spellman family.

■ ■ ■ ■

I quit for a second time, but it didn't stick. My announcement was met with a silent acceptance. Or so I believed. Later I discovered that the entire family (David included) had started a betting pool on how long it would take me to return.

Uncle Ray, the seasoned gambler, won with a wager on three days, the three longest days of my life. I wore a suit with a crisp white shirt and high heels and answered phones at a brokerage firm in the financial district. Within the first five minutes, I was desperate for my old job. Desperate. But pride forced me to endure as long as I could, which was the aforementioned three days.

I returned to my parents' employ with a list of demands that I explained were non-negotiable and further explained that if any demand was not fully met, I would seek work with the competition. The list, before I had David turn it into a binding legal document, read as follows:

- No matchmaking with lawyers.
- Section 5, clause (d) null and void.
- No background checks on future ex-

boyfriends.
- Personal privacy must be respected.

My parents agreed to all my demands and every member of the Spellman family signed the document.

A few weeks later, Rae and I worked our first surveillance job together since her disappearance. As I wove through traffic, struggling to maintain a tail on Joseph Baumgarten, Case #07-427, Rae turned to me and asked what I supposed had been on her mind for weeks.

"Izzy, why did you come back?"

I answered without contemplating the question. "Because I don't know how to do anything else."

What I didn't say was that I didn't want to do anything else. That I had a choice and I finally made it. That I had always loved the job, I just hadn't always liked who I became doing it. That I had grown tired of trying to be someone I was not.

Rae's days of recreational surveillance, lock picking, mass sugar consumption, and Uncle Ray taunting came to an abrupt halt. She became, for the first time ever, a typical adolescent. Who, yes, still worked in the family business, but certainly didn't run it.

One might have expected that the change

in Rae's status would have her railing against this newfound authority. But that was not the case. Because, in the end, in spite of or because of what my sister had done, she got exactly what she wanted. I came back and the family was once again together as it used to be.

Two months after Rae's safe return home, David and Petra announced their engagement. Uncle Ray quickly popped a bottle of champagne to celebrate. Rae watched him with quiet acceptance as he downed half the bottle and then went out to the corner store for a six-pack of beer.

Petra spent the next several weeks ordering me to try on various bridesmaid's dresses at department stores scattered throughout the city. Each dress was markedly puffier and brighter than the last. And just when I was convinced that she was suffering from some kind of bridal-magazine brainwashing, I received a brown envelope in the mail with an array of embarrassing photographs of me — scowling — adorned in the motley assortment of bloated pastels and chiffon. I discovered that my mother was behind the charade — in a feeble attempt to resurrect some of the joy she derived from section 5, clause (d) — and briefly considered that surreptitious photographs of me were in direct violation of my contract, but I let it slide. Because what was I going to do? Quit?

Three months into Rae's probation, upon hearing the news that her investigation resulted in indictments, she promptly went to see Inspector Stone.

This was not their first visit. She had been visiting him at least once a week since her probation began. Each time he would remind her that she was assigned a court-ordered psychologist and that she should be speaking to her. But Rae would stay, try to negotiate down her sentence, and when that failed, begin chatting about other matters — family, friends, the pitfalls of curfew. Each time Rae dropped by Inspector Stone's office, he would reluctantly see her and then promptly telephone me to pick her up.

"She's here again" is how all our conversations would begin.

"Who?" I'd ask, because it amused me.

"Your sister. Please come get her. I have work to do," Stone would reply with a pronounced professional air.

Usually I would drop whatever I was doing and go pick her up. By the time I arrived, Rae was typically sitting cross-legged in the worn black leather chair in front of his desk, doing homework at his insistence. And since he was the only supervising adult present, she assumed this meant he should help her with her assignments. Their exchanges would go something like this:

"Inspector, what does 'hirsute' mean?"

Stone would silently grab the dictionary from behind his desk and slide it over to Rae.

"So you don't know what it means, either," she'd say.

"I know what it means, but the assignment isn't to ask your local police inspector to do your homework."

"You're bluffing. You don't know."

"I know."

"No, you don't."

"It means 'covered with hair.' Now get back to work."

Then Rae would attempt to hide her self-satisfied grin and complete the entry in her homework assignment.

When I arrived, Stone would ask Rae to give us privacy and then he would suggest that I have another talk with her about these unannounced visits.

On her last visit, Stone insisted that he had done nothing to encourage her, but he had. Her instincts were dead-on. Stone could scowl and shake his head all he wanted, but if he secretly enjoyed her visits, she would know.

And so I explained to Stone that these visits were his fault alone. "She knows you like her deep down. She knows you look forward to her interrupting your day."

"But I don't," he insisted. "I have work to do."

"You must or she wouldn't come here," I insisted back.

Stone would sigh and say, "Talking to you and your sister is not unlike banging one's head against the wall."

"Then why is it that you call me every time she drops by and not my parents, who are, as you know, her legal guardians?"

Stone refused to answer the question. But I knew the answer and I knew then that this man would eventually be Ex-boyfriend #10. What a relief to begin a relationship without having to worry about sustaining a series of calculated lies.

Uncle Ray was a man of his word. He went to rehab for thirty days. During the time Ray was a resident at Green Leaf Recovery Center, he remained sober — to his great disappointment. It turns out there was no contraband-smuggling technique that the

Green Leaf staffers hadn't already seen.

Eventually he decided to make the most of his stay. He went for walks in the woods and exercised at the gym. He took whirlpool baths and saunas. He performed his designated chores — leaf raking, kitchen sweeping, bathroom cleaning — with calm acceptance. He labored at a snail's pace but was known as a peaceful and diligent worker. He went to group therapy and explained the deal he'd made with God. He further explained, with an honesty that surprised and disappointed his group leader, that he had no intention of maintaining his sobriety once the thirty days came to an end.

When those thirty days did come to an end, my father picked up Uncle Ray from Green Leaf, drove him two hours back to the city, and dropped him off at a Sleeper's Inn on Sloat Boulevard, where within five minutes, Ray drank two beers, smoked a cigar, bet one thousand dollars on a poker hand, and smacked the asses of at least three different women.

The healthy glow of thirty days' detox was erased by the subsequent three days' worth of debauchery. My sister gave him the silent treatment for a week as punishment. She finally spoke to him when he offered to teach her how to dust for fingerprints.

It could be said that the Spellmans returned to normal after that. However, there was no previous pattern of normalcy to judge it by. I moved out of the house and into Bernie Peterson's place when he finally agreed to move to Las Vegas and marry his ex-showgirl sweetheart. I sublet at Bernie's rent-controlled rate, since he continued to claim that "it would never last."

The new and improved Rae lasted only a few weeks, tops. Eventually the recreational surveillance and sugar highs returned, but she did manage to limit both activities to the weekend only. My parents never followed or paid anyone to follow me again. My father officially fired Jake Hand when he caught him looking down my mother's shirt. David got a tattoo with Petra's name on it as an engagement present. Once again, Petra railed against me for not stopping him. They continued to plan their September nuptials. And Uncle Ray went missing again.

THE LAST LOST
WEEKEND

It was officially Lost Weekend #27. He was last seen on a Thursday, and by Sunday my father and Rae began making the customary telephone calls. They tracked my uncle through a series of poker games in the city until the trail went cold. Dad then checked the activity on all of Uncle Ray's credit cards and found charges at the Golden Nugget resort in Reno, Nevada.

My mother and father had a new-client meeting in the morning and so the responsibility of collecting Uncle Ray fell to me. But I would not go alone. It is an essential rite of passage for all the Spellman children to, at one time or another, take a road trip to collect their uncle.

Within an hour of discovering Uncle Ray's whereabouts, Rae and I were packed and on the road. Four hours later we arrived in Reno and checked into the hotel. My father provided a letter detailing his credentials and references, which allowed the hotel to provide me with Uncle Ray's room number and an additional key.

As usual, the DO NOT DISTURB sign was hung on the door of room 62B. I knocked out of courtesy and waited for Ray to bellow out something along the lines of "Can't you read?" or "I'm conducting important business here." But there was no answer, which I assumed meant he was passed out.

I slid the card key into the door and opened it a crack. Just as quickly, I pulled the door shut. The smell was unmistakable. The brief whiff I got told me all that I needed to know.

"What's wrong?" Rae asked, sensing my tension.

I wasn't ready for her to know the truth and I was equally unsure of how to proceed. I needed to buy some time, to keep her unaware as long as I could.

"Uncle Ray's having sex," I said. Only after the fact did I realize that this was a lie of which my uncle would have wholly approved.

My sister promptly plugged her ears and started singing, "La la la la la la la." I took her by the arm and suggested we go to our room. Rae checked out the view and noticed the swimming pool three stories down. She asked if she could take a dip. I was grateful for the opportunity to make some phone calls in private and practically shoved her out the door.

I watched Rae from the balcony as she floated on her back in the pink-bottomed pool. I phoned the coroner and then my parents. I returned to Uncle Ray's room one more time to be sure.

According to the police, Uncle Ray died of asphyxiation. He had passed out in the bathtub approximately two days earlier. Ray had slipped housekeeping an extra twenty to give him his privacy. Prior to his death, he gambled away six thousand dollars at the Caribbean Poker tables. His death was determined to be an alcohol-related accident. There was no follow-up police investigation.

Rae returned from her swim as I was finishing up a conversation with the coroner's office that included words like *body, autopsy,* and *transport.* So she figured it out.

"He's dead, isn't he?"

"Yes."

Rae showered for two hours and then went to bed without uttering a single word, shattering all previous records. She finally spoke the following morning as we put our bags into the car.

"How will he get home?" Rae asked.

"Who?"

"Uncle Ray," she snarled.

"They'll fly him back when the autopsy is complete."

"Uncle Ray doesn't like flying."

"I don't think he'll mind now."

"Why can't we drive him back?"

"Because."

"Because why?"

"Because he's dead. Because he has begun to decompose. Because I don't want to hang around in Reno for three days until the coroner's office releases his body. Get in the car, Rae. This is nonnegotiable."

Rae responded with a frustrated sigh, got into the passenger seat, and slammed the door behind her.

The first hour along the barren stretch of I-80 was punctuated by sighing and gloomy stares out the window. It wasn't until she turned to me and snapped, "He shouldn't be dead," that I realized she was angry. She was angry because as long as she was able to witness it, no one had tried to stop Uncle Ray from poisoning himself. She saw only the second half of the story, which included an entire family turning a blind eye to his self-abuse.

I pulled off at the next rest stop and washed away the tears that had settled beneath my sunglasses. I returned to the car and found Rae on my cell phone, speaking with the coroner's office, trying to negotiate a car or train ride for the return of her uncle's body. I opened the passenger-side door, snapped the phone out of her hand, and kneeled down in front of her.

"We all have the right to destroy ourselves. He was a grown man and that was his choice."

Rae fell silent again as we got back on the road.

We crossed the Bay Bridge two hours, one hundred and forty-seven miles, and half a box of tissues later. It was only then that the silence was broken.

"Izzy?"

"Yes, Rae?"

"Can we get ice cream?"

ACKNOWLEDGMENTS

The fact that I can now put writer (or the more pretentious "author") as my occupation on all tax forms seems unbelievable. For a while there I was certain I wouldn't amount to anything. I am now certain that it would not have been possible if I had to do this all on my own. Therefore, I feel lengthy acknowledgments are appropriate. If you don't know me or anyone connected to me, don't feel obligated to read this. In fact, *don't* read this. It's personal and filled with inside jokes that won't make any sense and might make me seem weird.

First I must acknowledge the people directly responsible for turning my manuscript into a book. Stephanie Kip Rostan, my agent: I can't believe my good fortune in finding you. Your wit, perfect advice, and patience astound me. My genius editor, Marysue Rucci: You have made this book so much better than I ever thought possible and working with you has been effortless.[1] Simply to meet another person who finds the same things funny as you do is great; for that person to be your editor is like winning the lottery.[2] David Rosenthal, my publisher: You had me at "molestation charges."[3]

Also thanks to Carolyn Reidy, president of Simon & Schuster; your support of this book is invaluable and I am extremely grateful. Alexis Taines, Marysue's editorial assistant, thanks for answering all my questions past and to come. Also at Simon & Schuster, thank you, Victoria Meyer; Aileen Boyle; Deb Darrock; Leah Wasielewski; and Aja Pollock, my very overworked production editor. Thank you to everyone at Levine Greenberg Literary Agency, especially Daniel Greenberg, Elizabeth Fisher, Melissa Rowland, and Monika Verma for all their hard work. And finally, a big thanks to Sarah Self, at the Gersh Agency, who didn't bat an eye when I kept saying no.

Now, I would like to thank all of my friends who have supported me over the

[1] I know you cannot say the same for me, and I'm okay with that.
[2] And, yes, I kind of know what that feels like.
[3] Example of aforementioned inside joke.

years, but I am going to limit this list to only those who have *both* lent[4] me money and read drafts of scripts or manuscripts. To begin, Morgan Do,[5] boy were you wrong about the whole Westernville thing. It *was* a good idea. Steve Kim,[6] I couldn't ask for a better friend. Thanks for everything, especially for reminding me about the Cone of Silence. I owe you big. Rae Dox Kim,[7] thanks for letting me borrow your name; I'm going to need it just a bit longer. Julie Shiroishi,[8] thank you for telling me to write a novel, when actually it hadn't really occurred to me. Ronnie Wenker-Konner, you can stop blaming yourself for the other thing; I'm good. Now I'm just going to start listing people in no particular order because this could get really long if I don't: Julie Ul-

---

[4] 0% loans only will be mentioned.

[5] Has lent me *a lot* of money and read perhaps more than anyone, including my supercrappy early screenplays.

[6] Morgan's husband and therefore money-lending applies to him as well.

[7] She is only four, therefore, I have not borrowed money from her.

[8] I don't recall borrowing money from Julie, but she has bought me many drinks and employed me a few times.

mer,[9] Warren Liu,[10] Peter Kim,[11] David Hayward,[12] Devin Jindrich, Lilac Lane, Beth Hartman, and a special thanks to Lisa Chen, who is lending me money at the moment and gave me some great notes. An honorable mention goes to Francine Silverman, who I don't recall lending me money, but who read some of the strangest adolescent writing imaginable (and laughed), and Cyndi Klane, who gave me four pages of notes even though we had never met.

If you are a friend of mine and your name was not mentioned in the previous paragraph, it does not mean that I do not value your friendship, it simply means that you did not lend me enough money or read enough dreadful drafts to qualify for mentioning. Remember, there will be a second book, and I'm wiping the slate clean for that one. While I no longer need to borrow large

---

[9] Lent money, but didn't read all that many drafts. Will need to step up if she wants mentioning in second book's acknowledgments.

[10] No, I will not buy you a car.

[11] Lent money, read lots of drafts, *and* bought lots of drinks.

[12] Read lots and lots of drafts, lent money, *and* has given me large household appliances and furniture.

sums of money, you'll still have the opportunity to spot me a twenty every now
and again. As someone who knows me, you
also know that I don't like to carry around
cash.[13]

Now I'd like to mention my war buddies
from *Plan B:* Greg Yaitanes, Steven Hoffman, Matt Salinger, and William Lorton.
You made me feel like a writer, when I was
entirely unconvinced of that fact. Your kindness, respect, and loyalty I will never forget.
And, once again, I'm sorry. I'm really, really
sorry. While I'm on the subject of *Plan B,*
another thanks goes to J. K. Amalou. *Miruf-
shim,* as they say in your country.

Most importantly, I really must thank my
family. There is something decidedly fishy
about a person in her midthirties who
refuses to let go of an idea. To my mother,
Sharlene Lauretz, not once did you tell me
to get a real job and get on with my life[14]. I
might still be working on the novel if it
weren't for your generosity and belief in me.
To my aunt and uncle[15] Beverly Fienberg

---

[13] Any potential muggers who happen to be reading this should note this fact.

[14] This would, in fact, have been a reasonable
thing to do — all things considered.

[15] For the record, Uncle Ray was not modeled

and Mark Fienberg, thanks for employing me all those years, not complaining about my bad attitude, and giving me a place to crash when I got tired of paying rent. A big whopping thanks to my aunt and uncle[16] Eve and Jeff Golden. You gave me a home[17] in which to write. It was a dream come true, living in the middle of nowhere, working on my first novel. There are no words to express what you have done for me. Jay Fienberg, my cousin, please read the damn book. Dan Fienberg, also my cousin, thanks so much for all your help/advice/etc. Anastasia Fuller: We are all so lucky to have you in our family. Thanks for reading the sloppiest draft ever and thanks in advance for everything I'm going to make you read in the future.

This next person deserves her own paragraph. Kate Golden, my cousin, my first copy editor. Who knew so many words had hyphens? You are brilliant and will find great success. But I am so pleased I had time to exploit you in your impoverished youth.

Last, I must acknowledge my friends from Desvernine Associates[18]: Graham "Des"

after either one of my uncles.

[16] Ibid.

[17] Rent free!

[18] Except Mike Joffe. I'm not acknowledging him.

Desvernine, Pamela Desvernine, Pierre Merkl, Debra Crofoot Meisner,[19] and especially Yvonne Prentiss and Gretchen Rice, who have patiently read drafts, answered endless questions, and reminded me about a job I had all but forgotten. The Spellmans are pure fiction, but they could never have existed without you.

Note to reader: With the exception of my mother, I have paid everyone back.

---

[19] Seriously, this book is *not* about you.

ABOUT THE AUTHOR

Lisa Lutz attended UC Santa Cruz, UC Irvine, the University of Leeds in England, and San Francisco State University, although she still does not have a bachelor's degree. Lisa spent most of the 1990s hopping through a string of low-paying odd jobs while writing and rewriting the screenplay *Plan B,* a mob comedy. After the film was made in 2000, she vowed she would never write another screenplay. Though she's not on the lam, Lisa has not had a permanent residence in over two years. She's calling Seattle home, for now.

Visit www.spellmanfilesthebook.com